Richard Brautigan

Revenge of the Lawn

The Abortion

So the Wind Won't
Blow It All Away

Books by Richard Brautigan

NOVELS
Trout Fishing in America
A Confederate General from Big Sur
In Watermelon Sugar
The Abortion: An Historical Romance 1966
The Hawkline Monster: A Gothic Western
Willard and His Bowling Trophies: A Perverse Mystery
Sombrero Fallout: A Japanese Novel
Dreaming of Babylon: A Private Eye Novel 1942
The Tokyo-Montana Express
So the Wind Won't Blow It All Away

POETRY
The Galilee Hitch-Hiker
Lay the Marble Tea
The Octopus Frontier
All Watched Over by Machines of Loving Grace
Please Plant This Book
The Pill *versus* the Springhill Mine Disaster
Rommel Drives on Deep into Egypt
Loading Mercury with a Pitchfork
June 30th, June 30th

SHORT STORIES
Revenge of the Lawn

Richard Brautigan

Revenge of the Lawn

The Abortion

So the Wind Won't
Blow It All Away

(Three books in the manner of their original editions)

Houghton Mifflin / Seymour Lawrence

Boston   New York

For information about permission to reproduce selections from this book, write to Permissions, Houghton Mifflin Company, 215 Park Avenue South, New York, New York 10003.

Library of Congress Cataloguing-in-Publication Data
Brautigan, Richard.
    Revenge of the lawn ; The abortion ; So the wind won't blow it all away / Richard Brautigan.
        p.   cm.
      ISBN 0-395-70674-2
      I. Brautigan, Richard. Abortion. II. Brautigan, Richard. So the wind won't blow it all away..
    PS3503.R2736A6   1995
    813'.54 — dc20   94-26177   CIP

Printed in the United States of America

BP 10 9 8

Some of the stories in *Revenge of the Lawn* first appeared in *Rolling Stone, Playboy, Ramparts, New American Review, Vogue, Coyote's Journal, Mademoiselle, Nice, Tri-Quarterly, Esquire, Evergreen Review, Kulchur, Now Now, Sum, Jeopardy, R. C. Lion, Parallel,* and *Change.*

A portion of *The Abortion* originally appeared in *The Dutton Review,* volume 1.

REVENGE
of the
Lawn

REVENGE

of the

Lawn

STORIES

1962-1970

BY RICHARD BRAUTIGAN

This book is for
Don Carpenter

CONTAINING:

REVENGE OF
THE LAWN

My grandmother, in her own way, shines like a beacon down the stormy American past. She was a bootlegger in a little county up in the state of Washington. She was also a handsome woman, close to six feet tall who carried 190 pounds in the grand operatic manner of the early 1900s. And her specialty was bourbon, a little raw but a welcomed refreshment in those Volstead Act days.

She of course was no female Al Capone, but her bootlegging feats were the cornucopia of legend in her neck of the woods, as they say. She had the county in her pocket for years. The sheriff used to call her up every morning and give her the weather report and tell her how the chickens were laying.

I can imagine her talking to the sheriff: "Well, Sheriff, I hope your mother gets better soon. I had a cold and a bad sore throat last week myself. I've still got the sniffles. Tell her hello for me and to drop by the next time she's down this way. And if you want that case, you can pick it up or I can have it sent over as soon as Jack gets back with the car.

"No, I don't know if I'm going to the firemen's ball this year, but you know that my heart is with the firemen. If you don't see me there tonight, you tell the boys that. No, I'll try to get there, but I'm still not fully recovered from my cold. It kind of climbs on me in the evening."

My grandmother lived in a three-story house that was old even in those days. There was a pear tree in the front yard which was heavily eroded by rain from years of not having any lawn.

The picket fence that once enclosed the lawn was gone, too, and people just drove their cars right up to the porch. In the winter the front yard was a mud hole and in the summer it was hard as a rock.

Jack used to curse the front yard as if it were a living thing. He was the man who lived with my grandmother for thirty years. He was not my grandfather, but an Italian who came down the road one day selling lots in Florida.

He was selling a vision of eternal oranges and sunshine door to door in a land where people ate apples and it rained a lot.

Jack stopped at my grandmother's house to sell her a lot just a stone's throw from downtown Miami, and he was delivering her whiskey a week later. He stayed for thirty years and Florida went on without him.

Jack hated the front yard because he thought it was against him. There had been a beautiful lawn there when Jack came along, but he let it wander off into nothing. He refused to water it or take care of it in any way.

Now the ground was so hard that it gave his car flat tires in the summer. The yard was always finding a nail to put in one of his tires or the car was always sinking out of sight in the winter when the rains came on.

The lawn had belonged to my grandfather who lived out the end of his life in an insane asylum. It had been his pride and joy and was said to be the place where his powers came from.

My grandfather was a minor Washington mystic who in 1911 prophesied the exact date when World War I would start: June 28, 1914, but it had been too much for him. He never got to enjoy the fruit of his labor because they had to put him away in 1913 and he spent seventeen years in the state insane asylum believing he was a child and it was actually May 3, 1872.

He believed that he was six years old and it was a cloudy day about to rain and his mother was baking a chocolate cake. It stayed May 3, 1872 for my grandfather until he died in 1930. It took seventeen years for that chocolate cake to be baked.

There was a photograph of my grandfather. I look a great deal like him. The only difference being that I am over six feet tall and he was not quite five feet tall. He had a dark idea that being so short, so close to the earth and his lawn would help to prophesy the exact date when World War I would start.

It was a shame that the war started without him. If only he could have held back his childhood for another year, avoided that chocolate cake, all of his dreams would have come true.

There were always two large dents in my grandmother's house that had never been repaired and one of them came about this way: In the autumn the pears would get ripe on the tree in the front yard and the pears would fall on the ground and rot and bees would gather by the hundreds to swarm on them.

The bees somewhere along the line had picked up the habit of stinging Jack two or three times a year. They would sting him in the most ingenious ways.

Once a bee got in his wallet and he went down to the store to buy some food for dinner, not knowing the mischief that he carried in his pocket.

He took out his wallet to pay for the food.

"That will be 72 cents," the grocer said.

"AAAAAAAAAAAAAAAAAAAAAAAAA!" Jack replied, looking down to see a bee busy stinging him on the little finger.

The first large dent in the house was brought about by still another bee landing on Jack's cigar as he was driving the car into the front yard that peary autumn the stock market crashed.

The bee ran down the cigar, Jack could only stare at it cross-eyed in terror, and stung him on the upper lip. His reaction to this was to drive the car immediately into the house.

That front yard had quite a history after Jack let the lawn go to hell. One day in 1932 Jack was off running an errand or delivering something for my grandmother. She wanted to dump the old mash and get a new batch going.

Because Jack was gone, she decided to do it herself. Grandmother put on a pair of railroad overalls that she used for working around the still and filled a wheelbarrow with mash and dumped it out in the front yard.

She had a flock of snow-white geese that roamed outside the house and nested in the garage that had not been used to park the car since the time Jack had come along selling futures in Florida.

Jack had some kind of idea that it was all wrong for a car to have a house. I think it was something that he had learned in the Old Country. The answer was in Italian because that

was the only language Jack used when he talked about the
garage. For everything else he used English, but it was only
Italian for the garage.

After Grandmother had dumped the mash on the ground
near the pear tree, she went back to the still down in the
basement and the geese all gathered around the mash and
started talking it over.

I guess they came to a mutually agreeable decision because
they all started eating the mash. As they ate the mash their
eyes got brighter and brighter and their voices, in appreciation
of the mash, got louder and louder.

After a while one of the geese stuck his head in the mash
and forgot to take it out. Another one of the geese cackled
madly and tried to stand on one leg and give a W. C. Fields
imitation of a stork. He maintained that position for about a
minute before he fell on his tail feathers.

My grandmother found them all lying around the mash in
the positions that they had fallen. They looked as if they had
been machine-gunned. From the height of her operatic
splendor she thought they were all dead.

She responded to this by plucking all their feathers and
piling their bald bodies in the wheelbarrow and wheeling them
down to the basement. She had to make five trips to accom-
modate them.

She stacked them like cordwood near the still and waited
for Jack to return and dispose of them in a way that would
provide a goose for dinner and a small profit by selling the rest
of the flock in town. She went upstairs to take a nap after
finishing with the still.

It was about an hour later that the geese woke up. They
had devastating hangovers. They had all kind of gathered
themselves uselessly to their feet when suddenly one of the
geese noticed that he did not have any feathers. He informed

the other geese of their condition, too. They were all in despair.

They paraded out of the basement in a forlorn and wobbly gang. They were all standing in a cluster near the pear tree when Jack drove into the front yard.

The memory of the time he had been stung on the mouth by that bee must have come back to his mind when he saw the defeathered geese standing there, because suddenly like a madman he tore out the cigar he had stuck in his mouth and threw it away from him as hard as he could. This caused his hand to travel through the windshield. A feat that cost him thirty-two stitches.

The geese stood by staring on like some helpless, primitive American advertisement for aspirin under the pear tree as Jack drove his car into the house for the second and last time in the Twentieth Century.

★　　★　　★

The first time I remember anything in life occurred in my grandmother's front yard. The year was either 1936 or 1937. I remember a man, probably Jack, cutting down the pear tree and soaking it with kerosene.

It looked strange, even for a first memory of life, to watch a man pour gallons and gallons of kerosene all over a tree lying stretched out thirty feet or so on the ground, and then to set fire to it while the fruit was still green on the branches.

1692 COTTON MATHER
NEWSREEL

O 1939 Tacoma Washington witch, where are you now that
I am growing toward you? Once my body occupied a child's
space and doors had a large meaning to them and were almost
human. Opening a door meant something in 1939 and the
children used to make fun of you because you were crazy
and lived by yourself in an attic across the street from where
we sat in the gutter like two slum sparrows.

We were four years old.

I think you were about as old as I am now with the children
always teasing and calling after you, "The crazy woman!
Run! Run! The witch! The witch! Don't let her look at you in
the eye. She looked at me! Run! Help! Run!"

Now I am beginning to look like you with my long hippie
hair and my strange clothes. I look about as crazy in 1967
as you did in 1939.

Little children yell, "Hey, hippie!" at me in the San
Francisco mornings like we yelled, "Hey, crazy woman!" at
you plodding through Tacoma twilights.

I guess you got used to it as I've gotten used to it.

As a child I would always hang my hat on a dare. Dare me to do anything and I'd do it. Ugh! some of the things that I did following, like a midget Don Quixote, trails and visions of dares.

We were sitting in the gutter doing nothing. Perhaps we were waiting for the witch or anything to happen that would free us from the gutter. We had been sitting there for almost an hour: child's time.

"I dare you to go up to the witch's house and wave at me out the window," my friend said, finally to get things going.

I looked up at the witch's house across the street. There was one window in her attic facing down upon us like a still photograph from a horror movie.

"OK," I said.

"You've got guts," my friend said. I can't remember his name now. The decades have filed it off my memory, leaving a small empty place where his name should be.

I got up from the gutter and walked across the street and around to the back of the house where the stairs were that led to her attic. They were gray wooden stairs like an old mother cat and went up three flights to her door.

There were some garbage cans at the bottom of the stairs. I wondered what garbage can was the witch's. I lifted up one garbage can lid and looked inside to see if there was any witches' garbage in the can.

There wasn't.

The can was filled with just ordinary garbage. I lifted up the lid to the next garbage can but there wasn't any witches' garbage in that can either. I tried the third can but it was the same as the other two cans: no witches' garbage.

There were three garbage cans and there were three apartments in the house, including the attic where she lived. One of the cans had to be her garbage but there wasn't any difference between her garbage and the other people's garbage.

. . . so . . .

I walked up the stairs to the attic. I walked very carefully as if I were petting an old gray mother cat nursing her kittens.

I finally arrived at the witch's door. I didn't know whether she was inside or not. She could have been home. I felt like knocking but that didn't make any sense. If she were there, she'd just slam the door in my face or ask me what I wanted and I'd run screaming down the stairs, "Help! Help! She looked at me!"

The door was tall, silent and human like a middle-aged woman. I felt as if I were touching her hand when I opened the door delicately like the inside of a watch.

The first room in the house was her kitchen and she wasn't in it, but there were twenty or thirty vases and jars and bottles filled with flowers. They were on the kitchen table and on all the shelves and ledges. Some of the flowers were stale and some of the flowers were fresh.

I went inside the next room and it was the living room and she wasn't there either, but again there were twenty or thirty vases and jars and bottles filled with flowers.

The flowers made my heart beat faster.

Her garbage had lied to me.

I went inside the last room and it was her bedroom and she wasn't there either, but again the twenty or thirty vases and jars and bottles filled with flowers.

There was a window right next to the bed and it was the window that looked down on the street. The bed was made of brass with a patchwork quilt on it. I walked over to the window and stood there staring down at my friend who was sitting in the gutter looking up at the window.

He couldn't believe that I was standing there in the witch's window and I waved very slowly at him and he waved very slowly at me. Our waving seemed to be very distant travelling from our arms like two people waving at each other in different cities, perhaps between Tacoma and Salem, and our waving was merely an echo of their waving across thousands of miles.

Now the dare had been completed and I turned around in that house which was like a shallow garden and all my fears collapsed upon me like a landslide of flowers and I ran screaming at the top of my lungs outside and down the stairs. I sounded as if I had stepped in a wheelbarrow-sized pile of steaming dragon shit.

When I came screaming around the side of the house, my friend jumped up from the gutter and started screaming, too. I guess he thought that the witch was chasing me. We ran screaming through the streets of Tacoma, pursued by our own voices like a 1692 Cotton Mather newsreel.

This was a month or two before the German Army marched into Poland.

1/3, 1/3, 1/3

IT was all to be done in thirds. I was to get 1/3 for doing the typing, and she was to get 1/3 for doing the editing, and he was to get 1/3 for writing the novel.

We were going to divide the royalties three ways. We all shook hands on the deal, each knowing what we were supposed to do, the path before us, the gate at the end.

I was made a 1/3 partner because I had the typewriter.

I lived in a cardboard-lined shack of my own building across the street from the run-down old house the Welfare rented for her and her nine-year-old son Freddy.

The novelist lived in a trailer a mile away beside a sawmill pond where he was the watchman for the mill.

I was about seventeen and made lonely and strange by that Pacific Northwest of so many years ago, that dark, rainy land of 1952. I'm thirty-one now and I still can't figure out what I meant by living the way I did in those days.

She was one of those eternally fragile women in their late thirties and once very pretty and the object of much attention

in the roadhouses and beer parlors, who are now on Welfare
and their entire lives rotate around that one day a month when
they get their Welfare checks.

The word "check" is the one religious word in their lives,
so they always manage to use it at least three or four times in
every conversation. It doesn't matter what you are talking
about.

The novelist was in his late forties, tall, reddish, and looked
as if life had given him an endless stream of two-timing girlfriends, five-day drunks and cars with bad transmissions.

He was writing the novel because he wanted to tell a story
that had happened to him years before when he was working
in the woods.

He also wanted to make some money: 1/3.

My entrance into the thing came about this way: One day
I was standing in front of my shack, eating an apple and
staring at a black ragged toothache sky that was about to
rain.

What I was doing was like an occupation for me. I was that
involved in looking at the sky and eating the apple. You
would have thought that I had been hired to do it with a
good salary and a pension if I stared at the sky long enough.

"HEY, YOU!" I heard somebody yell.

I looked across the mud puddle and it was the woman. She
was wearing a kind of green Mackinaw that she wore all the
time, except when she had to visit the Welfare people downtown. Then she put on a shapeless duck-gray coat.

We lived in a poor part of town where the streets weren't
paved. The street was nothing more than a big mud puddle
that you had to walk around. The street was of no use to
cars any more. They travelled on a different frequency where
asphalt and gravel were more sympathetic.

She was wearing a pair of white rubber boots that she

always had on in the winter, a pair of boots that gave her
a kind of child-like appearance. She was so fragile and firmly
indebted to the Welfare Department that she often looked
like a child twelve years old.

"What do you want?" I said.

"You have a typewriter, don't you?" she said. "I've walked
by your shack and heard you typing. You type a lot at night."

"Yeah, I have a typewriter," I said.

"You a good typist?" she said.

"I'm all right."

"We don't have a typewriter. How would you like to go
in with us?" she yelled across the mud puddle. She looked
a perfect twelve years old, standing there in her white boots,
the sweetheart and darling of all mud puddles.

"What's 'go in' mean?"

"Well, he's writing a novel," she said. "He's good. I'm
editing it. I've read a lot of pocketbooks and the *Reader's
Digest*. We need somebody who has a typewriter to type it
up. You'll get 1/3. How does that sound?"

"I'd like to see the novel," I said. I didn't know what was
happening. I knew she had three or four boyfriends that were
always visiting her.

"Sure!" she yelled. "You have to see it to type it. Come
on around. Let's go out to his place right now and you can
meet him and have a look at the novel. He's a good guy. It's
a wonderful book."

"OK," I said, and walked around the mud puddle to where
she was standing in front of her evil dentist house, twelve
years old, and approximately two miles from the Welfare
office.

"Let's go," she said.

★   ★   ★

We walked over to the highway and down the highway past mud puddles and sawmill ponds and fields flooded with rain until we came to a road that went across the railroad tracks and turned down past half a dozen small sawmill ponds that were filled with black winter logs.

We talked very little and that was only about her check that was two days late and she had called the Welfare and they said they mailed the check and it should be there tomorrow, but call again tomorrow if it's not there and we'll prepare an emergency money order for you.

"Well, I hope it's there tomorrow," I said.

"So do I or I'll have to go downtown," she said.

Next to the last sawmill pond was a yellow old trailer up on blocks of wood. One look at that trailer showed that it was never going anywhere again, that the highway was in distant heaven, only to be prayed to. It was really sad with a cemetery-like chimney swirling jagged dead smoke in the air above it.

A kind of half-dog, half-cat creature was sitting on a rough plank porch that was in front of the door. The creature half-barked and half-meowed at us, "Arfeow!" and darted under the trailer, looking out at us from behind a block.

"This is it," the woman said.

The door to the trailer opened and a man stepped out onto the porch. There was a pile of firewood stacked on the porch and it was covered with a black tarp.

The man held his hand above his eyes, shielding his eyes from a bright imaginary sun, though everything had turned dark in anticipation of the rain.

"Hello, there," he said.

"Hi," I said.

"Hello, honey," she said.

He shook my hand and welcomed me to his trailer, then

he gave her a little kiss on the mouth before we all went inside.

The place was small and muddy and smelled like stale rain and had a large unmade bed that looked as if it had been a partner to some of the saddest love-making this side of The Cross.

There was a green bushy half-table with a couple of insect-like chairs and a little sink and a small stove that was used for cooking and heating.

There were some dirty dishes in the little sink. The dishes looked as if they had always been dirty: born dirty to last forever.

I could hear a radio playing Western music someplace in the trailer, but I couldn't find it. I looked all over but it was nowhere in sight. It was probably under a shirt or something.

"He's the kid with the typewriter," she said. "He'll get 1/3 for typing it."

"That sounds fair," he said. "We need somebody to type it. I've never done anything like this before."

"Why don't you show it to him?" she said. "He'd like to take a look at it."

"OK. But it isn't too carefully written," he said to me. "I only went to the fourth grade, so she's going to edit it, straighten out the grammar and commas and stuff."

There was a notebook lying on the table, next to an ash-tray that probably had 600 cigarette butts in it. The notebook had a color photograph of Hopalong Cassidy on the cover.

Hopalong looked tired as if he had spent the previous night chasing starlets all over Hollywood and barely had enough strength to get back in the saddle.

There were about twenty-five or thirty pages of writing in the notebook. It was written in a large grammar school sprawl: an unhappy marriage between printing and longhand.

"It's not finished yet," he said.

"You'll type it. I'll edit it. He'll write it," she said.

It was a story about a young logger falling in love with a waitress. The novel began in 1935 in a cafe in North Bend, Oregon.

The young logger was sitting at a table and the waitress was taking his order. She was very pretty with blond hair and rosy cheeks. The young logger was ordering veal cutlets with mashed potatoes and country gravy.

"Yeah, I'll do the editing. You can type it, can't you? It's not too bad, is it?" she said in a twelve-year-old voice with the Welfare peeking over her shoulder.

"No," I said. "It will be easy."

Suddenly the rain started to come down hard outside, without any warning, just suddenly great drops of rain that almost shook the trailer.

You sur lik veel cutlets dont you Maybell said she was ~~holding~~ holding her pensil up her mowth that was preti and red like an apl!

Onli wen you tak my oder Carl said he was a kind of bassful loger but big and strong lik his dead who ownd the starmill!

Ill mak sur you get plenti of gravi!

Just ten the caf door opend and in cam Rins Adams he was hansom and meen, everi bodi in thos parts was afrad of him but not Carl and his ~~dead~~ dad they wasnt afrad of him no sur!

Maybell shifard wen she saw him standing ther in his blac macinaw he smild at her and Carl felt his blod run hot lik scallding cofee and fiting mad!

Howdi ther Rins said Maybell blushed like a ~~flower~~ flouar while we were all sitting there in that rainy trailer, pounding at the gates of American literature.

THE GATHERING
OF A CALIFORNIAN

LIKE most Californians, I come from someplace else and was
gathered to the purpose of California like a metal-eating
flower gathers the sunshine, the rain, and then to the freeway
beckons its petals and lets the cars drive in, millions of cars
into but a single flower, the scent choked with congestion and
room for millions more.

California needs us, so it gathers us from other places. I'll
take you, you, you, and I from the Pacific Northwest: a
haunted land where nature dances the minuet with people and
danced with me in those old bygone days.

I brought everything I knew from there to California: years
and years of a different life to which I can never return nor
want to and seems at times almost to have occurred to another
body somehow vaguely in my shape and recognition.

It's strange that California likes to get her people from
every place else and leave what we knew behind and here
to California we are gathered as if energy itself, the shadow
of that metal-eating flower, had summoned us away from
other lives and now to do the California until the very end
like the Taj Mahal in the shape of a parking meter.

A SHORT STORY ABOUT
CONTEMPORARY LIFE
IN CALIFORNIA

THERE are thousands of stories with original beginnings. This is not one of them. I think the only way to start a story about contemporary life in California is to do it the way Jack London started *The Sea-Wolf*. I have confidence in that beginning.

It worked in 1904 and it can work in 1969. I believe that beginning can reach across the decades and serve the purpose of this story because this is California—we can do anything we want to do—and a rich young literary critic is taking a ferryboat from Sausalito to San Francisco. He has just finished spending a few days at a friend's cabin in Mill Valley. The friend uses the cabin to read Schopenhauer and Nietzsche during the winter. They all have great times together.

While travelling across the bay in the fog he thinks about writing an essay called "The Necessity for Freedom: A Plea for the Artist."

Of course Wolf Larsen torpedoes the ferryboat and captures the rich young literary critic who is changed instantly into a cabin boy and has to wear funny clothes and take a lot of shit off everybody, has great intellectual conversations with old Wolf, gets kicked in the ass, grabbed by the throat, promoted to mate, grows up, meets his true love Maud, escapes from Wolf, bounces around the damn Pacific Ocean in little better than a half-assed rowboat, finds an island, builds a stone hut, clubs seals, fixes a broken sailing ship, buries Wolf at sea, gets kissed, etc.: all to end this story about contemporary life in California sixty-five years later.

Thank God.

PACIFIC RADIO FIRE

THE largest ocean in the world starts or ends at Monterey, California. It depends on what language you are speaking. My friend's wife had just left him. She walked right out the door and didn't even say good-bye. We went and got two fifths of port and headed for the Pacific.

It's an old song that's been played on all the jukeboxes in America. The song has been around so long that it's been recorded on the very dust of America and it has settled on everything and changed chairs and cars and toys and lamps and windows into billions of phonographs to play that song back into the ear of our broken heart.

We sat down on a small corner-like beach surrounded by big granite rocks and the hugeness of the Pacific Ocean with all its vocabularies.

We were listening to rock and roll on his transistor radio and somberly drinking port. We were both in despair. I didn't know what he was going to do with the rest of his life either.

I took another sip of port. The Beach Boys were singing a song about California girls on the radio. They liked them.

His eyes were wet wounded rugs.

Like some kind of strange vacuum cleaner I tried to console him. I recited the same old litanies that you say to people when you try to help their broken hearts, but words can't help at all.

It's just the sound of another human voice that makes the only difference. There's nothing you're ever going to say that's going to make anybody happy when they're feeling shitty about losing somebody that they love.

Finally he set fire to the radio. He piled some paper around it. He struck a match to the paper. We sat there watching it. I had never seen anybody set fire to a radio before.

As the radio gently burned away, the flames began to affect the songs that we were listening to. A record that was #1 on the Top-40 suddenly dropped to #13 inside of itself. A song that was #9 became #27 in the middle of a chorus about loving somebody. They tumbled in popularity like broken birds. Then it was too late for all of them.

ELMIRA

I return as if in the dream of a young American duck hunting prince to Elmira and I am standing again on the bridge across the Long Tom River. It is always late December and the river is high and muddy and stirs dark leafless branches from its cold depths.

Sometimes it is raining on the bridge and I'm looking downstream to where the river flows into the lake. There is always a marshy field in my dream surrounded by an old black wooden fence and an ancient shed showing light through the walls and the roof.

I'm warm and dry under sweet layers of royal underwear and rain clothes.

Sometimes it is cold and clear and I can see my breath and there's frost on the bridge and I'm looking upstream into a tangle of trees that lead to the mountains many miles away where the Long Tom River starts its beginning.

Sometimes I write my name on the bridge in frost. I spell

my name out very carefully, and sometimes I write "Elmira" in frost, too, and just as carefully.

I'm always carrying a double-barrel sixteen-gauge shotgun with lots of shells in my pockets . . . perhaps too many shells because I am a teen-ager and it's easy to worry about running out of shells, so I'm weighed down with too many shells.

I'm almost like a deep-sea diver because my pockets are filled with such an abundance of lead. Sometimes I even walk funny because I've got so many shells in my pockets.

I'm always alone on the bridge and there's always a small flock of mallards that fly very high over the bridge and down toward the lake.

Sometimes I look both ways on the road to see if a car is coming and if a car isn't coming, I shoot at them, but they are too high for my shot to do anything but annoy them a little.

Sometimes a car is coming and I just watch the ducks fly down the river and keep the shooting to myself. It might be a game warden or a deputy sheriff. I have an idea somewhere in my head that it is against the law to shoot at ducks from a bridge.

I wonder if I am right.

Sometimes I don't look to see if there is a car on the road. The ducks are too high to shoot at. I know I'll just waste my ammunition, so I let them pass.

The ducks are always a flock of fat mallards just in from Canada.

Sometimes I walk through the little town of Elmira and everything is very quiet because it's so early in the morning and God forsaken with either rain or cold.

Whenever I walk through Elmira, I stand and look at the

Elmira Union High School. The classrooms are always empty and dark inside. It seems as if nobody ever studies there and the darkness is never broken because there is no reason to ever turn the lights on.

Sometimes I don't go into Elmira. I cross over the black wooden fence and go into the marshy field and walk past the ancient religious shed and follow the river down to the lake, hoping to hit some good duck hunting.

I never do.

Elmira is very beautiful but it is not a lucky place for me to hunt.

I always get to Elmira by hitch-hiking about twenty miles. I stand out there in the cold or the rain with my shotgun, wearing my royal duck hunting robes and people stop and pick me up, and that's how I get there.

"Where are you going?" people say when I get in. I sit beside them with my shotgun balanced like a scepter between my legs and the barrels pointing up at the roof. The gun is at an angle, so the barrels point toward the passenger side of the roof, and I'm always the passenger.

"Elmira."

COFFEE

SOMETIMES life is merely a matter of coffee and whatever intimacy a cup of coffee affords. I once read something about coffee. The thing said that coffee is good for you; it stimulates all the organs.

I thought at first this was a strange way to put it, and not altogether pleasant, but as time goes by I have found out that it makes sense in its own limited way. I'll tell you what I mean.

Yesterday morning I went over to see a girl. I like her. Whatever we had going for us is gone now. She does not care for me. I blew it and wish I hadn't.

I rang the door bell and waited on the stairs. I could hear her moving around upstairs. The way she moved I could tell that she was getting up. I had awakened her.

Then she came down the stairs. I could feel her approach in my stomach. Every step she took stirred my feelings and led indirectly to her opening the door. She saw me and it did not please her.

Once upon a time it pleased her very much, last week. I wonder where it went, pretending to be naive.

"I feel strange now," she said. "I don't want to talk."

"I want a cup of coffee," I said, because it was the last thing in the world that I wanted. I said it in such a way that it sounded as if I were reading her a telegram from somebody else, a person who really wanted a cup of coffee, who cared about nothing else.

"All right," she said.

I followed her up the stairs. It was ridiculous. She had just put some clothes on. They had not quite adjusted themselves to her body. I could tell you about her ass. We went into the kitchen.

She took a jar of instant coffee off a shelf and put it on the table. She placed a cup next to it, and a spoon. I looked at them. She put a pan full of water on the stove and turned the gas on under it.

All this time she did not say a word. Her clothes adjusted themselves to her body. I won't. She left the kitchen.

Then she went down the stairs and outside to see if she had any mail. I didn't remember seeing any. She came back up the stairs and went into another room. She closed the door after her. I looked at the pan full of water on the stove.

I knew that it would take a year before the water started to boil. It was now October and there was too much water in the pan. That was the problem. I threw half the water into the sink.

The water would boil faster now. It would take only six months. The house was quiet.

I looked out at the back porch. There were sacks of garbage there. I stared at the garbage and tried to figure out what she had been eating lately by studying the containers and peelings and stuff. I couldn't tell a thing.

It was now March. The water started to boil. I was pleased by this.

I looked at the table. There was the jar of instant coffee, the empty cup and the spoon all laid out like a funeral service. These are the things that you need to make a cup of coffee.

When I left the house ten minutes later, the cup of coffee safely inside me like a grave, I said, "Thank you for the cup of coffee."

"You're welcome," she said. Her voice came from behind a closed door. Her voice sounded like another telegram. It was really time for me to leave.

I spent the rest of the day not making coffee. It was a comfort. And evening came. I had dinner in a restaurant and went to a bar. I had some drinks and talked to some people.

We were bar people and said bar things. None of them remembered, and the bar closed. It was two o'clock in the morning. I had to go outside. It was foggy and cold in San Francisco. I wondered about the fog and felt very human and exposed.

I decided to go visit another girl. We had not been friends for over a year. Once we were very close. I wondered what she was thinking about now.

I went over to her house. She didn't have a door bell. That was a small victory. One must keep track of all the small victories. I do, anyway.

She answered the door. She was holding a robe in front of herself. She didn't believe that she was seeing me. "What do you want?" she said, believing now that she was seeing me. I walked right into the house.

She turned and closed the door in such a way that I could see her profile. She had not bothered to wrap the robe completely around herself. She was just holding the robe in front of herself.

I could see an unbroken line of body running from her head to her feet. It looked kind of strange. Perhaps because it was so late at night.

"What do you want?" she said.

"I want a cup of coffee," I said. What a funny thing to say, to say again for a cup of coffee was not what I really wanted.

She looked at me and wheeled slightly on the profile. She was not pleased to see me. Let the AMA tell us that time heals. I looked at the unbroken line of her body.

"Why don't you have a cup of coffee with me?" I said. "I feel like talking to you. We haven't talked for a long time."

She looked at me and wheeled slightly on the profile. I stared at the unbroken line of her body. This was not good.

"It's too late," she said. "I have to get up in the morning. If you want a cup of coffee, there's instant in the kitchen. I have to go to bed."

The kitchen light was on. I looked down the hall into the kitchen. I didn't feel like going into the kitchen and having another cup of coffee by myself. I didn't feel like going to anybody else's house and asking them for a cup of coffee.

I realized that the day had been committed to a very strange pilgrimage, and I had not planned it that way. At least the jar of instant coffee was not on the table, beside an empty white cup and a spoon.

They say in the spring a young man's fancy turns to thoughts of love. Perhaps if he has enough time left over, his fancy can even make room for a cup of coffee.

THE LOST CHAPTERS OF
TROUT FISHING IN AMERICA:
"REMBRANDT CREEK"
AND "CARTHAGE SINK"

THESE two chapters were lost in the late winter, early spring of 1961. I looked all over for them but I couldn't find them anywhere. I haven't the slightest idea why I didn't rewrite them as soon as I realized that they were gone. It's a real puzzler but I didn't and now eight years later, I've decided to return to the winter that I was twenty-six years old, living on Greenwich Street in San Francisco, married, had an infant daughter and wrote these two chapters toward a vision of America and then lost them. I'm going back there now to see if I can find them.

"REMBRANDT CREEK"

REMBRANDT Creek looked just like its name and it was in lonely country that had very bad winters. The creek started in a high mountain meadow surrounded by pine trees. That was about the only real light that creek ever saw because after it had gathered itself from some small springs in the meadow, it flowed off into the pines and down to a dark-tree-tangled canyon that went along the edge of the mountains.

The creek was filled with little trout so wild that they were barely afraid when you walked up to the creek and stood there staring down at them.

I never really went fishing for them in any classical or even functioning sense. The only reason I knew that creek was because that's where we camped when we went deer hunting.

No, it was not a fishing creek for me but just a place where we got water that we needed for our camp but I seemed to carry most of the water that we used and I think I washed a lot of dishes because I was the teen-ager and it was easier to have me do those things than the men who were older and wiser and needed time to think about places where deer might be and also to drink a little whiskey which seemed to aid thoughts of hunting and other things.

"Hey, kid, take your head out of your ass and see if you can do something about these dishes." That was one of the elders of the hunt speaking. His voice is remembered down trails of sound-colored hunting marble.

Often I think about Rembrandt Creek and how much it looked like a painting hanging in the world's largest museum with a roof that went to the stars and galleries that knew the whisk of comets.

I only fished it once.

I didn't have any fishing tackle, just a 30:30 Winchester, so I took an old rusty bent nail and tied some white string onto it like the ghost of my childhood and tried to catch a trout using a piece of deer meat for bait and I almost caught one, too, lifting it out of the water just before it fell off my nail and back into the painting that carried it from my sight, returning it to the Seventeenth Century where it belonged on the easel of a man named Rembrandt.

"CARTHAGE SINK"

THE Carthage River came roaring out of the ground at a fountainhead that was like a wild well. It flowed arrogantly a dozen miles or so through an open canyon and then just disappeared into the ground at a place that was called Carthage Sink.

The river loved to tell everybody (everybody being the sky, the wind, the few trees that grew around there, birds, deer and even the stars if you can believe that) what a great river it was.

"I come roaring from the earth and return roaring to the earth. I am the master of my waters. I am the mother and father of myself. I don't need a single drop of rain. Look at my smooth strong white muscles. I am my own future!"

The Carthage River kept this kind of talking up for thousands of years. Needless to say: Everybody (everybody being the sky, etc.) was bored up to here with that river.

Birds and deer tried to keep away from that part of the country if they could avoid it. The stars had been reduced to playing a waiting game and there was a dramatically noticeable lack of wind in that area, except of course for the Carthage River.

Even the trout that lived there were ashamed of the river and always glad when they died. Anything was better than living in that God-damn bombastic river.

One day the Carthage River in mid-breath telling about how great it was, dried up, "I am the master of my . . ." It just stopped.

The river couldn't believe it. Not one more drop of water came from the ground and its sink was soon just a trickle dripping back into the ground like the runny nose of a kid.

The Carthage River's pride vanished in an irony of water and the canyon turned into a good mood. Birds suddenly flew all over the place and took a happy look at what had happened and a great wind came up and it even seemed as if the stars were out earlier that night to take a look and then smile beatifically.

There was a summer rainstorm a few miles away in some mountains and the Carthage River begged for the rain to come to its rescue.

"Please," the river said with a voice that was now only the shadow of a whisper. "Help me. I need water for my trout. They're dying. Look at the poor little things."

The storm looked at the trout. The trout were very happy with the way things were now, though they would soon be dead.

The rainstorm made up some incredibly elaborate story about having to visit somebody's grandmother who had a broken ice-cream freezer and somehow lots of rain was needed to repair it, "But maybe in a few months we might get together. I'll call you on the telephone before I come over."

The next day which was of course August 17, 1921 a lot of people, townspeople and such, drove out in their cars and looked at the former river and shook their heads in wonder. They had a lot of picnic baskets with them, too.

There was an article in the local paper with two photographs showing two large empty holes that had been the fountainhead and the sink of the Carthage River. The holes looked like nostrils.

Another photograph was of a cowboy sitting on his horse,

holding an umbrella in one hand and pointing into the depths of the Carthage Sink with his other hand. He was looking very serious. It was a photograph to make people laugh and that's exactly what they did.

Well, there you have the lost chapters of *Trout Fishing in America*. Their style is probably a little different because I'm a little different now, I'm thirty-four, and they were probably written in a slightly different form, too. It's interesting that I didn't rewrite them back there in 1961 but waited until December 4, 1969, almost a decade later, to return and try to bring them back with me.

THE WEATHER IN
SAN FRANCISCO

IT was a cloudy afternoon with an Italian butcher selling a pound of meat to a very old woman, but who knows what such an old woman could possibly use a pound of meat for?

She was too old for that much meat. Perhaps she used it for a bee hive and she had five hundred golden bees at home waiting for the meat, their bodies stuffed with honey.

"What kind of meat would you like today?" the butcher said. "We have some good hamburger. It's lean."

"I don't know," she said. "Hamburger is something else."

"Yeah, it's lean. I ground it myself. I put a lot of lean meat in it."

"Hamburger doesn't sound right," she said.

"Yeah," the butcher said. "It's a good day for hamburger. Look outside. It's cloudy. Some of those clouds have rain in them. I'd get the hamburger," he said.

"No," she said. "I don't want any hamburger, and I don't think it's going to rain. I think the sun is going to come out, and it will be a beautiful day, and I want a pound of liver."

The butcher was stunned. He did not like to sell liver to old ladies. There was something about it that made him very nervous. He didn't want to talk to her any more.

He reluctantly sliced a pound of liver off a huge red chunk and wrapped it up in white paper and put it into a brown bag. It was a very unpleasant experience for him.

He took her money, gave her the change, and went back to the poultry section to try and get a hold of his nerves.

By using her bones like the sails of a ship, the old woman passed outside into the street. She carried the liver as if it were a victory to the bottom of a very steep hill.

She climbed the hill and being very old, it was hard on her. She grew tired and had to stop and rest many times before she reached the top.

At the top of the hill was the old woman's house: a tall San Francisco house with bay windows that reflected a cloudy day.

She opened her purse which was like a small autumn field and near the fallen branches of an old apple tree, she found her keys.

Then she opened the door. It was a dear and trusted friend. She nodded at the door and went into the house and walked down a long hall into a room that was filled with bees.

There were bees everywhere in the room. Bees on the chairs. Bees on the photograph of her dead parents. Bees on the curtains. Bees on an ancient radio that once listened to the 1930s. Bees on her comb and brush.

The bees came to her and gathered about her lovingly while she unwrapped the liver and placed it upon a cloudy silver platter that soon changed into a sunny day.

COMPLICATED BANKING
PROBLEMS

I have a bank account because I grew tired of burying my money in the back yard and something else happened. I was burying some money a few years ago when I came across a human skeleton.

The skeleton had the remains of a shovel in one hand and a half-dissolved coffee can in the other hand. The coffee can was filled with a kind of rustdust material that I think was once money, so now I have a bank account.

But most of the time that doesn't work out very well either. When I wait in line there are almost always people in front of me who have complicated banking problems. I have to stand there and endure the financial cartoon crucifixions of America.

It goes something like this: There are three people in front of me. I have a little check to cash. My banking will only take a minute. The check is already endorsed. I have it in my hand, pointed in the direction of the teller.

The person just being waited on now is a woman fifty years

old. She is wearing a long black coat, though it is a hot day. She appears to be very comfortable in the coat and there is a strange smell coming from her. I think about it for a few seconds and realize that this is the first sign of a complicated banking problem.

Then she reaches into the folds of her coat and removes the shadow of a refrigerator filled with sour milk and year-old carrots. She wants to put the shadow in her savings account. She's already made out the slip.

I look up at the ceiling of the bank and pretend that it is the Sistine Chapel.

The old woman puts up quite a struggle before she's taken away. There's a lot of blood on the floor. She bit an ear off one of the guards.

I guess you have to admire her spunk.

The check in my hand is for ten dollars.

The next two people in line are actually one person. They are a pair of Siamese twins, but they each have their own bank books.

One of them is putting eighty-two dollars in his savings account and the other one is closing his savings account. The teller counts out 3,574 dollars for him and he puts it away in the pocket on his side of the pants.

All of this takes time. I look up at the ceiling of the bank again but I cannot pretend that it is the Sistine Chapel any more. My check is sweaty as if it had been written in 1929.

The last person between me and the teller is totally anonymous looking. He is so anonymous that he's barely there.

He puts 237 checks down on the counter that he wants to deposit in his checking account. They are for a total of 489,000 dollars. He also has 611 checks that he wants to deposit in his savings account. They are for a total of 1,754,961 dollars.

His checks completely cover the counter like a success snow storm. The teller starts on his banking as if she were a long distance runner while I stand there thinking that the skeleton in the back yard had made the right decision after all.

A HIGH BUILDING
IN SINGAPORE

I⊤'s a high building in Singapore that holds the only beauty for this San Francisco day where I am walking down the street, feeling terrible and watching my mind function with the efficiency of a liquid pencil.

A young mother passes by talking to her little girl who is really too small to be able to talk, but she's talking anyway and very excitedly to her mother about something. I can't quite make out what she is saying because she's so little.

I mean, this is a tiny kid.

Then her mother answers her to explode my day with a goofy illumination. "It was a high building in Singapore," she says to the little girl who enthusiastically replies like a bright sound-colored penny, "Yes, it was a high building in Singapore!"

AN UNLIMITED SUPPLY
OF 35 MILLIMETER FILM

PEOPLE cannot figure out why he is with her. They don't understand. He's so good-looking and she's so plain. "What does he see in her?" they ask themselves and each other. They know it's not her cooking because she's not a good cook. About the only thing that she can cook is a halfway decent meat loaf. She makes it every Tuesday night and he has a meat loaf sandwich in his lunch on Wednesday. Years pass. They stay together while their friends break up.

The beginning answer, as in so many of these things, lies in the bed where they make love. She becomes the theater where he shows films of his sexual dreams. Her body is like soft rows of living theater seats leading to a vagina that is the warm screen of his imagination where he makes love to all the women that he sees and wants like passing quicksilver movies, but she doesn't know a thing about it.

All she knows is that she loves him very much and he always pleases her and makes her feel good. She gets excited around four o'clock in the afternoon because she knows that he will be home from work at five.

He has made love to hundreds of different women inside of her. She makes all his dreams come true as she lies there like a simple contented theater in his touching, thinking only of him.

"What does he see in her?" people go on asking themselves and each other. They should know better. The final answer is very simple. It's all in his head.

THE SCARLATTI TILT

"IT's very hard to live in a studio apartment in San Jose with a man who's learning to play the violin." That's what she told the police when she handed them the empty revolver.

THE WILD BIRDS
OF HEAVEN

I'd rather dwell in some dark holler
where the sun refuses to shine,
where the wild birds of heaven
can't hear me when I whine.

> *—Folk Song*

THAT'S right. The children had been complaining for weeks about the television set. The picture was going out and that death John Donne spoke so fondly about was advancing rapidly down over the edge of whatever was playing that night, and there were also static lines that danced now and then like drunken cemeteries on that picture.

Mr. Henly was a simple American man, but his children were reaching the end of their rope. He worked in an insurance office keeping the dead separated from the living. They were in filing cabinets. Everybody at the office said that he had a great future.

One day he came home from work and his children were

waiting for him. They laid it right on the line: either he bought a new television set or they would become juvenile delinquents.

They showed him a photograph of five juvenile delinquents raping an old woman. One of the juvenile delinquents was hitting her on the head with a bicycle chain.

Mr. Henly agreed instantly to the children's demands. Anything, just put away that awful photograph. Then his wife came in and said the kindest thing she had said to him since the children were born, "Get a new television set for the kids. What are you: some kind of human monster?"

The next day Mr. Henly found himself standing in front of the Frederick Crow Department Store, and there was a huge sign plastered over the window. The sign said poetically: TV SALE.

He went inside and immediately found a video pacifier that had a 42-inch screen with built-in umbilical ducts. A clerk came over and sold the set to him by saying, "Hi, there."

"I'll take it," Mr. Henly said.

"Cash or credit?"

"Credit."

"Do you have one of our credit cards?" The clerk looked down at Mr. Henly's feet. "No, you don't have one," he said. "Just give me your name and address and the television set will be home when you get there."

"What about my credit?" Mr. Henly said.

"That won't be any problem," the clerk said. "Our credit department is waiting for you."

"Oh," Mr. Henly said.

The clerk pointed the way back to the credit department. "They're waiting for you."

The clerk was right, too. There was a beautiful girl sitting at a desk. She was really lovely. She looked like a composite of all the beautiful girls you see in all the cigarette advertisements and on television.

Wow! Mr. Henly took out his pack and lit up. After all he was no fool.

The girl smiled and said, "May I help you?"

"Yes. I want to buy a television set on credit, and I'd like to open an account at your store. I have a steady job, three children and I'm buying a house and a car. My credit's good," he said. "I'm already 25,000 dollars in debt."

Mr. Henly expected the girl to make a telephone call to check on his credit or do something to see if he had been lying about the 25,000 dollars.

She didn't.

"Don't worry about anything," she said. She certainly did have a nice voice. "The set is yours. Just step in there."

She pointed toward a room that had a pleasant door. Actually the door was quite exciting. It was a heavy wooden door with a fantastic grain running through the wood, a grain like the cracks of an earthquake running across the desert sunrise. The grain was filled with light.

The doorknob was pure silver. It was the door that Mr. Henly had always wanted to open. His hand had dreamt its shape while millions of years had passed in the sea.

Above the door was a sign:

BLACKSMITH.

He opened the door and went inside and there was a man waiting for him. The man said, "Take off your shoes, please."

"I just want to sign the papers," Mr. Henly said. "I've got a steady job. I'll pay on time."

"Don't worry about it," the man said. "Just take off your shoes."

Mr. Henly took off his shoes.

"The socks, too."

He did this and then did not think it strange because after all he didn't have any money to buy the television set with. The floor wasn't cold.

"How tall are you?" the man asked.

"5-11."

The man walked over to a filing cabinet and pulled out the drawer that had 5-11 printed on it. The man took out a plastic bag and then closed the drawer. Mr. Henly thought of a good joke to tell the man but then immediately forgot it.

The man opened the bag and took out the shadow of an immense bird. He unfolded the shadow as if it were a pair of pants.

"What's that?"

"It's the shadow of a bird," the man said and walked over to where Mr. Henly was sitting and laid the shadow on the floor beside his feet.

Then he took a strange-looking hammer and pulled the nails out of Mr. Henly's shadow, the nails that fastened it to his body. The man folded up the shadow very carefully. He laid it on a chair beside Mr. Henly.

"What are you doing?" Mr. Henly said. He wasn't afraid. Just a little curious.

"Putting the shadow on," the man said and nailed the bird's shadow onto his feet. At least it didn't hurt.

"There you go," the man said. "You have 24 months to pay for the television set. When you finish paying for the set, we'll switch shadows. It looks pretty good on you."

Mr. Henly stared down at the shadow of a bird coming off his human body. It doesn't look bad, Mr. Henly thought.

When he left the room the beautiful girl behind the desk said, "My, how you've changed."

Mr. Henly liked having her talk to him. During many years of married life he had forgotten what sex was really about.

He reached into his pocket for a cigarette and discovered that he had smoked them all up. He felt very embarrassed. The girl stared at him as if he were a small child that had done something wrong.

WINTER RUG

MY credentials? Of course. They are in my pocket. Here: I've had friends who have died in California and I mourn them in my own way. I've been to Forest Lawn and romped over the place like an eager child. I've read *The Loved One, The American Way of Death, Wallets in Shrouds* and my favorite *After Many a Summer Dies the Swan.*

I have watched men standing beside hearses in front of mortuaries directing funerals with walky-talkies as if they were officers in a metaphysical war.

Oh, yes: I was once walking with a friend past a skid row hotel in San Francisco and they were carrying a corpse out of the hotel. The corpse was done tastefully in a white sheet with four or five Chinese extras looking on, and there was a very slow-moving ambulance parked out front that was prohibited by law from having a siren or to go any faster than thirty-seven miles an hour and from showing any aggressive action in traffic.

My friend looked at the lady or gentleman corpse as it went by and said, "Being dead is one step up from living in that hotel."

As you can see, I am an expert on death in California. My credentials stand up to the closest inspection. I am qualified to continue with another story told to me by my friend who also works as a gardener for a very wealthy old woman in Marin County. She had a nineteen-year-old dog that she loved deeply and the dog responded to this love by dying very slowly from senility.

Every day my friend went to work the dog would be a little more dead. It was long past the proper time for the dog to die, but the dog had been dying for so long that it had lost the way to death.

This happens to a lot of old people in this country. They get so old and live with death so long that they lose the way when it comes time to actually die.

Sometimes they stay lost for years. It is horrible to watch them linger on. Finally the weight of their own blood crushes them.

Anyway, at last the woman could not stand to watch the senile suffering of her dog any longer and called up a veterinarian to come and put the dog to sleep.

She instructed my friend to build a coffin for the dog, which he did, figuring it was one of the fringe clauses of gardening in California.

The death doctor drove out to her estate and was soon in the house carrying a little black bag. That was a mistake. It should have been a large pastel bag. When the old woman saw the little black bag, she paled visibly. The unnecessary reality of it scared her, so she sent the veterinarian away with a generous check in his pocket.

Alas, having the veterinarian go away did not solve the dog's basic problem: He was so senile that death had become a way of life and he was lost from the act of dying.

The next day the dog walked into the corner of a room and couldn't get out of it. The dog stood there for hours until it collapsed from exhaustion, which conveniently happened to be just when the old woman came into the room, looking for the keys to her Rolls-Royce.

She started crying when she saw the dog lying there like a mutt puddle in the corner. Its face was still pressed against the wall and its eyes were watering in some human kind of way that dogs get when they live with people too long and pick up their worst characteristics.

She had her maid carry the dog to his rug. The dog had a Chinese rug that he had slept on since he was a puppy in China before the fall of Chiang Kai-shek. The rug had been worth a thousand American dollars, then, having survived a dynasty or two.

The rug was worth a lot more now, being in rather excellent shape with actually no more wear and tear than it would get being stored in a castle for a couple of centuries.

The old woman called the veterinarian again and he arrived with his little black bag of tricks and how to find the way back to death after having lost it for years, years that led oneself to being trapped in the corner of a room.

"Where is your pet?" he said.

"On his rug," she said.

The dog lay exhausted and sprawled across beautiful Chinese flowers and things from a different world. "Please do it on his rug," she said. "I think he would like that."

"Certainly," he said. "Don't worry. He won't feel a thing. It's painless. Just like falling asleep."

"Good-bye, Charlie," the old woman said. The dog of course didn't hear her. He had been deaf since 1959.

After bidding the dog farewell, the old woman took to bed. She left the room just as the veterinarian was opening his little black bag. The veterinarian needed PR help desperately.

Afterward my friend took the coffin in the house to pick up the dog. A maid had wrapped the body in the rug. The old woman insisted that the dog be buried with the rug and its head facing West in a grave near the rose garden, pointing toward China. My friend buried the dog with its head pointing toward Los Angeles.

As he carried the coffin outside he peeked in at the thousand-dollar rug. Beautiful design, he said to himself. All you would have to do would be to vacuum it a little and it would be as good as new.

My friend is not generally known as a sentimentalist. Stupid dead dog! he said to himself as he neared the grave, Damn dead dog!

"But I did it," he told me. "I buried that dog with the rug and I don't know why. It's a question that I'll ask myself forever. Sometimes when it rains at night in the winter, I think of that rug down there in the grave, wrapped around a dog."

ERNEST HEMINGWAY'S
TYPIST

IT sounds like religious music. A friend of mine just came back from New York where he had Ernest Hemingway's typist do some typing for him.

He's a successful writer, so he went and got the very best, which happens to be the woman who did Ernest Hemingway's typing. It's enough to take your breath away, to marble your lungs with silence.

Ernest Hemingway's typist!

She's every young writer's dream come true with the appearance of her hands which are like a harpsichord and the perfect intensity of her gaze and all to be followed by the profound sound of her typing.

He paid her fifteen dollars an hour. That's more money than a plumber or an electrician gets.

$120 a day! for a typist!

He said that she does everything for you. You just hand her the copy and like a miracle you have attractive, correct spelling and punctuation that is so beautiful that it brings

tears to your eyes and paragraphs that look like Greek temples
and she even finishes sentences for you.
　She's Ernest Hemingway's
　She's Ernest Hemingway's typist.

HOMAGE
TO THE SAN FRANCISCO
YMCA

ONCE upon a time in San Francisco there was a man who really liked the finer things in life, especially poetry. He liked good verse.

He could afford to indulge himself in this liking, which meant that he didn't have to work because he was receiving a generous pension that was the result of a 1920s investment that his grandfather had made in a private insane asylum that was operating quite profitably in Southern California.

In the black, as they say and located in the San Fernando Valley, just outside of Tarzana. It was one of those places that do not look like an insane asylum. It looked like something else with flowers all around it, mostly roses.

The checks always arrived on the 1st and the 15th of every month, even when there was not a mail delivery on that day. He had a lovely house in Pacific Heights and he would go out and buy more poetry. He of course had never met a poet in person. That would have been a little too much.

One day he decided that his liking for poetry could not be

fully expressed in just reading poetry or listening to poets reading on phonograph records. He decided to take the plumbing out of his house and completely replace it with poetry, and so he did.

He turned off the water and took out the pipes and put in John Donne to replace them. The pipes did not look too happy. He took out his bathtub and put in William Shakespeare. The bathtub did not know what was happening.

He took out his kitchen sink and put in Emily Dickinson. The kitchen sink could only stare back in wonder. He took out his bathroom sink and put in Vladimir Mayakovsky. The bathroom sink, even though the water was off, broke out into tears.

He took out his hot water heater and put in Michael McClure's poetry. The hot water heater could barely contain its sanity. Finally he took out his toilet and put in the minor poets. The toilet planned on leaving the country.

And now the time had come to see how it all worked, to enjoy the fruit of his amazing labor. Christopher Columbus' slight venture sailing West was merely the shadow of a dismal event in the comparison. He turned the water back on again and surveyed the countenance of his vision brought to reality. He was a happy man.

"I think I'll take a bath," he said, to celebrate. He tried to heat up some Michael McClure to take a bath in some William Shakespeare and what happened was not actually what he had planned on happening.

"Might as well do the dishes, then," he said. He tried to wash some plates in "I taste a liquor never brewed," and found there was quite a difference between that liquid and a kitchen sink. Despair was on its way.

He tried to go to the toilet and the minor poets did not do at all. They began gossiping about their careers as he sat there trying to take a shit. One of them had written 197 sonnets about a penguin he had once seen in a travelling circus. He sensed a Pulitzer Prize in this material.

Suddenly the man realized that poetry could not replace plumbing. It's what they call seeing the light. He decided immediately to take the poetry out and put the pipes back in, along with the sinks, the bathtub, the hot water heater and the toilet.

"This just didn't work out the way I planned it," he said. "I'll have to put the plumbing back. Take the poetry out." It made sense standing there naked in the total light of failure.

But then he ran into more trouble than there was in the first place. The poetry did not want to go. It liked very much occupying the positions of the former plumbing.

"I look great as a kitchen sink," Emily Dickinson's poetry said.

"We look wonderful as a toilet," the minor poets said.

"I'm grand as pipes," John Donne's poetry said.

"I'm a perfect hot water heater," Michael McClure's poetry said.

Vladimir Mayakovsky sang new faucets from the bathroom, there are faucets beyond suffering, and William Shakespeare's poetry was nothing but smiles.

"That's well and dandy for you," the man said. "But I have to have plumbing, *real* plumbing in this house. Did you notice the emphasis I put on *real*? Real! Poetry just can't handle it. Face up to reality," the man said to the poetry.

But the poetry refused to go. "We're staying." The man offered to call the police. "Go ahead and lock us up, you illiterate," the poetry said in one voice.

"I'll call the fire department!"

"Book burner!" the poetry shouted.

The man began to fight the poetry. It was the first time

he had ever been in a fight. He kicked the poetry of Emily Dickinson in the nose.

Of course the poetry of Michael McClure and Vladimir Mayakovsky walked over and said in English and in Russian, "That won't do at all," and threw the man down a flight of stairs. He got the message.

That was two years ago. The man is now living in the YMCA in San Francisco and loves it. He spends more time in the bathroom than everybody else. He goes in there at night and talks to himself with the light out.

THE PRETTY OFFICE

WHEN first I passed by there, it was just an ordinary office with desks and typewriters and filing cabinets and telephones ringing and people answering the telephones. There were half a dozen women working there, but there was nothing to distinguish them from millions of other office workers across America, and none of them were pretty.

The men who worked in the office were all about middle age and they did not show any sign of ever having been handsome in their youth or actually anything in their youth. They all looked like people whose names you forget.

They did what they had to do in the office. There was no sign on the window or above the door telling what the office was about, so I never knew what those people were doing. Perhaps they were a division of a large business that was located someplace else.

The people all seemed to know what they were doing, and so I let it go at that, passing by there twice a day: on my way to work and on my way home from work.

A year or so passed and the office remained constant. The people were the same and a certain amount of activity went on: just another little place in the universe.

Then one day I passed by there on my way to work and all the ordinary women who had worked there were gone, vanished, as if the very air itself had given them new employment.

There was not even a trace of them, and in their wake were six very pretty girls: blondes and brunettes and on and on into the various pretty faces and bodies, into the exciting feminine of this and that, into form-fitting smart clothes.

There were large friendly-looking breasts and small pleasant breasts and behinds that were all enticing. Every place I looked in that office there was something nice happening in woman form.

What had happened? Where had the other women gone? Where had these women come from? They all looked new to San Francisco. Whose idea was this? Was this the ultimate meaning of Frankenstein? My God, we all guessed wrong!

And now it's been another year with passing by there five days a week and staring intently in the window, trying to figure it out: all these pretty bodies carrying on whatever they do in there.

I wonder if the boss's wife, whoever the boss is, which one he is, died and this is his revenge over years of dullness, getting even it's called, or maybe he just got tired of watching television in the evening.

Or just what happened, I don't know.

There is a girl with long blond hair answering the telephone. There is a cute brunette putting something away in a filing cabinet. There is a cheer leader type with perfect teeth erasing something. There is an exotic brunette carrying a book across the office. There is a mysterious little girl with very large breasts rolling a piece of paper into a typewriter. There is a tall girl with a perfect mouth and a grand behind, putting a stamp on an envelope.

It's a pretty office.

A NEED FOR GARDENS

WHEN I got there they were burying the lion in the back yard again. As usual, it was a hastily dug grave, not really large enough to hold the lion and dug with a maximum of incompetence and they were trying to stuff the lion into a sloppy little hole.

The lion as usual took it quite stoically. Having been buried at least fifty times during the last two years, the lion had gotten used to being buried in the back yard.

I remember the first time they buried him. He didn't know what was happening. He was a younger lion, then, and was frightened and confused, but now he knew what was happening because he was an older lion and had been buried so many times.

He looked vaguely bored as they folded his front paws across his chest and started throwing dirt in his face.

It was basically hopeless. The lion would never fit the hole. It had never fit a hole in the back yard before and it never would. They just couldn't dig a hole big enough to bury that lion in.

"Hello," I said. "The hole's too small."

"Hello," they said. "No, it isn't."

This had been our standard greeting now for two years.

I stood there and watched them for an hour or so struggling desperately to bury the lion, but they were only able to bury ¼ of him before they gave up in disgust and stood around trying to blame each other for not making the hole big enough.

"Why don't you put a garden in next year?" I said. "This soil looks like it might grow some good carrots."

They didn't think that was very funny.

THE OLD BUS

I do what everybody else does: I live in San Francisco. Sometimes I am forced by Mother Nature to take the bus. Yesterday was an example. I wanted to get some place beyond the duty of my legs, far out on Clay Street, so I waited for a bus.

It was not a hardship but a nice warm autumn day and fiercely clear. An old woman waited, too. Nothing unusual about that, as they say. She had a large purse and white gloves that fit her hands like the skins of vegetables.

A Chinese fellow came by on the back of a motorcycle. It startled me. I had just never thought about the Chinese riding motorcycles before. Sometimes reality is an awfully close fit like the vegetable skins on that old woman's hands.

I was glad when the bus came. There is a certain happiness sighted when your bus comes along. It is of course a small specialized form of happiness and will never be a great thing.

I let the old woman get on first and trailed behind in classic medieval tradition with castle floors following me onto the bus.

I dropped in my fifteen cents, got my usual transfer, even though I did not need one. I always get a transfer. It gives me something to do with my hands while I am riding the bus. I *need* activity.

I sat down and looked the bus over to see who was there, and it took me about a minute to realize that there was something very wrong with that bus, and it took the other people about the same period to realize that there was something very wrong with the bus, and the thing that was wrong was me.

I was young. Everybody else on the bus, about nineteen of them, were men and women in their sixties, seventies and eighties, and I only in my twenties. They stared at me and I stared at them. We were all embarrassed and uncomfortable.

How had this happened? Why were we suddenly the players in this cruel fate and could not take our eyes off one another?

A man about seventy-eight began to clutch desperately at the lapel of his coat. A woman maybe sixty-three began to filter her hands, finger by finger, through a white handkerchief.

I felt terrible to remind them of their lost youth, their passage through slender years in such a cruel and unusual manner. Why were we tossed this way together as if we were nothing but a weird salad served on the seats of a God-damn bus?

I got off the bus at the next possibility. Everybody was glad to see me go and none of them were more glad than I.

I stood there and watched after the bus, its strange cargo now secure, growing distant in the journey of time until the bus was gone from sight.

THE GHOST CHILDREN
OF TACOMA

THE children of Tacoma, Washington, went to war in December 1941. It seemed like the thing to do, following in the footsteps of their parents and other grown-ups who acted as if they knew what was happening.

"Remember Pearl Harbor!" they said.

"You bet!" we said.

I was a child, then, though now I look like somebody else. We were at war in Tacoma. Children can kill imaginary enemies just as well as adults can kill real enemies. It went on for years.

During World War II, I personally killed 352,892 enemy soldiers without wounding one. Children need a lot less hospitals in war than grown-ups do. Children pretty much look at it from the alldeath side.

I sank 987 battleships, 532 aircraft carriers, 799 cruisers, 2,007 destroyers and 161 transport ships. Transports were not too interesting a target: very little sport.

I also sank 5,465 enemy PT boats. I have no idea why I

sank so many of them. It was just one of those things. Every time I turned around for four years, I was sinking a PT boat. I still wonder about that. 5,465 are a lot of PT boats.

I only sank three submarines. Submarines were just not up my alley. I sank my first submarine in the spring of 1942. A lot of kids rushed out and sank submarines right and left during December and January. I waited.

I waited until April, and then one morning on my way to school: BANG! my first sub., right in front of a grocery store. I sank my second submarine in 1944. I could afford to wait two years before sinking another one.

I sank my last submarine in February 1945, a few days after my tenth birthday. I was not totally satisfied with the presents I got that year.

And then there was the sky! I ventured forth into the sky, seeking the enemy there, while Mount Rainier towered up like a cold white general in the background.

I was an ace pilot with my P-38 and my Grumman Wildcat, my P-51 Mustang and my Messerschmitt. That's right: Messerschmitt. I captured one and had it painted a special color, so my own men wouldn't try to shoot me down by mistake. Everybody recognized my Messerschmitt and the enemy had hell to pay for it.

I shot down 8,942 fighter planes, 6,420 bombers and 51 blimps. I shot down most of the blimps when the war was first in season. Later, sometime in 1943, I stopped shooting down blimps altogether. Too slow.

I also destroyed 1,281 tanks, 777 bridges and 109 oil refineries because I knew we were in the right.

"Remember Pearl Harbor!" they said.

"You bet!" we said.

I shot the enemy planes down by holding out my arms

straight from my body and running like hell, shouting at the top of my lungs: RAT-tattattattattattattattattattattat!

Children don't do that kind of stuff any more. Children do other things now and because children do other things now, I have whole days when I feel like the ghost of a child, examining the memory of toys played back into the earth again.

There was a thing I used to do that was also a lot of fun when I was a young airplane. I used to hunt up a couple of flashlights and hold them lit in my hands at night, with my arms straight out from my body and be a night pilot zooming down the streets of Tacoma.

I also used to play airplane in the house, too, by taking four chairs from the kitchen and putting them together: two chairs facing the same way for the fuselage and a chair for each wing.

In the house I played mostly at dive-bombing. The chairs seemed to do that best. My sister used to sit in the seat right behind me and radio urgent messages back to base.

"We only have one bomb left, but we can't let the aircraft carrier escape. We'll have to drop the bomb down the smokestack. Over. Thank you, Captain, we'll need all the luck we can get. Over and out."

Then my sister would say to me, "Do you think you can do it?" and I'd reply, "Of course, hang onto your hat."

Your Hat
Gone Now These
Twenty Years
January 1,
1965

TALK SHOW

I'M listening to a talk show on a new radio that I bought a few weeks ago. It's an AM/FM solid state white plastic radio. I very seldom buy anything new, so it was quite a surprise to my economy when I went into an Italian appliance store and bought this radio.

The salesman was very nice and told me that he had sold over four hundred of these radios to Italians who wanted to listen to an Italian language program that was on FM.

I don't know why but somehow that impressed me a great deal. It made me want to buy the radio, so that's how I surprised my economy.

The radio cost $29.95.

Now I'm listening to a talk show because it's raining hard outside and I've got nothing better to do with my ears. While I'm listening to this new radio, I'm remembering another new radio that lived in the past.

I think I was about twelve years old up in the Pacific Northwest where winter meant that it was always raining and muddy.

We had an old 1930s kind of radio that was in a huge cabinet that looked like a coffin and it scared me because old furniture can frighten children and make them think about dead people.

The radio was in pretty bad shape soundwise and it had become harder and harder to listen to my favorite programs on it.

The radio was beyond any kind of real repair job. It was holding onto a pathetic sound by the skin of its dial.

We had needed a new radio for a long while but we couldn't afford one because we were too poor. Finally we got enough money for the down payment to buy a radio on time and we walked over through the mud to the local radio store.

This was my mother and me and my sister and we all listened to brand-new radios as if we were in paradise until we had narrowed it down to the radio that we finally bought.

It was breathtakingly beautiful in a fine wooden cabinet that smelled like a lumberyard in heaven. The radio was a table model which was really nice, too.

We walked home with the radio down muddy streets that had no sidewalks. The radio was in a guarding cardboard box and I got to carry it. I felt so proud.

That was one of the happiest nights of my life listening to my favorite programs on a brand-new radio while a winter's rainstorm shook the house. Each program sounded as if it had been cut from a diamond. The hoof beats of the Cisco Kid's horse sparkled like a ring.

I'm sitting here now, baldingfatmiddleagedyearslater, listening to a talk show on the second brand-new radio of my life while shadows of the same storm shake the house.

I WAS TRYING
TO DESCRIBE YOU
TO SOMEONE

I was trying to describe you to someone a few days ago. You don't look like any girl I've ever seen before.

I couldn't say: "Well, she looks just like Jane Fonda except that she's got red hair and her mouth is different and of course she's not a movie star."

I couldn't say that because you don't look like Jane Fonda at all.

I finally ended up describing you as a movie I saw when I was a child in Tacoma, Washington. I guess I saw it in 1941 or '42: somewhere in there. I think I was seven or eight or six. It was a movie about rural electrification and a perfect 1930s New Deal morality kind of movie to show kids.

The movie was about farmers living in the country without electricity. They had to use lanterns to see by at night, for sewing and reading, and they didn't have any appliances, like toasters or washing machines, and they couldn't listen to the radio.

Then they built a dam with big electric generators and they

put poles across the countryside and strung wire over fields and pastures.

There was an incredible heroic dimension that came from the simple putting up of poles for the wires to travel along. They looked ancient and modern at the same time.

Then the movie showed Electricity like a young Greek god coming to the farmer to take away forever the dark ways of his life.

Suddenly, religiously, with the throwing of a switch the farmer had electric lights to see by when he milked his cows in the early black winter mornings.

The farmer's family got to listen to the radio and have a toaster and lots of bright lights to sew dresses and read the newspaper by.

It was really a fantastic movie and excited me like listening to "The Star-Spangled Banner" or seeing photographs of President Roosevelt or hearing him on the radio.

". . . The President of the United States . . ."

I wanted electricity to go everywhere in the world. I wanted all the farmers in the world to be able to listen to President Roosevelt on the radio.

That's how you look to me.

TRICK OR TREATING
DOWN TO THE SEA
IN SHIPS

As a child I used to play at Halloween as if I were a sailor and go trick or treating down to the sea in ships. My sack of candy and things were at the wheel and my Halloween mask was sails cutting through a beautiful autumn night with lights on front porches shining like ports of call.

Trickortreat was the captain of our ship, saying, "We are only going to be in this port for a short time. I want all of you to go ashore and have a good time. Just remember we sail on the morning tide." My God, he was right! We sailed on the morning tide.

BLACKBERRY MOTORIST

THE blackberry vines grew all around and climbed like green dragon tails the sides of some old abandoned warehouses in an industrial area that had seen its day. The vines were so huge that people laid planks across them like bridges to get at the good berries in the center of them.

There were many bridges reaching into the vines. Some of them were five or six planks long and it took careful balancing to get back in there because if you fell off, there were nothing but blackberry vines for fifteen feet or so beneath you, and you could really hurt yourself on their thorns.

This was not a place you went casually to gather a few blackberries for a pie or to eat with some milk and sugar on them. You went there because you were getting blackberries for the winter's jam or to sell them because you needed more money than the price of a movie.

There were so many blackberries back in there that it was hard to believe. They were huge like black diamonds but it took a lot of medieval blackberry engineering, chopping entrances and laying bridges, to be successful like the siege of a castle.

"The castle has fallen!"

Sometimes when I got bored with picking blackberries I used to look into the deep shadowy dungeon-like places way down in the vines. You could see things that you couldn't make out down there and shapes that seemed to change like phantoms.

Once I was so curious that I crouched down on the fifth plank of a bridge that I had put together way out there in the vines and stared hard into the depths where thorns were like the spikes on a wicked mace until my eyes got used to the darkness and I saw a Model A sedan directly underneath me.

I crouched on that plank for a long time staring down at the car until I noticed that my legs were cramped. It took me about two hours to tunnel my way with ripped clothes and many bleeding scratches into the front seat of that car with my hands on the steering wheel, a foot on the gas pedal, a foot on the brake, surrounded by the smell of castle-like upholstery and staring from twilight darkness through the windshield up into green sunny shadows.

Some other blackberry pickers came along and started picking blackberries on the planks above me. They were very excited. I think it was the first time they had ever been there and seen blackberries like that. I sat there in the car underneath them and listened to them talk.

"Hey, look at this blackberry!"

THOREAU RUBBER BAND

LIFE is as simple as driving through New Mexico in a bor-
rowed Jeep, sitting next to a girl who is so pretty that every
time I look at her I just feel good all over. It's been snowing
a lot and we've had to drive a hundred and fifty miles out of
our way because the snow like an hourglass has closed the
road that we needed.

Actually, I'm very excited because we are driving into the
little town of Thoreau, New Mexico, to see if Highway 56 is
open to Chaco Canyon. We want to see the Indian ruins
there.

The ground is covered with snow so heavy that it looks as
if it has just received its Government pension and is looking
forward to a long and cheerful retirement.

We see a cafe resting in the snow's leisure. I get out of the
Jeep and leave the girl sitting there while I go into the cafe
to find out about the road.

The waitress is middle-aged. She looks at me as if I am a
foreign movie that has just come in out of the snow starring

Jean-Paul Belmondo and Catherine Deneuve. The cafe smells like a fifty-foot-long breakfast. Two Indians are sitting at it, eating ham and eggs.

They are quiet and curious about me. They look at me sideways. I ask the waitress about the road and she tells me that it's closed. She says it in one quick final sentence. Well, that takes care of that.

I start out the door but one of the Indians turns and says sideways to me, "The road's open. I went over it this morning."

"Is it open all the way to Highway 44: the road over to Cuba?" I ask him.

"Yes."

The waitress suddenly turns her attention to the coffee. The coffee needs taking care of right now and that is what she is doing for the benefit of all the generations of coffee drinkers to come. Without her dedication, coffee might become extinct in Thoreau, New Mexico.

44:40

WHEN I knew Cameron he was a very old man and wore
carpet slippers all the time and didn't talk any more. He
smoked cigars and occasionally listened to Burl Ives' records.
He lived with one of his sons who was now a middle-aged
man himself and starting to complain about growing old.

"God-damn it, there's no getting around the fact that I'm
not as young as I used to be."

Cameron had his own easy chair in the front room. It was
covered with a wool blanket. Nobody else ever sat in that
chair, but it was always as if he were sitting there, anyway. His
spirit had taken command of that chair. Old people have a
way of doing that with the furniture they end their lives sitting
in.

He didn't go outside any more during the winter, but he
would sit out on the front porch sometimes in the summer
and stare past the rose bushes in the front yard to the street
beyond where life calendared its days without him as if he
had never existed out there at all.

That wasn't true, though. He used to be a great dancer and would dance all night long in the 1890s. He was famous for his dancing. He sent many a fiddler to an early grave and when the girls danced with him, they always danced better and they loved him for it and just the mention of his name in that county made the girls feel good and would get them blushing and giggling. Even the "serious" girls would get excited by his name or the sight of him.

There were a lot of broken hearts when he married the youngest of the Singleton girls in 1900.

"She's not that pretty," refrained the sore losers and they all cried at the wedding.

He was also a hell-of-a good poker player in a county where people played very serious poker for high stakes. Once a man sitting next to him was caught cheating during a game.

There was a lot of money on the table and a piece of paper that represented twelve head of cattle, two horses and a wagon. That was part of a bet.

The man's cheating was made public by one of the other men at the table reaching swiftly across without saying a word and cutting the man's throat.

Cameron automatically reached over and put his thumb on the man's jugular vein to keep the blood from getting all over the table and held him upright, though he was dying until the hand was finished and the ownership of the twelve head of cattle, two horses and a wagon was settled.

Though Cameron didn't talk any more, you could see events like that in his eyes. His hands had been made vegetable-like by rheumatism but there was an enormous dignity to their repose. The way he lit a cigar was like an act of history.

Once he had spent a winter as a sheepherder in 1889. He was a young man, not yet out of his teens. It was a long lonely winter job in God-forsaken country, but he needed the money to pay off a debt that he owed his father. It was one of those complicated family debts that it's best not to go into detail about.

There was very little exciting to do that winter except look at sheep but Cameron found something to keep his spirits up.

Ducks and geese flew up and down the river all winter and the man who owned the sheep had given him and the other sheepherders a lot, an almost surrealistic amount, of 44:40 Winchester ammunition to keep the wolves away, though there weren't any wolves in that country.

The owner of the sheep had a tremendous fear of wolves getting to his flock. It bordered on being ridiculous if you were to go by all the 44:40 ammunition he supplied his sheepherders.

Cameron heavily favored this ammunition with his rifle that winter by shooting at the ducks and geese from a hillside about two hundred yards from the river. A 44:40 isn't exactly the greatest bird gun in the world. It lets go with a huge slow-moving bullet like a fat man opening a door. Cameron wanted those kind of odds.

The long months of that family-debted-exile winter passed slowly day after day, shot after shot until it was finally spring and he had maybe fired a few thousand shots at those ducks and geese without hitting a single one of them.

Cameron loved to tell that story and thought it was very funny and always laughed during the telling. Cameron told that story just about as many times as he had fired at those birds years in front of and across the bridge of 1900 and up the decades of this century until he stopped talking.

PERFECT CALIFORNIA DAY

I was walking down the railroad tracks outside of Monterey on Labor Day in 1965, watching the Sierra shoreline of the Pacific Ocean. It has always been a constant marvel to me how much the ocean along there is like a high Sierra river with a granite shore and fiercely-clear water and turns of green and blue with chandelier foam shining in and out of the rocks like the currents of a river high in the mountains.

It's hard to believe that it's the ocean along there if you don't look up. Sometimes I like to think of that shore as a small river and carefully forget that it's 11,000 miles to the other bank.

I went around a bend in the river and there were a dozen or so frog people having a picnic on a sandy little beach surrounded by granite rocks. They were all in black rubber suits. They were standing in a circle eating big slices of watermelon. Two of them were pretty girls who wore soft felt hats on top of their suits.

The frog people were of course all talking frog people talk.

Often they were child-like and a summer of tadpole dialogue went by in the wind. Some of them had weird blue markings on the shoulders and down the arms of their suits like a brand-new blood system.

There were two German police dogs playing around the frog people. The dogs were not wearing black rubber suits and I did not see any suits lying on the beach for them. Perhaps their suits were behind a rock.

A frog man was floating on his back in the surf, eating a slice of watermelon. He swirled and eddied with the tide.

A lot of their equipment was leaning against a large theater-like rock that would have given Prometheus a run for his money. There were some yellow oxygen tanks lying next to the rock. They looked like flowers.

The frog people changed into a half-circle and then two of them ran into the sea and turned back to throw pieces of watermelon at the others and two of them started wrestling on the shore in the sand and the dogs were barking around them.

The girls were very pretty in their poured-on black rubber suits and gentle clowning hats. Eating watermelon, they sparkled like jewels in the crown of California.

THE POST OFFICES
OF EASTERN OREGON

DRIVING along in Eastern Oregon: autumn and the guns in the back seat and the shells in the jockey box or glove compartment, whatever you elect to call it.

I was just another kid going deer hunting in this land of mountains. We had come a long ways, leaving before it was dark. Then all night.

Now the sun was shining inside the car, hot like an insect, a bee or something, trapped and buzzing against the windshield.

I was very sleepy and asking Uncle Jarv, who was stuffed beside me in the front seat, about the country and the animals. I looked over at Uncle Jarv. He was driving and the steering wheel was awkwardly close in front of him. He weighed well over two hundred pounds. The car was barely enough room for him.

There in the half-light of sleep was Uncle Jarv, some Copenhagen in his mouth. It was always there. People used to like Copenhagen. There were signs all around telling you to buy some. You don't see those signs any more.

Uncle Jarv had once been a locally famous high school

athlete and later on, a legendary honky-tonker. He once had
four hotel rooms at the same time and a bottle of whiskey in
each room, but they had all left him. He had grown older.

Uncle Jarv lived quietly, reflectively now, reading Western
novels and listening to opera on the radio every Saturday
morning. He always had some Copenhagen in his mouth. The
four hotel rooms and the four bottles of whiskey had vanished.
Copenhagen had become his fate and his eternal condition.

I was just another kid pleasantly thinking about the two
boxes of 30:30 shells in the jockey box. "Are there any
mountain lions?" I asked.

"You mean cougars?" Uncle Jarv said.

"Yeah, cougars."

"Sure," Uncle Jarv said. His face was red and his hair was
thin. He had never been a good-looking man but that had
never stopped women from liking him. We kept crossing the
same creek over and over again.

We crossed it at least a dozen times, and it was always a
surprise to see the creek again because it was kind of pleasant,
the water low with long months of heat, going through country that had been partially logged off.

"Are there any wolves?"

"A few. We're getting close to town now," Uncle Jarv said.
We saw a farm house. Nobody lived there. It was abandoned
like a musical instrument.

There was a good pile of wood beside the house. Do ghosts
burn wood? I guess it's up to them, but the wood was the
color of years.

"How about wildcats? There's a bounty on them, isn't
there?"

We passed by a sawmill. There was a little log pond
dammed up behind the creek. Two guys were standing on the
logs. One of them had a lunch bucket in his hand.

"A few dollars," Uncle Jarv said.

We were now coming into the town. It was a small place. The houses and stores were rinky-tinky, and looked as if a lot of weather had been upon them.

"How about bears?" I said, just as we went around a bend in the road, and right in front of us was a pickup truck and there were two guys standing beside the truck, taking bears out of it.

"The country's filled with bears," Uncle Jarv said. "There are a couple of them right over there."

And sure enough . . . as if it were a plan, the guys were lifting the bears out, handling the bears as if they were huge pumpkins covered with long black hair. We stopped the car by the bears and got out.

There were people standing around looking at the bears. They were all old friends of Uncle Jarv's. They all said hello to Uncle Jarv, and where you been?

I had never heard so many people saying hello at once. Uncle Jarv had left the town many years before. "Hello, Jarv, hello." I expected the bears to say hello.

"Hello, Jarv, you old bad penny. What's that you're wearing around there for a belt? One of them Goodyears?"

"Ho-ho, let's take a look at the bears."

They were both cubs, weighing about fifty or sixty pounds. They had been shot up on Old Man Summers' Creek. The mother had gotten away. After the cubs were dead, she ran into a thicket, and hid in close with the ticks.

Old Man Summers' Creek! That's where we were going hunting. Up Old Man Summers' Creek! I'd never been there before. Bears!

"She'll be mean," one of the guys standing there said. We were going to stay at his house. He was the guy who shot the bears. He was a good friend of Uncle Jarv's. They had played together on the high school football team during the Depression.

A woman came by. She had a sack of groceries in her arms. She stopped and looked at the bears. She got up very close, leaning over toward the bears, shoving celery tops in their faces.

They took the bears and put them on the front porch of an old two-story house. The house had wooden frosting all around the edges. It was a birthday cake from a previous century. Like candles we were going to stay there for the night.

The trellis around the porch had some kind of strange-looking vines growing on it, with even stranger-looking flowers. I'd seen those vines and the flowers before, but never on a house. They were hops.

It was the first time that I had ever seen hops growing on a house. That was an interesting taste in flowers. But it took a little while to get used to them.

The sun was shining out front and the shadow of the hops lay across the bears as if they were two glasses of dark beer. They were sitting there, backs against the wall.

"Hello, gentlemen. What would you like to drink?"

"A couple of bears."

"I'll check the icebox and see if they're cold. I put some in there a little while ago . . . yeah, they're cold."

The guy who shot the bears decided that he didn't want them, so somebody said, "Why don't you give them to the mayor? He likes bears." The town had a population of three hundred and fifty-two, including the mayor and the bears.

"I'll go tell the mayor there are some bears over here for him," somebody said and went to find the mayor.

Oh, how good those bears would taste: roasted, fried, boiled or made into spaghetti, bear spaghetti just like the Italians make.

Somebody had seen him over at the sheriff's. That was about an hour ago. He might still be there. Uncle Jarv and I went over and had lunch at a little restaurant. The screen door was badly in need of repair, and opened like a rusty bicycle. The waitress asked us what we wanted. There were some slot machines by the door. The county was wide open.

We had some roast beef sandwiches with mashed potatoes and gravy. There were hundreds of flies in the place. Quite a crew of them had found some strips of flypaper that were hanging here and there like nooses in the restaurant, and were making themselves at home.

An old man came in. He said he wanted a glass of milk. The waitress got one for him. He drank it and put a nickel in a slot machine on his way out. Then he shook his head.

After we finished eating, Uncle Jarv had to go over to the post office and send a postcard. We walked over there and it was just a small building, more like a shack than anything else. We opened the screen door and went in.

There was a lot of post office stuff: a counter and an old clock with a long drooping hand like a mustache under the sea, swinging softly back and forth, keeping time with time.

There was a large nude photograph of Marilyn Monroe on the wall. The first one I had ever seen in a post office. She was lying on a big piece of red. It seemed like a strange thing to have on the wall of a post office, but of course I was a stranger in the land.

The postmistress was a middle-aged woman, and she had copied on her face one of those mouths they used to wear during the 1920s. Uncle Jarv bought a postcard and filled it up on the counter as if it were a glass of water.

It took a couple of moments. Halfway through the postcard Uncle Jarv stopped and glanced up at Marilyn Monroe. There was nothing lustful about his looking up there. She just as well could have been a photograph of mountains and trees.

I don't remember whom he was writing to. Perhaps it was to a friend or a relative. I stood there staring at the nude photograph of Marilyn Monroe for all I was worth. Then Uncle Jarv mailed the postcard. "Come on," he said.

We went back to the house where the bears were, but they were gone. "Where did they go?" somebody said.

A lot of people had gathered around and they were all talking about the missing bears and were kind of looking for the bears all over the place.

"They're dead," somebody said, trying to be reassuring, and pretty soon we were looking inside the house, and a woman went through the closets, looking for bears.

After a while the mayor came over and said, "I'm hungry. Where are my bears?"

Somebody told the mayor that they had disappeared into thin air and the mayor said, "That's impossible," and got down and looked under the porch. There were no bears there.

An hour or so passed and everybody gave up looking for the bears, and the sun went down. We sat outside on the front porch where once upon a time, there had been bears.

The men talked about playing high school football during the Depression, and made jokes about how old and fat they had grown. Somebody asked Uncle Jarv about the four hotel rooms and the four bottles of whiskey. Everybody laughed except Uncle Jarv. He smiled instead. Night had just started when somebody found the bears.

They were on a side street sitting in the front seat of a car. One of the bears had on a pair of pants and a checkered shirt. He was wearing a red hunting hat and had a pipe in the mouth and two paws on the steering wheel like Barney Old-field.

The other bear had on a white silk negligee, one of the kind you see advertised in the back pages of men's magazines, and a pair of felt slippers stuck on the feet. There was a pink bonnet tied on the head and a purse in the lap.

Somebody opened up the purse, but there wasn't anything inside. I don't know what they expected to find, but they were disappointed. What would a dead bear carry in its purse, anyway?

★   ★   ★

Strange is the thing that makes me recall all this again: the bears. It's a photograph in the newspaper of Marilyn Monroe, dead from a sleeping pill suicide, young and beautiful, as they say, with everything to live for.

The newspapers are filled with it: articles and photographs and the like—her body being taken away on a cart, the body wrapped in a dull blanket. I wonder what post office wall in Eastern Oregon will wear this photograph of Marilyn Monroe.

An attendant is pushing the cart out a door, and the sun is shining under the cart. Venetian blinds are in the photograph and the branches of a tree.

PALE MARBLE MOVIE

THE room had a high Victorian ceiling and there was a marble fireplace and an avocado tree growing in the window, and she lay beside me sleeping in a very well-built blond way.

And I was asleep, too, and it was just starting to be dawn in September.

1964.

Then suddenly, without any warning, she sat up in bed, waking me instantly, and she started to get out of bed. She was very serious about it.

"What are you doing?" I said.

Her eyes were wide open.

"I'm getting up," she said.

They were a somnambulist blue.

"Get back in bed," I said.

"Why?" she said, now halfway out of bed with one blond foot touching the floor.

"Because you're still asleep," I said.

"Ohhh . . . OK," she said. That made sense to her and

she got back into bed and pulled the covers around herself and cuddled up close to me. She didn't say another word and she didn't move.

She lay there sound asleep with her wanderings over and mine just beginning. I have been thinking about this simple event for years now. It stays with me and repeats itself over and over again like a pale marble movie.

PARTNERS

I like to sit in the cheap theaters of America where people live and die with Elizabethan manners while watching the movies. There is a theater down on Market Street where I can see four movies for a dollar. I really don't care how good they are either. I'm not a critic. I just like to watch movies. Their presence on the screen is enough for me.

The theater is filled with black people, hippies, senior citizens, soldiers, sailors and the innocent people who talk to the movies because the movies are just as real as anything else that has ever happened to them.

"No! No! Get back in the car, Clyde. Oh, God, they're killing Bonnie!"

I am the poet-in-residence at these theaters but I don't plan on getting a Guggenheim for it.

Once I went into the theater at six o'clock in the evening and got out at one o'clock in the morning. At seven I crossed my legs and they stayed that way until ten and I never did stand up.

In other words, I am not an art film fan. I do not care to be esthetically tickled in a fancy theater surrounded by an audience drenched in the confident perfume of culture. I can't afford it.

I was sitting in a two-pictures-for-seventy-five-cents theater called the Times in North Beach last month and there was a cartoon about a chicken and a dog.

The dog was trying to get some sleep and the chicken was keeping him awake and what followed was a scrics of adventures that always ended up in cartoon mayhem.

There was a man sitting next to me.

He was WHITEWHITEWHITE: fat, about fifty years old, balding sort of and his face was completely minus any human sensitivity.

His baggy no-style clothes covered him like the banner of a defeated country and he looked as if the only mail he had ever gotten in his life were bills.

Just then the dog in the cartoon let go with a huge yawn because the chicken was still keeping him awake and before the dog had finished yawning, the man next to me started yawning, so that the dog in the cartoon and the man, this living human being, were yawning together, partners in America.

GETTING TO KNOW
EACH OTHER

SHE hates hotel rooms. It's like a Shakespearean sonnet. I mean, the childwoman or Lolita thing. It's a classic form:

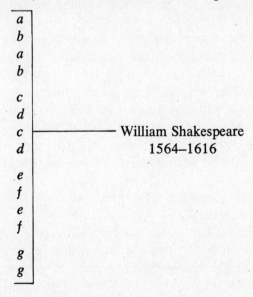

a
b
a
b

c
d
c ———————— William Shakespeare
d   1564–1616

e
f
e
f

g
g

She hates hotel rooms. It's the light in the morning that really bothers her. She doesn't like to wake up surrounded by that kind of light.

The morning light in hotel rooms is always synthetic, harshly clean as if the maid had let herself so quietly in, like a maidmouse, and put the light there by making phantom beds with strange sheets hanging in the very air itself.

She used to lie in bed and pretend that she was still asleep, so as to catch the maid coming in with the morning light folded in her arms, but she never caught her and finally gave it up.

Her father is asleep in the other room with a new lover. Her father is a famous movie director and in town to promote one of his pictures.

This trip to San Francisco he is promoting a horror movie that he has just finished directing called *The Attack of the Giant Rose People*. It is a film about a mad gardener and the results of his handiwork in the greenhouse working with experimental fertilizers.

She thinks the giant rose people are a bore. "They look like a bunch of funky valentines," she recently told her father.

"Why don't you go fuck yourself?" had been his reply.

That afternoon he would have lunch with Paine Knickerbocker of the *Chronicle* and later on in the afternoon he would be interviewed by Eichelbaum of the *Examiner* and a few days later her father's same old line of bullshit would appear in the papers.

Last night he rented a suite at the Fairmont but she wanted to stay at a motel on Lombard.

"Are you crazy? This is San Francisco!" he'd said.

She likes motels a lot better than she does hotels, but she doesn't know why. Maybe it's the light in the morning. That probably has something to do with it. The light in motel rooms is more natural. It's not as if the maid had put it there.

She got out of bed. She wanted to see who her father was sleeping with. It was a little game of hers. She liked to see if she could guess who her father was in bed with, but it was a kind of silly game and she knew it because the women that her father went to bed with always looked just like her.

She wondered where her father kept finding them.

Some of his friends and other people liked to make little jokes about it. They liked to say that his lovers and his daughter always looked like sisters. Sometimes she felt as if she were the member of a strange and changing family of sisters.

She was 5-7, had straight blond hair that went almost down to her ass. She weighed 113 pounds. She had *very* blue eyes.

She was fifteen years old but she could have been any age. With just the turn of a whim she could look anywhere between thirteen and thirty-five.

Sometimes she would deliberately look thirty-five, so that young men in their early twenties would be attracted to her and consider her to be an older, experienced woman.

She could perform perfectly the role of a still glamorous but fading thirty-five-year-old woman, having studied so many of them in Hollywood, New York, Paris, Rome, London, etc.

She'd already had three affairs with young men in their early twenties without them ever catching on that she was only fifteen.

It had become a little hobby of hers.

She could invent whole lifetimes for herself and it was as if she had lived them in a kind of dreamy telescope way. She could be a thirty-four-year-old matron with three children in Glendale married to a Jewish dentist and having a lost youth fling on the side or she could be a thirty-one-year-old spinster literary editor from New York trying to escape the clutches of an insane lesbian lover and needing a young man to provide her salvation from perversion or she could be a thirty-year-old divorcée with an incurable but attractive disease and wanting to have one more chance at romance before . . .

She loved it.

She got out of bed and tiptoed without any clothes on into the living room and went over to the door of her father's bedroom and stood there listening to see if they were awake or making love.

Her father and his lover were sound asleep. She could feel it through the door. It was like a chunk of warm frozen space in their bedroom.

She opened the door a crack and saw the blond hair of the woman spilling over the side of the bed like the sleeve of a yellow shirt.

She smiled and closed the door.

And that's where we leave her.

We know a little about her.

And she knows a lot about us.

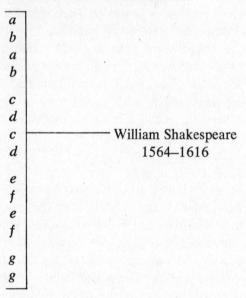

William Shakespeare
1564–1616

A SHORT HISTORY
OF OREGON

I would do things like that when I was sixteen. I'd hitch-hike fifty miles in the rain to go hunting for the last hours of the day. I'd stand alongside the road with a 30:30 and my thumb out and think nothing of it, expecting to be picked up and I always was.

"Where are you going?"

"Deer hunting."

That meant something in Oregon.

"Get in."

It was raining like hell when I got out of the car at the top of the ridge. The driver couldn't believe it. I saw a draw half-full of trees, sloping down into a valley obscured by rain mist.

I hadn't the slightest idea where the valley led to. I'd never been there before and I didn't care.

"Where are you going?" the driver said, hardly believing that I was getting out of the car in the rain.

"Down there."

When he drove off I was alone in the mountains and that

was how I wanted it to be. I was waterproofed from head to toe and had some candy bars in my pocket.

I walked down through the trees, trying to kick a deer out of the dry thickets, but it didn't really make any difference if I saw one or not.

I just wanted the awareness of hunting. The thought of the deer being there was just as good as the deer actually being there.

There was nothing stirring in the thickets. I didn't see any sign of a deer or the sign of a bird or the sign of a rabbit or anything.

Sometimes I would just stand there. The trees were dripping. There was only the sign of myself: alone, so I ate a candy bar.

I had no idea of the time. The sky was dark with winter rain. I only had a couple of hours when I started and I could feel that they were nearly at an end and soon it would be night.

I came out of a thicket into a patch of stumps and a logging road that curved down into the valley. They were new stumps. The trees had been cut sometime that year. Perhaps in the spring. The road curved into the valley.

The rain slackened off, then stopped and a strange kind of silence settled over everything. It was twilight and wouldn't last long.

There was a turn in the logging road and suddenly, without warning, there was a house right there in the middle of my private nowhere. I didn't like it.

The house was more of a large shack than anything else with a lot of old cars surrounding it and there was all sorts of logging junk and things that you need and then abandon after using.

I didn't want the house to be there. The rain mist lifted and I looked back up the mountain. I'd come down only about half a mile, thinking all the time I was alone.

That was a joke.

There was a window in the house-shack facing up the road toward me. I couldn't see anything in the window. Even though it was starting to get night, they hadn't turned their lights on yet. I knew there was somebody home because heavy black smoke was coming out of the chimney.

As I got closer to the house, the front door slammed open and a kid ran out onto a crude makeshift porch. He didn't have any shoes or a coat on. He was about nine years old and his blond hair was disheveled as if the wind were blowing all the time in his hair.

He looked older than nine and was immediately joined by three sisters who were three, five and seven. The sisters weren't wearing any shoes either and they didn't have any coats on. The sisters looked older than they were.

The quiet spell of the twilight broke suddenly and it started raining again, but the kids didn't go into the house. They just stood there on the porch, getting all wet and looking at me.

I'll have to admit that I was a strange sight coming down their muddy little road in the middle of God-damn nowhere with darkness coming on and a 30:30 cradled down in my arms, so the night rain wouldn't get in the barrel.

The kids didn't say a word as I walked by. The sisters' hair was unruly like dwarf witches'. I didn't see their folks. There was no light on in the house.

A Model A truck lay on its side in front of the house. It was next to three empty fifty-gallon oil drums. They didn't have a purpose any more. There were some odd pieces of rusty cable. A yellow dog came out and stared at me.

I didn't say a word in my passing. The kids were soaking wet now. They huddled together in silence on the porch. I had no reason to believe that there was anything more to life than this.

A LONG TIME AGO
PEOPLE DECIDED TO
LIVE IN AMERICA

I'M wandering along, thinking about how I'd like to get laid by somebody new. It's a cold winter afternoon and just another thought, almost out of my mind when—

A tall, God-I-love the tall-ones girl comes walking up the street, casual as a young animal with Levi's on. She must be 5-9, wearing a blue sweater. Her breasts are loose beneath it and move in firm youthful tide.

She has no shoes on.

She's a hippie girl.

Her hair is long.

She doesn't know how pretty she is. I like that. It always turns me on, which isn't very hard to do right now because I'm already thinking about girls.

Then as we pass each other she turns toward me, a thing totally unexpected and she says, "Don't I know you?"

Wow! She is standing beside me now. She's really tall!

I look closely at her. I try to see if I know her. Maybe she's a former lover or somebody else I've met or made a pass at when I've been drunk. I look carefully at her and she is beautiful in a fresh young way. She has the nicest blue eyes, but I don't recognize her.

"I know I've seen you before," she says, looking up into my face. "What's your name?"

"Clarence."

"Clarence?"

"Yeah, Clarence."

"Oh, then I don't know you," she says.

That was kind of fast.

Her feet are cold on the pavement and she's hunched in a cold-like way toward me.

"What is your name?" I ask, maybe I'm going to make a pass at her. That's what I should be doing right now. Actually, I'm about thirty seconds late in doing it.

"Willow Woman," she says. "I'm trying to get out to the Haight-Ashbury. I just got into town from Spokane."

"I wouldn't," I say. "It's very bad out there."

"I have friends in the Haight-Ashbury," she says.

"It's a bad place," I say.

She shrugs her shoulders and looks helplessly down at her feet. Then she looks up and her eyes have a friendly wounded expression in them.

"This is all I have," she says.

(Meaning what she is wearing.)

"And what's in my pocket," she says.

(Her eyes glance furtively toward the left rear pocket of her Levi's.)

"My friends will help me out when I get there," she says.

(Glancing in the direction of the Haight-Ashbury three miles away.)

Suddenly she has become awkward. She doesn't know exactly what to do. She has taken two steps backward. They are in the direction of going up the street.

"I . . . ," she says.

"I . . . ," looking down at her cold feet again.

She takes another half-step backward.

"I."

"I don't want to whine," she says.

She's really disgusted with what's happening now. She's ready to leave. It didn't work out the way she wanted.

"Let me help you," I say.

I reach into my pocket.

She steps toward me, instantly relieved as if a miracle has happened.

I give her a dollar, having totally lost somewhere the thread of making a pass at her, which I had planned on doing.

She can't believe it's a dollar and throws her arms around me and kisses me on the cheek. Her body is warm, friendly and giving.

We could make a nice scene together. I could say the words that would cause it to be, but I don't say anything because I've lost the thread of making a pass at her and don't know where it's gone, and she departs beautifully toward all the people that she will ever meet, at best I will turn out to be a phantom memory, and all the lives that she will live.

We've finished living this one together.

She's gone.

A SHORT HISTORY
OF RELIGION
IN CALIFORNIA

THERE'S only one way to get into it: We saw the deer in the meadow. The deer turned in a slow circle and then broke the circle and went toward some trees.

There were three deer in the meadow and we were three people. I, a friend and my daughter 3½ years old. "See the deer," I said, pointing the way to the deer.

"Look the deer! There! There!" she said and surged against me as I held her in the front seat. A little jolt of electricity had come to her from the deer. Three little gray dams went away into the trees, celebrating a TVA of hoofs.

She talked about the deer as we drove back to our camp in Yosemite. "Those deer are really something," she said. "I'd like to be a deer."

When we turned into our campground there were three deer standing at the entrance, looking at us. They were the same deer or they were three different ones.

"Look the deer!" and the same electrical surge against me, enough perhaps to light a couple of Christmas tree lights or make a fan turn for a minute or toast half a slice of bread.

The deer followed close behind the car as we drove at deer speed into the camp. When we got out of the car, the deer were there. My daughter took out after them. Wow! The deer!

I slowed her down. "Wait," I said. "Let Daddy take your hand." I didn't want her to scare them or get hurt by them either, in case they should panic and run over her, a next to impossible thing.

We followed after the deer, a little ways behind and then stopped to watch them cross the river. The river was shallow and the deer stopped in the middle and looked in three different directions.

She stared at them, not saying anything for a while. How quiet and beautiful they looked and then she said, "Daddy, take off the deer's head and put it on my head. Take off the deer's feet, put them on my feet. And I'll be the deer."

The deer stopped looking in three different directions. They all looked in one direction toward the trees on the other side of the river and moved off into those trees.

So the next morning there was a band of Christians camping beside us because it was Sunday. There were about twenty or thirty of them seated at a long wooden table. They were singing hymns while we were taking down our tent.

My daughter watched them very carefully and then walked over to peek out at them from behind a tree as they sang on. There was a man leading them. He waved his hands in the air. Probably their minister.

My daughter watched them very carefully and then moved out from behind the tree and slowly advanced until she was right behind their minister, looking up at him. He was standing out there alone and she was standing out there alone with him.

I pulled the metal tent stakes out of the ground and put them together in a neat pile, and I folded the tent and put it beside the tent stakes.

Then one of the Christian women got up from the long table and walked over to my daughter. I was watching this. She gave her a piece of cake and asked her if she wanted to sit down and listen to the singing. They were busy singing something about Jesus doing something good for them.

My daughter nodded her head and sat down on the ground. She held the piece of cake in her lap. She sat there for five minutes. She did not take a bite out of the piece of cake.

They were now singing about Mary and Joseph doing something. In the song it was winter and cold and there was straw in the barn. It smelled good.

She listened for about five minutes and then she got up, waved good-bye in the middle of "We Three Kings of Orient Are" and came back with the piece of cake.

"Well, how was that?" I said.

"Singing," she said, pointing they are singing.

"How's the cake?" I said.

"I don't know," she said and threw it on the ground. "I've already had breakfast." It lay there.

I thought about the three deer and the Christians singing. I looked at the piece of cake and to the river where the deer had been gone for a day.

The cake was very small on the ground. The water flowed over the rocks. A bird or an animal would eat the cake later on and then go down to the river for a drink of water.

A little thing came to my mind and having no other choice: it pleased me, so I hugged my arms around a tree and my cheek sailed to the sweet bark and floated there for a few gentle moments in the calm.

APRIL IN GOD-DAMN

THIS early April in God-damn God-damn begins with a note on the front door, left by a young lady. I read the note and wonder what the hell's up.

I'm too old for this kind of stuff. I can't keep track of everything, and so I go pick up my daughter and do the best I can on that front: take her to play in the park.

I really don't want to get out of bed, but I have to go to the toilet. Returning from the toilet, I see something a note or something fastened to the glass window on the front door. It leaves a shadow on the glass.

I don't give a damn. Let somebody else handle these complicated things in early April. It's enough for me to have gone to the toilet. I go back to bed.

I dream that somebody I don't like is walking their dog. The dream takes hours. The person is singing to their dog but I can't make out what the song is and I have to listen too hard and never get it, anyway.

I wake up totally bored. What am I going to do with the

rest of my life? I'm twenty-nine. I get the note off the door
and go back to bed.

I read it with the sheet pulled up over my head. The light
is not very good but it is better than anything else I've come
across today. It's from a girl. She came by so quietly this
morning and left it on my door.

The note is an apology for a bad scene she made the other
night. It is in the form of a riddle. I can't figure it out. I never
cared for riddles, anyway. Fuck her.

I go get my daughter and take her to the playground at
Portsmouth Square. I have been watching her for the last
hour. From time to time I have paused to write this down.

I wonder if my daughter will ever leave a note on some
man's door in early April God-damn God-damn and he'll
read it in bed with the sheet pulled up over his head and then
take his daughter to the park and look up as I just did to see
her playing with a blue bucket in the sand.

ONE AFTERNOON
IN 1939

THIS is a constant story that I keep telling my daughter who is four years old. She gets something from it and wants to hear it again and again.

When it's time for her to go to bed, she says, "Daddy, tell me about when you were a kid and climbed inside that rock."

"OK."

She cuddles the covers about her as if they were controllable clouds and puts her thumb in her mouth and looks at me with listening blue eyes.

"Once when I was a little kid, just your age, my mother and father took me on a picnic to Mount Rainier. We drove up there in an old car and saw a deer standing in the middle of the road.

"We came to a meadow where there was snow in the shadows of the trees and snow in the places where the sun didn't shine.

"There were wild flowers growing in the meadow and they looked beautiful. In the middle of the meadow there was a huge round rock and Daddy walked over to the rock and found a hole in the center of it and looked inside. The rock was hollow like a small room.

"Daddy crawled inside the rock and sat there staring out at the blue sky and the wild flowers. Daddy really liked that rock and pretended that it was a house and he played inside the rock all afternoon.

"He got some smaller rocks and took them inside the big rock. He pretended that the smaller rocks were a stove and furniture and things and he cooked a meal, using wild flowers for food."

That's the end of the story.

Then she looks up at me with her deep blue eyes and sees me as a child playing inside a rock, pretending that wild flowers are hamburgers and cooking them on a small stove-like rock.

She can never get enough of this story. She has heard it thirty or forty times and always wants to hear it again.

It's very important to her.

I think she uses this story as a kind of Christopher Columbus door to the discovery of her father when he was a child and her contemporary.

CORPORAL

ONCE I had visions of being a general. This was in Tacoma during the early years of World War II when I was a child going to grade school. They had a huge paper drive that was brilliantly put together like a military career.

It was very exciting and went something like this: If you brought in fifty pounds of paper you became a private and seventy-five pounds of paper were worth a corporal's stripes and a hundred pounds to be a sergeant, then spiralling pounds of paper leading upward until finally you arrived at being a general.

I think it took a ton of paper to be a general or maybe it was only a thousand pounds. I can't remember the exact amount but in the beginning it seemed so simple to gather enough paper to be a general.

I started out by gathering all the loose paper that was lying innocently around the house. That added up to three or four pounds. I'll have to admit that I was a little disappointed. I don't know where I got the idea that the house was just filled with paper. I actually thought there was paper all over the place. It's an interesting surprise that paper can be deceptive.

I didn't let it throw me, though. I marshalled my energies and went out and started going door to door asking people if they had any newspapers or magazines lying around that could be donated to the paper drive, so that we could win the war and destroy evil forever.

An old woman listened patiently to my spiel and then she gave me a copy of *Life* magazine that she had just finished reading. She closed the door while I was still standing there staring dumbfoundedly at the magazine in my hands. The magazine was warm.

At the next house, there wasn't any paper, not even a used envelope because another kid had already beaten me to it.

At the next house, nobody was home.

That's how it went for a week, door after door, house after house, block after block until finally I got enough paper together to become a private.

I took my God-damn little private's stripe home in the absolute bottom of my pocket. There were already some paper officers, lieutenants and captains, on the block. I didn't even bother to have the stripe sewed on my coat. I just threw it in a drawer and covered it up with some socks.

I spent the next few days cynically looking for paper and lucked into a medium pile of *Collier's* from somebody's basement which was enough to get my corporal's stripes that immediately joined my private's stripe under the socks.

The kids who wore the best clothes and had a lot of spending money and got to eat hot lunch every day were already generals. They had known where there were a lot of magazines and their parents had cars. They strutted military airs around the playground and on their way home from school.

Shortly after that, like the next day, I brought a halt to my glorious military career and entered into the disenchanted paper shadows of America where failure is a bounced check or a bad report card or a letter ending a love affair and all the words that hurt people when they read them.

LINT

I'M haunted a little this evening by feelings that have no vocabulary and events that should be explained in dimensions of lint rather than words.

I've been examining half-scraps of my childhood. They are pieces of distant life that have no form or meaning. They are things that just happened like lint.

A COMPLETE HISTORY
OF GERMANY AND JAPAN

A few years ago (World War II) I lived in a motel next to a Swift packing plant which is a nice way of saying slaughterhouse.

They killed pigs there, hour after hour, day after day, week after week, month after month until spring became summer and summer became fall, by cutting their throats after which would follow a squealing lament equal to an opera being run through a garbage disposal.

Somehow I thought that killing all those pigs had something to do with winning the war. I guess that was because everything else did.

For the first week or two that we lived in the motel it really bothered me. All that screaming was hard to take, but then I grew used to it and it became like any other sound: a bird singing in a tree or the noon whistle or the radio or trucks driving by or human voices or being called for dinner, etc.

"You can play after dinner!"

Whenever the pigs weren't screaming, the silence sounded as if a machine had broken down.

THE AUCTION

It was a rainy Pacific Northwest auction with kids running all over the place getting into things and farm women interested in buying boxes of used fruit jars, secondhand dresses, and perhaps some furniture for the house while the men were interested in saddles and farm equipment and livestock.

The auction was in a kind of old warehousebarn-like building with used excitement everywhere on Saturday afternoon. It smelled like the complete history of America.

The auctioneer was selling things so fast that it was possible to buy stuff that wouldn't be for sale until next year. He had false teeth that sounded like crickets jumping up and down inside the jaws of a skeleton.

Whenever there was a box of old toys put up for auction, the kids would bother the hell out of their folks until they were threatened with the strap if they didn't shut up, "Stop pestering me or you won't be able to sit down for a week."

There were always cows and sheep, horses and rabbits

waiting to get new owners or a farmer somberly contemplating some chickens while blowing his nose.

It was great on a rainy winter afternoon because the auction had a tin roof and there was a beautiful wet closeness to everything inside.

An ancient case made out of dusty glass and long yellow wood like a pioneer's mustache contained boxes of stale candy bars. They were fifty cents a box and really stale but for some kid reason I liked to gnaw away on them and would work up a quarter and find somebody to go in with me on a box and I'd end up with twelve stale candy bars in 1947.

THE ARMORED CAR
For Janice

I lived in a room that had a bed and a telephone. That was all. One morning I was lying in bed and the telephone rang. The window shades were pulled down and it was raining hard outside. It was still dark.

"Hello," I said.

"Who invented the revolver?" a man asked.

Before I could hang the telephone up my own voice escaped me like an anarchist and said, "Samuel Colt."

"You just won a cord of wood," the man said.

"Who are you?" I asked.

"This is a contest," he said. "You just won a cord of wood."

"I don't have a stove," I said. "I live in a rented room. There's no heat."

"Is there anything else you would want besides a cord of wood?" he said.

"Yeah, a fountain pen."

"Good, we'll send you one. What's the address there?"

I gave him my address and then I asked him who was sponsoring the contest.

"Never mind," he said. "The pen will be in the mail tomorrow morning. Oh, yes, is there any particular color you like? I almost forgot."

"Blue would be fine."

"We're all out of blue. Any other color? Green? We have a lot of green pens."

"All right, green, then."

"It'll be in the mail tomorrow morning," he said.

It wasn't. It never came.

The only thing I ever won in my life and actually received was an armored car. When I was a child I had a paper route that went for miles along the rough edge of town.

I would have to ride my bicycle down a hill, following a road that had fields of grass on both sides and an old plum orchard at the end of the road. They had chopped down part of the trees and built four new houses there.

Parked in front of one house was an armored car. It was a small town and every day after work the driver took the armored car home with him. He parked it out in front of his house.

I would pass there before six o'clock in the morning and everybody would be asleep in the houses. When there was light in the morning I could see the armored car from a quarter of a mile or so.

I liked the armored car and would get off my bicycle and walk over and take a look at it, knock on the heavy metal, look in the bulletproof windows, kick the tires.

Because everybody was asleep in the morning and I alone out there, after a while I considered the armored car to be mine and treated it as such.

One morning I got into the armored car and delivered the

rest of my papers from it. It looked kind of strange to see a kid delivering newspapers from an armored car.

I rather enjoyed it and started doing it regularly.

"Here comes that kid in the armored car delivering papers," the early risers said. "Yeah, he's a nut."

That was the only thing I ever won.

THE LITERARY LIFE
IN CALIFORNIA/1964

1

I was sitting in a bar last night talking to a friend who was from time to time looking down the bar at his wife. They had been separated for two years: no hope.

She was palling it up with another man. They looked as if they were having a lot of fun.

My friend turned and asked me about two books of my poetry. I'm a minor poet, even so, people sometimes ask me questions like that.

He said he used to have the books but he didn't have them any more. They were gone. I said that one of the books was out of print and copies of the other book were down at City Lights Bookstore.

He took a look down at his wife. She was laughing at something the other man had said, who was then quite pleased with himself, and so it goes.

"I have a confession to make," my friend said. "Remember that night I came home from work and found you and my wife drunk together on sweet vermouth in the kitchen?"

I remembered the evening, though nothing had happened. We were just sitting there in the kitchen, listening to the phonograph and drunk on sweet vermouth. There were probably thousands like us all across America.

"Well, when you left I went and got those two books of poetry out of the bookcase and tore them up and threw the pieces on the floor. All the king's horses and all the king's men couldn't have put those books of poetry back together again."

"Win a few, lose a few," I said.

"What?" he said.

He was a little drunk. There were three empty beer bottles in front of him on the bar. Their labels had been carefully scratched off.

"I just write the poetry," I said. "I'm not a shepherd of the pages. I can't look after them forever. It wouldn't make sense."

I was also a little drunk.

"Anyway," my friend said. "I would like to have those books again. Where can I get them?"

"One of them has been out of print for five years. The other one you can get at City Lights," I said, busy putting together and filming in my mind what went on after I left the kitchen and went home, glowing like a lantern in sweet vermouth.

What he said to her before he went and got the books of poetry and tore them up. What she said, what he said, which book went first, the way he tore it. Oh, a lovely act of healthy outrage and what was taken care of after that.

2

I was at City Lights a year ago and saw somebody looking at one of my books of poetry. He was pleased with the book, but there was a reluctance to his pleasure.

He looked at the cover again and turned the pages again. He stopped the pages as if they were the hands of a clock and he was pleased at what time it was. He read a poem at seven o'clock in the book. Then the reluctance came again and clouded up the time.

He put the book back on the shelf, then he took it off the shelf. His reluctance had become a form of nervous energy.

Finally he reached in his pocket and took out a penny. He placed the book in the crook of his arm. The book was now a nest and the poems were eggs. He threw the penny up in the air, caught it and slapped it on the back of his hand. He took his other hand away.

He put the book of poetry back on the shelf and left the bookstore. As he walked out he looked very relaxed. I walked over and found his reluctance lying there on the floor.

It was like clay but nervous and fidgeting. I put it in my pocket. I took it home with me and shaped it into this, having nothing better to do with my time.

BANNERS OF MY
OWN CHOOSING

DRUNK laid and drunk unlaid and drunk laid again, it makes
no difference. I return to this story as one who has been away
but one who was always destined to return and perhaps that's
for the best.

I found no statues nor bouquets of flowers, no beloved to
say: "Now we will fly new banners from the castle, and they
will be of your own choosing," and to hold my hand again,
to take my hand in yours.

None of that stuff for me.

My typewriter is fast enough as if it were a horse that's just
escaped from the ether, plunging through silence, and the
words gallop in order while outside the sun is shining.

Perhaps the words remember me.

It is the fourth day of March 1964. The birds are singing
on the back porch, a bunch of them in an aviary, and I try
to sing with them: Drunk laid and drunk unlaid and drunk
laid again, I'm back in town.

FAME
IN CALIFORNIA/1964

1

IT'S really something to have fame put its feathery crowbar under your rock and then upward to the light release you, along with seven grubs and a sow bug.

I'll show you what happens, then. A friend of mine came up to me a few months ago .and said, "You're a character in the novel I just finished."

It really set me up when he said that. I had an immediate vision of myself as the romantic lead or the villain: "He put his hand on her breast and his hot breath fogged up her glasses," or "He laughed as she cried, then he kicked her down the stairs like a sack of dirty laundry."

"What do I do in your novel?" I said, waiting to hear great words.

"You open a door," he said.

"What else do I do?"

"That's all."

"Oh," I said, my fame diminishing. "Couldn't I have done

something else? Maybe opened two doors? Kissed somebody?"

"That one door was enough," he said. "You were perfect."

"Did I say anything when I opened the door?" still hoping
a little.

"No."

2

I met a photographer friend of mine last week. We were
making the rounds of the bars. He took some photographs.
He is a careful young photographer and conceals his camera
under his coat like a pistol.

He doesn't want people to know what he is doing. Wants
to capture them in real life poses. Doesn't want to make them
nervous and begin acting like movie stars.

Then he whips out his camera like the bank robber that
got away: that simple Indiana boy that's now living in Swit-
zerland among royalty and big business and who has culti-
vated a foreign accent.

Yesterday I met the young photographer and he had some
large prints of the photographs he had taken that night.

"I took a picture of you," he said. "I'll show it to you."

He showed me through a dozen or so prints and then he
turned to the next one and said, "See!" It was the photograph
of an old woman drinking a rather silly martini.

"There you are," he said.

"Where?" I said. "I'm not an old woman."

"Of course not," he said. "That's your hand on the table."

I looked very carefully into the photograph and sure
enough, but now I wonder what happened to the seven grubs
and the sow bug.

I hope they made out a little better than I did after that

feathery crowbar lifted us to the light. Perhaps they have their own television show and are coming out with an LP and are having their novels published by Viking, and *Time* will ask them about themselves, "Just tell us how you got started. In your own words."

MEMORY OF A GIRL

I cannot look at the Fireman's Fund Insurance Company building without thinking of her breasts. The building is at Presidio and California Streets in San Francisco. It is a red brick, blue and glass building that looks like a minor philosophy plopped right down on the site of what was once one of California's most famous cemeteries:

Laurel Hill Cemetery
1854–1946

Eleven United States Senators were buried there.

They, and everybody else were moved out years ago, but there are still some tall cypress trees standing beside the insurance company.

These trees once cast their shadows over graves. They

were a part of daytime weeping and mourning, and nighttime silence except for the wind.

I wonder if they ask themselves questions like: Where did everybody go who was dead? Where did they take them? And where are those who came here to visit them? Why were we left behind?

Perhaps these questions are too poetic. Maybe it would be best just to say: There are four trees standing beside an insurance company out in California.

SEPTEMBER CALIFORNIA

SEPTEMBER 22 means that she is lying on the beach in a black bathing suit and she is very carefully taking her own temperature.

She is beautiful: long and white and obviously a secretary from Montgomery Street who went to San Jose State College for three years and this is not the first time that she has taken her own temperature in a black bathing suit at the beach.

She seems to be enjoying herself and I cannot take my eyes off her. Beyond the thermometer is a ship passing out of San Francisco Bay, bound for cities on the other side of the world, those places.

Her hair is the same color as the ship. I can almost see the captain. He is saying something to one of the crew.

Now she takes the thermometer out of her mouth, looks at it, smiles, everything is all right, and puts it away in a little lilac carrying case.

The sailor does not understand what the captain said, so the captain has to repeat it.

A STUDY IN
CALIFORNIA FLOWERS

OH, suddenly it's nothing to see on the way and it's nothing when I get there, and I'm in a coffeehouse, listening to a woman talk who's wearing more clothes than I have money in the world.

She is adorned in yellow and jewelry and a language that I cannot understand. She is talking about something that is of no importance, insisting on it. I can tell all this because the man who is with her will buy none of it, and stares absent-mindedly at the universe.

The man has not spoken a word since they sat down here with cups of espresso coffee accompanying them like small black dogs. Perhaps he does not care to speak any more. I think he is her husband.

Suddenly she breaks into English. She says, "He should know. They're his flowers," in the only language I understand and there's no reply echoing all the way back to the beginning where nothing could ever have been any different.

I was born forever to chronicle this: I don't know these people and they aren't my flowers.

THE BETRAYED KINGDOM

THIS love story took place during the last spring of the Beat Generation. She must be in her middle thirties and I wonder what she's doing now and if she still goes to parties.

Her name slips my memory. It has joined all the other names that I have forgotten that swirl through my head like a tide pool of discontinued faces and invisible syllables.

She lived in Berkeley and I saw her often at the parties I attended that spring.

She'd come to a party all sexied up and really move it around and drink wine and flirt until midnight came and then she'd lay her scene on whomever was trying to get into her pants, which happened to be a lot of my friends who had cars. One after another they answered the fate that she had waiting for them.

"Is anyone driving to Berkeley? I need a ride to Berkeley," she would always announce erotically. She wore a little gold watch to keep track of the midnight.

One of my friends would always say yes behind too much

wine and drive her to Berkeley and she'd let them into her little apartment and then tell them that she wouldn't go to bed with them, that she didn't sleep with anybody, but if they wanted to, they could sleep on her floor. She had an extra wool blanket.

My friends would always be too drunk to drive back to San Francisco, so they would sleep on her floor, curled around that green army blanket and wake up in the morning, stiff and grouchy as a coyote with rheumatism. Neither coffee nor breakfast was ever offered and she had gotten another ride to Berkeley.

A few weeks later you'd see her at another party and come the midnight she'd sing her little song, "Is anybody driving to Berkeley? I need a ride to Berkeley." And some poor son-of-a-bitch, always one of my friends, would fall for it and keep an appointment with that blanket on her floor.

Obviously, I was never able to understand the attraction that existed for her because she did nothing to me. Of course, I didn't have a car. That was probably it. You had to have a car to understand her charms.

I remember one evening when everybody was drinking wine and having a good time, listening to music. Oh, those Beat Generation days! talking, wine and jazz!

Miss Berkeley Floor was drifting through the place spreading joy wherever she went, except among those friends of mine who had already availed themselves of her hospitality.

Then midnight came! and, "Is anybody driving to Berkeley." She always used the same words. I guess because they worked so well: perfectly.

A friend of mine who had told me of his adventures with her looked at me and smiled as another friend, a virgin to the experience and quite aroused behind an evening's wine, took the hook.

"I'll give you a ride home," he said.

"Wonderful," she said with a sexy smile.

"I hope he enjoys sleeping on the floor," my friend half-whispered to me, loud enough for her to hear but not quite loud enough for him to hear because he was kismeted to make an acquaintance with a Berkeley floor.

In other words, this girl's scene had become a *very* in-joke among the stung and they were always amused to see somebody else take that carnival ride to Berkeley.

She went and got her coat and out they traipsed but she had drunk a little too much wine herself and she got sick when they got to his car and she puked all over his front fender.

After she had emptied her stomach and was feeling a little better, my friend drove her to Berkeley and she made him sleep on the floor wrapped up in that God-damn blanket.

He came back to San Francisco the next morning: stiff, hung over and so fucking mad at her that he never washed her puke off that fender. He drove around San Francisco for months with that stuff residing there like a betrayed kingdom until it wore itself away.

This might have been a funny story if it weren't for the fact that people need a little loving and, God, sometimes it's sad all the shit they have to go through to find some.

WOMEN WHEN THEY
PUT THEIR CLOTHES ON
IN THE MORNING

IT's really a very beautiful exchange of values when women put their clothes on in the morning and she is brand-new and you've never seen her put her clothes on before.

You've been lovers and you've slept together and there's nothing more you can do about that, so it's time for her to put her clothes on.

Maybe you've already had breakfast and she's slipped her sweater on to cook a nice bare-assed breakfast for you, padding in sweet flesh around the kitchen, and you both discussed in length the poetry of Rilke which she knew a great deal about, surprising you.

But now it's time for her to put her clothes on because you've both had so much coffee that you can't drink any more and it's time for her to go home and it's time for her to go to work and you want to stay there alone because you've got some things to do around the house and you're going outside together for a nice walk and it's time for *you* to go home and it's time for *you* to go to work and she's got some things that she wants to do around the house.

Or . . . maybe it's even love.

But anyway: It's time for her to put her clothes on and it's so beautiful when she does it. Her body slowly disappears and comes out quite nicely all in clothes. There's a virginal quality to it. She's got her clothes on, and the beginning is over.

HALLOWEEN
IN DENVER

SHE didn't think that she would get any trick or treaters, so she didn't buy anything for them. That seems simple enough, doesn't it? Well, let's see what can happen with that. It might be interesting.

We'll start off with me reacting to her diagnosis of the situation by saying, "Hell, get something for the kids. After all, you're living on Telegraph Hill and there are a lot of kids in the neighborhood and some of them are certain to stop here."

I said it in such a way that she went down to the store and came back a few minutes later with a carton of gum. The gum was in little boxes called Chiclets and there were a lot of them in the carton.

"Satisfied?" she said.

She's an Aries.

"Yes," I said.

I'm an Aquarius.

We also had two pumpkins: both Scorpios.

So I sat there at the kitchen table and carved a pumpkin. It was the first pumpkin that I had carved in many years. It was kind of fun. My pumpkin had one round eye and one triangular eye and a not-very-bright witchy smile.

She cooked a wonderful dinner of sweet red cabbage and sausages and had some apples baking in the oven.

Then she carved her pumpkin while dinner was cooking beautifully away. Her pumpkin looked very modernistic when she was through. It looked more like an appliance than a jack-o'-lantern.

All the time that we were carving pumpkins the door bell did not ring once. It was completely empty of trick or treaters, but I did not panic, though there were an awful lot of Chiclets waiting anxiously in a large bowl.

We had dinner at 7:30 and it was so good. Then the meal was eaten and there were still no trick or treaters and it was after eight and things were starting to look bad. I was getting nervous.

I began to think that it was every day except Halloween.

She of course looked beatifically down upon the scene with an aura of Buddhistic innocence and carefully did not mention the fact that no trick or treaters had darkened the door.

That did not make things any better.

At nine o'clock we went in and lay down upon her bed and we were talking about this and that and I was in a kind of outrage because we had been forsaken by all trick or treaters, and I said something like, "Where are those little bastards?"

I had moved the bowl of Chiclets into the bedroom, so I could get to the trick or treaters faster when the door bell rang. The bowl sat there despondently on a table beside the bed. It was a very lonely sight.

At 9:30 we started fucking.

About fifty-four seconds later we heard a band of kids come running up the stairs accompanied by a cyclone of Halloween shrieking and mad door bell ringing.

I looked down at her and she looked up at me and our eyes met in laughter, but it wasn't too loud because suddenly we weren't at home.

We were in Denver, holding hands at a street corner, waiting for the light to change.

ATLANTISBURG

THERE were a couple of pool tables in the back and a table full of drunks nearby. I was talking to a young man who'd just gotten fired from his job and he was happy about it, but bored with the evening and the thought of looking for work next week. He was also quite disturbed about his home situation and went into it at great length.

We talked for a while, both of us leaning up against a pinball machine. There was a game of pool going on in the back. A little black Lesbian with a bull cut to her was playing pool with an old Italian, a sort of working type. Maybe he worked with vegetables or he was something else. The Lesbian was a seaman. They were locked in their game.

One of the drunks at the table spilled his drink all over the table and all over himself.

"Get a bar rag," another drunk said.

The spiller got up unevenly and went over to the bar and asked the bartender for a rag. The bartender leaned over the bar and said something to him that we couldn't hear.

The drunk came back and sat down. He did not have a bar rag.

"Where's the rag?" the other drunk said.

"He said I owe him forty-five dollars and sixty cents. My tab . . ."

"Well, I don't owe him forty-five dollars and sixty cents. I'll go over and get a bar rag. This table is a mess," and gets up to prove that he doesn't owe the bartender forty-five dollars and sixty cents.

The table was returned to normal. They started talking about something that I know about.

Finally my friend said, "What a God-damn boring night. I think I'll watch that dike play pool."

"I think I'll stay here and listen to these drunks for a while," I said.

He walked over and watched the black Lesbian play pool with the old Italian. I stood there leaning up against the pin-ball machine, listening to the drunks talk about lost cities.

THE VIEW FROM
THE DOG TOWER

". . . three German shepherd puppies wandered away from
their home up near the County line."

—North County Journal
Serving Northern Santa Cruz County

I have been thinking about this little item that I read in the
North County Journal for a couple of months now. It contains
the boundaries of a small tragedy. I know we are surrounded
by so much blossoming horror in the world (Vietnam, starva-
tion, rioting, living in hopeless fear, etc.) that three puppies
wandering off isn't very much, but I worry about it and see
this simple event as the possible telescope for a larger agony.

". . . three German shepherd puppies wandered away
from their home up near the County line." It sounds like
something from a Bob Dylan song.

Perhaps they vanished playing, barking and chasing each
other, into the woods where lost they are to this very day,

cringing around like scraps of dogs, looking for any small thing to eat, intellectually unable to comprehend what has happened to them because their brains are welded to their stomachs.

Their voices are used now only to cry out in fear and hunger, and all their playing days are over, those days of careless pleasure that led them into the terrible woods.

I fear that these poor lost dogs may be the shadow of a future journey if we don't watch out.

GREYHOUND TRAGEDY

SHE wanted her life to be a movie magazine tragedy like the death of a young star with long lines of people weeping and a corpse more beautiful than a great painting, but she was never able to leave the small Oregon town that she was born and raised in and go to Hollywood and die.

Though it was the Depression, her life was comfortable and untouched because her father was the manager of the local Penney's and financially compassionate to his family.

Movies were the religion of her life and she attended every service with a bag of popcorn. Movie magazines were her Bible that she studied with the zealousness of a doctor of divinity. She probably knew more about movies than the Pope.

The years passed like the subscriptions to her magazines: 1931, 1932, 1933, 1934, 1935, 1936, 1937, until September 2, 1938.

Finally it was time to make her move if she were ever going to go to Hollywood. There was a young man who wanted to marry her. Her parents were very enthusiastic about his prospects. They approved of him because he was a Ford salesman. "It's a company with a fine tradition," her father said. Things did not look good for her.

She spent months building up the courage to go down to the bus station to find out how much the fare to Hollywood cost. Sometimes she spent whole days thinking about the bus station. A few times she even got dizzy and had to sit down. It never dawned on her that she could have called on the telephone.

She made it a point during those nervous months never to go by the bus station. Thinking about it all the time was one thing but actually seeing it was another.

Once she was driving downtown with her mother and her mother turned onto the street where the bus station was located and she asked her mother to *please* turn down another street because she wanted to buy something at a store on that street.

Some shoes.

Her mother thought nothing of it and made the turn. She didn't think to ask her daughter why her face was red but that was not unusual because she seldom thought to ask her anything.

One morning she was going to talk to her about all the movie magazines that came in the mail. Some days they would jam up the mailbox, so that she would have to use a screwdriver to get the mail out. But her mother had forgotten about it by noon. Her mother's memory had never been able to last until twelve. It usually pooped out around 11:30, but she was a good cook if the recipes were simple.

Time was running out like the popcorn at a Clark Gable picture. Her father had been dropping a lot of "hints" lately about her being out of high school for three years and perhaps it was time for her to think about doing something with her life.

He was not the local manager of Penney's for nothing. Recently, actually about a year ago, he had become tired of watching his daughter sit around the house all the time reading movie magazines with her eyes wide as saucers. He had begun to think of her as a bump on a log.

Her father's hints happened to coincide with the young Ford salesman's fourth proposal of marriage. She had turned down the other three saying that she needed time to think it over which really meant that she was trying to build up enough courage to go down to the bus station and find out what the fare to Hollywood cost.

At last the pressure of her own longings and her father's "hints" made her leave the house early one warm twilight, after getting out of doing the dinner dishes, and walk slowly down to the bus station. From March 10, 1938 until the evening of September 2, 1938, she had been wondering what a bus ticket to Hollywood cost.

The bus station was stark, unromantic and very distant from the silver screen. Two old people were sitting there on a bench waiting for a bus. The old people were tired. They wanted to be now at wherever they were going. Their suitcase was like a burned-out light bulb.

The man who sold the tickets looked as if he could have sold anything. He could just as well be selling washing machines or lawn furniture as tickets to other places.

She was red-faced and nervous. Her heart felt out of place in the bus station. She tried to act as if she were waiting for somebody to come in on the next bus, an aunt, as she worked desperately to build up enough courage to go ask how much it cost to go to Hollywood but it didn't make any difference to anybody else what games she pretended.

Nobody looked at her, though she could have rented herself out as an earthquake beet. They simply didn't care. It was a stupid night in September and she just didn't have enough nerve to find out how much the fare to Hollywood cost.

She cried all the way home through the warm gentle Oregon night, wanting to die every time her feet touched the ground. There was no wind and all the shadows were comforting. They were like cousins to her, so she married the young Ford salesman and drove a new car every year except for the Second World War.

She had two children that she named Jean and Rudolph and tried to let her beautiful movie star death go at that, but now, thirty-one years later, she still blushes when she passes the bus station.

CRAZY OLD WOMEN
ARE RIDING THE BUSES
OF AMERICA TODAY
For Marcia Pacaud

THERE is one of them sitting behind me right now. She is wearing an old hat that's got plastic fruit on it, and her eyes dart back and forth across her face like fruit flies.

The man sitting next to her is pretending that he is dead.

The crazy old woman talks to him in one continuous audio breath that passes out of her mouth like a vision of angry bowling alleys on Saturday night with millions of pins crashing off her teeth.

The man sitting next to her is an old, very little Chinese man and he's wearing the clothes of a teen-ager. His coat, pants, shoes and cap belong to a fifteen-year-old boy. I've seen a lot of old Chinese men wearing teen-age clothes. It must be strange when they go to the store and buy them.

The Chinese man has scrunched himself up next to the window, and you can't even tell he's breathing. She doesn't care if he's dead or alive.

He was alive before she sat down beside him and started telling him about her children that came to no good and her husband who is an alcoholic and the leak in the God-damn car roof that he won't fix because he's always drunk, the son-of-a-bitch, and she's too tired to do anything because she works all the time at a cafe, I must be the oldest waitress in the world, and her feet can't take it any more and her son's in the penitentiary and her daughter is living with an alcoholic truck driver and they've got three little bastards running around the house and she wishes she had a television because she can't listen to the radio any more.

She stopped listening to the radio ten years ago because she couldn't find any programs on it. All there is is music and news now and I don't like the music and I can't understand the news and she doesn't care if this fucking Chinaman is alive or dead.

She ate some Chinese food twenty-three years ago in Sacramento and crapped for five days afterwards and all she can see is one ear facing her mouth.

The ear looks like a little yellow dead horn.

THE CORRECT TIME

I'LL do a bubble the best I can and perhaps a few more. Not that they are overly important and would change things, except for the one that got hit by the Number 30 Stockton bus. That's another story.

My girlfriend was late, so I went to the park alone. I got tired of waiting, of standing there in a bookstore reading a novel about people who make love all the time in wealthy surroundings. She was good-looking, but I was also growing older, jaded.

It was one of those typical summer afternoons that we do not get in San Francisco until the autumn. The park was as usual: Children were playing these-are-the-days-of-my-youth, and old people were sunning now what the grave would darken soon enough and the beatniks were lying here and there like stale rugs on the grass, waiting for the great hip rug merchant to come along.

I walked all around the park before I sat down: a long slow circle gathered gently to its end. Then I sat down but before I could examine the territory of where I was at, an old man asked me what time it was.

"A quarter of three," I said, though I did not know what time it was. I just wanted to be helpful.

"Thank you," he said, and flashed an antique smile of relief.

A quarter of three was the correct time for that old man for that was the time he wanted, the time that pleased him the most. I felt pretty good.

I sat there for a few moments and saw nothing else to remember and nothing to forget. I got up and went away, leaving a happy old man behind.

The Boy Scouts of America taught me all I know, and I had done my good deed for the day, and all I needed now so that I could dwell in perfection would be to find an enfeebled fire engine and help it across the street.

"Thank you, son," with its arthritic red paint smelling of old age, and its ladder covered with white hair, and a slight cataract over its siren.

There were children playing a game with bubbles at the place I had chosen to leave the park. They had a jar of magic bubble stuff and little rods with metal rings to cast the bubbles away with, to join them with the air.

Instead of leaving the park, I stood and watched the bubbles leave the park. They had a very high mortality pulse. I saw them again and again suddenly die above the sidewalk and the street: their rainbow profiles ceasing to exist.

I wondered what was happening and then looked closer to see that they were colliding with insects in the air. What a lovely idea! and then one of the bubbles was hit by the Number 30 Stockton bus.

WHAM! like the collision between an inspired trumpet and a great concerto, and showed all those other bubbles how to go out in the grand style.

HOLIDAY IN GERMANY

LET'S put it up front right now: I'm not an expert on holidays. I just don't have that kind of money. You might even go so far as to say that I am poor. I don't mind because it's true.

I am thirty, and my average income has been around $1400 a year for the last ten years. America is a very wealthy country, so sometimes I feel anti-American. I mean, I feel as if I am letting America down because I'm not making enough money to justify my citizenship.

Anyway, it's hard to holiday on $1400 a year and yesterday I was taking the Greyhound bus to Monterey to stay for a couple of weeks as a kind of exile from San Francisco.

I won't go into the reasons why. I am afraid that too much humor would ruin this story because actually it has very little to do with me. I just went along for the ride.

It concerns the two German boys that were on the bus. They were in their early twenties and sitting in the seat in front of me. They were in America for a three-week vacation. It was almost over: too bad.

They were yakking it up in German and touristing away, pointing out this and that as the bus rolled toward Monterey.

The German boy sitting next to the window also had a deep interest in the contents of American automobiles, especially the female contents. Whenever he would spot a good-looking girl driving along, he would point her out to his friend as part of their itinerary in America.

They were healthy, normal sex fiends.

A Volkswagen sedan came by the German boy on the window and he immediately got his friend's attention by pointing out two good-looking young girls in the Volkswagen. The German boys really had their faces pressed against the window now.

The girl on the passenger side, she was right beneath us, had short blond hair and a gentle white neck. The Volkswagen and the bus were travelling at the same rate of speed.

As the German boys continued to stare down at her, she grew kind of nervous, self-conscious, but she did not know why this was happening because she couldn't see us. She was now playing with her hair as women are prone to do under such conditions, even if they don't know quite what's up.

The lane of traffic in front of the Volkswagen slowed down and our bus went roaring ahead of the car. We were gone from each other for about a minute when the Volkswagen came up on us again.

The German boys picked up on this instantly and their faces were pressed against the window, participating in the age-old Candy-Store-Sex-Window Syndrome.

This time the girl looked up and saw the German boys staring down, all big smiles and flirting. The girl returned a kind of ambiguous half-smile. She was a perfect freeway Mona Lisa.

We hit another scramble of traffic and the Volkswagen

suffered from it and fell back, but a couple of minutes later it was up with us again. We were both moving about sixty miles an hour.

This time when she of the blond hair, the gentle white neck looked up and saw the German boys flirting away, she gave them a great big smile and waved enthusiastically. They had shattered her cool.

The German boys were waving like a convention of flags with mile-a-minute flirting and smiling. They were very happy: Ah, America!

The girl had a lovely smile. Her friend waved, too, driving the Volkswagen with one hand. She was also a good-looking girl: another blonde, but with long hair.

The German boys were having a fine holiday in America. Too bad there was no way they could get out of that bus and into the Volkswagen to meet the girls, but things like that are impossible.

Soon the girls took an off ramp to Palo Alto and disappeared forever, not unless of course, they take a holiday next year in Germany and are driving along the autobahn in a bus.

SAND CASTLES

STRANGE fences grow on Point Reyes Peninsula which is fastened like a haunted fingerprint to the California coast. Odd perspectives are constantly drifting out of sight or becoming too intimate in this place where white medieval Portuguese dairies suddenly appear cradled by cypress trees and then disappear as if they had never really been there at all.

Hawks circle in the sky like the lost springs of old railroad watches looking for correct protein wandering somewhere below to swoop down upon and devour chronologically.

It is not often that I journey to Point Reyes because, frankly, my mind is seldom in that place, but when I do go there I always enjoy myself. That is, if enjoy is the right word, driving down a road lined with fences that look like cemeteries lost in half-vague and half-mercuric spiritual density.

I usually end up going to a place called McClures Beach at the end of the peninsula. There's a parking lot where you leave your car and then it's a good hike down a gradual canyon to the beach, following a small creek.

Watercress grows luxuriously in the creek.

There are many peculiar flowers as step by step you disappear down into the turns of the canyon until at last you arrive at the Pacific Ocean and a dramatic beach like a photograph if they'd had cameras in the days when Christ lived, and now you are a part of the photograph, but sometimes you have to pinch yourself to make sure that you are really there.

I remember one afternoon many years ago I went with a friend to Point Reyes where my mind was exactly in that kind of place and stared at the fences as we drove deeper and deeper into the peninsula which of course unfolded like layers of abstraction and intimacy constantly being circled by hawks.

We parked at McClures Beach. I remember very clearly the sound of the car being parked. It made a lot of noise. There were some other cars parked there. Even after our car was parked, totally silent, it was still making noise.

Warm fog swirled in the canyon as we gradually descended. A hundred feet in front of us everything was lost in the fog and a hundred feet behind us everything was lost in the fog. We were walking in a capsule between amnesias.

There were hushed flowers all around us. The flowers looked as if they had been painted by a Fourteenth Century anonymous French painter. My friend and I had not said anything to each other for a long time. Perhaps our tongues had joined the brushes of that painter.

I stared at the watercress in the creek. It looked wealthy. Whenever I see watercress, which isn't very often, I think of the rich. I think they are the only people who can afford it and they use watercress in exotic recipes that they keep hidden in vaults from the poor.

Suddenly we went around a turn in the canyon and there were five handsome teen-age boys in swimming suits burying five pretty teen-age girls in the sand. They were all carved from classical California physical marble.

The girls had arrived at various stages of being buried. One of them was completely buried with only her head above the sand. She was very beautiful with long black hair stretched out along the sand as if it were some kind of dark water, perhaps jade, flowing out of her head.

The girls were all very happy being buried in the sand and so were the boys who were burying them in the sand. It was a teen-age graveyard party because they had run out of everything else to do. They were surrounded by towels, beer cans, beach baskets, picnic leftovers, etc.

They gave us no particular attention as we walked by and down to the Pacific Ocean where I mentally pinched myself to make sure that I was still in this Christ-powered photograph.

FORGIVEN

THIS story is a close friend or perhaps even a lover to a story called "Elmira." They both deal in a way with the Long Tom River and the time when I was young, a teen-ager, and somehow the Long Tom River was a part of my spiritual DNA.

I really needed that river. It was the beginning answers to some very complicated questions in my life that I am still trying to work out.

I'm quite aware that Richard Brautigan has written a novel called *Trout Fishing in America* that deals thoroughly with trout fishing and its kaleidoscope of environments, so I'm a little embarrassed to try something in the same theme, but I'm going to go ahead because this is a story that I have to tell.

I used to go fishing on the Long Tom River way back in the mountains where the river in parts wasn't much wider than a coffee table with a best seller sitting on it.

The trout were little cutthroats between six and ten inches long and a lot of fun to catch. I really got good at fishing the Long Tom and could take my limit of ten fish in little over an hour if I had any kind of luck at all.

The Long Tom River was forty miles away. I usually hitch-hiked there late in the afternoon and would leave in the twilight to hitch-hike the forty miles back home.

A few times I hitch-hiked there in the rain and fished in the rain and hitch-hiked back in the rain. I travelled eighty miles in a wet circle.

I'd get out at a bridge across the Long Tom and fish down half a mile to another bridge across the river. It was a wooden bridge that looked like an angel. The river was sort of murky. It was gentle fishing between the bridges, down through a lazy dripping landscape.

Below the second bridge, which looked like a white wooden angel, the Long Tom River flowed into very strange ways. It was dark and haunting and went something like this: Every hundred yards or so there was a large open swamp-like pool and then the river flowed out of the pool into a fast shallow run covered over closely with trees like a shadowy knitted tunnel until it reached the next swampy pool and very seldom did I let the Long Tom River call me down into there.

But late one August afternoon I had fished down to the angel bridge and the fishing hadn't been very good. I only had four or five trout.

It was raining and very warm up there in the mountains and edging toward sundown and actually it may have been early twilight. I couldn't tell exactly what time it was because of the rain.

Anyway: I was taken by some goofy kid reason to try a little fishing down below the bridge into those knitted river tunnels and big swampy open pools.

It was really too late to go down into there and I should have just turned around and got out of there and hitch-hiked the forty miles back home through the rain.

I should have let well enough alone.

But, Oh no, I started fishing down into there. It was tropical in the tunnels and I was catching trout where the tunnels flowed into the big swampy pools. Then I'd have to wade around the pools through deep warm mud.

I lost a trout that went about thirteen inches long and that really got my excitement up, so I continued fishing down further and further until I was six swampy pools past the wooden angel bridge when suddenly, out of nowhere, the light just dropped away within a few moments, falling into total night and there I was halfway around the sixth swampy pool in the dark, and in front of me there was nothing but darkness and water, and behind me was nothing but darkness and water.

The strangest God-damn feeling of fear shook through me. It was just like a crystal chandelier made out of adrenaline swaying wildly in an earthquake, and I turned around and fled up the river, splashing like an alligator around the big swampy pools and running like a dog up the shallow tunnels.

Every horror in the world was at my back, at my sides and directly in front of me and they were all without names and had no shape but perception itself.

When at last I ran out of the final tunnel and saw the dim white outline of the bridge standing out against the night, my soul was born again through a vision of rescue and sanctuary.

As I got closer and closer, the bridge bloomed like a white wooden angel in my eyes until I was sitting on the bridge, resting and soaking wet but not at all cold in the constant rain of the mountain evening.

I hope that Richard Brautigan will forgive me for writing this story.

AMERICAN FLAG DECAL

THIS story begins with an American flag decal on the rear window of a pickup truck, but you can barely see it because the truck is far away and then it turns off the highway onto a side road and it's gone, but somehow we have started again.

It's good to be back in California after a very unhappy month in the East: New York, etc. . . . with too much drunkenness, days and days of cold autumn rain and love affairs that were breathing mirrors of my unhappiness.

Now out here driving through the California countryside with a friend all we have to do is find somebody to repair his broken cesspool. It's a mess. We need somebody right now whose living is made from the knowing and handling of cesspools.

We drive down one road and then another, looking for a particular cesspool man. We stop at a place where we think he lives, but we are very wrong by about a million miles. It's a place that sells honey.

We don't know how we made the mistake. It's a long ways

from a cesspool man to some women behind a screen door selling honey.

We think it's amusing and so do they. We laugh at ourselves and they laugh at us. We are funny and drive away talking about the inner and outer roads that a man travels down to arrive at owning a grocery store or being a doctor or knowing cesspools intimately or how somebody else decides to sell honey but then is mistaken for a cesspool man.

A short, humorously spiritual distance away we find a cesspool man who's at home surrounded by all the equipment that he needs to successfully exercise cesspools.

Three men are fixing a broken truck. They stop working and turn to look at us. They are very serious in a country-casual way.

"No, not today. We got to fix this truck, so we can go bear hunting."

And that's it and there you have it: They want to fix the truck, so they can go bear hunting. Our cesspool is transparent, child-like. Bears are more important. I'm glad to be back in California.

THE WORLD WAR I
LOS ANGELES AIRPLANE

HE was found lying dead near the television set on the front room floor of a small rented house in Los Angeles. My wife had gone to the store to get some ice cream. It was an early-in-the-night-just-a-few-blocks-away store. We were in an ice-cream mood. The telephone rang. It was her brother to say that her father had died that afternoon. He was seventy. I waited for her to come home with the ice cream. I tried to think of the best way to tell her that her father was dead with the least amount of pain but you cannot camouflage death with words. Always at the end of the words somebody is dead.

She was very happy when she came back from the store.

"What's wrong?" she said.

"Your brother just called from Los Angeles," I said.

"What happened?" she said.

"Your father died this afternoon."

That was in 1960 and now it's just a few weeks away from 1970. He has been dead for almost ten years and I've done a lot of thinking about what his death means to all of us.

1. He was born from German blood and raised on a farm in South Dakota. His grandfather was a terrible tyrant who completely destroyed his three grown sons by treating them exactly the way he treated them when they were children. They never grew up in his eyes and they never grew up in their own eyes. He made sure of that. They never left the farm. They of course got married but he handled all of their domestic matters except for the siring of his grandchildren. He never allowed them to discipline their own children. He took care of that for them. Her father thought of his father as another brother who was always trying to escape the never-relenting wrath of their grandfather.

2. He was smart, so he became a schoolteacher when he was eighteen and he left the farm which was an act of revolution against his grandfather who from that day forth considered him dead. He didn't want to end up like his father, hiding behind the barn. He taught school for three years in the Midwest and then he worked as an automobile salesman in the pioneer days of car selling.

3. There was an early marriage followed by an early divorce with feelings afterward that left the marriage hanging like a skeleton in her family's closet because he tried to keep it a secret. He probably had been very much in love.

4. There was a horrible automobile accident just before the First World War in which everybody was killed except him. It was one of those automobile accidents that leave deep spiritual scars like historical landmarks on the family and friends of the dead.

5. When America went into the First World War in 1917, he decided that he wanted to be a pilot, though he was in his late twenties. He was told that it would be impossible because

he was too old but he projected so much energy into his desire to fly that he was accepted for pilot training and went to Florida and became a pilot.

In 1918 he went to France and flew a De Havilland and bombed a railroad station in France and one day he was flying over the German lines when little clouds began appearing around him and he thought that they were beautiful and flew for a long time before he realized that they were German antiaircraft guns trying to shoot him down.

Another time he was flying over France and a rainbow appeared behind the tail of his plane and every turn that the plane made, the rainbow also made the same turn and it followed after him through the skies of France for part of an afternoon in 1918.

6. When the war was over he got out a captain and he was travelling on a train through Texas when the middle-aged man sitting next to him and with whom he had been talking for about three hundred miles said, "If I was a young man like you and had a little extra cash, I'd go up to Idaho and start a bank. There's a good future in Idaho banking."

7. That's what her father did.

8. He went to Idaho and started a bank which soon led to three more banks and a large ranch. It was by now 1926 and everything was going all right.

9. He married a schoolteacher who was sixteen years his junior and for their honeymoon they took a train to Philadelphia and spent a week there.

10. When the stock market crashed in 1929 he was hit hard by it and had to give up his banks and a grocery store that he had picked up along the way, but he still had the ranch, though he had to put a mortgage on it.

11. He decided to go into sheep raising in 1931 and got a big flock and was very good to his sheepherders. He was so

good to them that it was a subject of gossip in his part of Idaho. The sheep got some kind of horrible sheep disease and all died.

12. He got another big flock of sheep in 1933 and added more fuel to the gossip by continuing to be so good to his men. The sheep got some kind of horrible sheep disease and all died in 1934.

13. He gave his men a big bonus and went out of the sheep business.

14. He had just enough money left over after selling the ranch to pay off all his debts and buy a brand-new Chevrolet which he put his family into and he drove off to California to start all over again.

15. He was forty-four, had a twenty-eight-year-old wife and an infant daughter.

16. He didn't know anyone in California and it was the Depression.

17. His wife worked for a while in a prune shed and he parked cars at a lot in Hollywood.

18. He got a job as a bookkeeper for a small construction company.

19. His wife gave birth to a son.

20. In 1940 he went briefly into California real estate, but then decided not to pursue it any further and went back to work for the construction company as a bookkeeper.

21. His wife got a job as a checker in a grocery store where she worked for eight years and then an assistant manager quit and opened his own store and she went to work for him and she still works there.

22. She has worked twenty-three years now as a grocery checker for the same store.

23. She was very pretty until she was forty.

24. The construction company laid him off. They said he

was too old to take care of the books. "It's time for you to go out to pasture," they joked. He was fifty-nine.

25. They rented the same house they lived in for twenty-five years, though they could have bought it at one time with no down payment and monthly payments of fifty dollars.

26. When his daughter was going to high school he was working there as the school janitor. She saw him in the halls. His working as a janitor was a subject that was very seldom discussed at home.

27. Her mother would make lunches for both of them.

28. He retired when he was sixty-five and became a very careful sweet wine alcoholic. He liked to drink whiskey but they couldn't afford to keep him in it. He stayed in the house most of the time and started drinking about ten o'clock, a few hours after his wife had gone off to work at the grocery store.

29. He would get quietly drunk during the course of the day. He always kept his wine bottles hidden in a kitchen cabinet and would secretly drink from them, though he was alone.

He very seldom made any bad scenes and the house was always clean when his wife got home from work. He did though after a while take on that meticulous manner of walking that alcoholics have when they are trying very carefully to act as if they aren't drunk.

30. He used sweet wine in place of life because he didn't have any more life to use.

31. He watched afternoon television.

32. Once he had been followed by a rainbow across the skies of France while flying a World War I airplane carrying bombs and machine guns.

33. "Your father died this afternoon."

The Abortion: An Historical
Romance 1966

RICHARD BRAUTIGAN

THE Abortion:
An Historical Romance 1966

DEDICATION

Frank :

come on in—
        read novel—
        it's on table
        in front room.
I'll be back
        in about
        2 hours.

                Richard

Contents

BOOK 1: Buffalo Gals, Won't You Come Out Tonight?

The Library

THIS is a beautiful library, timed perfectly, lush and American. The hour is midnight and the library is deep and carried like a dreaming child into the darkness of these pages. Though the library is "closed" I don't have to go home because this is my home and has been for years, and besides, I have to be here all the time. That's part of my position. I don't want to sound like a petty official, but I am afraid to think what would happen if somebody came and I wasn't here.

I have been sitting at this desk for hours, staring into the darkened shelves of books. I love their presence, the way they honor the wood they rest upon.

I know it's going to rain.

Clouds have been playing with the blue style of the sky all day long, moving their heavy black wardrobes in, but so far nothing rain has happened.

I "closed" the library at nine, but if somebody has a

book to bring in, there is a bell they can ring by the door that calls me from whatever I am doing in this place: sleeping, cooking, eating or making love to Vida who will be here shortly.

She gets off work at 11:30.

The bell comes from Fort Worth, Texas. The man who brought us the bell is dead now and no one learned his name. He brought the bell in and put it down on a table. He seemed embarrassed and left, a stranger, many years ago. It is not a large bell, but it travels intimately along a small silver path that knows the map to our hearing.

Often books are brought in during the late evening and the early morning hours. I have to be here to receive them. That's my job.

I "open" the library at nine o'clock in the morning and "close" the library at nine in the evening, but I am here twenty-four hours a day, seven days a week to receive the books.

An old woman brought in a book a couple of days ago at three o'clock in the morning. I heard the bell ringing inside my sleep like a small highway being poured from a great distance into my ear.

It woke up Vida, too.

"What is it?" she said.

"It's the bell," I said.

"No, it's a book," she said.

I told her to stay there in bed, to go back to sleep,

that I would take care of it. I got up and dressed myself in the proper attitude for welcoming a new book into the library.

My clothes are not expensive but they are friendly and neat and my human presence is welcoming. People feel better when they look at me.

Vida had gone back to sleep. She looked nice with her long black hair spread out like a fan of dark lakes upon the pillow. I could not resist lifting up the covers to stare at her long sleeping form.

A fragrant odor rose like a garden in the air above the incredibly strange thing that was her body, motionless and dramatic lying there.

I went out and turned on the lights in the library. It looked quite cheerful, even though it was three o'clock in the morning.

The old woman waited behind the heavy glass of the front door. Because the library is very old-fashioned, the door has a religious affection to it.

The woman had a look of great excitement. She was very old, eighty I'd say, and wore the type of clothing that associates itself with the poor.

But no matter . . . rich or poor . . . the service is the same and could never be any different.

"I just finished it," she said through the heavy glass before I could open the door. Her voice, though slowed down a great deal by the glass, was bursting with joy, imagination and almost a kind of youth.

13

"I'm glad," I said back through the door. I hadn't quite gotten it open yet. We were sharing the same excitement through the glass.

"It's done!" she said, coming into the library, accompanied by an eighty-year-old lady.

"Congratulations," I said. "It's so wonderful to write a book."

"I walked all the way here," she said. "I started at midnight. I would have gotten here sooner if I weren't so old."

"Where do you live?" I said.

"The Kit Carson Hotel," she said. "And I've written a book." Then she handed it proudly to me as if it were the most precious thing in the world. And it was.

It was a loose-leaf notebook of the type that you find everywhere in America. There is no place that does not have them.

There was a heavy label pasted on the cover and written in broad green crayon across the label was the title:

GROWING FLOWERS BY CANDLELIGHT
IN HOTEL ROOMS
BY
MRS. CHARLES FINE ADAMS

"What a wonderful title," I said. "I don't think we have a book like this in the entire library. This is a first."

She had a big smile on her face which had turned

old about forty years ago, eroded by the gases and exiles of youth.

"It has taken me five years to write this book," she said. "I live at the Kit Carson Hotel and I've raised many flowers there in my room. My room doesn't have any windows, so I have to use candles. They work the best.

"I've also raised flowers by lanternlight and magnifying glass, but they don't seem to do well, especially tulips and lilies of the valley.

"I've even tried raising flowers by flashlight, but that was very disappointing. I used three or four flashlights on some marigolds, but they didn't amount to much.

"Candles work the best. Flowers seem to like the smell of burning wax, if you know what I mean. Just show a flower a candle and it starts growing."

I looked through the book. That's one of the things I get to do here. Actually, I'm the only person who gets to do it. The book was written in longhand with red, green and blue crayons. There were drawings of her hotel room with the flowers growing in the room.

Her room was very small and there were many flowers in it. The flowers were in tin cans and bottles and jars and they were all surrounded by burning candles.

Her room looked like a cathedral.

There was also a drawing of the former manager of the hotel and a drawing of the hotel elevator. The elevator looked like a very depressing place.

In her drawing of the hotel manager, he appeared to be very unhappy, tired and looked as if he needed a vacation. He also seemed to be looking over his shoulder at something that was about to enter his vision. It was a thing he did not want to see and it was just about there. Under the drawing was written this:

MANAGER OF THE KIT CARSON HOTEL
UNTIL HE GOT FIRED
FOR DRINKING IN THE ELEVATOR
AND FOR STEALING SHEETS

The book was about forty pages long. It looked quite interesting and would be a welcomed addition to our collection.

"You're probably very tired," I said. "Why don't you sit down and I'll make you a cup of instant coffee?"

"That would be wonderful," she said. "It took me five years to write this book about flowers. I've worked very hard on it. I love flowers. Too bad my room doesn't have any windows, but I've done the best I can with candles. Tulips do all right."

Vida was sound asleep when I went back to my room. I turned on the light and it woke her up. She was blinking and her face had that soft marble quality to it that beautiful women have when they are suddenly awakened and are not quite ready for it yet.

"What's happening?" she said. "It's another book," she replied, answering her own question.

"Yes," I said.

"What's it about?" she said automatically like a gentle human phonograph.

"It's about growing flowers in hotel rooms."

I put the water on for the coffee and sat down beside Vida who curled over and put her head on my lap, so that my lap was entirely enveloped in her watery black hair.

I could see one of her breasts. It was fantastic!

"Now what's this about growing flowers in hotel rooms?" Vida said. "It couldn't be that easy. What's the real story?"

"By candlelight," I said.

"Uh-huh," Vida said. Even though I couldn't see her face, I knew she was smiling. She has funny ideas about the library.

"It's by an old woman," I said. "She loves flowers but she doesn't have any windows in her hotel room, so she grows them by candlelight."

"Oh, baby," Vida said, in that tone of voice she always uses for the library. She thinks this place is creepy and she doesn't care for it very much.

I didn't answer her. The coffee water was done and I took a spoonful of instant coffee and put it out in a cup.

"Instant coffee?" Vida said.

"Yes," I said. "I'm making it for the woman who just brought the book in. She's very old and she's walked a great distance to get here. I think she needs a cup of instant coffee."

17

"It sounds like she does. Perhaps even a little amyl nitrate for a chaser. I'm just kidding. Do you need any help? I'll get up."

"No, honey," I said. "I can take care of it. Did we eat all those cookies you baked?"

"No," she said. "The cookies are over there in that sack." She pointed toward the white paper bag on the table. "I think there are a couple of chocolate cookies left."

"What did you put them in the sack for?" I said.

"I don't know," she said. "Why does anyone put cookies in a sack? I just did."

Vida was resting her head on her elbow and watching me. She was unbelievable: her face, her eyes, her . . .

"Strong point," I said.

"Am I right?" she said, sleepily.

"Yup," I said.

I took the cup of coffee and put it on a small wooden tray, along with some canned milk and some sugar and a little plate for the cookies.

Vida had given me the tray as a present. She bought it at Cost Plus Imports and surprised me with it one day. I like surprises.

"See you later," I said. "Go back to sleep."

"OK," and pulled the covers up over her head. Farewell, my lovely.

I took the coffee and cookies out to the old woman. She was sitting at a table with her face resting on her

18

elbow and she was half asleep. There was an expression of dreaming on her face.

I hated to interrupt her. I know how much a dream can be worth, but, alas . . . "Hello," I said.

"Oh, hello," she said, breaking the dream cleanly.

"It's time for some coffee," I said.

"Oh, how nice," she said. "It's just what I need to wake me up. I'm a little tired because I walked so far. I guess I could have waited until tomorrow and taken the bus here, but I wanted to bring the book out right away because I just finished it at midnight and I've been working on it for five years.

"Five Years," she repeated, as if it were the name of a country where she was the President and the flowers growing by candlelight in her hotel room were her cabinet and I was the Secretary of Libraries.

"I think I'll register the book now," I said.

"That sounds wonderful," she said. "These are delicious cookies. Did you bake them yourself?"

I thought that was a rather strange question for her to ask me. I have never been asked that question before. It startled me. It's funny how people can catch you off guard with a question about cookies.

"No," I said. "I didn't bake these cookies. A friend did."

"Well, whoever baked them knows how to bake cookies. The chocolate tastes wonderful. So chocolatey."

"Good," I said.

Now it was time to register the book. We register all the books we receive here in our Library Contents Ledger. It is a record of all the books we get day by day, week by week, month by month, year by year. They all go into the Ledger.

We don't use the Dewey decimal classification or any index system to keep track of our books. We record their entrance into the library in the Library Contents Ledger and then we give the book back to its author who is free to place it anywhere he wants in the library, on whatever shelf catches his fancy.

It doesn't make any difference where a book is placed because nobody ever checks them out and nobody ever comes here to read them. This is not that kind of library. This is another kind of library.

"I just love these cookies," the old woman said, finishing the last cookie. "Such a good chocolate flavor. You can't buy these in a store. Did a friend bake them?"

"Yes," I said. "A very good friend."

"Well, good for them. There isn't enough of that thing going on now, if you know what I mean."

"Yes," I said. "Chocolate cookies are good."

Vida baked them.

By now the old woman had finished the last drops of coffee in her cup, but she drank them again, even though they were gone. She wanted to make sure that she did not leave a drop in the cup, even to the point of drinking the last drop of coffee twice.

I could tell that she was preparing to say good-bye because she was trying to rise from her chair. I knew that she would never return again. This would be her only visit to the library.

"It's been so wonderful writing a book," she said. "Now it's done and I can return to my hotel room and my flowers. I'm very tired."

"Your book," I said, handing it to her. "You are free to put it anywhere you want to in the library, on any shelf you want."

"How exciting," she said.

She took her book very slowly over to a section where a lot of children are guided by a subconscious track of some kind to place their books on that shelf.

I don't remember ever seeing anyone over fifty put a book there before, but she went right there as if guided by the hands of the children and placed her book about growing flowers by candlelight in hotel rooms in between a book about Indians (pro) and an illustrated, highly favorable tract on strawberry jam.

She was very happy as she left the library to walk very slowly back to her room in the Kit Carson Hotel and the flowers that waited for her there.

I turned out the lights in the library and took the tray back to my room. I knew the library so well that I could do it in the dark. The returning path to my room was made comfortable by thoughts of flowers, America and Vida sleeping like a photograph here in the library.

The Automobile Accident

THIS library came into being because of an overwhelming need and desire for such a place. There just simply had to be a library like this. That desire brought into existence this library building which isn't very large and its permanent staffing which happens to be myself at the present time.

The library is old in the San Francisco post-earthquake yellow-brick style and is located at 3150 Sacramento Street, San Francisco, California 94115, though no books are ever accepted by mail. They must be brought in person. That is one of the foundations of this library.

Many people have worked here before me. This place has a fairly rapid turnover. I believe I am the 35th or 36th librarian. I got the job because I was the only person who could fulfill the requirements and I was available.

I am thirty-one years old and never had any formal library training. I have had a different kind of training which is quite compatible with the running of this library. I have an understanding of people and I love what I am doing.

I believe I am the only person in America who can perform this job right now and that's what I'm doing. After I am through with my job here, I'll find something else to do. I think the future has quite a lot in store for me.

The librarian before me was here for three years and finally had to quit because he was afraid of children. He thought they were up to something. He is now living in an old folks' home. I got a postcard from him last month. It was unintelligible.

The librarian before him was a young man who took a six-months leave of absence from his motorcycle gang to put in his tenure here. Afterward he returned to his gang and never told them where he had been.

"Where have you been the last six months?" they asked him.

"I've been taking care of my mother," he said. "She was sick and needed lots of hot chicken soup. Any more questions?" There were no more questions.

The librarian before him was here for two years, then moved suddenly to the Australian bush. Nothing has been heard from him since. I've heard rumors that he's alive, but I've also heard rumors that he's dead, but whatever he's doing, dead or alive, I'm certain he's still in the Australian bush because he said he wasn't coming back and if he ever saw another book again, he'd cut his throat.

The librarian before him was a young lady who quit because she was pregnant. One day she caught the glint in a young poet's eye. They are now living together in the Mission District and are no longer young. She has a beautiful daughter, though, and he's on unemployment. They want to move to Mexico.

I believe it's a mistake on their part. I have seen too many couples who went to Mexico and then immediately broke up when they returned to America. I believe if they want to stay together they shouldn't go to Mexico.

The librarian before her was here for one year. He was killed in an automobile accident. An automobile went out of control and crashed into the library. Somehow it killed him. I have never been able to figure this out because the library is made of bricks.

The 23

Ah, it feels so good to sit here in the darkness of these books. I'm not tired. This has been an average evening for books being brought in: with 23 finding their welcomed ways onto our shelves.

I wrote their titles and authors and a little about the receiving of each book down in the Library Contents Ledger. I think the first book came in around 6:30.

MY TRIKE by Chuck. The author was five years old and had a face that looked as if it had been struck by a tornado of freckles. There was no title on the book and no words inside, just pictures.

"What's the name of your book?" I said.

The little boy opened the book and showed me the drawing of a tricycle. It looked more like a giraffe standing upside down in an elevator.

"That's my trike," he said.

"Beautiful," I said. "And what's your name?"

"That's my trike."

"Yes," I said. "Very nice, but what's your name?"

"Chuck."

He reached the book up onto the desk and then headed for the door, saying, "I have to go now. My mother's outside with my sister."

I was going to tell him that he could put the book on any shelf he wanted to, but then he was gone in his small way.

LEATHER CLOTHES AND THE HISTORY OF MAN by S. M. Justice. The author was quite motorcyclish and wearing an awful lot of leather clothes. His book was made entirely of leather. Somehow the book was printed. I had never seen a 290-page book printed on leather before.

When the author turned the book over to the library, he said, "I like a man who likes leather."

LOVE ALWAYS BEAUTIFUL by Charles Green. The author was about fifty years old and said he had been trying to find a publisher for his book since he was seventeen years old when he wrote the book.

"This book has set the world's record for rejections," he said. "It has been rejected 459 times and now I am an old man."

THE STEREO AND GOD by the Reverend Lincoln Lincoln. The author said that God was keeping his eye on our stereophonic phonographs. I don't know what he meant by that but he slammed the book down very hard on the desk.

PANCAKE PRETTY by Barbara Jones. The author was seven years old and wearing a pretty white dress.

"This book is about a pancake," she said.

SAM SAM SAM by Patricia Evens Summers. "It's a book of literary essays," she said. "I've always admired Alfred Kazin and Edmund Wilson, especially Wilson's theories on The Turn of the Screw." She was a woman in her late fifties who looked a great deal like Edmund Wilson.

A HISTORY OF NEBRASKA by Clinton York. The author was a gentleman about forty-seven who said he had never been to Nebraska but he had always been interested in the state.

"Ever since I was a child it's been Nebraska for me. Other kids listened to the radio or raved on about their bicycles. I read everything I could find on Nebraska. I don't know what got me started on the thing. But, any way, this is the most complete history ever written about Nebraska."

The book was in seven volumes and he had them in a shopping bag when he came into the library.

HE KISSED ALL NIGHT by Susan Margar. The author was a very plain middle-aged woman who looked as if she had never been kissed. You had to look twice to see if she had any lips on her face. It was a surprise to find her mouth almost totally hidden beneath her nose.

"It's about kissing," she said.

I guess she was too old for any subterfuge now.

MOOSE by Richard Brautigan. The author was tall and blond and had a long yellow mustache that gave him an anachronistic appearance. He looked as if he would be more at home in another era.

This was the third or fourth book he had brought to the library. Every time he brought in a new book he looked a little older, a little more tired. He looked quite young when he brought in his first book. I can't remember the title of it, but it seems to me the book had something to do with America.

"What's this one about?" I asked, because he looked as if he wanted me to ask him something.

"Just another book," he said.

I guess I was wrong about him wanting me to ask him something.

IT'S THE QUEEN OF DARKNESS, PAL by Rod Keen. The author was wearing overalls and had on a pair of rubber boots.

"I work in the city sewers," he said, handing the book to me. "It's science-fiction."

YOUR CLOTHES ARE DEAD by Les Steinman. The author looked like an ancient Jewish tailor. He was very old and looked as if he had made some shirts for Don Quixote.

"They are, you know," he said, showing the book to me as if it were a piece of cloth, a leg from a pair of trousers.

JACK, THE STORY OF A CAT by Hilda Simpson. The author was a girl about twelve years old, just entering into puberty. She had lemon-sized breasts against a green sweater. She was awakening to adolescence in a delightful way.

"What do you have with you this evening?" I said. Hilda had brought in five or six books previously.

"It's a book about my cat Jack. He's really a noble animal. I thought I would put him down in a book, bring it here and make him famous," she said, smiling.

THE CULINARY DOSTOEVSKI by James Fallon. The author said the book was a cookbook of recipes he had found in Dostoevski's novels.

"Some of them are very good," he said. "I've eaten everything Dostoevski ever cooked."

MY DOG by Bill Lewis. The author was seven years old and said thank you when he put his book on a shelf.

HOMBRE by Canton Lee. The author was a Chinese gentleman about seventy.

"It's a Western," he said. "About a horse thief. Reading Westerns is my hobby, so I decided to write one myself. Why not? I spent thirty years cooking in a restaurant in Phoenix."

VIETNAM VICTORY by Edward Fox. The author was a very serious young man who said that victory could only be achieved in Vietnam by killing everybody there. He recommended that after we had killed everybody there we turn the country over to Chiang Kai-shek, so he could attack Red China, then.

"It's only a matter of time," he said.

PRINTER'S INK by Fred Sinkus. The author was a former journalist whose book was almost illegibly written in longhand with his words wrapped around whiskey.

"That's it," he said, handing the book to me. "Twenty years." He left the library unevenly, barely under his own power.

I stood there looking down at twenty years in my hands.

BACON DEATH by Marsha Paterson. The author was a totally nondescript young woman except for a look of anguish on her face. She handed me this fantastically greasy book and fled the library in terror. The book actually looked like a pound of bacon. I was going to open it and see what it was about, but I changed my mind. I didn't know whether to fry the book or put it on the shelf.

Being a librarian here is sometimes a challenge.

UFO VERSUS CBS by Susan DeWitt. The author was an old woman who told me that her book, which was written in Santa Barbara at her sister's house, was about a Martian conspiracy to take over the Columbia Broadcasting System.

"It's all here in my book," she said. "Remember all those flying saucers last summer?"

"I think so," I said.

"They're all in here," she said. The book looked quite handsome and I'm certain they were all in there.

THE EGG LAYED TWICE by Beatrice Quinn Porter. The author said this collection of poetry summed up the wisdom she had found while living twenty-six years on a chicken ranch in San Jose.

"It may not be poetry," she said. "I never went to college, but it's sure as hell about chickens."

BREAKFAST FIRST by Samuel Humber. The author said that breakfast was an absolute requisite for travelling and was overlooked in too many travel books, so he decided that he would write a book about how important breakfast was in travelling.

31

THE QUICK FOREST by Thomas Funnell. The author was about thirty years old and looked scientific. His hair was thinning and he seemed eager to talk about the book.

"This forest is quicker than an ordinary forest," he said.

"How long did it take you to write it?" I said, knowing that authors seem to like that question.

"I didn't write it," he said. "I stole it from my mother. Serves her right, too. The God-damn bitch."

THE NEED FOR LEGALIZED ABORTION by Doctor O. The author was doctory and very nervous in his late 30s. The book had no title on the cover. The contents were very neatly typed, about 300 pages long.

"It's all I can do," he said.

"Do you want to put it on a shelf yourself?" I said.

"No," he said. "You take care of that yourself. There's nothing else that I can do. It's all a God-damn shame."

It has just started to rain now outside the library. I can hear it splash against the windows and echo among the books. They seem to know it's raining here in the beautiful darkness of lives as I wait for Vida.

Buffalo Gals, Won't
You Come Out Tonight?

I MUST tell you right now that most of the library isn't here. This building is not large and couldn't begin to hold all the books that have been brought in over the years.

The library was in existence before it came to San Francisco in the late 1870s, and the library didn't lose a book during the earthquake and fire of 1906. While everybody else was running around like a bunch of chickens with their heads cut off, we were careful: no panic.

This library rests upon a sloping lot that runs all the way through the block down from Clay to Sacramento Street. We use just a small portion of the lot and the rest of it is overgrown with tall grass and bushes and flowers and wine bottles and lovers' trysts.

There are some old cement stairs that pour through green and busy establishments down from the Clay Street side and there are ancient electric lamps, friends of Thomas Edison, mounted on tall metal asparagus stalks.

They are on what was once the second landing of the stairs. The lights don't work any more and everything is so overgrown that it's hard to tell why anything ever existed in the first place.

The back of the library lies almost disappearing in green at the bottom of the stairs.

The front lawn is neat, though. We don't want this place to look totally like a jungle. It might frighten people away.

A little Negro boy comes and mows the lawn every month or so. I don't have any money to pay him but he doesn't mind. He does it because he likes me and he knows that I have to stay inside here, that I can't mow the lawn myself. I always have to be in here ready to welcome a new book.

Right now the lawn has many dandelions on it and thousands of daisies sprawled here and there together like a Rorschach dress pattern designed by Rudi Gernreich.

The dandelions are loners and pretty much stay off by themselves, but those daisies! I know all this by looking out the heavy glass door.

This place is constantly bathed in the intermediate barking of dogs from early in the morning when the dogs wake up and continuing until late at night when the dogs go to sleep and sometimes they bark in between.

We are just a few doors down from a pet hospital and, though I can't see the hospital, I am seldom without the barking of dogs and I have grown used to it.

At first I hated their damn barking. It had always been a thing with me: a dislike for dogs. But now in my third year here, I've grown accustomed to their barking and it doesn't bother me any more. Actually, I like it sometimes.

There are high arched windows here in the library above the bookshelves and there are two green trees towering into the windows and they spread their branches like paste against the glass.

I love those trees.

Through the glass door and across the street is a big white garage with cars coming and going all the time in hours of sickness and need. There is a big word in blue on the front of the garage: GULF.

Before the library came to San Francisco, it was in Saint Louis for a while, then in New York for a long time. There are a lot of Dutch books somewhere.

Because this building is so small, we have been forced to store thousands of books at another place. We moved into this little brick building after the '06 business to be on the safe side, but there just isn't enough room here.

There are so many books being written that end up here, either by design or destiny. We have accepted 114 books on the Model T Ford, fifty-eight books on the history of the banjo and nineteen books on buffalo-skinning since the beginning of this library.

We keep all the ledgers here that we use to record the acceptance of each book in, but most of the books themselves are in hermetically-sealed caves in Northern California.

I have nothing to do with the storing of the books in the caves. That's Foster's job. He also brings me my food because I can't leave the library. Foster hasn't been around for a few months, so I guess he's off on another drunk.

Foster loves to drink and it's always easy for him to find somebody to drink with. Foster is about forty years old and always wears a T-shirt, no matter what the weather is about, rain or shine, hot or cold, it's all the same to his T-shirt because his T-shirt is an eternal garment that only death will rob from his body.

Foster has long buffalo-heavy blond hair and I have never seen Foster when he wasn't sweating. He's very friendly in an overweight sort of style, jolly you might say, and has a way of charming people, total strangers, into buying him drinks. He goes off on month-long drunks in the logging towns near the caves, raises hell with the loggers and chases the Indian girls through the woods.

I imagine he'll be down here one of these days, red-faced and hung-over, full of excuses and driving his big green van and all ready to fill it up with another load of books for the caves.

BOOK 2: Vida

Vida

WHEN I first met Vida she had been born inside the wrong body and was barely able to look at people, wanting to crawl off and hide from the thing that she was contained within.

This was late last year in San Francisco.

She came to the library one evening after she got off work. The library was "closed" and I was in my room making some coffee and thinking about the books that had come into the library that day.

One of the books was about a great octopus that had leather wings and flew through abandoned school yards at night, demanding entrance into the classrooms.

I was putting some sugar into my coffee when I heard the bell ring ever so slightly, but always just enough to alert me and to summon me.

I went out and turned on the light in the library and

there was a young girl at the door, waiting behind the heavy religious glass.

She startled me.

Besides having an incredibly delicate face, beautiful, with long black hair that hung about her shoulders like bat lightning, there was something very unusual about her, but I could not quite tell what that thing was because her face was like a perfect labyrinth that led me momentarily away from a very disturbing thing.

She did not look directly at me as she waited for me to unlock the door and let her in. She was holding something under her arm. It was in a brown paper bag and looked like a book.

Another one for the caves.

"Hello," I said. "Please come in."

"Thank you," she said, coming very awkwardly into the library. I was surprised that she was so awkward. She did not look directly at me and she did not look at the library either. She seemed to be looking at something else. The thing that she was looking at was not in front of me nor behind me nor at the side of me.

"What do you have there? A book?" I said, wanting to sound like a pleasant librarian and make her feel at ease.

Her face was so delicate: the mouth, the eyes, the nose, the chin, the curve of her cheeks all beautiful. She was almost painful to gaze upon.

"Yes," she said. "I hope I didn't disturb you. It's late."

"No," I said. "Not at all. No. Please come over here to the desk and we'll register your book in the Library Contents Ledger. That's how we do it here."

"I was wondering how you were going to do it," she said.

"Did you come far?" I said.

"No," she said. "I just got off work."

She wasn't looking at herself either. I do not know what she was looking at, but she was looking at something very intently. I believe the thing that she was looking at was inside of herself. It had a shape that only she could see.

She moved very awkwardly over to the desk, stunningly awkward, but again the almost tide-pool delicacy of her face led me away from the source of her awkwardness.

"I hope I'm not disturbing you. I know it's late," she said, kind of hopelessly, and then broke away from the thing that she was looking at, to glance lightspeed at me.

She *was* disturbing me, but not in the way she thought. There was a dynamically incongruous thing about her, but I still couldn't find it. Her face, like a circle of mirrors, led me away from it.

"No, not at all," I said. "This is my job and I love doing it. There's no place I would rather be than where I am now."

"What?" she said.

"I love my work," I said.

"It's good you're happy," she said. She said the word happy as if she were looking at it from a great distance through a telescope. The word sounded celestial upon her mouth, stark and Galilean.

Then I noticed what was so extraordinarily strange about her. Her face was so delicate, perfect, but her body was fantastically developed for the fragility of her face.

She had very large fully realized breasts and an incredibly tiny waist and large full hips that tapered down into long majestic legs.

Her body was very sensual, inciting one to think of lust, while her face was Botticellian and set your mind to voyaging upon the ethereal.

Suddenly she sensed my recognition of her body. She blushed bitterly and reached into the paper bag and took out her book.

"This is my book," she said.

She put it down on the desk and almost stepped back when she did it. She was going to step back but then she changed her mind. She glanced at me again and I could feel somebody inside of her looking out as if her body were a castle and a princess lived inside.

The book had a plain brown wrapper on it and there was no title. The book looked like a stark piece of ground burning with frozen heat.

"What's it about?" I said, holding the book in my hand, feeling almost a hatred coming from within the book.

"It's about this," she said and suddenly, almost hysterically, she unbuttoned her coat and flung it open as if it were a door to some horrible dungeon filled with torture instruments, pain and dynamic confession.

She was wearing a blue sweater and skirt and a pair of black leather boots in the style of this time. She had a fantastically full and developed body under her clothes that would have made the movie stars and beauty queens and showgirls bitterly ooze dead make-up in envy.

She was developed to the most extreme of Western man's desire in this century for women to look: the large breasts, the tiny waist, the large hips, the long *Playboy* furniture legs.

She was so beautiful that the advertising people would have made her into a national park if they would have gotten their hands on her.

Then her blue eyes swirled like a tide pool and she started crying.

"This book is about my body," she said. "I hate it. It's too big for me. It's somebody else's body. It's not mine."

I reached into my pocket and took out a handkerchief and a candy bar. When people are troubled or worried, I always tell them that it will be all right and give them a candy bar. It surprises them and it's good for them.

"Everything's going to be all right," I said.

I gave her a Milky Way. She held it in her startled

43

hand, staring at it. And I gave her the handkerchief.

"Wipe your eyes," I said. "And eat the candy bar while I get you a glass of sherry."

She fumbled abstractedly with the candy bar wrapper as if it were a tool from a distant and future century while I went and got some sherry for us. I figured that we would both need it.

When I came back she was eating the candy bar. "Now isn't that good," I said, smiling.

The ludicrousness of me giving her a candy bar made her smile, ever so slightly, and almost look directly at me.

"Please sit down over here," I said, motioning toward a table and some chairs. She sat down as if her body were six inches larger than she was. After she had sat down, her body was still sitting down.

I poured us each a glass of Gallo sherry, all the library could afford, and then there was a kind of awkward silence as we sat there sipping our sherry.

I was going to tell her that she was a beautiful girl and she shouldn't feel bad about it, that she was all wrong in denouncing herself, but then I changed my mind instantly.

That was not what she wanted to hear and that wasn't really what I wanted to say. After all, I have a little more sense than that. We both didn't want to hear what I first thought of telling her.

"What's your name?" I said.

"Vida. Vida Kramar."

"Do you like to be called V-(ee)-da or V-(eye)-da?"

That made her smile.

"V-(eye)-da."

"How old are you?"

"Nineteen. Soon I'll be twenty. On the tenth."

"Do you go to school?"

"No, I work at night. I went to State for a while, then UC, but I don't know. Now I'm working at night. It's OK."

She was almost looking at me.

"Did you just finish your book?" I said.

"Yes, I finished it yesterday. I wanted to tell how it is to be like me. I figured it was the only thing left for me to do. When I was eleven years old, I had a thirty-six-inch bust. I was in the sixth grade.

"For the last eight years I've been the object, veneration and butt of at least a million dirty jokes. In the seventh grade they called me 'points.' Isn't that cute? It never got any better.

"My book is about my body, about how horrible it is to have people creeping, crawling, sucking at something I am not. My older sister looks the way I really am.

"It's horrible.

"For years I had a recurrent dream that I got up in the middle of the night and went into my sister's bedroom and changed bodies with her. I took off my body and put on her body. It fit perfectly.

"When I woke up in the morning, I had on my own

45

true body and she had this terrible thing I'm wearing now. I know it's not a nice dream, but I had it all during my early teens.

"You'll never know how it is to be like I am. I can't go anywhere without promoting whistles, grunts, howls, minor and major obscenities and every man I meet wants to go to bed instantly with me. I have the wrong body."

She was staring directly at me now. Her vision was unbroken and constant as a building with many windows standing fully here in this world.

She continued: "My whole life has just been one torment. I, I don't know. I wrote this book to tell how horrible physical beauty is, the full terror of it.

"Three years ago a man was killed in an automobile accident because of my body. I was walking along a highway. I had gone to the beach with my family, but I couldn't stand it any longer.

"They demanded that I put on a bathing suit. 'Don't be bashful, just relax and enjoy yourself.' I was miserable with all the attention I was getting. When an eighty-year-old man dropped his ice-cream cone on his foot, I put my clothes back on and went for a walk along the highway up from the beach. I had to go somewhere.

"A man came driving by in his car. He slowed down and was gawking at me. I tried to ignore him but he was very persistent. He forgot all about where he was

46

and what he was doing and drove his car right into a train.

"I ran over and he was still alive. He died in my arms, still staring at me. It was horrible. There was blood all over both of us and he wouldn't take his eyes off me. Part of the bone was sticking out of his arm. His back felt funny. When he died, he said, 'You're beautiful.' That's just what I needed to make me feel perfect forever.

"When I was fifteen a student in a high-school chemistry class drank hydrochloric acid because I wouldn't go out with him. He was a little crazy, anyway, but that didn't make me feel any better. The principal prohibited me from wearing a sweater to school.

"It's this," Vida said, gesturing rain-like toward her body. "It's not me. I can't be responsible for what it does. I don't attempt to use my body to get anything from anyone and I never have.

"I spend all my time hiding from it. Can you imagine spending your whole life hiding from your own body as if it were a monster in a Grade B movie, but still every day having to use it to eat, sleep and get from one place to another?

"Whenever I take a bath I always feel as if I'm going to vomit. I'm in the wrong skin."

All the time she told me these things she did not take her eyes off me. I felt like a statue in a park. I poured her another glass of sherry and one for myself. I had a feeling that we were going to need a lot of sherry before the night was over.

"I don't know what to say," I said. "I'm just a librarian. I can't pretend that you are not beautiful. That would be like pretending that you are someplace else in the world, say China or Africa, or that you are some other kind of matter, a plant or a tire or some frozen peas or a bus transfer. Do you understand?"

"I don't know," she said.

"It's the truth. You're a very pretty girl and you're not going to change, so you might as well settle down and get used to it."

She sighed and then awkwardly slipped her coat off and let it hang on the chair behind her like a vegetable skin.

"I once tried wearing very baggy formless clothes, muu muus, but that didn't work because I got tired of looking like a slob. It's one thing to have this fleshy thing covering me but it's another thing to be called a beatnik at the same time."

Then she gave me a great big smile and said, "Anyway, that's my problem. Where do we go from here? What's next? Got any more candy bars?"

I pretended to get one from my pocket and she laughed out loud. It was a pleasing thing.

Suddenly she turned her attention upon me in a very strong way. "Why are you here in this funny library?" she said. "This place where losers bring their books. I'm curious about you now. What's your story, Mr. Candyman Librarian?"

She was smiling as she said these things.

"I work here," I said.

"That's too easy. Where did you come from? Where are you going?"

"Well, I've done all sorts of things," I said, sounding falsely old. "I worked in canneries, sawmills, factories, and now I'm here."

"Where do you live?"

"Here," I said.

"You live here in the library?" she said.

"Yes. I have a large room in the back with a small kitchen and toilet."

"Let me see it," she said. "I'm suddenly curious about you. A young-old man like yourself working in a creepy place like this doesn't show that you've come out too far ahead of the game either."

"You're really laying it on the line," I said, because she had really gotten to me.

"I'm that way," she said. "I may be sick, but I'm not stupid. Show me your room."

"Well," I said, dogging a little. "That's a little irregular."

"You're kidding," she said. "You mean there's something irregular for this place? I don't know how to break it to you, but you've got a pretty far-out operation going on here. This library is a little on the whacky side."

49

She stood up and stretched awkwardly, but it's hard to describe the rest of it. I had never in my life seen a woman graced with such a perfect body whose spell was now working on me. As certain as the tides in the sea rush to the shore, I showed her my room.

"I'd better get my coat," she said. She folded her coat over her arm. "After you, Mr. Librarian."

"I've never done this before," I said, faraway-like as if to no one.

"Neither have I," she said. "It will be a different thing for both of us."

I started to say something else, but abstraction clouded my tongue and made it distant and useless.

"The library isn't really open now, is it?" she said. "I mean, it's after midnight and it's only open for special books, latecomers like myself, right?"

"Yes, it's 'closed' but—"

"But what?" she said.

I don't know where that "but" came from but it vanished just as fast, returning to some conjunctional oblivion.

"But nothing," I said.

"You had better turn out the lights, then," she said. "You don't want to waste electricity."

"Yes," I said, feeling a door close behind me, knowing that somehow this at first-appearing shy unhappy girl was turning, turning into something strong that I did not know how to deal with.

"I'd better turn the lights out," I said.

"Yes," she said.

I turned the lights out in the library and turned the light on in my room. That was not all I was turning on as a door closed behind us and a door opened in front of us.

"Your room is very simple," she said, putting her coat down on my bed. "I like that. You must live a very lonely life with all the losers and dingalings, myself included, that bring their books in here."

"I call it home," I said.

"That's sad," she said. "How long have you been here?"

"Years," I said. What the hell.

"You're too young to have been here that long," she said. "How old are you?"

"Thirty-one."

"That's a good age."

She had her back to me and was staring at the cupboard in my kitchen.

"It's all right to look at me," she said, without turning her head the slightest. "For some strange reason I don't mind your looking at me. Actually, it makes me feel good, but stop acting like a bandit when you do it."

I laughed at that.

Suddenly she turned around and looked half at me, then directly at me and smiled gently. "I really have had a hard time of it."

"I think I can almost understand," I said.

51

"That's nice," she said. She reached up and brushed her long black hair, causing a storm of bat lightning to flash past her ears.

"I'd like some coffee," she said, looking at me.

"I'll put it on," I said.

"No, let me," she said. "I know how to make good coffee. It's my specialty. Just call me Queen Caffeine."

"Well, damn," I said, a little embarrassed. "I'm sorry but I only have instant."

"Then instant it is," she said. "That's the name of the game. Perhaps I have a way with instant coffee, too. You never can tell," smiling.

"I'll get the stuff for you," I said.

"Oh, no," she said. "Let me do it. I'm a little curious about this kitchen of yours. I want to find out more about you, and this little kitchen is a good place to start. I can see at a glance, though, that you are something like me. You're not at home in the world."

"At least let me get the coffee for you," I said. "It's—"

"Sit down," she said. "You make me nervous. Only one person can make instant coffee at a time. I'll find everything."

I sat down on the bed next to her coat.

She found everything and made the coffee as if she were preparing a grand meal. I have never seen such care and eloquence applied to a cup of instant coffee. It was almost as if making a cup of instant coffee were a ballet and she were a ballerina pirouetting between the spoon, the cups, the jar, and the pan full of boiling water.

She cleared the clutter from my table, but then decided that we should have our coffee on the bed, because it was more comfortable.

We sat there on the bed, cozy as two bugs in a rug, drinking coffee and talking about our lives. She worked as a laboratory technician for a small institute that was studying the effects of various experiments on dogs in an attempt to solve some of the more puzzling questions of science.

"How did you get the job?" I said.

"Through an ad in the *Chronicle*."

"What happened at San Francisco State?"

"I got tired of it. One of my English teachers fell in love with me. I told him to buzz off, so he failed me. That made me mad, so I transferred to UC."

"And UC?"

"The same story. I don't know what it is about English teachers and me, but they fall like guillotines when they see me coming."

"Where were you born?"

"Santa Clara. All right, I've answered enough of your questions. Now tell me how you got this job. What's your story, Mr. Librarian?"

"I assumed possession of it."

"I take it then that there was no ad in the paper."

"Nope."

"How did you assume possession of it?"

"The fellow who was here before me couldn't stand children. He thought they were going to steal his shoes. I came in here with a book I had written and while he was writing it down in the Library Contents Ledger, a couple of children came in and he flipped, so I told him that I had better take over the library and he had better do something that didn't involve children. He told me he thought he was cracking up, too, and that's how I got this job."

"What did you do before you started working here?"

"I kicked around a lot: canneries, sawmills, factories. A woman supported me for a couple of years, then she got tired of it and kicked my ass out. I don't know," I said. "It was all pretty complicated before I started working here."

"What are you going to do after you quit here or do you plan on quitting?"

"I don't know," I said. "Something will come up. Maybe I'll get another job or find a woman to support me again or maybe I'll write a novel and sell it to the movies."

That amused her.

We had finished our coffee. It was funny because suddenly we both noticed that we did not have any more coffee to drink and we were sitting together on the bed.

"What are we going to do now?" she said. "We can't drink any more coffee and it's late."

"I don't know," I said.

"I guess it would be too corny for us to go to bed together," she said. "But I can't think of anything else that would be better to do. I don't want to go home and sleep by myself. I like you. I want to stay here with you tonight."

"It's a puzzler," I said.

"Do you want to sleep with me?" she said, not looking at me, but not looking away either. Her eyes were somewhere in between half-looking at me and half-thinking about something else.

"We don't have any place else to go," I said. "I'd feel like a criminal if you left tonight. It's hard to sleep with strangers. I gave it up years ago, but I don't think we are really strangers. Do you?"

She turned her eyes 3/4 toward me.

"No, we're not strangers."

"Do you want to sleep with me?" I asked.

"I don't know what it is about you," she said. "But you make me feel nice."

"It's my clothes. They're relaxing. They've always been this way. I know how to get clothes that make people feel better when they're with me."

"I don't want to sleep with your clothes," she said, smiling.

"Do you want to sleep with me?" I said.

"I've never slept with a librarian before," she said, 99% toward me. The other 1% was waiting to turn. I saw it starting to turn.

"I brought a book in here tonight denouncing my own body as grotesque and elephant-like, but now I want to take this awkward machine and lie down beside you here in this strange library."

Counting toward Tijuana

WHAT an abstract thing it is to take your clothes off in front of a stranger for the very first time. It isn't really what we planned on doing. Your body almost looks away from itself and is a stranger to this world.

We live most of our lives privately under our clothes, except in a case like Vida whose body lived outside of herself like a lost continent, complete with dinosaurs of her own choosing.

"I'll turn the lights out," she said, sitting next to me on the bed.

I was startled to hear her panic. She seemed almost relaxed a few seconds before. My, how fast she could move the furniture about in her mind. I responded to this by firmly saying, "No, please don't."

Her eyes stopped moving for a few seconds. They came to a crashing halt like blue airplanes.

"Yes," she said. "That's a good idea. It will be very

hard, but I have no other choice. I can't go on like this forever."

She gestured toward her body as if it were far away in some lonesome valley and she, on top of a mountain, looking down. Tears came suddenly to her eyes. There was now rain on the blue wings of the airplanes.

Then she stopped crying without a tear having left her eyes. I looked again and all the tears had vanished. "We have to leave the lights on," she said. "I won't cry. I promise."

I reached out and, for the first time in two billion years, I touched her. I touched her hand. My fingers went carefully over her fingers. Her hand was almost cold.

"You're cold," I said.

"No," she said. "It's only my hand."

She moved slightly, awkwardly toward me and rested her head on my shoulder. When her head touched me, I could feel my blood leap forward, my nerves and muscles stretch like phantoms toward the future.

My shoulder was drenched in smooth white skin and long bat-flashing hair. I let go of her hand and touched her face. It was tropical.

"See," she said, smiling faintly. "It was only my hand."

It was fantastic trying to work around her body, not wanting to startle her like a deer and have her go running off into the woods.

I poetically shifted my shoulder like the last lines of

a Shakespearean sonnet (Love is a babe; then might I not say so, / To give full growth to that which still doth grow.) and at the same time lowered her back onto the bed.

She lay there looking up at me as I crouched forward, descending slowly, and kissed her upon the mouth as gently as I could. I did not want that first kiss to have attached to it the slightest gesture or flower of the meat market.

The Decision

Iᴛ's a hard decision whether to start at the top or the bottom of a girl. With Vida I just didn't know where to begin. It was really a problem.

After she reached up awkwardly and put my face in a small container which was her hands and kissed me quietly again and again, I had to start somewhere.

She stared up at me all the time, her eyes never leaving me as if I were an airfield.

I changed the container and her face became a flower in my hands. I slowly let my hands drift down her face while I kissed her and then further down her neck to her shoulders.

I could see the future being moved in her mind while I arrived at the boundaries of her bosom. Her breasts were so large, so perfectly formed under her sweater that my stomach was standing on a stepladder when I touched them for the first time.

Her eyes never left me and I could see in her eyes
the act of my touching her breasts. It was like brief
blue lightning.

I was almost hesitant in a librarian sort of way.

"I promise," she said, reaching up and awkwardly
pressing my hands harder against her breasts. She of
course had no idea what that did to me. The stepladder
started swirling.

She kissed me again, but this time with her tongue.
Her tongue slid past my tongue like a piece of hot glass.

A Continuing Decision

WELL, it had been my decision to start at the top and I was going to have to carry it out and soon we arrived at the time to take off her clothes.

I could tell that she didn't want to have anything to do with it. She wasn't going to help. It was all up to me.

Damn it.

It wasn't exactly what I had planned on doing when I started working at the library. I just wanted to take care of the books because the other librarian couldn't do it any more. He was afraid of children, but of course it was too late now to think about his fears. I had my own problems.

I had gone further than taking this strange awkward beautiful girl's book. I was now faced with taking her body which lay before me and had to have its clothes taken off, so we could join our bodies together like a bridge across the abyss.

"I need your help," I said.

She didn't say anything. She just continued staring at me. That brief blue lightning flashed again in her eyes, but it was relaxed at the edges.

"What can I do?" she said.

"Sit up, please," I said.

"All right."

She sat up awkwardly.

"Please put your arms up," I said.

"It's that simple, isn't it?" she said.

Whatever was happening I was certainly getting down to it. It would have been much simpler just to have kindly taken her book for the library and sent her on her way but that was history now or like the grammar of a forgotten language.

"How's this?" she said and then smiled. "I feel like a San Francisco bank teller."

"That's right," I said. "Just do what the note says," and I started her sweater gently off. It slid up her stomach and went on over her breasts, getting briefly caught on one of them, so I had to reach down and help it over the breast, and then her neck and face disappeared in the sweater and came out again when the sweater went off her fingers.

It was really fantastic the way she looked. I could have been hung up for a long time there, but I kept moving on, had to. It was my mission in life to take her bra off.

"I feel like a child," she said. She turned sideways

63

from me, so I could get at the brassiere clasp in the back. I fumbled at the clasp for a few moments. I've never had much luck with brassieres.

"Want me to help?" she said.

"No, I can get it," I said. "It may take me a few days but I'll get it. Don't dishearten. There . . . *AH!*"

That made Vida laugh.

She did not need a bra at all. Her breasts stayed right up there after the bra left them like an extra roof on a house and joined her sweater. It was a difficult pile of clothes. Each garment was won in a strange war.

Her nipples were small and delicately colored in relationship to the large full expansion of her breasts. Her nipples were very gentle. They were another incongruity fastened like a door to Vida.

Then at the same time we both looked down at her boots, long and black and leather like a cloud of animals gathered about her feet.

"I'll take your boots off," I said.

I had finished with the top of her and now it was time to start on the bottom. There certainly are a lot of parts to girls.

I took off her boots and then I took off her socks. I liked the way my hands ran along her feet like water over a creek. Her toes were the cutest pebbles I have ever seen.

"Stand up, please," I said. We were really moving along now. She got awkwardly to her feet and I unzipped her skirt. I brought it down her hips to the floor and she stepped out of it and I put it on the pile of other battles.

I looked into her face before I took her panties off. Her features were composed and though there still flashed bolts of brief blue lightning in her eyes, her eyes remained gentle at the edges and the edges were growing.

I took her panties off and the deed was done. Vida was without clothes, naked, there.

"See?" she said. "This isn't me. I'm not here." She reached out and put her arms about my neck. "But I'll try to be here for you, Mr. Librarian."

Two (37-19-36) Soliloquies

"**I** JUST don't understand why women want bodies like this. The grotesqueness of them and they try so very hard to get these bodies, moving hell and high water with dieting, operations, injections, obscene undergarments to arrive at one of these damn things and then if they try everything and still can't get one, the dumb cunts fake it. Well, here's one they can have for free. Come and get it, you bitches.

"They don't know what they're getting into or maybe they like it. Maybe they're all pigs like the women who use these bodies to turn the tides of money: the movie stars, models, whores.

"Oh, Christ!

"I just can't see the fatal attraction that bodies like this hold for men and women. My sister has my body: tall and skinny. All these layers are beyond me. These aren't my breasts. These aren't my hips. This isn't my ass. I'm inside of all this junk. Can you see me? Look hard. I'm in here, Mr. Librarian."

She reached out and put her arms about my neck and I put my hands upon her hips. We stood there looking at each other.

"I think you're wrong," I said. "Whether you like it or not, you're a very beautiful woman and you've got a grand container. It may not be what you want, but this body is in your keeping and you should take good care of it and with pride, too. I know it's hard but don't worry about what other people want and what they get. You've got something that's beautiful and try to live with it.

"Beauty is the hardest damn thing in the world to understand. Don't buy the rest of the world's juvenile sexual thirsts. You're a smart young lady and you'd better start using your head instead of your body because that's what you're doing.

"Don't be a fatalist winner. Life's a little too short to haul that one around. This body is you and you'd better get used to it because this is all she wrote for this world and you can't hide from yourself.

"This is you.

"Let your sister have her own body and start learning how to appreciate and use this one. I think you might enjoy it if you let yourself relax and get your mind out of other people's sewers.

67

"If you get hung up on everybody else's hang-ups, then the whole world's going to be nothing more than one huge gallows."

We kissed.

BOOK 3: Calling the Caves

Calling the Caves

FORTUNATELY, I was able to get in touch with Foster up at the caves when Vida discovered that she was pregnant. Vida and I talked it over. The decision to have the abortion was arrived at without bitterness and was calmly guided by gentle necessity.

"I'm not ready to have a child yet," Vida said. "And neither are you, working in a kooky place like this. Maybe another time, perhaps for certain another time, but not now. I love children, but this isn't the time. If you can't give them the maximum of yourself, then it's best to wait. There are too many children in the world and not enough love. An abortion is the only answer."

"I think you're right," I said. "I don't know about this library being a kooky place, but we're not ready for a child yet. Perhaps in a few years. I think you should use the pill after we have the abortion."

71

"Yes," she said. "It's the pill from now on."

Then she smiled and said, "It looks like our bodies got us."

"It happens sometimes," I said.

"Do you know anything about this kind of business?" Vida said. "I know a little bit. My sister had an abortion last year in Sacramento, but before she had the abortion, she went to a doctor in Marin County who gave her some hormone shots, but they didn't work because it was too late. The shots work if you take them soon enough and they're quite a bit cheaper than an abortion."

"I think I'd better call Foster," I said. "He got into a thing like this last year and had to go down to Tijuana with one of his Indian girls."

"Who's Foster?" Vida said.

"He takes care of the caves," I said.

"What caves?"

"This building is too small," I said.

"What caves?" she said.

I guess I was rattled by the events in Vida's stomach. I hadn't realized it. I calmed myself down a little bit and said, "Yes, we have some caves up in Northern California where we store most of our books because this building is too small for our collection.

"This library is very old. Foster takes care of the caves. He comes down here every few months and loads his van up with books and stores them in the caves.

"He also brings me food and the little things that I need. The rest of the time he stays drunk and chases the local women, mostly Indians. He's quite a guy. A regular explosion of a man.

"He had to go down to Tijuana last year. He told me all about it. He knows a very good doctor there. There's a telephone at the caves. I'll give him a ring. I've never done it before. Never had to. Things are usually pretty calm down here. We might as well get this thing going. Would you watch the library while I do it?"

"Yes," Vida said. "Of course. It would be a privilege. I never thought that I would end up being the librarian of this place, but I guess I should have had an inkling when I came in here with my book under my arm."

She was smiling and wearing a short green dress. Her smile was on top of the dress. It looked like a flower.

"It will only take a few minutes," I said. "I think there's a pay telephone down at the corner. That is, if it's still there. I haven't been out of here in so long that they may have moved it."

"No, it's still there," Vida said, smiling. "I'll take care of everything. Don't worry. Your library is in good hands."

She held her hands out to me and I kissed them.

"See?" she said.

"You know how to put the books down in the Library Contents Ledger?" I said.

73

"Yes," she said. "I know how to do it and I'll give anyone who brings in a book the royal carpet treatment. Don't worry. Everything's going to be all right. Stop worrying, Mr. Librarian. I think you have been in here too long. I think I'll kidnap you soon."

"You could ask them to wait," I said. "I'll only be gone for a few minutes."

"Come on now!" Vida said. "Let your granny gland relax a little and slow down those rocking chair secretions."

Outside (Briefly)

Gee, it had been a long time. I hadn't realized that being in that library for so many years was almost like being in some kind of timeless thing. Maybe an airplane of books, flying through the pages of eternity.

Actually being outside was quite different from looking out the window or the door. I walked down the street, feeling strangely awkward on the sidewalk. The concrete was too hard, aggressive or perhaps I was too light, passive.

It was something to think about.

I had a lot of trouble opening the telephone booth door but finally I got inside and started to call Foster up at the caves when suddenly I realized that I didn't have any money with me. I searched all my pockets but, alas, not a cent. I didn't need money in the library.

"Back already?" Vida said. She looked very pretty

behind the counter in her green dress with her flower-like head.

"I don't have any money," I said.

After she stopped laughing, which took about five minutes, very funny, she went and got her purse and gave me a handful of change.

"You're too much," she said. "Are you sure you haven't forgotten how to use money? You hold it like this." She held an imaginary coin between her fingers and started laughing all over again.

I left. I had my dime.

Foster's Coming

I CALLED Foster up at the caves. I could hear his telephone ringing. It rang seven or eight times and then Foster answered it.

"What's happening?" Foster said. "Who is this? What are you up to, you son-of-a-bitch? Don't you know it's one o'clock in the afternoon. What are you? A vampire?"

"It's me," I said. "You old drunk!"

"Oh," he said. "The kid. Hell, why didn't you say so? What's up down there? Somebody bring in an elephant with a book written on it? Well, feed it some hay and I'll be down with the van."

"Very funny, Foster," I said.

"Not bad," he said. "Nothing's impossible at that loony bin you've got down there. What's up, kid?"

"I've got a problem."

"You?" he said. "How in the hell can you have a

problem? You're inside all the time. Is that prison pallor of yours beginning to flake?"

"No," I said. "My girlfriend is pregnant."

"DINGALING CUCKOO!" Foster said and the conversation stopped for a moment while Foster laughed so hard it almost shook the telephone booth hundreds of miles away.

Finally he stopped laughing and said, "It sounds like you've really been working hard at the library, but when did fornication become one of its services? Girlfriend, huh? Pregnant, huh? Cuckoo, kid!"

He started to laugh all over again. It was everybody's day to laugh except mine.

"Well, what do you need?" he said. "A little trip down to Tijuana? A short visit with my abortionist buddy, Dr. Garcia?"

"Something like that," I said.

"Well, I'll have a few drinks for breakfast," he said. "And get in the van and be in sometime late this evening."

"Good," I said. "That's what I need."

Then there was a slight pause at the cave end of the telephone.

"You don't have any money, do you, kid?" Foster said.

"Are you kidding?" I said. "Where would I get any money? This is the lowest-paying job in the world because it doesn't. I had to borrow this dime from my girlfriend to call you collect."

"I guess I'm still gorgonized," he said. "I don't know what I was thinking. I was probably thinking that I spent all my money last night on drink or was it last week? and I haven't got a cent. Cuckoo, have I been out of it!"

"What about my food?" I said, realizing that he had spent my food money, too.

"Is she good-looking?" Foster said. "Will she do in a dust storm at midnight with a candle?"

"What?" I said.

"I'll bring the money, then," he said. "It costs a couple of hundred if you make the good doctor toe the line. He likes to speculate sometimes—it's the businessman in him—but you can hold him down by putting the two hundred in his hand.

"Let's see: You'll need airplane tickets and walking around money and you might need a hotel room for her to rest up after she sees Dr. Garcia.

"I'll go down to the bar and turn a couple of the patrons upside down and see what I can shake out of their pockets, so you hang on, kid, and I'll be in late this evening and we'll get this show on the road.

"I never thought you had it in you, kid. Tell your young lady hello for me and that everything will be all right. Foster's coming."

Masturbation

THAT Foster! I went back to the library. Somebody was just leaving as I arrived. It was a young boy, maybe sixteen. He looked awfully tired and nervous. He hurried past me.

"Thank God, darling, you didn't get lost," Vida said. "I was worried that you wouldn't be able to find your way back up the block. It's great to see you, honey."

She came out from behind the desk and moved breathlessly to where I was given a great big lingering kiss. She had lost about 80% of her awkwardness since she had come to the library that evening late last year. The 20% she had left was very intriguing.

"How did it go?" she said.

"Fine," I said. "Here's your dime. Foster's on his way down. He'll be in late this evening."

"Good," she said. "I'll be glad when this thing is over. I wouldn't like to wait for an abortion. I'm glad we're doing it right now."

"So am I. Foster knows a great doctor," I said. "Everything will be all right. Foster's going to take care of everything."

"Fine, just fine," she said. "What about money? I have—"

"No, no," I said. "Foster will get the money."

"You're sure, because—"

"No, I'm sure," I said. "Who was that boy who was leaving?"

"Some kid who brought in a book," she said. "I welcomed it in my most pleasing manner and recorded it in my best handwriting in the Library Contents Ledger."

"Gee," I said. "This is the first time I haven't received a book in years."

"Oh, honey," she said. "You aren't that old, even though you try to be, but that kind of thinking is going to make you an old man if you work at it hard enough."

She kissed me again.

"I'll take a look at it," I said.

"Your old age?" she said.

"No, the book."

She stood there and smiled after me as I walked over behind the desk and opened the Library Contents Ledger and read:

THE OTHER SIDE OF MY HAND by Harlow
Blade, Jr. The author was about sixteen and seemed a
little sadder than he should have been for his age. He
was very shy around me. The poor dear. He kept looking at me out of the corner of his eye.

Finally he said, "Are *you* the librarian?"

"Yes," I said.

"I expected a man."

"He's out," I said. "So I'll just have to do. I don't
bite."

"You're not a man," he said.

"What's your name?"

"What?"

"Your name, please? I have to write it down here in
the ledger before we can take your book. You do have
a name, don't you?"

"Yes. Harlow Blade, Jr."

"Now what's your book about? I have to have that,
too. Just tell me what it's about and I'll write it down
here in the ledger."

"I was expecting a man," he said.

"What's your book about? The subject, please?"

"Masturbation. I'd better be going now."

I started to thank him for bringing his book in and
tell him that he could put it anywhere he wanted to in
the library, but he left without saying anything else.
Poor kid.

What a strange place this library is, but I guess it's

the only place you can bring a book in the end. I brought mine here and I'm still here.

Vida trailed over to the desk and moved behind it with me and put her arm around me and read the entry over my shoulder after I finished reading it.

"I think it sounds pretty good," she said.

Gee, the handwriting of a different librarian lay before me on the desk. It was the first book I hadn't welcomed and recorded there myself in years.

I looked over at Vida for a moment. I must have looked at her kind of strangely because she said, "Oh, no. No, no, no."

Foster

FOSTER arrived at midnight. We were in my room, sitting around drinking coffee and talking about small casual things that are never remembered afterward, except perhaps in the twilight moments of our lives.

Foster never bothered to ring the bell on the front door. He said it made him think he was going into some kind of church and he'd had enough of that to last him forever.

BANG! BANG! BANG! he just slugged the door with his fist and I could always hear him and was afraid that he would break the glass. Foster couldn't be overlooked nor forgotten.

"What's that?" Vida said, jumping up startled from the bed.

"That's Foster," I said.

"It sounds like an elephant," she said.

"He never touches the stuff," I said.

We went out into the library and turned on the lights and there was Foster on the other side of the door, still banging away with that big fist of his.

There was a large smile on his face and he was wearing his traditional T-shirt. He never wore a shirt or a coat or a sweater. It didn't make any difference what the weather did. Cold, wind or rain, Foster always wore his T-shirt. He was of course sweating like a dam and his buffalo-heavy blond hair hung almost down to his shoulders.

"Hello!" he said. His voice came booming through as if the glass door were made of tissue paper. "What's going on in there?"

I opened the door for him and could see the van parked out in front. The van was big and strange and looked like a prehistoric animal asleep in front of the library.

"Well, here I am," he said and threw an arm around me and gave me a big hug. There was a bottle of whiskey in his other hand and half the whiskey was gone.

"How's it going, kid? Cheer up. Foster's here. Hey, *hello* there!" he said to Vida. "My, aren't you a pretty girl! Damn, am I glad I drove down here! Every mile was worth it. My God, ma'am, you're so pretty I'd walk ten miles barefooted on a freezing morning to stand in your shit."

Vida broke up. There was a big smile on her face. I could tell that she liked him instantly.

My, how her body had relaxed these few months we'd been going together. She was still a little awkward, but now instead of treating it as a handicap, she treated it as a form of poetry and it was fantastically charming.

Vida came over and put her arm around Foster. He gave her a great big hug, too, and offered her a drink from his bottle of whiskey.

"It's good for you," he said.

"All right, I'll give it a try," she said.

He wiped the mouth of the bottle off with his hand in the grand manner and offered her the bottle and she took a delicate nip.

"Hey, kid. You try some of this stuff, too. It'll grow hair on your books."

I took a drink.

Wow!

"Where did you get this whiskey?" I said.

"I bought it from a dead Indian."

The A D Standoff

"LEAD the way," Foster said.

He had his arm around Vida. They were like two peas in a pod. I was very pleased that they were getting along so well together. We went back to my room to relax and make our plans for Tijuana.

"Where have you been all my life?" Foster said.

"Not on the reservation," Vida said.

"Wonderful!" Foster said. "Where did you find this girl?"

"She came along," I said.

"I should be working down here at the library," Foster said. "Not up at the caves. I got up on the wrong side of the map. Hey, hey, you're the prettiest thing I've ever seen in my life. My God, you're even prettier than my mother's picture."

"It's the whiskey," Vida said. "I always look better through amber-colored fluid."

"Damn, it's the whiskey. You're pulling my 86 proof. I think I'll take over this library for a while and you kids can go up and dust off those God-damn books and live at the caves. It's real nice up there. But don't mention to anyone that you know me. Jesus Christ and old Foster wore out their welcome at the same time. I only survive on my good looks these days."

The Plan for Tijuana

WE went back to my room and we all sat down on the bed together and drank a little whiskey and made plans for Tijuana. I usually don't drink but I figured the present condition of our lives merited a little drink.

"Well, it's a little abortion, huh?" Foster said. "You're sure now?"

"Yeah," I said. "We talked it over. That's what we want."

Foster looked over at Vida.

"Yes," she said. "We're too immature right now to have a child. It would only confuse us and this confusion would not be good for a child. It's hard enough being born into this world without having immature and confused parents. Yes, I want the abortion."

"OK, then," Foster said. "There's nothing to be afraid of. I know a good doctor: Dr. Garcia. He won't hurt you and there will be no complications. Everything will be just fine."

"I trust you," she said.

Vida reached over and took my hand.

"The arrangements are very simple," Foster said. "You'll take a plane down there. There's one that leaves at 8:15 tomorrow morning for San Diego. I've got you both round-trip tickets. I called the doctor and he'll be waiting for you. You'll be in TJ before noon and the thing will be over in a short while.

"You can come back in the evening on the plane if you feel up to it, but if you want to stay over in San Diego, I've got a reservation for you at the Green Hotel. I know the guy who runs the place. He's a good guy. You'll feel a little weak after the abortion, so it's up to you if you want to stay. It just depends on how you feel, but don't push it if you feel too woozy, just stay over at the hotel.

"Sometimes Dr. Garcia tries to speculate on the price of the abortion, but I told him you were coming and you only had 200 dollars and there was no more and he said, 'OK, Foster, will do.' He doesn't speak very good English but he's very kind and very good. He's a regular doctor. He did me a good turn with that Indian girl last year. Any questions or anything? Damn! you're a pretty girl."

He gave Vida a nice hug.

"I think you've probably covered it all," I said.

"Vida?" he said.

"No, I can't think of anything."

"What about the library?" I said.

"*Whatabout* the library?" Foster said.

"Who's going to watch it? There has to be somebody here. That's a big part of this library. Somebody has to be here twenty-four hours a day to receive and welcome books. It's the very foundation of this library. We can't close it. It has to remain open."

"You mean me?" Foster said. "Oh, no. I'm strictly a caveman. You'll have to get another boy."

"But there has to be somebody here," I said, looking hard at him.

"Oh, no," Foster said.

"But," I said.

Vida was awfully amused by the whole thing. I was fully aware that Vida did not share the intensity of my feeling toward the library. I could understand that it was a rather strange calling that I had answered, but it was a thing I had to do.

"I'm a caveman," Foster said.

"This is our job," I said. "This is what we were hired to do. We have to take care of this library and the people that need its services."

"I was meaning to bring that up," Foster said. "This is a kind of slow-paying operation. I haven't been paid in two years. I'm supposed to make $295.50 a month."

"Foster!" I said.

"I was just joking," Foster said. "Just a little joke. Here, have some more whiskey."

"Thanks."

"Vida?" Foster said.

"Yes," she said. "Another sip would be just wonderful. It's relaxing."

"It's the old Indian tranquilizer," Foster said.

"You can take care of this place for a day or so while we're down in Mexico getting the abortion," I said. "It won't kill you to actually put in a day's work. It's been years since you've turned a wheel."

"I have my work up at the caves," he said. "It's quite a responsibility lugging books up there and putting them away, guarding them and making sure cave seepage doesn't get to them."

"Cave seepage!" I said, horrified.

"Forget I said that," Foster said. "I don't want to go into it right now, but OK, I'll stay here and take care of the library until you get back. I don't like it but I'll do it."

"Cave seepage?" I repeated.

"What do I have to do around here?" Foster said. "How do I deal with the nuts that bring their books in? What do you do here, anyway? Have some whiskey. Tell me all about it."

Vida was very amused by what was going on. She certainly was pretty. We were all very relaxed lying

92

there on the bed. The whiskey had made us mud-puddly at the edges of our bodies and the edges of our minds.

"This is delightful," Vida said.

Foster's Girl #1

"WHAT's that?" Foster said, almost moving on the bed.

"That's the bell," I said. "Somebody is out there with a new book for the library. I'll show you how we honor a book into the library. 'Welcome it' is the phrase I use."

"Sounds like a funeral parlor," Foster said. "Damn, what time is it?" Foster looked around the room. "I can hear it ticking."

I looked over at the clock. Foster couldn't see it because of the way he was lying on the bed.

"After midnight."

"That's kind of late to bring a book in, isn't it? Midnight? That's twelve."

"We're open twenty-four hours a day, seven days a week. We never close," I said.

"Good God!" Foster said.

"See what I mean?" Vida said.

"Do I," Foster said. "This boy needs a rest."

Then he looked over at Vida. He appraised her in a classic computerized masculine manner without being obvious or sensual and he liked what he saw.

Vida looked at him smiling gently without disturbing her mouth. It remained unchanged by her smile. I believe this thing has been gone into before.

She was not the same girl who had brought her book in a few months before. She had become somebody else with her body.

"Yes," Foster said, finally. "Yes, maybe we had better go out and see who's bringing in a book. We don't want to keep her, I mean, them waiting. It's cold outside."

Foster had never been aware of cold in his entire life, so he was a little drunk and his imagination had just gone into full gallop.

"What do you do out there?" Foster said. "Maybe I'll just go out there and take care of it myself. You kids can sit here and relax. No reason to stop being comfortable when old Foster's around. I'll take care of that book myself. Besides, I have to find out what's going on here if I'm going to run this asylum while you're in TJ."

Vida's smile had opened until now you could see the immaculate boundaries of her teeth. Her eyes had small friendly lightning walking across them.

I was smiling, too.

"What do you do out there? You write down the title of the book and the name of the writer and a little something about the book into that big black ledger, huh?"

"That's right," I said. "And you have to be friendly, too. That's important. To make the person and the book feel wanted because that's the main purpose of the library and to gather pleasantly together the unwanted, the lyrical and haunted volumes of American writing."

"You're kidding," Foster said. "You have to be kidding."

"Come on, Foster," I said. "Or I'll bring up 'cave seepage' again. You know 'cave seepage.' "

"All right. All right. All right, cuckoo," Foster said. "I'll be on my best and besides, who knows: I might want to be on my best. I'm not such a bad guy. Come to think of it, I've got a lot of friends. They may not admit it, but I'm a big place in their hearts."

The bell was still ringing but it was growing weak and needed immediate attention. Foster was by now off the bed. He ran his hand through his buffalo-heavy blond hair as if to comb it before going out to the library.

Blank like Snow

WHILE Foster went into the library to welcome his first book, Vida and I continued lying there on the bed taking little nips from the bottle of whiskey he had graciously left behind. After a while Vida and I were so relaxed that we both could have been rented out as fields of daisies.

Suddenly, we had lost track of time, Foster came slamming into the room. He was very angry in his overweight T-shirt sweating kind of way.

"I think we'd better close this nuthouse while you're south," he said, demanding whiskey with his right hand. "Come to think of it, we should close this God-damn place forever. Everybody go home. Pick up their marbles. That is, if they have any left."

Foster gobbled down a big turkey slug of whiskey. He grimaced and shook when it hit his stomach.

"That's better," he said, wiping his hand across his mouth.

"What happened?" Vida said. "It looks like your library vaccination didn't take."

"You're telling me. More whiskey!" Foster said, addressing the bottle as if it were a healing hand of balm.

"I hope you didn't frighten them," I said. "That's not the purpose of this library. It's a service, not a demand that we perform here."

"Frighten them? Are you kidding, kid? It was the other God-damn way around. Hell, I usually get along with people."

"What happened?" Vida repeated.

"Well, I went out there and it wasn't exactly who I expected would be there. I mean, they were standing outside and—"

"Who was it?" Vida said.

"A woman?" I said, a little mercilessly.

"It's not important," Foster said. "Let me continue, damn it! Yes, there was a woman out there and I use the word woman with serious reservation. She was ringing the bell and she had a book under her arm, so I opened the door. That was a mistake."

"What did she look like?" I said.

"It's not important," Foster said.

"Come on," Vida said. "Tell us."

Ignoring us, Foster continued telling the story in his own manner, "When I opened the door she opened her mouth at the same time. 'Who are you?' she demanded to know in a voice just like a car wreck. What the hell!

" 'I'm Foster,' I said.

" 'You don't look like any Foster I've ever seen,' she said. 'I think you're somebody else because you're no Foster.'

" 'That's my name,' I said. 'I've always been Foster.'

" 'Haa! but enough of you. Where's my mother?' she demanded.

" 'What do you mean, your mother? You're too old to have a mother,' I said. I was tired of humoring the bag.

" 'What do you want done with that book?' I said.

" 'That's none of your God-damn business, you impostor Foster. Where's she at?'

" 'Good night,' I said.

" 'What do you mean, good night? I'm not going anywhere. I'm staying right here until you tell me about my mother.'

" 'I don't know where your mother is and frankly, to quote Clark Gable in *Gone with the Wind*, "I don't give a damn." '

" 'Call my mother Clark Gable!' she said, and then she tried to slap me. Well, that was quite enough out of her, so I grabbed her hand in mid-flight and spun her around and gave her a big shove out the door. She went flying out that door like a garbage can on the wing.

99

" 'Let my mother go free!' she yelled. 'My mother! My mother!'

"I started to close the door. It was getting kind of dreamlike about this time. I didn't know whether to wake up or slug the bitch.

"She made a threatening motion toward the glass, so I went outside and escorted her down the stairs. We had a little struggle along the way, but I laid a little muscle on her arm and she cooled it and at the same time I gentlemanly offered to break her chicken neck if she didn't take out down the street as fast as her clothes-hanger legs would take her.

"The last I saw of her she was yelling, 'It isn't right that I should end up like this, doing these crazy things that I do, feeling the way I do, saying these things,' and she was tearing pages out of the book and throwing them over her head like a bride at a wedding reception."

"Like a bride at a wedding?" Vida said.

"The flowers," Foster said.

"Oh, I didn't understand," she said.

"I don't understand either," Foster said. "I went down and picked up some of the pages to see what kind of book they came from, but the pages didn't have any writing on them. They were blank like snow."

"That's how it goes here sometimes," I said. "We get some disturbed authors, but most of the time it's quiet. All you have to do is be patient with them and write down the author of the book, its title and a little description in the Library Contents Ledger, and let them put the book any place they want in the library."

"That's easy enough with this one," Foster said.

I started to say something—

"The description," Foster said.

I started to say something—

"Blank like snow," Foster said.

The Van

"**I**'LL sleep in my van," Foster said.

"No, there's room in here for you," I said.

"Please stay," Vida said.

"No, no," Foster said. "I'm more comfortable in my van. I always sleep there. I got a little mattress and a sleeping bag and it makes me cozy as a bug in a rug.

"No, it's already settled. It's the van for old Foster. You kids get a good night's sleep because you have to leave early on the plane. I'll take you down to the air-field."

"No, you can't do that," I said. "We'll have to take the bus because you have to stay here and watch the library. Remember? It has to remain open all the time we're gone. You'll have to stay until we get back."

"I don't know about that," Foster said. "After that experience I had a little while ago, I don't know. You couldn't get somebody to come in from one of those temporary employment agencies to handle it, a Kelly Girl or something like that, huh? Hell, I'd pay for it out of my own pocket. They can take care of the library while I go down to North Beach and take in a few topless shows while I'm here."

"No, Foster," I said. "We can't trust this library to just anyone. You'll have to stay here while we're gone. We're not going to be gone long."

"Humor him, Foster," Vida said.

"OK. I wonder what the next nut will be about who brings a book in."

"Don't worry," I said. "That was an exception. Things will run smoothly while we're gone."

"I'll bet."

Foster got ready to go outside. "Here, have another drink of whiskey," Foster said. "I'm going to take the bottle with me."

"When does the plane leave?" Vida said.

"8:15," Foster said. "Our pal here can't drive, so I guess you'll have to take the bus because the Library Kid here wants me to stay and tend his garden of nuts."

"I can drive," Vida said, looking smoothly-beautiful and young.

"Can you drive a van?" Foster said.

"I think so," she said. "I used to drive trucks and pickups one summer when I was on a ranch in Montana. I've always been able to drive anything that's got four wheels, sports cars, anything. I even drove a school bus once, taking some kids on a picnic."

103

"A van's different," Foster said.

"I've driven a horse van," Vida said.

"This isn't a horse van," Foster said, now somewhat outraged. "There's never been a horse in my van!"

"Foster," Vida said. "Don't get mad, dear. I was just telling you that I can drive it. I can drive anything. I've never been in an accident. I'm a good driver. That's all. You have a beautiful van."

"It is a good one," Foster said, now placated. "Well, I guess I don't see any harm in it and it would get you out there a lot faster than the bus and you could get back here faster. It would be a lot smoother ride. Buses are horrible, and you can park it right out there at the airfield. I guess I won't need the van while I'm working at this God-damn madhouse. Sure, you can take it, but drive carefully. There's only one van like that in the whole world and she's mine and I love her."

"Don't worry," Vida said. "I'll love it, too."

"Good deal," Foster said. "Well, I guess I'd better go out and get to bed. Any more whiskey here?"

"No, I think we've had enough," I said.

"OK."

"Do you want us to wake you?" Vida said.

"No, I'll be up," Foster said. "I can get up when I want to, down to the minute. I've got an alarm clock in my head. It always gets me up. Oh, I almost forgot to tell you something. Don't eat anything for breakfast tomorrow. It's against the rules."

Johnny Cash

AFTER Foster left to go out and spend the night in his van, we started getting ready for tomorrow. We wouldn't have much time in the morning when we woke up.

Vida had enough clothes there at the library, so she wouldn't have to go home. Even though she only lived a block from the library, I of course had never been there. Sometimes in the past I had been curious about her place and she told me about it.

"It's very simple," she told me. "I don't have much. All I have is a few books on a shelf, a white rug, a little marble table on the floor, and some records for my stereo: Beatles, Bach, Rolling Stones, Byrds, Vivaldi, Wanda Landowska, Johnny Cash. I'm not a beatnik. It's just that I always considered my body to be more possessions than I ever needed and so everything else had to be simple."

She packed a few clothes for us in an old KLM bag and our toothbrushes and my razor in case we had to stay overnight in San Diego.

"I've never had an abortion before," Vida said. "I hope we don't have to stay overnight in San Diego. I was there once and I didn't like it. There are too many unlaid sailors there and everything is either stone stark or neon cheap. It's not a good town."

"Don't worry about it," I said. "We'll just play it by ear and if everything's all right, we'll come back tomorrow evening."

"That sounds reasonable," Vida said, finishing with our simple packing.

"Well, let's have a kiss, honey, and go to bed. We need some sleep," I said. "We're both tired and we have to get up early in the morning."

"I'll have to take a bath and a douche," Vida said. "And put a little dab of perfume behind my ears."

I took Vida in my arms and gathered the leaves and blossoms of her close, a thing she returned to me, delicate and bouquet-like.

Then we took off our clothes and got into bed. I put out the light and she said, "Did you set the clock, honey?"

"Oh, I forgot," I said. "I'll get up."

"I'm sorry," she said.

"No," I said. "I should have remembered to set the clock. What time do you want to wake up? Six?"

"No, I think you'd better make it 5:30. I want to

take care of my 'female complaints' before Foster wakes up, so I can cook a good breakfast for all of us. It'll be a long day and we'll need a solid start."

"The lady is not for breakfast," I said. "Remember what Foster said?"

"Oh. Oh, that's right. I forgot," Vida said.

It was hard for a minute and then we both smiled across the darkness at what we were doing. Though we could not see our smiles, we knew they were there and it comforted us as dark-night smiles have been doing for thousands of years for the problemed people of the earth.

I got up and turned the light on. Vida was still smiling softly as I set the clock for 5:30. It was absolutely too late for remorse now or to cry against the Fates. We were firmly in the surgical hands of Mexico.

"Genius"

Vida did not look at all pregnant as she got into her bath. Her stomach was still so unbelievably thin that it was genius and I wondered how there could be enough intestines in there to digest any food larger than cookies or berries.

Her breasts were powerful but delicate and wet at the nipples.

She had put a pot of coffee on before she had gotten into the tub and I was standing there watching it perk and watching her bathe at the same time through the open door of the bathroom.

She had her hair piled and pinned on top of her head. It looked beautiful resting on the calm of her neck.

We were both tired, but not as nervous as we could have been facing the prospects of the day, because we had gone into a gentle form of shock that makes it easier to do one little thing after another, fragile step by fragile step, until you've done the big difficult thing waiting at the end, no matter what it is.

I think we have the power to transform our lives into brand-new instantaneous rituals that we calmly act out when something hard comes up that we must do.

We become like theaters.

I was taking turns watching the coffee perk and watching Vida at her bath. It was going to be a long day but fortunately we would get there only moment by moment.

"Is the coffee done yet?" Vida said.

I smelled the coffee fumes that were rising like weather from the spout. They were dark and heavy with coffee. Vida had taught me how to smell coffee. That was the way she made it.

I had always been an instant man, but she had taught me how to make real coffee and it was a good thing to learn. Where had I been all those years, thinking in terms of coffee as dust?

I thought about making coffee for a little while as I watched it perk. It's strange how the simple things in life go on while we become difficult.

"Honey, did you hear me?" Vida said. "The coffee. Stop daydreaming and get on the coffee, dear. Is it done?"

"I was thinking about something else," I said.

Foster's Bell

Vida put on a simple but quite attractive white blouse with a short blue skirt—you could see easily above her knees—and a little half-sweater thing on over the blouse. I've never been able to describe clothes so that anyone knows what I am talking about.

She did not have any make-up on except for her eyes. They looked dark and blue in the way that we like eyes to look in these last years of the seventh decade of the Twentieth Century.

I heard the silver bell ringing on the library door. The bell was ringing rapidly in a kind of shocked manner. The bell seemed almost frightened and crying for help.

It was Foster.

Foster had never really taken to that bell. He had always insisted that it was a sissy bell and always offered to put a bell up himself. He continued the thing as I let him in. I opened the door but he stood there with his hand on the bell rope, though he was not ringing the bell any more.

It was still dark and Foster was wearing his eternal T-shirt and his buffalo-heavy blond hair hung about his shoulders.

"You should take my advice," he said. "Get rid of this damn bell and let me put a real bell up for you."

"We don't want a bell that will frighten people," I said.

"What do you mean frighten people? How in the hell can a bell frighten people?"

"We need a bell that fits the service we offer, that blends in with the library. We need a gentle bell here."

"No roughneck bells, huh?" Foster said.

"I wouldn't put it that way," I said.

"Hell," Foster said. "This bell rings like a Goddamn queer down on Market Street. What are you running here?"

"Don't worry about it," I said.

"Well, I'm just trying to look out for your best interests. That's all, kid." He reached over and gave the bell a little tap on its butt.

"Foster!" I said.

"Hell, kid, a tin can and a spoon make a great bell."

"What about a fork and a knife and a bowl of soup to go with it, Foster? A little mashed potatoes and gravy and maybe a turkey leg? What about that? Wouldn't that make a good bell?"

"Forget it," Foster said. He reached over and gave the bell another little tap on its silver butt and said, "Good-bye, sweetie."

The TJ Briefing

VIDA cooked Foster and me a good breakfast, though she didn't have anything with us except some coffee.

"You certainly look pretty this morning," Foster said. "You look like a dream I've never had before."

"I bet you tell that to all the girls," Vida said. "I can see that you're a flirt from way back."

"I've had a girlfriend or two," Foster said.

"Some more coffee?" Vida said.

"Yeah, another cup of coffee would be fine. Sure is good coffee. Somebody here knows their way around coffee beans."

"What about you, honey?" Vida said.

"Sure."

"There you go."

"Thank you."

Vida sat back down.

"Well, you know what you're supposed to do,"

Foster said after breakfast. "There's nothing to worry about. Dr. Garcia is a wonderful doctor. There will be no pain or fuss. Everything will go just beautifully. You know how to get there. It's just a few blocks off the Main Street of town.

"The doc may want to try and get a few extra bucks out of you, but hold the line and say, 'Well, Doctor Garcia, Foster said that it was 200 dollars and that's all we brought and here it is,' and take it out of your pocket.

"He'll look a little nervous and then he'll take it and put it in his pocket without counting it and then he's just like the best doctor in the whole wide world. Have faith in him and do what he says and relax and everything will be all right.

"He's a wonderful doctor. He saves a lot of people a lot of trouble."

The Library Briefing

". . . ," I said.

"I promise I won't take down that swishy little bell of yours with the silver pants and put up a tin can with a spoon, which would be the best bell for this asylum. Have you ever heard one?" Foster said.

". . . ," I said.

"I'm sorry about that. It's an awfully pretty sound. So beautiful to the spirit and so soothing to the nerves."

". . . ," I said.

"That's a real shame," Foster said.

". . . ," I said.

"I didn't know you felt that way about it," Foster said.

". . . ," I said.

"Don't worry, I won't harm a brick on this library's head. I'll treat your library like a child's birthday cake in a little yellow box that I'm carrying home in my arms from the bakery because carrying it by the string would be too risky.

"I've got to be careful of that dog up ahead. He might bite me and I'd drop the cake. There, I'm past him. Good dog.

"Oh, oh, there's a little lady coming toward me. Got to be careful. She might have a heart attack and collapse in front of me and I might trip over her body. I won't take my eyes off her. There, she's passing me. Everything's going to be all right. Your library is safe," Foster said.

". . . ," Vida said, laughing.

"Thank you, honey," Foster said.

". . . ," I said.

"I love this place," Foster said.

". . . ," I said.

"I'll treat your patrons like saintly eggshells. I won't break one of them," Foster said.

". . . ," Vida said, laughing.

"Oh, honey, you're too nice," Foster said.

". . . ," I said.

"Stop worrying, kid. I know what I'm supposed to do and I'll do it the best I can and that's all I can say," Foster said.

". . . ," Vida said.

"Isn't it the truth and he's not old either. He's just a kid," Foster said.

". . . ," I said.

"I don't think I ever really appreciated the peace and

quiet, the downhomeness of the caves until now. You've opened up a whole new world for me, kid. I should get down on my hands and knees and thank you with all my heart for what you've done."

". . . ," I said.

"Ah, California!" Foster said.

Foster's Heart

FOSTER insisted on carrying our bag out to the van. It was light and halfway through the dawn. Foster was busy sweating away in his T-shirt, even though we found the morning to be a little chilly.

During the years that I had known Foster, I'd never seen him when he wasn't sweating. It was probably brought about by the size of his heart. I was always certain that his heart was as big as a cantaloupe and sometimes I went to sleep thinking about the size of Foster's heart.

Once Foster's heart appeared to me in a dream. It was on the back of a horse and the horse was going into a bank and the bank was being pushed off a cloud. I couldn't see what was pushing the bank off, but it's strange to think *what* would push a bank off a cloud with Foster's heart in it, falling past the sky.

"What do you have in this bag?" Foster said. "It's

so light I don't think there's anything in it."

He was following after Vida who led the way with a delightful awkwardness, looking so perfect and beautiful as not to be with us, as to be alone in some different contemplation of the spirit or an animal stepladder to religion.

"Never you mind our secrets," Vida said, not turning back.

"How would you like to visit my rabbit trap someday?" Foster said.

"And be your Bunny girl?" Vida said.

"I guess you've heard that one," Foster said.

"I've heard them all."

"I'll bet you have," Foster said, falling cleanly past the sky.

Vida Meets the Van

THERE were leftover pieces of blank white paper on the sidewalk from the woman last night. They looked terribly alone. Foster put our little bag in the van.

"There's your bag in the van. Now you're sure you know how to drive this thing?" Foster said. "It's a van."

"Yes, I know how to drive a van. I know how to drive anything that has wheels. I've even flown an airplane," Vida said.

"An airplane?" Foster said.

"I flew one up in Montana a few summers ago. It was fun," Vida said.

"You don't look like the airplane-flying type," Foster said. "Hell, a few summers ago you were in the cradle. Are you sure you weren't flying a stuffed toy?"

"Don't worry about your van," Vida said, returning the conversation from the sky to the ground.

"You've got to drive carefully," Foster said. "This van has its own personality."

"It's in good hands," Vida said. "My God, you're almost as bad with your van as he is with his library."

"Damn! all right," Foster said. "Well, I've told you what to do and now I guess you'd better go and do it. I'll stay here and take care of the asylum while you're gone. I imagine it won't be dull if that lady I met last night is any example of what's going on here."

There were pieces of white paper on the ground.

Foster put his arms around both of us and gave us a very friendly, consoling hug as if to say with his arms that everything was going to be all right and he would see us in the evening.

"Well, kids, good luck."

"Thank you very much," Vida said, turning and giving Foster a kiss on the cheek. They looked hero-ically like father and daughter around each other's arms and cheek to cheek in the classic style that has brought us to these years.

"In you go," Foster said.

We got into the van. It suddenly felt awfully strange for me to be in a vehicle again. The metallic egg-like quality of the van was very surprising and in some ways I had to discover the Twentieth Century all over again.

Foster stood there on the curb carefully watching Vida at the controls of the van.

"Ready?" she said, turning toward me with a little smile on her face.

"Yeah, it's been a long time," I said. "I feel as if I'm in a time machine."

"I know," she said. "Just relax. I know what I'm doing."

"All right," I said. "Let's go."

Vida started the van as if she had been born to the instrument panel, to the wheel and to the pedals.

"Sounds good," Vida said.

Foster was pleased with her performance, nodding at her as if she were an equal. Then he gave her the go signal and she took it and we were off to visit Dr. Garcia who was waiting for us that very day in Tijuana, Mexico.

BOOK 4: Tijuana

The Freewayers

I HAD forgotten how the streets in San Francisco go to get to the freeway. Actually, I had forgotten how San Francisco went.

It was really a surprise to be outside again, travelling in a vehicle again. It had been almost three years. My God, I was twenty-eight when I went into the library and now I was thirty-one years old.

"What street is this?" I said.

"Divisadero," Vida said.

"Oh, yeah," I said. "It's Divisadero all right."

Vida looked over at me very sympathetically. We were stopped at a red light, next to a place that sold flying chickens and spaghetti. I had forgotten that there were places like that.

Vida took one hand off the wheel and gave me a little pat on the knee. "My poor dear hermit," she said.

We drove down Divisadero and saw a man washing

the windows of a funeral parlor with a garden hose. He was spraying the hose against the second-floor windows. It was not a normal thing to see, so early in the morning.

Then Vida made a turn off Divisadero and went around the block. "Oak Street," she said. "You remember Oak Street? It'll take us to the freeway and down to the airport. You remember the airport, don't you?"

"Yes," I said. "But I've never been on an airplane. I've gone out there with friends who were going on airplanes, but that was years ago. Have the airplanes changed any?"

"Oh, honey," she said. "When we're through with all this, I've got to get you out of that library. I think you've been there long enough. They'll have to get somebody else."

"I don't know," I said, trying to drop the subject. I saw a Negro woman pushing an empty Safeway grocery cart on Oak Street. The traffic was very good all around us. It frightened me and excited me at the same time. We were headed for the freeway.

"By the way," Vida said. "Who do you work for?"

"What do you mean?" I said.

"I mean, who pays the bills for your library?" she said. "The money that it takes to run the place? The tab."

"We don't know," I said, pretending that was the answer to the question.

"What do you mean, you don't know?" Vida said. It hadn't worked.

"They send Foster a check from time to time. He never knows when it's coming or how much it will be. Sometimes they don't send us enough."

"They?" she said, keeping right on it.

We stopped for a red light. I tried to find something to look at. I didn't like talking about the financial structure of the library. I didn't like to think in terms of the library and money together. All I saw was a Negro man delivering papers from still another cart.

"Who are you talking about?" Vida said. "Who picks up the tab?"

"It's a foundation. We don't know who's behind it."

"What's the name of the foundation?" Vida said.

I guess that wasn't enough.

"The American Forever, Etc."

"The American Forever, Etc.," Vida said. "Wow! That sounds like a tax dodge. I think your library is a tax write-off."

Vida was now smiling.

"I don't know," I said. "All I know is that I have to be there. It's my job. I have to be there."

"Honey, I think you've got to get some new work. There must be something else that you can do."

"There are a lot of things I can do," I said, a little defensively.

Just then we slammed onto the freeway and my

stomach flew into birds with snakes curling at their wings and we joined the mainstream of American motor thought.

It was frightening after so many years. I felt like a dinosaur plucked from my grave and thrust into competition with the freeway and its metallic fruit.

"If you don't want to work, honey," Vida said. "I think I can take care of us until you feel like it, but you've got to get out of that library as soon as possible. It's not the right place for you any more."

I looked out the window and saw a sign with a chicken holding a gigantic egg.

"I've got other things on my mind right now," I said, trying to get away. "Let's talk about it in a few days."

"You're not worried about the abortion are you, honey?" Vida said. "Please don't be. I have perfect faith in Foster and his doctor. Besides, my sister had an abortion last year in Sacramento and she went to work the next day. She felt a little tired but that was all, so don't worry. An abortion is a rather simple thing."

I turned and looked at Vida. She was staring straight ahead after saying that, watching the traffic in front of us as we roared out of San Francisco down the freeway past Potrero Hill and toward the airplane that waited to fly us at 8:15 down California to land in San Diego at 9:45.

"Maybe when we get back we can go live at the

caves for a while," Vida said. "It'll be spring soon. They should be pretty."

"Seepage," I said.

"What?" Vida said. "I didn't hear you. I was watching that Chevrolet up there to see what it was going to do. What did you say now, honey?"

"Nothing," I said.

"Anyway," she said. "We've got to get you out of that library. Maybe the best thing would be just to give the whole thing up, forget the caves and start someplace new together. Maybe we can go to New York or we'll move to Mill Valley or get an apartment on Bernal Heights or I'll go back to UC and get my degree and we'll get a little place in Berkeley. It's nice over there. You'd be a hero."

Vida seemed to be more interested in getting me out of the library than worrying about the abortion.

"The library is my life," I said. "I don't know what I'd do without it."

"We're going to fix you up with a new life," Vida said.

I looked down the freeway to where the San Francisco International Airport waited, looking almost medieval in the early morning like a castle of speed on the entrails of space.

The San Francisco
International Airport

Vida parked the van near the Benny Bufano statue of Peace that waited for us towering above the cars like a giant bullet. The statue looked at rest in that sea of metal. It is a steel thing with gentle mosaic and marble people on it. They were trying to tell us something. Unfortunately, we didn't have time to listen.

"Well, here we are," Vida said.

"Yeah."

I got our bag and we left the van there quite early in the morning, planning, if everything went well, to pick it up that evening. The van looked kind of lonesome like a buffalo next to the other cars.

We walked over to the terminal. It was filled with hundreds of people coming and going on airplanes. The air was hung with nets of travelling excitement and people were entangled within them and we became a part of the catch.

The San Francisco International Airport Terminal is gigantic, escalator-like, marble-like, cybernetic-like and wants to perform a thing for us that we don't know if we're quite ready for yet. It is also very *Playboy*.

We went over—over being very large—and got our tickets from the Pacific Southwest Airlines booth. There was a young man and woman there. They were beautiful and efficient. The girl looked as if she would look good without any clothes on. She did not like Vida. They both had pins with half-wings on their chests like amputated hawks. I put our tickets in my pocket.

Then I had to go to the toilet.

"Wait here for me, honey," I said.

The toilet was so elegant that I felt as if I should have been wearing a tuxedo to take a leak.

Three men made passes at Vida while I was gone. One of them wanted to marry her.

We had forty-five minutes or so before our airplane left for San Diego, so we went and got a cup of coffee. It was so strange to be among people again. I had forgotten how complex they were in large units.

Everybody was of course looking at Vida. I had never seen a girl attract so much attention before. It was just as she said it would be: plus so.

A young handsome man in a yellow coat like a God-damn maître d' showed us to a table that was next to a plant with large green leaves. He was extremely interested in Vida, though he tried not to be obvious about it.

131

The basic theme of the restaurant was red and yellow with a surprising number of young people and the loud clatter of dishes. I had forgotten that dishes could be that noisy.

I looked at the menu, even though I wasn't hungry. It had been years since I had looked at a menu. The menu said good morning to me and I said good morning back to the menu. We could actually end our lives talking to menus.

Every man in the restaurant had been instantly alerted to Vida's beauty and the women, too, in a jealous sort of way. There was a green aura about the women.

A waitress wearing a yellow dress with a cute white apron took our order for a couple cups of coffee and then went off to get them. She was pretty but Vida made her pale.

We looked out the window to see airplanes coming and going, joining San Francisco to the world and then taking it away again at 600 miles an hour.

There were Negro men in white uniforms doing the cooking while wearing tall white hats, but there were no Negroes in the restaurant eating. I guess Negroes don't take airplanes early in the morning.

The waitress came back with our coffee. She put the coffee on the table and left. She had lovely blond hair but it was to no avail. She took the menu with her: good-bye, good morning.

Vida knew what I was thinking because she said,

"You're seeing it for the first time. It really used to bother me until I met you. Well, you know all about that."

"Have you ever thought about going into the movies or working here at the airport?" I said.

That made Vida laugh which caused a boy about twenty-one years old to spill his coffee all over himself and the pretty waitress to rush a towel over to him. He was cooking in his own coffee.

It was time now to catch our airplane, so we left the restaurant. I paid a very pretty cashier at the front of the cafe. She smiled at me as she took the money. Then she looked at Vida and she stopped smiling.

There was much beauty among the women working in the terminal, but Vida was chopping it down almost as if it weren't even there. Her beauty, like a creature unto itself, was quite ruthless in its own way.

We walked to catch our plane causing people in pairs to jab each other with their elbows to bring the other's attention to Vida. Vida's beauty had probably caused a million black and blue marks: Ah, de Sade, thy honeycomb of such delights.

Two four-year-old boys walking with their mother suddenly became paralyzed from the neck up as they passed us. They did not take their eyes off Vida. They couldn't.

We walked down to the PSA pre-flight lounge stimulating pandemonium among the males our path chanced to cross. I had my arm around Vida, but it

133

wasn't necessary. She had almost totally overcome the dread of her own body.

I had never seen anything like it. A middle-aged man, perhaps a salesman, was smoking a cigarette as we came upon him. He took one look at Vida and missed his mouth with the cigarette.

He stood there staring on like a fool, not taking his eyes off Vida, even though her beauty had caused him to lose control of the world.

PSA

THE jet was squat and leering and shark-like with its tail. It was the first time I had ever been on an airplane. It was a strange experience climbing into that thing.

Vida caused her usual panic among the male passengers as we got into our seats. We immediately fastened our seat belts. Everybody who got on the airplane joined the same brotherhood of nervousness.

I looked out the window and we were sitting over the wing. Then I was surprised to find a rug on the floor of the airplane.

The walls of the airplane had little California scenes on them: cable cars, Hollywood, Coit Tower, the Mount Palomar telescope, a California mission, the Golden Gate Bridge, a zoo, a sailboat, etc. and a building that I couldn't recognize. I looked very hard at the building. Perhaps it was built while I was in the library.

The men continued to stare at Vida, though the air-

135

plane was filled with attractive stewardesses. Vida made the stewardesses invisible, which was probably a rare thing for them.

"I really can't believe it," I said.

"They can have it all if they want it. I'm not trying to do anything," Vida said.

"You're really a prize," I said.

"Only because I'm with you," she said.

Before taking off a man talked to us over the plane's PA system. He welcomed us aboard and told us too much about the weather, the temperature, clouds, the sun and the wind and what weather waited for us down California. We didn't want to hear that much about the weather. I hoped he was the pilot.

It was gray and cold outside without any hope for the sun. We were now taking off. We started moving down the runway, slow at first, then faster, faster, faster: my God!

I looked at the wing below me. The rivets in the wing looked awfully gentle as if they were not able to hold anything up. The wing trembled from time to time ever so gently, but just enough to put the subtle point across.

"How does it feel?" Vida said. "You look a little green around the edges."

"It's different," I said.

A medieval flap was hanging down from the wing as we took off. It was the metal intestine of some kind of bird, retractable and visionary.

136

We flew above the fog clouds and right into the sun. It was fantastic. The clouds were white and beautiful and grew like flowers to the hills and mountains below, hiding with blossoms the valleys from our sight.

I looked down on my wing and saw what looked like a coffee stain as if somebody had put a cup of coffee down on the wing. You could see the ring stain of the cup and then a big splashy sound stain to show that the cup had fallen over.

I was holding Vida's hand.

From time to time we hit invisible things in the air that made the plane buck like a phantom horse.

I looked down at the coffee stain again and I liked it with the world far below. We were going to land at Burbank in Los Angeles in less than an hour to let off and pick up more passengers, then on to San Diego.

We were travelling so fast that it only took a few moments before we were gone.

The Coffee Stain

I was beginning to love the coffee stain on my wing. Somehow it was perfect for the day: like a talisman. I started to think about Tijuana, but then I changed my mind and went back to the coffee stain.

Things were going on in the airplane with the stewardesses. They were taking tickets and offering coffee inside the plane, and making themselves generally liked.

The stewardesses were like beautiful *Playboy* nuns coming and going through the corridors of the airplane as if the airplane were a nunnery. They wore short skirts to show off lovely knees, beautiful legs, but their knees and legs became invisible in front of Vida, who sat quietly in her seat next to me, holding my hand, thinking about her body's Tijuana destination.

There was a perfect green pocket in the mountains.

It was perhaps a ranch or a field or a pasture. I could have loved that pocket of green forever.

The speed of the airplane made me feel affectionate.

After a while the clouds reluctantly gave up the valleys, but it was a very desolate land we were travelling over, not even the clouds wanted it. There was nothing human kind below, except a few roads that ran like long dry angleworms in the mountains.

Vida remained quiet, beautiful.

The sun kept swinging back and forth on my wing. I looked down beyond my coffee stain to see that we were flying now above a half-desolate valley that showed the agricultural designs of man in yellow and in green. But the mountains had no trees in them and were barren and sloped like ancient surgical instruments.

I looked at the medieval intestinal flap of the wing, rising to digest hundreds of miles an hour, beside my coffee stain talisman.

Vida was perfect, though her eyes were dreaming south.

The people on the other side of the airplane were looking down below at something. I wondered what it was and looked down my side to see a small town and land that looked gentler and there were more towns. The towns began magnifying one another. The gentleness of the land became more and more towns and grew sprawling into Los Angeles and I was looking for a freeway.

The man I hoped was the pilot or involved in some official capacity with the airplane told us that we were going to land in two minutes. We suddenly flew into a cloudy haze that became the Burbank airport. The sun was not shining and everything was murky. It was a yellow murk whereas back in San Francisco it was a gray murk.

The airplane grew empty and then became full again. Vida got a lot of visual action while this was going on. One of the stewardesses lingered for a minute a few seats away and stared at Vida as if to make sure she were really there.

"How do you feel?" I said

"Fine," Vida said.

A small airliner about the size of a P-38 with rusty-looking propellers taxied by to take off. Its windows were filled with terrified passengers.

Some businessmen were now sitting in front of us. They were talking about a girl. They all wanted to go to bed with her. She was a secretary in a branch office in Phoenix. They were talking about her, using business language. "I'd like to get her account! Ha-ha! Ha-ha! Ha-ha! Ha-ha-ha-ha!"

The "pilot" welcomed the new people aboard and told us too much about the weather again. Nobody wanted to hear what he had to say.

"We'll be landing in San Diego in twenty-one minutes," he said, finishing his weather report.

As we took off from Burbank, a train was running

parallel with us across from the airport. We left it behind as if it weren't there and the same with Los Angeles.

We climbed through the heavy yellow haze and then suddenly the sun was shining calmly away on the wing and my coffee stain looked happy like a surfer, but it was only a passing thing.

Bing-Bonging to San Diego

BING-BONG!

The trip to San Diego was done mostly in the clouds. From time to time a bell tone was heard in the airplane. I didn't know what it was about.

Bing-bong!

The stewardesses wanted more tickets and people to like them. The smiles never left their faces. They were smiling even when they weren't smiling.

Bing-bong!

I thought about Foster and the library, then I very rapidly changed the subject in my mind. I didn't want to think about Foster and the library: *grimace*.

Bing-bong!

Then we flew into heavy fog and the plane made funny noises. The noises were fairly solid. I almost thought that we had landed in San Diego and were moving along the runway when a stewardess told us that we *were* going to land shortly, so we were still in the air.

Hmmmmmmmm . . .

Bing-bong!

Hot Water

FROM San Francisco our speed had been amazing. We had gathered hundreds of miles effortlessly, as if guided by lyrical poetry. Suddenly we broke out into the clear to find that we had been over the ocean. I saw white waves below breaking against the shore and there was San Diego. I saw a thing that looked like a melting park and my ears were popping and we were going down.

The airplane stopped and there were many warships anchored across from the airport and they were in a low gray mist that was the color of their bodies.

"You can stop being green now," Vida said.

"Thank you," I said. "I'm new at the tree game. Perhaps it's not my calling."

We got off the airplane with Vida causing her customary confusion among the male passengers and resentment among the female passengers.

Two sailors looked as if their eyes had been jammed with pinball machines and we went on into the terminal. It was small and old-fashioned.

And I had to go to the toilet.

The difference between the San Francisco International Airport and the San Diego International Airport is the men's toilet.

In the San Francisco International Airport the hot water stays on by itself when you wash your hands, but in the San Diego International Airport, it doesn't. You have to hold the spigot all the time you want hot water.

While I was making hot water observations, Vida had five passes made at her. She brushed them off like flies.

I felt like having a drink, a very unusual thing for me, but the bar was small, dark and filled with sailors. I didn't like the looks of the bartender. It didn't look like a good bar.

There was more confusion and distraction among the men in the terminal. One man actually fell down. I don't know how he did it, but he did it. He was lying there on the floor staring up at Vida just as I decided not to have a drink in the bar but a cup of coffee in the cafe instead.

"I think you've affected his inner ear," I said.

"Poor man," Vida said.

Flying Backwards

THE basic theme of the San Diego airport cafe was small and casual with a great many young people and boxes full of wax flowers.

The cafe was also filled with a lot of airplane folks: stewardesses and pilots and people talking about airplanes and flight.

Vida had her effect on them while I ordered two cups of coffee from a waitress in a white uniform. She was not young or pretty and she was not quite awake either.

The cafe windows were covered with heavy green curtains that held the light out and you couldn't see anything outside, not even a wing.

"Well, here we are," I said.

"That's for certain," Vida said.

"How do you feel?" I said.

"I wish it were over," Vida said.

"Yeah."

There were two men sitting next to us talking about airplanes and the wind and the number eighty kept coming up again and again. They were talking about miles per hour.

"Eighty," one of them said.

I lost track of what they were saying because I was thinking about the abortion in Tijuana and then I heard one of them say, "At eighty you'd actually be flying the plane backwards."

Downtown

IT was an overcast nothing day in San Diego. We took a Yellow Cab downtown. The driver was drinking coffee. We got in and he took a long good look at Vida while he finished with his coffee.

"Where to?" he said, more to Vida than to me.

"The Green Hotel," I said. "It's—"

"I know where it's at," he said to Vida.

He drove us onto a freeway.

"Do you think the sun will come out?" I said, not knowing what else to say. Of course I didn't have to say anything, but he was really staring at Vida in his rear-view mirror.

"It will pop out around twelve or so, but I like it this way," he said to Vida.

So I took a good look at his face in the mirror. He looked as if he had been beaten to death with a wine bottle, but by doing it with the contents of the bottle.

"Here we are," he said to Vida, finally pulling up in front of the Green Hotel.

The fare was one dollar and ten cents, so I gave him a twenty-cent tip. This made him very unhappy. He was staring at the money in his hand as we walked away from the cab and into the Green Hotel.

He didn't even say good-bye to Vida.

The Green Hotel

THE Green Hotel was a four-story red brick hotel across the street from a parking lot and next to a bookstore. I couldn't help but look at the books in the window. They were different from the books that we had in the library.

The desk clerk looked up as we came into the hotel. The hotel had a big green plant in the window with enormous leaves.

"Hello, there!" he said. He was very friendly with a lot of false teeth in his mouth.

"Hello," I said.

Vida smiled.

That really pleased him because he became twice as friendly, which was hard to do.

"Foster sent us," I said.

"Oh, Foster!" he said. "Yes. Yes. Foster. He called and said you were coming and here you are! Mr. and

Mrs. Smith. Foster. Wonderful person! Foster, yes."

He was really smiling up a storm now. Maybe he was the father of an airline stewardess.

"I have a lovely room with a bath and view," he said. "It's just like home. You'll adore it," he said to Vida. "It's not like a hotel room."

For some reason he did not like the idea of Vida staying in a hotel room, though he ran a hotel, and that was only the beginning.

"Yeah, it's a beautiful room," he said. "Very lovely. It'll help you enjoy your stay in San Diego. How long will you be here? Foster didn't say much over the telephone. He just said you were coming and here you are!"

"Just a day or so," I said.

"Business or pleasure?" he said.

"We're visiting her sister," I said.

"Oh, that sounds nice. She has a small place, huh?"

"I snore," I said.

"Oh," the desk clerk said.

I signed Mr. and Mrs. Smith of San Francisco on the hotel register. Vida watched me as I signed our new instant married name. She was smiling. My! how beautiful she looked.

"I'll show you to your room," the desk clerk said. "It's a beautiful room. You'll be happy in it. The walls are thick, too. You'll be at home."

"Good to hear," I said. "My affliction has caused me a lot of embarrassment in the past."

"Really a loud snorer?" he said.

"Yes," I said. "Like a sawmill."

"If you'll please wait a minute," he said. "I'll ring my brother and have him come down and watch the desk while I'm taking you upstairs to the room."

He pushed a silent buzzer that summoned his brother down the elevator a few moments later.

"Some nice people here. Mr. and Mrs. Smith. Friends of Foster," the desk clerk said. "I'm going to give them Mother's room."

The brother clerk gave Vida a solid once-over as he went behind the desk to take over the wheel from his brother who stepped out and he stepped in.

They were both middle-aged.

"That's good," the brother desk clerk said, satisfied. "They'll love Mother's room."

"Your mother lives here?" I said, now a little confused.

"No, she's dead," the desk clerk said. "But it was her room before she died. This hotel has been in the family for over fifty years. Mother's room is just the way it was when she died. God bless her. We haven't touched a thing. We only rent it out to nice people like yourselves."

We got into an ancient dinosaur elevator that took us up to the fourth floor and Mother's room. It was a nice room in a dead mother kind of way.

"Beautiful, isn't it?" the desk clerk said.

"Very comfortable," I said.

"Lovely," Vida said.

"You'll enjoy San Diego even more with this room," he said.

He pulled up the window shade to show us an excellent view of the parking lot, which was fairly exciting if you'd never seen a parking lot before.

"I'm sure we will," I said.

"If there's anything you want, just let me know and we'll take care of it: a call in the morning, anything, just let us know. We're here to make your stay in San Diego enjoyable, even if you can't stay at your sister's because you snore."

"Thank you," I said.

He left and we were alone in the room.

"What's the snoring thing you told him about?" Vida said, sitting down on the bed.

She was smiling.

"I don't know," I said. "It just seemed like the proper thing to do."

"You are a caution," Vida said. Then she freshened herself up a little, washed the air travel off and we were ready to go visit Dr. Garcia in Tijuana.

"Well, I guess we'd better go," I said.

"I'm ready," Vida said.

The ghost of the dead mother watched us as we left. She was sitting on the bed knitting a ghost thing.

The Bus to Tijuana

I DON'T like San Diego. We walked the few blocks to the Greyhound bus depot. There were baskets of flowers hanging from the light posts.

There was almost a small town flavor to San Diego that morning except for the up-all-night tired sailors or just-starting-out sailors walking along the streets.

The Greyhound bus depot was jammed with people and games of amusement and vending machines and there were more Mexicans in the bus depot than on the streets of San Diego. It was almost as if the bus depot were the Mexican part of town.

Vida's body, perfect face and long lightning hair performed their customary deeds among the men in the bus depot, causing a thing that was just short of panic.

"Well," I said.

Vida replied with a silence.

The bus to Tijuana left every fifteen minutes and cost sixty cents. There were a lot of Mexican men in the line wearing straw and cowboy hats in sprawled laziness to Tijuana.

A jukebox was playing square pop tunes from the time that I had gone into the library. It was strange to hear those old songs again.

There was a young couple waiting for the bus in front of us. They were very conservative in dress and manner and seemed to be awfully nervous and bothered and trying hard to hold on to their composure.

There was a man standing in the line, holding a racing form under his arm. He was old with dandruff on the lapels and shoulders of his coat and on his racing form.

I had never been to Tijuana before but I had been to a couple of other border towns: Nogales and Juarez. I didn't look forward to Tijuana.

Border towns are not very pleasant places. They bring out the worst in both countries, and everything that is American stands out like a neon sore in border towns.

I noticed the middle-aged people, growing old, that you always see in crowded bus depots but never in empty ones. They exist only in numbers and seem to live in crowded bus depots. They all looked as if they were enjoying the old records on the jukebox.

One Mexican man was carrying a whole mess of stuff in a Hunt's tomato sauce box and in a plastic bread wrapper. They seemed to be his possessions and he was going home with them to Tijuana.

Slides

As we drove the short distance to Tijuana it was not a very pleasant trip. I looked out the window to see that there was no wing on the bus, no coffee stain out there. I missed it.

San Diego grew very poor and then we were on a freeway. The country down that way is pretty nothing and not worth describing.

Vida and I were holding hands. Our hands were together in our hands as our real fate moved closer to us. Vida's stomach was flat and perfect and it was going to remain that way.

Vida looked out the window at what is not worth describing, but even more so and done in cold cement freeway language. She didn't say anything.

The young conservative couple sat like frozen beans in their seats in front of us. They were really having a bad time of it. I pretty much guessed why they were going to Tijuana.

The man whispered something to the woman. She nodded without saying anything. I thought she was going to start crying. She bit her lower lip.

I looked down from the bus into cars and saw things in the back seats. I tried hard not to look at the people but instead to look at the things in the back seats. I saw a paper bag, three coat hangers, some flowers, a sweater, a coat, an orange, a paper bag, a box, a dog.

"We're on a conveyer belt," Vida said.

"It's easier this way," I said. "It will be all right. Don't worry."

"I know it will be all right," she said. "But I wish we were there. Those people in front of us are worse than the idea of the abortion."

The man started to whisper something to the woman, who continued staring straight ahead, and Vida turned and looked out the window at the nothing leading to Tijuana.

The Man from Guadalajara

THE border was a mass of cars coming and going in excitement and confusion to pass under an heroic arch into Mexico. There was a sign that said something like: WELCOME TO TIJUANA THE MOST VISITED CITY IN THE WORLD.

I had a little trouble with that one.

We just walked across the border into Mexico. The Americans didn't even say good-bye and we were suddenly in a different way of doing things.

First there were Mexican guards wearing those .45 caliber automatic pistols that Mexicans love, checking the cars going into Mexico.

Then there were other men who looked like detectives standing along the pedestrian path to Mexico. They didn't say a word to us, but they stopped two people behind us, a young man and woman, and asked them what nationality they were and they said Italian.

"We're Italians."

I guess Vida and I looked like Americans.

The arch, besides being heroic, was beautiful and modern and had a nice garden with many fine river rocks in the garden, but we were more interested in getting a taxi and went to a place where there were many taxis.

I noticed that famous sweet acrid dust that covers Northern Mexico. It was like meeting a strange old friend again.

"TAXI!"

"TAXI!"

"TAXI!"

The drivers were yelling and motioning a new supply of gringos toward them.

"TAXI!"

"TAXI!"

"TAXI!"

The taxis were typically Mexican and the drivers were shoving them like pieces of meat. I don't like people to try and use the hard sell on me. I'm not made for it.

The conservative young couple came along, looking very frightened, and got into a taxi and disappeared toward Tijuana that lay flat before us and then sloped up into some hazy yellow poor-looking hills with a great many houses on them.

The air was beginning electric with the hustle for the Yankee dollar and its biblical message. The taxi drivers seemed to be endless like flies trying to get you into their meat for Tijuana and its joys.

"Hey, beau-ti-ful girl and BE-atle! Get in!" a driver yelled at us.

"Beatle?" I said to Vida. "Is my hair that long?"

"It is a little long," Vida said, smiling.

"Hey, BE-atle and hey, beauty!" another driver yelled.

There was a constant buzzing of TAXI! TAXI! TAXI! Suddenly everything had become speeded up for us in Mexico. We were now in a different country, a country that just wanted to see our money.

"TAXI!"

"TAXI!"

(Wolf whistle.)

"BE-atle!"

"TAXI!"

"HEY! THERE!"

"TAXI!"

"TIJUANA!"

"SHE'S GOOD-LOOKING!"

"TAXI!"

(Wolf whistle.)

"TAXI!"

"TAXI!"

"SENORITA! SENORITA! SENORITA!"

"HEY, BEATLE! TAXI!"

And then a Mexican man walked quietly up to us. He seemed a little embarrassed. He was wearing a business suit and was about forty years old.

"I have a car," he said. "Would you like a ride downtown? It's right over there."

It was a ten-year-old Buick, dusty, but well kept up and seemed to want us to get into it.

"Thank you," I said. "That would be very nice."

The man looked all right, just wanting to be helpful, so it seemed. He didn't look as if he were selling anything.

"It's right over here," he repeated, to show that the car was something that he took pride in owning.

"Thank you," I said.

We walked over to his car. He opened the door for us and then went around and got in himself.

"It's noisy here," he said, as we started driving the mile or less to Tijuana. "Too much noise."

"It is a little noisy," I said.

After we left the border he kind of relaxed and turned toward us and said, "Did you come across for the afternoon?"

"Yes, we thought we'd take a look at Tijuana while we're visiting her sister in San Diego," I said.

"It's something to look at all right," he said. He didn't look too happy when he said that.

"Do you live here?" I said.

"I was born in Guadalajara," he said. "That's a beautiful city. That's my home. Have you ever been there? It's beautiful."

162

"Yes," I said. "I was there five or six years ago. It is a lovely city."

I looked out the window to see a small carnival lying abandoned by the road. The carnival was flat and stagnant like a mud puddle.

"Have you ever been to Mexico before, Señora?" he said, fatherly.

"No," Vida said. "This is my first visit."

"Don't judge Mexico by this," he said. "Mexico is different from Tijuana. I've been working here for a year and in a few months I'll go back home to Guadalajara, and I'm going to stay there this time. I was a fool to leave."

"What do you do?" I said.

"I work for the government," he said. "I'm taking a survey among the Mexican people who come and go across the border into your country."

"Are you finding out anything interesting?" Vida said.

"No," he said. "It's all the same. Nothing is different."

A Telephone Call
from Woolworth's

THE government man, whose name we never got, left us on the Main Street of Tijuana and pointed out the Government Tourist Building as a place that could tell us things to do while we were in Tijuana.

The Government Tourist Building was small and glass and very modern and had a statue in front of it. The statue was a gray stone statue and did not look at peace. It was taller than the building. The statue was a pre-Columbian god or fella doing something that did not make him happy.

Though the building was quite attractive, there was nothing the people in that little building could do for us. We needed another service from the Mexican people.

Everybody was shoving us for dollars, trying to sell us things that we didn't want: kids with gum, people wanting us to buy border junk from them, more taxi-

cab drivers shouting that they wanted to take us back
to the border, even though we had just gotten there, or
to other places where we would have some fun.

"TAXI!"

"BEAUTIFUL GIRL!"

"TAXI!"

"BEATLE!"

(Wolf whistle.)

The taxicab drivers of Tijuana remained constant in
their devotion to us. I had no idea my hair was so long
and of course Vida had her thing going.

We went over to the big modern Woolworth's on
the Main Street of Tijuana to find a telephone. It was
a pastel building with a big red Woolworth's sign and
a red brick front and big display windows all filled up
with Easter stuff: lots and lots and lots of bunnies and
yellow chicks bursting happily out of huge eggs.

The Woolworth's was so antiseptic and clean and
orderly compared to the outside which was just a few
feet away or not away at all if you looked past the
bunnies in the front window.

There were very attractive girls working as sales girls,
dark and young and doing lots of nice things with their
eyes. They all looked as if they should work in a bank
instead of Woolworth's.

I asked one of the girls where the telephone was and
she pointed out the direction to me.

"It's over there," she said in good-looking English.

I went over to the telephone with Vida spreading

erotic confusion like missile jam among the men in the store. The Mexican women, though very pretty, were no match for Vida. She shot them down without even thinking about it.

The telephone was beside an information booth, next to the toilet, near a display of leather belts and a display of yarn and the women's blouse section.

What a bunch of junk to remember, but that's what I remember and look forward to the time I forget it.

The telephone operated on American money: a nickel like it used to be in the good old days of my childhood.

A man answered the telephone.

He sounded like a doctor.

"Hello, Dr. Garcia?" I said.

"Yes."

"A man named Foster called you yesterday about our problem. Well, we're here," I said.

"Good. Where are you?"

"We're at Woolworth's," I said.

"Please excuse my English. Isn't so good. I'll get the girl. Her English is . . . better. She'll tell you how to get here. I'll be waiting. Everything is all right."

A girl took over the telephone. She sounded very young and said, "You're at Woolworth's."

"Yes," I said.

"You're not very far away," she said.

That seemed awfully strange to me.

"When you leave Woolworth's, turn right and walk down three blocks and then turn left on Fourth Street, walk four blocks and then turn left again off Fourth Street," she said. "We are in a green building in the middle of the block. You can't miss it. Did you get that?"

"Yes," I said. "When we leave Woolworth's, we turn right and walk three blocks down to Fourth Street, then we turn left on Fourth Street, and walk four blocks and then turn left again off Fourth Street, and there's a green building in the middle of the block, and that's where you're at."

Vida was listening.

"Your wife hasn't eaten, has she?"

"No," I said.

"Good, we'll be waiting for you. If you should get lost, telephone again."

We left Woolworth's and followed the girl's directions amid being hustled by souvenir junk salesmen, the taxi drivers and gum kids of Tijuana, surrounded by wolf whistles, cars cars cars, and cries of animal consternation and HEY, BEATLE!

Fourth Street had waited eternally for us to come as we were always destined to come, Vida and me, and now we'd come, having started out that morning in San Francisco and our lives many years before.

The streets were filled with cars and people and a fantastic feeling of excitement. The houses did not have any lawns, only that famous dust. They were our guides to Dr. Garcia.

There was a brand-new American car parked in front

of the green building. The car had California license plates. I didn't have to think about that one too much to come up with an answer. I looked in the back seat. There was a girl's sweater lying there. It looked helpless.

Some children were playing in front of the doctor's office. The children were poor and wore unhappy clothes. They stopped playing and watched us as we went in.

We were no doubt a common sight for them. They had probably seen many gringos in this part of town, going into this green adobe-like building, gringos who did not look very happy. We did not disappoint them.

BOOK 5: My Three Abortions

Furniture Studies

THERE was a small bell to ring on the door. It was not like the silver bell of my library, so far away from this place. You rang this bell by pressing your finger against it. That's what I did.

We had to wait a moment for someone to answer. The children stayed away from their play to watch us. The children were small, ill-dressed and dirty. They had those strange undernourished bodies and faces that make it so hard to tell how old children are in Mexico.

A child that looks five will turn out to be eight. A child that looks seven will actually be ten. It's horrible.

Some Mexican mother women came by. They looked at us, too. Their eyes were expressionless, but showed in this way that they knew we were *abortionistas*.

Then the door to the doctor's office opened effortlessly as if it had always planned to open at that time and it was Dr. Garcia himself who opened the door for us. I didn't know what he looked like, but I knew it was him.

"Please," he said, gesturing us in.

"Thank you," I said. "I just called you on the telephone. I'm Foster's friend."

"I know," he said, quietly. "Follow, please."

The doctor was small, middle-aged and dressed perfectly like a doctor. His office was large and cool and had many rooms that led like a labyrinth far into the back and places that we knew nothing about.

He took us to a small reception room. It was clean with modern linoleum on the floor and modern doctor furniture: an uncomfortable couch and three chairs that you could never really fit into.

The furniture was the same as the furniture you see in the offices of American doctors. There was a tall plant in the corner with large flat cold green leaves. The leaves didn't do anything.

There were some other people already in the room: a father, a mother and a young teen-age daughter. She obviously belonged to the brand-new car parked in front.

"Please," the doctor said, gesturing us toward the two empty chairs in the room. "Soon," he said, smiling gently. "Wait, please. Soon."

He went away across the corridor and into another room that we could not see, leaving us with the three people. They were not talking and it was strangely quiet all through the building.

Everybody looked at everybody else in a nervous kind of way that comes when time and circumstance reduce us to seeking illegal operations in Mexico.

The father looked like a small town banker in the San Joaquin Valley and the mother looked like a woman who participated in a lot of social activities.

The daughter was pretty and obviously intelligent and didn't know what to do with her face as she waited for her abortion, so she kept smiling in a rapid knife-like way at nothing.

The father looked very stern as if he were going to refuse a loan and the mother looked vaguely shocked as if somebody had said something a little risqué at a social tea for the Friends of the DeMolay.

The daughter, though she possessed a narrow budding female body, looked as if she were too young to have an abortion. She should have been doing something else.

I looked over at Vida. She also looked as if she were too young to have an abortion. What were we all doing there? Her face was growing pale.

Alas, the innocence of love was merely an escalating physical condition and not a thing shaped like our kisses.

My First Abortion

ABOUT forever or ten minutes passed and then the doctor came back and motioned toward Vida and me to come with him, though the other people had been waiting when we came in. Perhaps it had something to do with Foster.

"Please," Dr. Garcia said, quietly.

We followed after him across the hall and into a small office. There was a desk in the office and a typewriter. The office was dark and cool, the shades were down, with a leather chair and photographs of the doctor and his family upon the walls and the desk.

There were various certificates showing the medical degrees the doctor had obtained and what schools he had graduated from.

There was a door that opened directly into an operating room. A teen-age girl was in the room cleaning up and a young boy, another teen-ager, was helping her.

A big blue flash of fire jumped across a tray full of surgical instruments. The boy was sterilizing the instruments with fire. It startled Vida and me. There was a table in the operating room that had metal things to hold your legs and there were leather straps that went with them.

"No pain," the doctor said to Vida and then to me. "No pain and clean, all clean, no pain. Don't worry. No pain and clean. Nothing left. I'm a doctor," he said.

I didn't know what to say. I was so nervous that I was almost in shock. All the color had drained from Vida's face and her eyes looked as if they could not see any more.

"250 dollars," the doctor said. "Please."

"Foster said it would be 200 dollars. That's all we have," I heard my own voice saying. "200. That's what you told Foster."

"200. That's all you have?" the doctor said.

Vida stood there listening to us arbitrate the price of her stomach. Vida's face was like a pale summer cloud.

"Yes," I said. "That's all we have."

I took the money out of my pocket and gave it to the doctor. I held the money out and he took it from my hand. He put it in his pocket, without counting it, and then he became a doctor again, and that's the way he stayed all the rest of the time we were there.

He had only stopped being a doctor for a moment. It was a little strange. I don't know what I expected. It was very good that he stayed a doctor for the rest of the time.

Foster was of course right.

He became a doctor by turning to Vida and smiling and saying, "I won't hurt you and it will be clean. Nothing left after and no pain, honey. Believe me. I'm a doctor."

Vida smiled 1/2: ly.

"How long has she been?" the doctor said to me and starting to point at her stomach but not following through with it, so his hand was a gesture that didn't do anything.

"About five or six weeks," I said.

Vida was now smiling 1/4: ly.

The doctor paused and looked at a calendar in his mind and then he nodded affectionately at the calendar. It was probably a very familiar calendar to him. They were old friends.

"No breakfast?" he said, starting to point again at Vida's stomach but again he failed to do so.

"No breakfast," I said.

"Good girl," the doctor said.

Vida was now smiling 1/37: ly.

After the boy finished sterilizing the surgical instruments, he took a small bucket back through another large room that was fastened to the operating room.

The other room looked as if it had beds in it. I moved my head a different way and I could see a bed in it and there was a girl lying on the bed asleep and there was a man sitting in a chair beside the bed. It looked very quiet in the room.

A moment after the boy left the operating room, I heard a toilet flush and water running from a tap and then the sound of water being poured in the toilet and the toilet was flushed again and the boy came back with the bucket.

The bucket was empty.

The boy had a large gold wristwatch on his hand.

"Everything's all right," the doctor said.

The teen-age girl, who was dark and pretty and also had a nice wristwatch, came into the doctor's office and smiled at Vida. It was that kind of smile that said: It's time now; please come with me.

"No pain, no pain, no pain," the doctor repeated like a nervous nursery rime.

No pain, I thought, how strange.

"Do you want to watch?" the doctor asked me, gesturing toward an examination bed in the operating room where I could sit if I wanted to watch the abortion.

I looked over at Vida. She didn't want me to watch and I didn't want to watch either.

"No," I said. "I'll stay in here."

"Please come, honey," the doctor said.

The girl touched Vida's arm and Vida went into

the operating room with her and the doctor closed the door, but it didn't really close. It was still open an inch or so.

"This won't hurt," the girl said to Vida. She was giving Vida a shot.

Then the doctor said something in Spanish to the boy who said OK and did something.

"Take off your clothes," the girl said. "And put this on."

Then the doctor said something in Spanish and the boy answered him in Spanish and the girl said, "Please. Now put your legs up. That's it. Good. Thank you."

"That's right, honey," the doctor said. "That didn't hurt, did it? Everything's going to be all right. You're a good girl."

Then he said something to the boy in Spanish and then the girl said something in Spanish to the doctor who said something in Spanish to both of them.

Everything was very quiet for a moment or so in the operating room. I felt the dark cool of the doctor's office on my body like the hand of some other kind of doctor.

"Honey?" the doctor said. "Honey?"

There was no reply.

Then the doctor said something in Spanish to the boy and the boy answered him in something metallic, surgical. The doctor used the thing that was metallic and surgical and gave it back to the boy who gave him something else that was metallic and surgical.

Everything was either quiet or metallic and surgical in there for a while.

Then the girl said something in Spanish to the boy who replied to her in English. "I know," he said.

The doctor said something in Spanish.

The girl answered him in Spanish.

A few moments passed during which there were no more surgical sounds in the room. There was now the sound of cleaning up and the doctor and the girl and the boy talked in Spanish as they finished up.

Their Spanish was not surgical any more. It was just casual cleaning-up Spanish.

"What time is it?" the girl said. She didn't want to look at her watch.

"Around one," the boy said.

The doctor joined them in English. "How many more?" he said.

"Two," the girl said.

"¿Dos?" the doctor said in Spanish.

"There's one coming," the girl said.

The doctor said something in Spanish.

The girl answered him in Spanish.

"I wish it was three," the boy said in English.

"Stop thinking about girls," the doctor said, jokingly.

Then the doctor and the girl were involved in a brief very rapid conversation in Spanish.

This was followed by a noisy silence and then the

sound of the doctor carrying something heavy and un-conscious out of the operating room. He put the thing down in the other room and came back a moment later.

The girl walked over to the door of the room I was in and finished opening it. My dark cool office was suddenly flooded with operating room light. The boy was cleaning up.

"Hello," the girl said, smiling. "Please come with me."

She casually beckoned me through the operating room as if it were a garden of roses. The doctor was sterilizing his surgical instruments with the blue flame.

He looked up at me from the burning instruments and said, "Everything went OK. I promised no pain, all clean. The usual." He smiled. "Perfect."

The girl took me into the other room where Vida was lying unconscious on the bed. She had warm covers over her. She looked as if she were dreaming in another century.

"It was an excellent operation," the girl said. "There were no complications and it went as smoothly as pos-sible. She'll wake up in a little while. She's beautiful, isn't she?"

"Yes."

The girl got me a chair and put it down beside Vida. I sat down in the chair and looked at Vida. She was so alone there in the bed. I reached over and touched her cheek. It felt as if it had just come unconscious from an operating room.

The room had a small gas heater that was burning quietly away in its own time. The room had two beds in it and the other bed where the girl had lain a short while before was now empty and there was an empty chair beside the bed, as this bed would be empty soon and the chair I was now sitting in: to be empty.

The door to the operating room was open, but I couldn't see the operating table from where I was sitting.

My Second Abortion

THE door to the operating room was open, but I couldn't see the operating table from where I was sitting. A moment later they brought in the teen-age girl from the waiting room.

"Everything's going to be all right, honey," the doctor said. "This won't hurt." He gave her the shot himself.

"Please take off your clothes," the girl said.

There was a stunned silence for a few seconds that bled into the awkward embarrassed sound of the teen-age girl taking her clothes off.

After she took off her clothes, the girl assistant who was no older than the girl herself said, "Put this on."

The girl put it on.

I looked down at the sleeping form of Vida. She was wearing one, too.

Vida's clothes were folded over a chair and her shoes

were on the floor beside the chair. They looked very sad because she had no power over them any more. She lay unconscious before them.

"Now put your legs up, honey," the doctor was saying. "A little higher, please. That's a good girl."

Then he said something in Spanish to the Mexican girl and she answered him in Spanish.

"I've had six months of Spanish I in high school," the teen-age girl said with her legs apart and strapped to the metal stirrups of this horse of no children.

The doctor said something in Spanish to the Mexican girl and she replied in Spanish to him.

"Oh," he said, a little absentmindedly to nobody in particular. I guess he had performed a lot of abortions that day and then he said to the teen-age girl, "That's nice. Learn some more."

The boy said something very rapidly in Spanish.

The Mexican girl said something very rapidly in Spanish.

The doctor said something very rapidly in Spanish and then he said to the teen-age girl, "How do you feel, honey?"

"Nothing," she said, smiling. "I don't feel anything. Should I feel something right now?"

The doctor said something very rapidly to the boy in Spanish. The boy did not reply.

"I want you to relax," the doctor said to the teen-age girl. "Please take it easy."

All three of them had a very rapid go at it in Spanish. There seemed to be some trouble and then the doctor said something very rapidly in Spanish to the Mexican girl. He finished it by saying, "¿Como se dice treinta?"

"Thirty," the Mexican girl said.

"Honey," the doctor said. He was leaning over the teen-age girl. "I want you to count to, to thirty for us, please, honey."

"All right," she said, smiling, but for the first time her voice sounded a little tired.

It was starting to work.

"1, 2, 3, 4, 5, 6 . . ." There was a pause here. "7, 8, 9 . . ." There was another pause here, but it was a little longer than the first pause.

"Count to, to thirty, honey," the doctor said.

"10, 11, 12."

There was a total stop.

"Count to thirty, honey," the boy said. His voice sounded soft and gentle just like the doctor's. Their voices were the sides of the same coin.

"What comes after 12?" the teen-age girl giggled. "I know! 13." She was very happy that 13 came after 12. "14, 15, 15, 15."

"You said 15," the doctor said.

"15," the teen-age girl said.

"What's next, honey?" the boy said.

"15," the teen-age girl said very slowly and triumphantly.

"What's next, honey?" the doctor said.

"15," the girl said. "15."

"Come on, honey," the doctor said.

"What's next?" the boy said.

"What's next?" the doctor said.

The girl didn't say anything.

They didn't say anything either. It was very quiet in the room. I looked down at Vida. She was very quiet, too.

Suddenly the silence in the operating room was broken by the Mexican girl saying, "16."

"What?" the doctor said.

"Nothing," the Mexican girl said, and then the language and silences of the abortion began.

Chalkboard Studies

Vida lay there gentle and still like marble dust on the bed. She had not shown the slightest sign of consciousness, but I wasn't worried because her breathing was normal.

So I just sat there listening to the abortion going on in the other room and looking at Vida and where I was at: this house in Mexico, so far away from my San Francisco library.

The small gas heater was doing its thing because it was cool within the adobe walls of the doctor's office.

Our room was in the center of a labyrinth.

There was a little hall on one side of the room, running back past the open door of the toilet and ending at a kitchen.

The kitchen was about twenty feet away from where Vida lay unconscious with her stomach vacant like a chalkboard. I could see the refrigerator and a sink in the kitchen and a stove with some pans on it.

On the other side of our room was a door that led into a huge room, almost like a small gym, and I could see still another room off the gym.

The door was open and there was the dark abstraction of another bed in the room like a large flat sleeping animal.

I looked down at Vida still submerged in a vacuum of anesthesia and listened to the abortion ending in the operating room.

Suddenly there was a gentle symphonic crash of surgical instruments and then I could hear the sounds of cleaning up joined to another chalkboard.

My Third Abortion

THE doctor came through the room carrying the teenage girl in his arms. Though the doctor was a small man, he was very strong and carried the girl without difficulty.

She looked very silent and unconscious. Her hair hung strangely over his arm in a blond confusion. He took the girl through the small gym and into the adjoining room where he lay her upon the dark animal-like bed.

Then he came over and closed the door to our room and went into the forward reaches of the labyrinth and came back with the girl's parents.

"It went perfect," he said. "No pain, all clean."

They didn't say anything to him and he came back to our room. As he passed through the door, the people were watching him and they saw Vida lying there and me sitting beside her.

I looked at them and they looked at me before the door was closed. Their faces were a stark and frozen landscape.

The boy came into the room carrying the bucket and he went into the toilet and flushed the fetus and the abortion leftovers down the toilet.

Just after the toilet flushed, I heard the flash of the instruments being sterilized by fire.

It was the ancient ritual of fire and water all over again to be all over again and again in Mexico today.

Vida still lay there unconscious. The Mexican girl came in and looked at Vida. "She's sleeping," the girl said. "It went fine."

She went back into the operating room and then the next woman came into the operating room. She was the "one" coming the Mexican girl had mentioned earlier. I didn't know what she looked like because she had come since we'd been there.

"Has she eaten today?" the doctor said.

"No," a man said sternly, as if he were talking about dropping a hydrogen bomb on somebody he didn't like.

The man was her husband. He had come into the operating room. He had decided that he wanted to watch the abortion. They were awfully tense people and the woman said only three words all the time she was there. After she had her shot, he helped her off with her clothes.

He sat down while her legs were strapped apart on

the operating table. She was unconscious just about the time they finished putting her in position for the abortion because they started almost immediately.

This abortion was done automatically like a machine. There was very little conversation between the doctor and his helpers.

I could feel the presence of the man in the operating room. He was like some kind of statue sitting there looking on, waiting for a museum to snatch him and his wife up. I never saw the woman.

After the abortion the doctor was tired and Vida was still lying there unconscious. The doctor came into the room. He looked down at Vida.

"Not yet," he said, answering his own question.

I said no because I didn't have anything else to do with my mouth.

"It's OK," he said. "Sometimes it's like this."

The doctor looked like an awfully tired man. God only knows how many abortions he had performed that day.

He came over and sat down on the bed. He took Vida's hand and he felt her pulse. He reached down and opened one of her eyes. Her eye looked back at him from a thousand miles away.

"It's all right," he said. "She'll be back in a few moments."

He went into the toilet and washed his hands. After he finished washing his hands, the boy came in with the bucket and took care of that.

The girl was cleaning up in the operating room. The doctor had put the woman on the examination bed in the operating room.

He had quite a thing going just taking care of the bodies.

"OHHHHHHHHHH!" I heard a voice come from behind the gym door where the doctor had taken the teen-age girl. "OHHHHHHHHHH!" It was a sentimental drunken voice. It was the girl. "OHH-HHHHHHHH!

"16!" she said. "I-OHHHHHHHHHH!"

Her parents were talking to her in serious, hushed tones. They were awfully respectable.

"OHHHHHHHHHHHHHHHHHHHHHHH!"

They were acting as if she had gotten drunk at a family reunion and they were trying to cover up her drunkenness.

"OHHHHHHHHHH! I feel funny!"

There was total silence from the couple in the operating room. The only sound was the Mexican girl. The boy had come back through our room and had gone somewhere else in the building. He never came back.

After the girl finished cleaning up the operating room, she went into the kitchen and started cooking a big steak for the doctor.

She got a bottle of Miller's beer out of the refrigerator and poured the doctor a big glass of it. He sat down in the kitchen. I could barely see him drinking the beer.

Then Vida started stirring in her sleep. She opened

her eyes. They didn't see anything for a moment or so and then they saw me.

"Hi," she said in a distant voice.

"Hi," I said, smiling.

"I feel dizzy," she said, coming in closer.

"Don't worry about it," I said. "Everything is fine."

"Oh, that's good," she said. There.

"Just lie quietly and take it easy," I said.

The doctor got up from the table in the kitchen and came in. He was holding the glass of beer in his hand.

"She's coming back," he said.

"Yes," I said.

"Good," he said. "Good."

He took his glass of beer and went back into the kitchen and sat down again. He was very tired.

Then I heard the people in the outside gym room dressing their daughter. They were in a hurry to leave. They sounded as if they were dressing a drunk.

"I can't get my hands up," the girl said.

Her parents said something stern to her and she got her hands up in the air, but they had so much trouble putting her little brassiere on that they finally abandoned trying and the mother put the brassiere in her purse.

"OHHHHHHHHHH! I'm so dizzy," the girl said as her parents half-carried her, half-dragged her out of the place.

I heard a couple of doors close and then everything was silent, except for the doctor's lunch cooking in the kitchen. The steak was being fried in a very hot pan and it made a lot of noise.

"What's that?" Vida said. I didn't know if she was talking about the noise of the girl leaving or the sound of the steak cooking.

"It's the doctor having lunch," I said.

"Is it that late?" she said.

"Yes," I said.

"I've been out a long time," she said.

"Yes," I said. "We're going to have to leave soon but we won't leave until you feel like it."

"I'll see what I can do," Vida said.

The doctor came back into the room. He was nervous because he was hungry and tired and wanted to close the place up for a while, so he could take it easy, rest some.

Vida looked up at him and he smiled and said, "See, no pain, honey. Everything wonderful. Good girl."

Vida smiled very weakly and the doctor returned to the kitchen and his steak that was ready now.

While the doctor had his lunch, Vida slowly sat up and I helped her get dressed. She tried standing up but it was too hard, so I had her sit back down for a few moments.

While she sat there, she combed her hair and then she tried standing up again but she still didn't have it and sat back down on the bed again.

"I'm still a little rocky," Vida said.

"That's all right."

The woman in the other room had come to and her husband was dressing her almost instantly, saying, "Here. Here. Here. Here," in a painful Okie accent.

"I'm tired," the woman said, using up 2/3 of her vocabulary.

"Here," the man said, helping her put something else on.

After he got her dressed he came into our room and stood there looking for the doctor. He was very embarrassed when he saw Vida sitting on the bed, combing her hair.

"Doctor?" he said.

The doctor got up from his steak and stood in the doorway of the kitchen. The man started to walk toward the doctor, but then stopped after taking only a few steps.

The doctor came into our room.

"Yes," he said.

"I can't remember where I parked my car," the man said. "Can you call me a taxi?"

"You lost your auto?" the doctor said.

"I parked it next to Woolworth's, but I can't remember where Woolworth's is," the man said. "I can find Woolworth's if I can get downtown. I don't know where to go."

"The boy's coming back," the doctor said. "He'll take you there in his auto."

"Thank you," the man said, returning to his wife in the other room. "Did you hear that?" he said to her.

"Yes," she said, using it all up.

"We'll wait," he said.

Vida looked over at me and I smiled at her and took her hand to my mouth and kissed it.

"Let's try again," she said.

"All right," I said.

She tried it again and this time it was all right. She stood there for a few moments and then said, "I've got it. Let's go."

"Are you sure you have it?" I said.

"Yes."

I helped Vida on with her sweater. The doctor looked at us from the kitchen. He smiled but he didn't say anything. He had done what he was supposed to do and now we did what we were supposed to do. We left.

We wandered out of the room into the gym and worked our way to the front of the place, passing through layers of coolness to the door.

Even though it had remained a gray overcast day, we were stunned by the light and everything was instantly noisy, car-like, confused, poor, rundown and Mexican.

It was as if we had been in a time capsule and now were released again to be in the world.

The children were still playing in front of the doctor's office and again they stopped their games of life to watch two squint-eyed gringos holding, clinging, holding to each other walk up the street and into a world without them.

BOOK 6: The Hero

Woolworth's Again

WE slowly, carefully and abortively made our way back to downtown Tijuana surrounded and bombarded by people trying to sell us things that we did not want to buy.

We had already gotten what we'd come to Tijuana for. I had my arm around Vida. She was all right but she was a little weak.

"How do you feel, honey?" I said.

"I feel all right," she said. "But I'm a little weak."

We saw an old man crouching like a small gum-like piece of death beside an old dilapidated filling station.

"HEY, a pretty, pretty girl!"

Mexican men kept reacting to Vida's now pale beauty.

Vida smiled faintly at me as a taxicab driver dramatically stopped his cab in front of us and leaned out the window and gave a gigantic wolf whistle and said, "WOW! You need a taxi, honey!"

We made our way to the Main Street of Tijuana and found ourselves in front of Woolworth's again and the bunnies in the window.

"I'm hungry," Vida said. She was tired. "So hungry."

"You need something to eat," I said. "Let's go inside and see if we can get you some soup."

"That would be good," she said. "I need something."

We went off the confused dirty Main Street of Tijuana into the clean modern incongruity of Woolworth's. A very pretty Mexican girl took our order at the counter. She asked us what we wanted.

"What would you like?" she said.

"She'd like some soup," I said. "Some clam chowder."

"Yes," Vida said.

"What would you like?" the waitress said in very good Woolworth's English.

"I guess a banana split," I said.

I held Vida's hand while the waitress got our orders. She leaned her head against my shoulder. Then she smiled and said, "You're looking at the future biggest fan The Pill ever had."

"How do you feel?" I said.

"Just like I've had an abortion."

Then the waitress brought us our food. While Vida slowly worked her soup, I worked my banana split. It was the first banana split I'd had in years.

It was unusual fare for the day, but it was no different

from anything else that had happened since we'd come to the Kingdom of Tijuana to avail ourselves of the local recreational facilities.

The taxicab driver never took his eyes off Vida as we drove back to America. His eyes looked at us from the rear-view mirror as if he had another face and it was a mirror.

"Did you have a good time in Tijuana?" he said.

"Lovely," I said.

"What did you do?" he said.

"We had an abortion," I said.

"HAHAHAHAHAHAHAVERYFUNNYJOKE!"
the driver laughed.
Vida smiled.
Farewell, Tijuana.
Kingdom of Fire and Water.

The Green Hotel Again

OUR desk clerk was waiting for us, agog with smiles and questions. I had an idea that he drank on the job. There was something about how friendly he was.

"Did you see your sister?" he asked Vida with a big falseteeth smile.

"What?" Vida said. She was tired.

"Yes, we saw her," I said. "She was just as we remembered her."

"Even more so," Vida said, catching the game by the tail.

"That's good," the clerk said. "People should never change. They should always be the same. They are happier that way."

I tried that one on for size and was able to hold a straight face. It had been a long day.

"My wife's a little tired," I said. "I think we'll go up to our room."

"Relatives can be tiring. The excitement of it all. Re-
newing family ties," the desk clerk said.

"Yes," I said.

He gave us the key to his mother's room.

"I can take you up to the room if you don't remember the way," he said.

"No, that's not necessary," I said. "I remember the
way." I headed him off by saying, "It's such a beautiful
room."

"Isn't it?" he said.

"Very lovely room," Vida said.

"My mother was so happy there," he said.

We took the old elevator upstairs and I opened the
door with the key. "Get off the bed," I said as we went
into the room. "Off," I repeated.

"What?" Vida said.

"The Mother Ghost," I said.

"Oh."

Vida lay down on the bed and closed her eyes. I took
her shoes off, so she could be more comfortable.

"How do you feel?" I said.

"A little tired."

"Let's take a nap," I said, putting her under the
covers and joining her.

We slept for an hour or so and then I woke up. The
Mother Ghost was brushing her teeth and I told her to
get into the closet until we were gone. She got into the
closet and closed the door after her.

"Hey, baby," I said. Vida stirred in her sleep and then opened her eyes.

"What time is it?" she said.

"About the middle of the afternoon," I said.

"What time does our plane leave?" she said.

"6:25," I said. "Do you feel you can make it? If you don't, we'll spend the night here."

"No, I'm all right," she said. "Let's go back to San Francisco. I don't like San Diego. I want to get out of here and leave all this behind."

We got up and Vida washed her face and straightened herself up and felt a lot better, though she was still a little weak.

I told the hotel ghost mother good-bye in the closet and Vida joined me. "Good-bye, ghost," she said.

We went down the elevator to the waiting desk clerk whom I suspected of drinking on the job.

He was startled to see me standing there holding the KLM bag in my hand and returning the room key to him.

"You're not spending the night?" he said.

"No," I said. "We've decided to stay with her sister."

"What about your snoring?" he said.

"I'm going to see a doctor about it," I said. "I can't hide from this all my life. I can't go on living like this forever. I've decided to face it like a man."

Vida gave me a little nudge with her eyes to tell me that I was carrying it a little too far, so I retreated by saying, "You have a lovely hotel here and I'll recommend it to all my friends when they visit San Diego. What do I owe you?"

"Thank you," he said. "Nothing. You're Foster's friend. But you didn't even spend the night."

"That's all right," I said. "You've been very friendly. Thank you and good-bye."

"Good-bye," the desk clerk said. "Come again when you can spend the night."

"We will," I said.

"Good-bye," Vida said.

Suddenly he got a little desperate and paranoid. "There was nothing wrong with the room, was there?" he said. "It was my mother's room."

"Nothing," I said. "It was perfect."

"A wonderful hotel," Vida said. "A beautiful room. A truly beautiful room."

Vida seemed to have calmed him down because he said to us as we were going out the door, "Say hello to your sister for me."

That gave us something to think about as we drove out to the San Diego airport sitting very close together in the back seat of a cab where the driver, American this time, did not take his eyes off Vida in the mirror.

When we first got into the cab, the driver said, "Where to?"

I thought it would be fairly simple just to say, "The International Airport, please."

It wasn't.

"That's the San Diego International Airport, isn't it? That's where you want to go, huh?"

"Yes," I said, knowing that something was wrong.

"I just wanted to be sure," he said. "Because I had a fare yesterday that wanted to go to the International Airport, but it was the Los Angeles International Airport he wanted to go to. That's why I was checking."

Oh, yeah.

"Did you take him?" I said. I didn't have anything else to do and my relationship with the cab driver was obviously out of control.

"Yes," he said.

"He was probably afraid of flying," I said.

The cab driver didn't get the joke because he was watching Vida in the rear-view mirror and Vida was watching me after that one.

The driver continued staring at Vida. He paid very little attention to his driving. It was obviously dangerous to ride in a cab with Vida.

I made a mental note of it for the future, not to have Vida's beauty risk our lives.

The San Diego
(Not Los Angeles)
International Tipping Abyss

UNFORTUNATELY, the cab driver was very unhappy with the tip I gave him. The fare was again one dollar and ten cents and remindful of the experience we'd had earlier in the day with that first cab driver, I raised the tip-ante to thirty cents.

He was startled by the thirty-cent tip and didn't want to have anything else to do with us. Even Vida didn't make any difference when he saw that thirty cents.

What *is* the tip to the San Diego airport?

Our plane didn't leave for an hour. Vida was quite hungry, so we had something to eat in the cafe. It was about 5:30.

We had hamburgers. It was the first time I'd had a hamburger in years, but it turned out not to be very good. It was flat.

Vida said her hamburger was good, though.

"You've forgotten how a hamburger is supposed to

taste," Vida said. "Too many years in the monastery have destroyed your better judgment."

There were two women sitting nearby. One of them had platinum hair and a mink coat. She was middle-aged and talking to a young, blandly pretty girl who was talking in turn about her wedding and the little caps that were being designed for the bridesmaids.

The girl was nice in the leg department but a little short in the titty line or was I spoiled? They departed their table without leaving a tip.

This made the waitress mad.

She was probably a close relative to the two cab drivers I'd met that day in San Diego.

She stared at the tipless table as if it were a sex criminal. Perhaps she was their mother.

Farewell, San Diego

I TOOK a closer look at the San Diego airport. It was petite, uncomplicated with no *Playboy* stuff at all. The people were there to work, not to look pretty.

There was a sign that said something like: Animals arriving as baggage may be claimed in the airline air freight areas in the rear of bldg.

You can bet your life that you don't see signs like that in the San Francisco International Airport.

A young man with crutches, accompanied by three old men, came along as we were going out to wait for our airplane. They all stared at Vida and the young man stared the hardest.

It was a long way from the beautiful PSA pre-flight lounge in San Francisco to just standing outside, beside a wire fence in San Diego, waiting to get on our airplane that was shark-like and making a high whistling steam sound, wanting very much to fly.

The evening was cold and gray coming down upon us with some palm trees, nearby, by the highway. The palm trees somehow made it seem colder than it actually was. They seemed out of place in the cold.

There was a military band playing beside one of the airplanes parked on the field, but it was too far away to see why they were playing. Maybe some big wig was coming or going. They sounded like my hamburger.

My Secret Talisman Forever

W<small>E</small> got our old seats back over the wing and I was sitting again next to the window. Suddenly it was dark in twelve seconds. Vida was quiet, tired. There was a little light on the end of the wing. I became quite fond of it out there in the dark like a lighthouse burning twenty-three miles away and I made it my secret talisman forever.

A young priest was sitting across the aisle from us. He was quite smitten by Vida for the short distance to Los Angeles.

At first he tried not to be obvious about it, but after a while he surrendered himself to it and one time he leaned across the aisle and was going to say something to Vida. He was actually going to say something to her, but then he changed his mind.

I will probably go on for a long time wondering what he would have said to my poor aborted darling who, though weak and tired from the ways of Tijuana, was the prettiest thing going in the sky above California, the rapidly moving sky to Los Angeles.

I went from the priest's interest in Vida to wondering about Foster at the library, how he was handling the books that were coming in that day.

I hoped he was welcoming them the right way and making the authors feel comfortable and wanted as I made them feel.

"Well, we'll be home soon," Vida said to me after a long silence that was noisy with thought. The priest's composure vibrated with tension when Vida spoke.

"Yes," I said. "I was just thinking about that."

"I know," she said. "I could hear the noise in your mind. I think everything's all right at the library. Foster's doing a good job."

"You're doing a good job yourself," I said.

"Thank you," she said. "It will be good to get home. Back to the library and some sleep."

I was very pleased that she considered the library her home. I looked out the window at my talisman. I loved it as much as the coffee stain flying down.

Perhaps and Eleven

THINGS are different at night. The houses and towns far below demand their beauty and get it in distant lights twinkling with incredible passion. Landing at Los Angeles was like landing inside a diamond ring.

The priest didn't want to get off the plane at Los Angeles, but he had to because that's where he was going. Perhaps Vida reminded him of somebody. Perhaps his mother was very beautiful and he didn't know how to handle it and that's what drove him to the Cloth and now to see that beauty again in Vida was like swirling back through the mirrors of time.

Perhaps he was thinking about something completely different from what I have ever thought about in my life and his thoughts were of the highest nature and should have been made into a statue . . . perhaps. To quote Foster, "Too many perhapses in the world and not enough people."

I was suddenly wondering about my library again and missed the actual departure of the priest to become part of Los Angeles, to add his share to its size and to take memories of Vida into whatever.

"Did you see that?" Vida said.

"Yes," I said.

"This has been happening ever since I was eleven," she said.

Fresno, Then 3 1/2 Minutes to Salinas

THE stewardesses on this flight were fantastically shallow and had been born from half a woman into a world that possessed absolutely no character except chrome smiles. All of them were of course beautiful.

One of them was pushing a little cart down the aisle, trying to sell us cocktails. She had a singsong inhuman voice that I'm positive was prerecorded by a computer.

"Purchase a cocktail.

"Purchase a cocktail.

"Purchase a cocktail."

While pushing her little cart down the sky.

"Purchase a cocktail.

"Purchase a cocktail.

"Purchase a cocktail."

There were no lights below.

Shine on, O talisman!

I pushed my face against the window and looked

very hard and saw a star and I made a wish but I won't tell. Why should I? Purchase a cocktail from pretty Miss Zero and find your own star. There's one for everyone in the evening sky.

There were two women behind us talking about nail polish for the thirty-nine minute way to San Francisco. One of them thought that fingernails without polish should be put under rocks.

Vida had no polish on her fingernails but she didn't care and gave the women's conversation no attention.

From time to time the airplane was bucked by an invisible horse in the sky but it didn't bother me because I was falling in love with the 727 jet, my sky home, my air love.

The pilot or some male voice told us that if we looked out the window, we could see the lights of Fresno and were 3½ minutes away from the lights of Salinas.

I was already looking for Salinas, but something happened on the plane. One of the women spilt her fingernail polish on a cat ten years ago and I looked away for a moment to wonder about that and missed Salinas, so I pretended my talisman was Salinas.

The Saint of Abortion

WE were about to land at San Francisco when the women behind us finished their conversation about fingernail polish.

"I wouldn't be caught dead without fingernail polish," one of them said.

"You're right," the other one said.

We were only three miles away from landing and I couldn't see the wing that led like a black highway to my talisman. It seemed as if we were going to land without a wing, only a talisman.

Ah, the wing appeared magically just as we touched the ground.

There were soldiers everywhere in the terminal. It was as if an army were encamped there. They flipped when they saw Vida. She was increasing the United States Army sperm count by about three tons as we walked through the place, heading toward the van in the parking lot.

Vida also affected the civilian population by causing a man who looked like a banker to walk directly into an Oriental woman, knocking the woman down. She was rather surprised because she had just flown in from Saigon and didn't expect this to happen on her first visit to America.

Alas, another victim of Vida's thing.

"Do you think you can take it?" Vida said.

"We ought to bottle what you've got," I said.

"Vida Pop," Vida said.

"How do you feel?" I said with my arm around her.

"Glad to be home," she said.

Even though the San Francisco International Airport acted like a *Playboy* cybernetic palace wanting to do things for us that we were not quite ready to have done, at that moment I felt that the International Airport was our first home back from Tijuana.

I was also anxious to get back to the library and see Foster.

The Bufano statue waited for us with a peace that we couldn't understand with its strange people fastened projectile-like upon a huge bullet.

As we got into the van, I thought there should be a statue for the Saint of Abortion, whoever that was, somewhere in the parking lot for the thousands of women who had made the same trip Vida and I had just finished, flying into the Kingdom of Fire and

Water, the waiting and counting hands of Dr. Garcia and his associates in Mexico.

Thank God, the van had an intimate, relaxed human feeling to it. The van reflected Foster in its smells and ways of life. It felt very good to be in the van after having travelled the story of California.

I put my hand on Vida's lap and that's where it stayed following the red lights of cars in front of us shining back like roses into San Francisco.

A New Life

WHEN we arrived back at the library the first thing we saw was Foster sitting out on the steps in his traditional T-shirt, even though it was now dark and cold.

The lights were on in the library and I wondered what Foster was doing sitting outside on the steps. That didn't seem to be the correct way to run a library.

Foster stood up and waved that big friendly wave of his.

"Hello, there, strangers," he said. "How did it go?"

"Fine," I said, getting out of the van. "What are you doing out here?"

"How's my baby?" Foster said to Vida.

"Great," she said.

"Why aren't you inside?" I said.

"Tired, honey?" Foster said to Vida. He put his arm gently around her.

"A little," she said.

"Well, that's the way it should be, but it won't last long."

"The library?" I said.

"Good girl," Foster said to Vida. "Am I glad to see you! You look like a million dollars in small change. What a sight!" giving her a kiss on the cheek.

"The library?" I said.

Foster turned toward me. "I'm sorry about that," he said, then turning to Vida, "Oh, what a girl!"

"You're sorry about what?" I said.

"Don't worry," Foster said. "It's for the best. You need a rest, a change of scene. You'll be a lot happier now."

"Happier, what? What's going on?"

"Well," Foster said. He had his arm around Vida and she was looking up at him as he tried to explain what was going on.

There was a slight smile on her face that grew large and larger as Foster continued, "Well, it happened this way. I was sitting there minding your asylum when this lady came in with a book and she—"

I looked away from Foster toward the library where its friendly light was shining out and I looked inside the glass door and I could see a woman sitting behind the desk.

I couldn't see her face but I could see that it was a woman and her form looked quite at home. My heart and my stomach started doing funny things in my body.

"You mean?" I said, unable to find the words.

"That's right," Foster said. "She said the way that I was handling the library was a disgrace and I was a slob and she would take it over now: thank you.

"I told her that you'd been here for years and that you were great with the library and I was just watching it during an emergency. She said that didn't make any difference, that if you had turned the library over to me, even for a day, you didn't deserve to be in charge of the library any more.

"I told her that I worked at the caves and she said that I didn't work there any more, that her brother would take care of it from now on, that I should think of doing something else like getting a job.

"Then she asked me where the living quarters were and I pointed out the way and she went in and packed all your stuff. When she found Vida's things there, she said, 'I got here just in time!' Then she had me take it all out here and I've been sitting here ever since."

I looked down at my meager possessions piled on the steps. I hadn't even noticed them.

"I can't believe it," I said. "I'll go tell her that it's all a mistake, that—"

Just then the woman got up from behind the desk and strolled very aggressively to the front door and opened the door without stepping outside and she yelled at me, "Get your God-damn stuff out of here right now and never come back, not unless you've got a book under your arm!"

"There's been a mistake," I said.

"Yes," she said. "I know and you are it. Farewell, creep!"

She turned and the front door closed behind her as if it were obeying her.

I stood there like Lot's wife on one of her bad days.

Vida was laughing like hell and Foster was, too. They started doing a little dance on the sidewalk around me.

"There must be a mistake," I cried in the wilderness.

"You heard the lady," Foster said. "Damn! Damn! Damn! am I glad to be out of the cave business. I thought I was going to get TB."

"Oh, darling," Vida said, breaking the dance to throw her arms around me while Foster started loading our stuff into the van. "You've just been fired. You're going to have to live like a normal human being."

"I can't believe it," I sighed. Then they loaded me into the van.

"Well, what are we going to do?" Foster said.

"Let's go to my place," Vida said. "It's just around the block on Lyon Street."

"I can always sleep in the van," Foster said.

"No, there's plenty of room in my place for all of us," Vida said.

Somehow Vida had ended up driving the van and

she parked it in front of a big red shingled house that had an ancient iron fence in front of it. The fence looked quite harmless. Time had removed its ferocity and Vida lived in the attic.

Her place was nice and simple. There was practically no furniture and the walls were painted white and there was nothing on them.

We sat on the floor on a thick white rug that had a low marble table in the center of it.

"Do you want a drink?" Vida said. "I think we all need a drink."

Foster smiled.

She made us some very dry vodka martinis in glasses full of ice. She didn't put any vermouth in them. The drinks were done off with twists of lemon peel. The lemon lay there like flowers in the ice.

"I'll put something on the stereo," Vida said. "Then I'll start some dinner."

I was shocked by losing my library and surprised at being inside a real house again. Both feelings were passing like ships in the night.

"Damn, does that vodka taste good!" Foster said.

"No, honey," I said. "I think you'd better rest. I'll cook up something."

"No," Foster said. "A little logger breakfast is what we all need now. Some fried potatoes and onions and eggs all cooked together with a gallon of catsup on top. Do you have the makings?"

"No," Vida said. "But there's a store open down at California and Divisadero."

"OK," Foster said.

He put some more vodka in his mouth.

"Ah, do you kids have any money left? I'm flat."

I gave Foster a couple of dollars that I had left and he went to the store.

Vida put a record on the phonograph. It was the Beatles' album *Rubber Soul*. I had never heard the Beatles before. That's how long I was in the library.

"I want you to hear this one first," Vida said.

We sat there quietly listening to the record.

"Who sang that?" I said.

"John Lennon," she said.

Foster came back with the food and started cooking our dinnerbreakfast thing. Soon the whole attic was filled with the smell of onions.

That was months ago.

It's now the last of May and we're all living together in a little house in Berkeley. It has a small back yard. Vida's working at a topless place over in North Beach, so she'll have some money to go back to school next fall. She's going to give English another try. Foster has a girlfriend who is an exchange student from Pakistan. She's twenty and majoring in sociology.

She's in the other room now cooking up a big Pakistani dinner and Foster is watching her with a can of beer in his hand. He's got a job at Bethlehem Steel over in San Francisco at night working on an aircraft carrier that's in dry dock being fixed. Today is Foster's day off.

Vida is off doing something or other and will be home soon. She doesn't work tonight either. I've spent the afternoon at a table across from Sproul Hall where they took all those hundreds of Free Speech kids off to jail in 1964. I've been gathering contributions for The American Forever, Etc.

I like to set my table up around lunch time near the fountain, so I can see the students when they come pouring through Sather Gate like the petals of a thousand-colored flower. I love the joy of their intellectual perfume and the political rallies they hold at noon on the steps of Sproul Hall.

It's nice near the fountain with green trees all around and bricks and people that need me. There are even a lot of dogs that hang around the plaza. They are of all shapes and colors. I think it's important that you find things like this at the University of California.

Vida was right when she said that I would be a hero in Berkeley.

So the Wind
Won't
Blow It All
Away

Richard Brautigan

So the Wind Won't Blow It All Away

This book is for
Portia Crockett
and Marian Renken.

I didn't know that afternoon that the ground was waiting to become another grave in just a few short days. Too bad I couldn't grab the bullet out of the air and put it back into the .22 rifle barrel and have it spiral itself back down the barrel and into the chamber and refasten itself to the shell and be as if it had never been fired or even loaded into the gun.

I wish the bullet was back in its box with the other 49 brother and sister bullets and the box was safely on the shelf in the gunshop, and I had just walked by the shop on that rainy February afternoon and never gone inside.

I wish I had been hungry for a hamburger instead of bullets. There was a restaurant right next to the gunshop. They had very good hamburgers, but I wasn't hungry.

For the rest of my life I'll think about that hamburger. I'll be sitting there at the counter, holding it in my hands with tears streaming down my cheeks. The waitress will be looking away because she doesn't like to see kids crying when they are eating hamburgers, and also she doesn't want to embarrass me.

I am the only customer in the restaurant.

She doesn't need this.

She has her own problems.

Her boyfriend left her last week for a redhead from Chicago. This is the second time in a year this has happened to her. She can't believe it. It has to be more than a coincidence. How many redheads are there in Chicago?

She takes a rag and cleans up an imaginary stain far down the counter, wiping up something spilled that isn't there. I'll continue on with this story:

So the Wind Won't Blow It All Away
Dust . . . American . . . Dust

It was the second year after World War II ended, when they rattled down a rutted, mud-hardened road toward the pond in an old pickup truck that had their fishing furniture piled on the back. It was always around 7 o'clock in the summer evenings of 1947 when they pulled up beside the pond and began taking their furniture off the truck.

First, they took the couch off. It was a big heavy couch but it was no problem for them because they were both big heavy people. She was just about as big as he was. They put the couch down on the grass right beside the pond, so they could sit there and fish off the couch.

They always took the couch off first and then they got the rest of the furniture. It took them no time at all to set up their things. They were very efficient at it and obviously had been doing this for years before I saw them and began waiting for them to arrive at the pond and became, in my own small way, a part of their life.

Sometimes I would arrive early and wait for them.

As I sit here on August 1st, 1979, my ear is pressed up against the past as if to the wall of a house that no longer exists.

I can hear the sound of redwing blackbirds and the wind blowing hard against the cattails. They rustle in the wind like ghost swords in battle and there is the steady lapping of the pond at the shore's edge, which I belong to with my imagination.

The blackbirds sound like melancholy exclamation marks typed on the summer late afternoon, which has a feeling of bored exhaustion because a hot wind is blowing from the south. That kind of wind is always tiring and gets on my nerves.

A plank has been crudely engineered with the help of a small log at the end and some stake-like pilings to form at best the world's saddest fishing dock.

It's really pathetic, and all of my own design and construction, so there's really no one else to blame, and I'm standing on the end of it, about twelve feet away from the shore. The plank cuts a narrow corridor through the cattails to get to the open water of the pond. The plank sags in the middle, so it's covered with three inches of water, and it's not solid enough to jump over.

My clown-like dock would collapse if I tried that, so I have to wade through the water to get to the dry end of the plank to fish.

Fortunately, twelve-year-old boys don't care if they get their tennis shoes wet. It means practically nothing to them. They couldn't care less, so I'm standing there with wet feet, fishing into the southern wind, listening to the blackbirds and the dry sword-like rustling of the cattails and the steady lapping of the water against where the pond ends and the shore of the world begins.

I'm fishing directly across the pond from where they will come in a few hours and set up their furniture.

I'm waiting for them by watching my bobber bobbing up and down like a strange floating metronome and slowly drowning a worm because the fish are not interested in the slightest with its plight.

The fish just aren't biting, but I don't care.

I'm just waiting and this is as good a way to wait

as any other way to wait because waiting's all the same anywait.

The sun is shining on the water in front of me, so I have to keep looking away. Whenever I look at the sun, it is reflected back to me like a shiny bed-spread whose design is hundreds of wind-driven roller coasters.

There is no freshness to the sun.

The sun turned boring in the middle of the after-noon, as it does so often for children, and was almost out of style like old clothes that were poorly and unin-terestingly designed from the very beginning. Maybe He should have thought twice about it.

The sun was burning me slightly but I didn't care. My face felt a little flushed. I wasn't wearing a hat. I seldom wore hats when I was a child. Hats were to come later on.

I had almost albino white hair.

Kids called me "Whitey."

I had been standing there so long that my tennis shoes were almost dry. They were at their half-life, which is the best time for tennis shoes. They felt as if they were truly a part of me like an extension of my soles. They were alive at the bottoms of my feet.

I didn't like it when my tennis shoes completely wore out and we didn't have any money to buy another pair. I always felt as if I had done something bad and was being punished for it.

I must be a better kid!

This was how God was punishing me: by making me wear fucked-up old tennis shoes, so that I was embarrassed to look at my own feet.

I was too young and naive then to link up the meaning of those ridiculingly defunct tennis shoes that I was forced to wear with the reality that we were on Welfare and Welfare was not designed to provide a child with any pride in its existence.

When I got a new pair of tennis shoes, my outlook on life immediately changed. I was a new person and proud to walk on the earth again and thanked God in my prayers for helping me get a new pair of tennis shoes.

But in the meantime it was the summer of 1947, and I got bored waiting for them to come with their furniture and decided to go visit an old man who was a night watchman at a small sawmill nearby.

He lived in a little shack by the sawmill and drank beer. He drank a lot of beer while he watched the sawmill, so that no one took anything. The sawmill was very, very quiet after the workers went home. He watched it with a bottle of beer in his hand. I think you could have stolen the entire sawmill and he wouldn't have noticed it.

I would often visit him and he would give me his empty beer bottles and I would return them to the store and get a penny apiece deposit for them.

Collecting his beer bottles was a good idea.

It beat looking into the sun.

I waded back across the plank and my feet were wet again. It took only a few seconds to make it as if they had never been dry, that they had always been wet, but I didn't care.

I had to make the decision whether to take my bamboo fishing pole with me because there was a place along the way where I sometimes jigged for frogs or hide it in the bushes. I stood there and took about ten seconds longer to make that decision than I should have.

I hid my pole in some bushes.

The idea of frogs was as boring as the sun.

I would pick it up when I came back to join the man and the woman in their open fishing house across the pond. I was now ahead of them in time, so I would give them a couple of hours to catch up.

There were other things that I could do besides not catch fish until they came and the night watchman's beer bottles was one of them.

While I walked a quarter of a mile to the sawmill, my mind was occupied with fantasies of empty beer bottles. Maybe he had two cases of them or perhaps even three. I hadn't visited him in a week or so and maybe he had been drinking more beer than usual. I hoped that was the case. Then I had the sobering thought that maybe another kid had already visited

him and gotten all the beer bottles that should right-
fully have been mine.

I didn't like the idea of that kid.

I vowed to make it a regular part of my life to visit
that old man at least every four days and get all of his
beer bottles for myself.

The loss of that revenue was no laughing matter,
especially if part of your life you had to wear shitty tennis shoes.

During those years just after World War II, I
could be quite a formidable collector of beer bottles if I put my mind to it. They were worth a penny
apiece for the small ones and two cents apiece for
quarts.

When I was in a very serious beer-bottle mood,
I would take an old baby buggy with me. It was made
out of wicker and had a huge hood. I could put a lot
of beer bottles in that buggy.

Sometimes I would spend a whole day pushing it
around, collecting abandoned beer bottles. Within a
mile of where we lived, there were many opportunities
for a young beer-bottle capitalist if he pushed his baby
buggy hard and long enough.

There was a highway to be explored. People liked
to drink beer in their cars and throw the bottles out
the windows where they would land in my baby buggy
a week later.

The highway stretched between cities and went

all the way across the state, but I used only a mile of it as part of my beer-bottle empire.

That mile was on the edge of town where I lived with my mother and two sisters in a cabin at an auto court, but we didn't have an automobile. We never had one. We were autoless guests of the Welfare Department. It was strange all those people coming and going to and from different places when we were going nowhere.

My mother and my sisters won't be mentioned again because they are not really a part of this story. That of course is a lie. They will be mentioned later on. I don't know why I just told this lie. It was really a silly and useless thing for me to do, but sometimes people do silly and useless things. They can't help themselves. They are often at the mercy of unknown vectors.

I have corrected it, though, and now we can continue on without, I hope, too much loss of credibility, and please remember that I could have changed this story to cover my lie and *actually* have left them out and substituted an aunt and two cousins in their place.

So please accept my apology and be prepared for them to reappear on page 12.

The highway went right past the auto court and I followed it out of town with my baby buggy. I got the baby buggy from an old woman who said she'd give me something if I went to the store for her. I said

OK, and she gave me a list of things she wanted and the money to pay for them.

"Can I trust you?" she said, pausing a very old hand on the clasp of an equally old black leather purse.

"Yes," I said, already holding the list in my hand. We had already gone that far with the deal, so she was holding onto the last flickering doubts of an already negotiated deal. All I needed was the money. We were both very aware of this. She sighed and opened the purse at the same time, saying, "I wish my husband wasn't dead."

"What did he die of?" I said, not really caring but knowing that I had to say something. You can't leave a remark like that alone without an attending comment, or so I thought at the time.

"A heart attack. He died in bed. He was an older man."

She handed me two dollars.

"When?" I chirped like a little death sparrow.

The money was old and crumpled like the woman. She must have had it for a very long time. Maybe she slept on it while dreaming of her dead husband. Old people are supposed to do that: sleep on their money, snoring on top of thousands of George Washingtons and Abraham Lincolns.

"March 3, 1916."

I did some primitive arithmetic in my mind which

has not been too good at arithmetic, anyway, and then said, "He's been dead for a long time."

"Too long," she said. "I can hardly remember what it was like."

I didn't know the full meaning of what she was saying.

I do now.

When I came back with the sack of groceries, she gave me the baby buggy. It was in a garage full of other old things right beside the weather-worn house that she lived in. The paint had fallen off the house years before, so the house just stood there in the neighborhood, hardly noticed any more.

The garage was very complicated in the light of a 15 watt globe fastened to a piece of yellow string that looked as if it had come off a mummy.

There were many perfectly packed boxes of the past in the garage and there were hundreds of things that were mostly shadows. Its reality was only the memories now of children grown up and away from the buggy.

"I think you can just wheel it out," she said.

I walked very carefully over to the baby buggy. I didn't want to stumble over the past and break my present-tense leg that might leave me crippled in the future.

I took the handle of the baby buggy and pulled it away from the 1900s and into the year 1947.

Though I was in the garage for just a short time, when I emerged pushing the baby buggy, the afternoon seemed extraordinarily bright. It was a cloudy day but it seemed as if the sun were out and shining in full magnitude.

I helped her close the garage door. She was just about too old to do it by herself. I guess when she got too old to close the garage door, she'd go live in an old folks home with other people who were too old to close their garage doors.

She padlocked the door with a very ancient and fragile lock. The lock was only a symbol of privacy and protection, but that meant something in those days. If that lock were around today, a thief would just walk up to it and blow it off with his breath.

"Do you want me to come back and do some more errands for you?" I said.

"No," she said.

I shrugged my shoulders and pushed the baby buggy away into my life where I pretended that it was a covered wagon for a while and pulled my sisters* and other kids around in it. I pretended that I was at the head of a wagon train of baby buggies crossing the Great Plains going West in the pioneer days to homestead Oregon.

There were many perils to be overcome: hostile

*I kept my word. See page 9.

Indians, the burning sun and lack of water, and also sudden unexplainable snowstorms that we got lost in and had to find the trail all over again.

After a week the romantic possibilities of baby-buggy pioneer days wore out my imagination and I changed it into a beer-bottle carrier.

The baby buggy gave me a tremendous ease of mobility and the chance, because of its capacity, to become a beer-bottle millionaire.

Before I got the buggy, I used gunnysacks to transport the bottles. Now with the baby buggy, I was breathing on the neck of John D. Rockefeller.

Maybe I was thinking about that as I walked over to the sawmill to investigate the night watchman's capacity for beer drinking and how it could help me see a John Wayne movie or experience the awkward joy of trying to keep one lick ahead of an ice-cream cone on a hot summer day. Shitty tennis shoes were not a problem at this time.

In the area just around the pond where the people came in the evening and set up their furniture, there were two other ponds and half-a-dozen sawmills with their accompanying log ponds.

The center of the area was an overpass on the highway.

Underneath the overpass travelling north and south was a railroad line that the sawmills used to supply America with houses. Coal-burning trains were constantly coming and going along the tracks. I used to pretend that pieces of coal that fell off the tenders were gigantic black diamonds and I was the richest kid in the world and bought everything a child could use or imagine with the coal that fell off the passing trains.

Besides the sawmill activities that went on in the area, there were also open fields and some agricultural lands with livestock: horses and cows and sheep. There were two previously planted and domesticated orchards that had been totally ignored, abandoned for reasons unknown and had reverted to the wild, bearing apples and pears and plums and cherries that had a tremendous amount of character. They made the fruit that you bought in the store seem like a bunch of sissies.

All of this started when I opened the front door of the auto court cabin where I lived and I never got to explore all of it because it just kept unfolding new territories until my childhood ended when I was twelve years old on February 17th, 1948, in yet another abandoned orchard five miles away in the opposite direction where I was always headed, though I did not know it at the time.

But now it was still the summer of 1947 and I cut over from the pond to the railroad tracks and walked north along the tracks toward the possible beer-bottle riches of a used-up old man who watched a sawmill at night, so nobody would drive carefully up in a truck with its lights out and steal the saw which would cause a lot of commotion when the mill hands came to work the next morning.

"Where's the saw?"

There were three sawmills north of the overpass along the tracks and the night watchman's was the last sawmill. It was just past quitting time when I arrived there. He had a shack to the side of the mill. There were a hell-of-a-lot of tall weeds growing around the shack. There were millions of weeds in that area, but these weeds were so tall that they attracted attention where normally that would not have happened. They would have just been another patch of weeds and gone very unnoticed.

The old man was sitting on the front porch of the shack surrounded by his weeds. He had a bottle of beer in his hand. That was a good sign. There was an empty bottle lying on its side next to the chair he was sitting in. That was even a better sign. The old man didn't know that as I walked toward him all I really saw was two cents.

"Hello, kid," he said. "Come to pay me a little visit?"

The dry gray chair he was sitting in looked just like another weed. Sometimes I thought about that. I wondered if it was possible to make a chair out of weeds. If they had ever made one, he was sitting in it.

"Yes, sir," I said.

"Nineteen empties," he said.

"What?" I said.

"You've got that empty-beer-bottle look in your eyes," the old man said and then repeated, "Nineteen empties."

"Oh," I said, looking down at the ground that somehow seemed very far away. I didn't know that it was that obvious. I wondered what I could do about it and then realized that there was nothing I could do about it. It was the truth and would always be the truth, so I looked up from the distant ground.

"Nice day," I said, trying hard to assert my twelve-year-old personality.

"They're on the back porch in a gunnysack," he said. "Why don't you get them while I take a real good look at this nice day of yours. Just go right through the house and I'll tell you what I think when you get back."

"Thank you," I said.

"Don't thank me," he said. "Just thank the fact that I'm an alcoholic."

I knew that did not need a reply, so I walked up the five weed-attacked steps to the front porch where the old man was sitting in a chair that the weeds had already conquered, with a bottle of beer in his hand which he very carefully drew to his mouth to take a sip. Rembrandt could not have drawn a more direct or finer line.

Before I open the screen door and go into the shack I'd like to make an observation. I keep referring to the sawmill night watchman alcoholic as an "old man." But looking back down upon that long-ago past now from the 1979 mountainside of this August afternoon, I think the "old man" was younger than I am now. He was about maybe thirty-five, nine years younger than I am now. To the marshy level of my human experience back then, he seemed to be very old, probably the equivalent of an eighty-year-old man to me now.

Also, drinking beer all the time didn't make him look any younger.

I knew very little about him. I knew that somehow he had gotten out of the Army and had spent the rest of the War in Mobile, Alabama, where he drank a lot of beer and married a woman who left him after two years of marriage because she didn't want to be around a man who drank so much beer.

She thought that there were better things in life, so she divorced him. He had loved her very much, so the divorce just contributed to him drinking more beer.

Once when he was talking about her to me with his inevitable bottle of beer in hand, I realized that he never spoke of her by name, so I asked him what her name was. He took a very long sip of beer before replying. Then he said after what seemed like an hour

to me that her name was not important and to just
think of her as the woman who had broken his heart.

I didn't say anything to that either.

I knew that didn't require an answer either.

I opened the screen door and walked into his little
one-room shack, which for some strange reason was
very tidy. He may have been a drunk but he was neat.

Besides a few sticks of elemental furniture, there
were very few personal effects in the shack. A picture
of Jesus on the wall seemed out of place, but that was
his and His business, not mine. The picture of Jesus
was hanging crookedly, so I didn't think that he was
much of a Christian.

Maybe the picture of Jesus covered a crack in the
wall.

He had some letters on the table. They were always the same two letters. They had both been opened
very neatly. One of the letters was from Pensacola,
Florida, and it was postmarked September 1, 1939. I
guess if he drank as much beer as he did, people didn't
write to him that often.

There were no bills on the table.

He had very carefully arranged a lifestyle that denied even the remotest possibility of getting a bill.

I never touched his mail. I wasn't that kind of kid.
I mean, of course, I was a sneak, but not that kind of
sneak. The imagination was where I snuck around.

I always walked very slowly and close to the table

and nonchalantly glanced at his mail. That was as far as I carried it. Another letter was from Little Rock, Arkansas, and it was postmarked April 4, 1942.

It was from a man named Edgar Peters. I wonder why that name still sticks in my mind after all these years. I've forgotten a lot more important things. I've even forgotten things that I don't even know that I knew. They are totally gone, but there's Edgar Peters like a Las Vegas neon sign someplace in my brain.

There was a postcard tacked to the wall beside the kitchen sink which was right next to the back door that always led me to empty beer bottles.

The postcard was extremely intriguing to me and I always eagerly waited to see it again. The contents of the postcard were facing the wall, so I don't know who it was from except that the card was postmarked July 12, 1938, and it was mailed from New Orleans, and the postmark should have been on the other side.

The picture on that postcard probably meant more to me than the existence of that "old man" other than his capacity to make me money by drinking beer.

It was a color photograph of a flatbed truck with a huge catfish on it that took up the whole bed. The catfish was maybe the size of a whale. Think about Moby Dick to my twelve-year-old way of looking at things and you're very close to the truth. The postcard was some kind of trick photography, but 50% of me believed that it was real.

Once that 50% gained total control of my mind and I asked him if that was a real catfish. Maybe I had spent too much time fishing in the sun that day.

"Are you kidding?" he replied.

"I guess so," I said. "How did they do that?"

"I don't know," he said. "If I knew how they did that I wouldn't be the night watchman of a half-assed sawmill out in the middle of nowhere."

No reply from me was forthcoming.

Another thing about him that I was aware of back then and it gave me pause to think, not long but a little, was that all the few personal references to his life had something to do with the South.

He had spent the War in Mobile, Alabama.

He had a catfish postcard from New Orleans.

He had married a Southern woman.

He had one letter from Pensacola, Florida, and another letter from Little Rock, Arkansas.

He had all these things that related him to the South, but he didn't have a Southern accent, not even in the slightest. The sound of his voice was at least a billion miles away from Robert E. Lee.

So I thought about it briefly sometimes, but not that often. If I had something better to think about other than the fact that an "old" alcoholic sawmill night watchman didn't have a Southern accent, I would think about whatever that was gladly.

I opened the screen door and stepped out onto

the back porch into an army of huge weeds that grew over the porch, almost trying to get into the shack and find out why that "old man" didn't have a Southern accent and maybe even the name of his wife who had left him in 1944 because he drank so much beer and she didn't want to sleep beside another beer fart in the middle of a hot Mobile night with the wind not stirring at all.

I picked up the sack of beer bottles and journeyed back through the house to the "old man" waiting for me on the front porch with probably something cynical to say about my "nice day" observation, but I didn't care because I had his beer bottles and I had looked at his catfish postcard and his letter from Edgar Peters, writing to him about something that will always remain a mystery to me. Maybe the contents of the letter told him to stop drinking so much beer all the time or his friends would give up on him.

When I came out the other side of the shack onto the front porch, lugging my beer bottles, he totally surprised me by saying, "You're right. It is a nice day and you've got nineteen fine beer bottles in that sack. I had a lot more last week. Three cases or so. Too bad you didn't come by then. You'd be rolling in dough."

He smiled when he said that.

Three cases! I thought.

"Some other kid got them," he said.

"Who was that?" I said, trying to sound casual

while mentally running through a list of kid enemies in my mind. Sometimes other kids got to the "old man's" beer bottles before I did. Anyone who took his bottles other than myself was not a friend of mine.

It's interesting that the "old man" never returned any of the bottles himself because I knew that he wasn't rich. I guess he just went to the store and got the beer and brought it back to the sawmill and sat there and drank it and then waited for us kids to come and scavenge the bottles away like empty-beer-bottle hyenas.

"It was some kid you don't know," he said, lowering my curiosity. "He lives in the opposite direction from you. I think he lives somewhere near Melody Ranch."

Melody Ranch was a cheap roadhouse dance hall where there were a lot of fistfights on the weekend between drunken men who would never sit in the chair where Harry Truman was sitting. It was out of my territory, so the kid was an unknown competitor, just another vulture circling the alcoholism of this "old" night watchman.

I used to wonder what he would do if somebody actually came to the sawmill at night and tried to steal something. He had a thin beer-brittle physique. Some men get fat when they drink a lot of beer. Others just get thinner until their bones come to resemble dried-out weeds. He was that type.

Also, there is something else that I haven't mentioned about him. He was a very fancy dresser and his clothes were immaculately neat and clean.

Sometimes he wore a suit with a tie while he watched the sawmill with a faithful bottle of beer in his hand. He looked like an insurance agent instead of a night watchman. I wondered about his capability and desire to defend the sawmill against sawmill thieves because he looked as if he couldn't defend a marshmallow against a three-year-old.

Perhaps he had a gun.

I asked him about that once.

"What do I need a gun for?" was his reply.

I didn't pursue that subject but finally I had to ask him what he would do if somebody came and tried to steal something.

"I'd let them steal the whole God-damn sawmill. I wouldn't help them load it, though. I wouldn't want to get my clothes dirty. They only pay me fifty dollars a month to watch this God-forsaken place, plus I get to live in this shack for nothing and they take care of my utilities."

He laughed when he said the words: "my utilities." Then he said them again but this time much louder, "My utilities!" and laughing even louder. I tried to think what was so funny, but I couldn't, so I left.

Anyway, that was a few months ago and this was

now and I had a sack of beer bottles and I was ready to go on my way again. I had to get back to the pond.

The people who brought their furniture with them when they went fishing would be arriving soon, and they were much more interesting than this carefully dressed "old" beer-drinking sawmill night watchman who didn't give a damn if thieves came and took the whole place, mill, pond, logs, lumber, and just left him there drinking beer with everything gone except for his little shack and his weed-like chair on the front porch.

"I have to be going," I said, taking a step back and away from his world.

"Well, don't go to Mobile, Alabama," he said, starting to laugh.

My second step was a little more hurried.

"Mobile, Alabama!" he repeated:

So the Wind Won't Blow It All Away
Dust . . . American . . . Dust

The afternoon sun was appropriately lower in the sky and the wind was beginning to die down and there was an advanced feeling of evening approaching with its refreshing contents and renewed hope after a long hot summer afternoon.

While I'm a quarter of a mile away, walking back to the pond with a sack of beer bottles over my shoulder, I'll talk about something else that is more interesting than just walking along various well-worn paths and then railroad tracks leading to a final path ending or perhaps beginning at the pond again.

As a child I was very interested when other children died. There was no doubt about it that I was a morbid kid and when other children died, it always fanned the flames of my forensic curiosity.

Later, in February of 1948, this curiosity would become a personal reality and engulf and turn my life upside down and inside out like *Alice in Wonderland* taking place in a cemetery with the white rabbit as an undertaker and Alice wearing a grave-eaten shroud to play her games in.

But in my life before that was to happen, I was fascinated by dead children and the aftermath of their passing. I think it all perhaps began in 1940 when we moved into an apartment that was annexed to a funeral parlor.

The apartment had once been a functioning part of the mortuary. I don't know exactly what part, but the undertaker to get a little extra cash had changed the former dead space of his funeral parlor into an apartment where we lived for a few months in the late spring of 1940.

I used to get up in the mornings and watch the

funerals out the window. I had to stand on a chair because I was five years old and I wanted a good view.

I seem to remember they held some funerals early in the morning because everybody would still be asleep in the apartment and I would be wearing my pajamas.

To get at the funerals I had to roll up a window shade that was particularly difficult for my dexterity to handle, but somehow I managed it and then pulled a chair over and stood on top of it and watched the funerals.

We moved into the apartment late one afternoon and the next morning while everybody was still asleep, I got up and wandered into the front room. I looked sleepily under the window shade and there was my first funeral as big as death.

The hearse was parked maybe thirty feet away. Can you imagine how big that hearse seemed? That's very close for a hearse to be to a five-year-old. It seemed to me to be the size of a movie that for some very strange reason they had painted black.

That's when I first went and got the chair and pulled the window shade up after quite a struggle and moved the chair into a very good funeral-viewing position and climbed on top of it.

I did this all very quietly because I didn't want to wake anybody up in the house. Adults always like to disrupt what kids are doing, no matter what it is except if it's something the kid doesn't like. If the kid doesn't like it, the adults will let him keep on doing it forever, but if the kid likes it . . .

The hearse was filled with flowers.

There were so many flowers in the hearse that ever since then flowers have always made me feel uneasy. I like flowers but sometimes I feel uncomfortable being in their presence. I've never let it get out of control, but I've had it ever since that morning in 1940 when I watched my first funeral.

For a while the hearse and all its flowers were just standing there alone except for two men dressed in black who seemed not to be in a hurry, just waiting. They could almost have been flowers themselves: some kind of black daffodils.

One of them was smoking a cigarette. He had smoked it down so short that it looked as if the butt were going to set his hand on fire. The other one kept stroking a long very black moustache that looked as if it had jumped off the hearse and right onto his face, but it didn't seem to bother him.

You probably want to know how I knew I was watching a funeral if I was only five years old and I had never seen this sort of thing before and nobody had told me about such goings on. The answer to this is very simple: I saw one in the movies, just a week before and figured it out for myself.

After a while the two men who were waiting beside the hearse went into the funeral parlor and then people started coming out. The people were all very somber and moved appropriately. They seemed to be in slow motion. Though I was close to them, standing on my chair, it was difficult to hear what they were say-ing.

This was becoming very interesting.

I could hardly wait to see what would happen next.

The two men in black came back out with some other men carrying the coffin. They put it in the back of the hearse. Actually, they had to sort of stuff it in because of all the flowers, but somehow they managed it and the two men got into the front seat where the living travelled.

The mourners walked very *s l o w l y* and started getting into parked cars. The cars all had one-word signs on their windshields, but I didn't know what the word said. It would be years before I figured it out.

Pretty soon everybody was gone and the street was very quiet in the wake of their departure. The first thing I heard after they were gone was a bird singing just outside the window.

I got down from the chair and went back to my bed. I lay there staring at the ceiling and digesting what I had just seen. I stayed in bed until everybody else woke up.

When I heard them moving around in the kitchen,

I got up and joined them. They were still sleepy and making some coffee to begin the war of another day.

They asked me if I'd had a good night's sleep.

For an unknown reason I pondered their question, which really didn't even need a reply. I mean, I could have said any little thing and that would have been OK, but I stood there, thinking hard about it.

They continued what they were already doing and immediately forgot that they had asked me something. People aren't really interested for any length of time if a five-year-old had a good night's sleep, and that's what was happening to me.

"Yes, I did," I finally said.

"Did what?" they asked.

"Had a good night's sleep."

"Oh," they said, looking at me curiously because they had forgotten what they had asked me. Adults are always doing that with children.

Anyway, I got up early and watched the funerals after that. There of course wasn't a funeral every morning and I was disappointed when there wasn't one. I went back to bed and hoped that there would be a funeral the next morning.

There were other funerals going on during the day but I didn't care about them very much.

I was strictly a morning funeral child.

For the first two weeks I did that, everybody stayed asleep in the apartment. Then one morning somebody got up early and found me standing on a chair in the front room, with my pajamas on, looking out the window at a funeral.

They came up quietly behind me and looked at what I was watching with total attention, so much so that I didn't even hear them come up.

I must have been a very strange sight.

"What are you doing?" they asked, but they could see what I was doing, so in a way, it was a wasted question.

"Looking out the window," I said.

"Looking out the window at a funeral. You're a weird kid."

I have to agree that observation was right on the money.

They said that they wanted to have a serious conversation with me later on, but they forgot about it and so the serious conversation never took place.

The undertaker had a wife and a little daughter. They lived in the funeral parlor along with the dead people. The daughter was a year older than I. She was six and had very cold hands. I guess living in a funeral parlor gave a person cold hands.

I wondered what her life was like in there with dead people coming and going like somber wind. When we played we always played outside. I didn't ask her if she wanted to come into my house and play because I was afraid she would ask me to come and play in her house.

Once I asked her if she was ever afraid of having dead people around the house.

"Why should I?" she said. "They're dead. They can't hurt anybody."

That was one way of looking at it, but it was not mine.

I also once asked if she ever listened to *Inner Sanctum*. I thought it would be very terrifying to listen to *Inner Sanctum* in a funeral parlor. It would be one of the worst experiences a person could ever have because listening to *Inner Sanctum* was scary enough but inside a funeral parlor! How could you stop from screaming or ever get to sleep again.

"Sure," she said. "But my favorite program is *Grand Central Station*. I like the sound of the trains and the people coming and going. They have interesting stories."

"What about *Inner Sanctum*?" I said, returning to the subject of *Inner Sanctum* which was the most important thing on my mind. At a time like this who wanted to hear about *Grand Central Station*?

"*Inner Sanctum* is . . ." she said, pausing, ". . . corny."

CORNY! *INNER SANCTUM.* CORNY!

I was stunned.

"Corny," she repeated, almost whispering it to get a certain dramatic effect.

If *Inner Sanctum* was corny, then how in the hell did she get such cold hands. Where did they come from? A Cracker Jack box? So when I played with her, I always avoided games that required hand holding.

She had long blond hair, but her hair wasn't cold, only her hands were cold and I treated them like the plague. Once she wanted to play ring-around-the-rosy, just the two of us, holding hands. I told her my mother was sick and I had to go get her a glass of water.

"I didn't know your mother was sick," she said. "You didn't mention it until now. How come?" The undertaker's daughter was too smart for her own good.

I was hard pressed for a reply.

If my mother had really been sick, that's the kind of thing kids tell each other right off the bat. A sick mother is a newsworthy topic. I kept thinking as hard as I could. Meanwhile, avoiding her cold hands by putting my hands safely in my pockets and taking a couple of steps backwards toward my house.

But I couldn't think of a God-damn thing to say.

I just stood there like an idiot with an imaginary sick mother who didn't need tending to.

"I've got to get her a glass of water," I finally said, desperately and ran into the house.

Someday I would be six years old, too, and be able to come up with fast questions, too.

"What are you doing in here?" my mother said when I came into the house. "It's a beautiful day. Go outside and play."

"I have to go to the toilet," I said.

"Oh," she said, rapidly losing her interest in me. "Well, go to the toilet and then go back outside and play. I don't want to see you in here. It's too nice a day."

I had no plans to stay inside. It was only a last ditch stand to keep away from the hands of the undertaker's daughter. I started toward a meaningless and unneeded pee-pee when there was a knock at the door.

My mother went to answer it.

Though I hadn't the slightest idea who was there, I knew that somehow it did not bring good tidings.

My mother opened the door.

I was sort of half-hidden on my way back to the toilet, watching my mother answer the door. Perhaps, I only thought I was hidden. I may have just been standing there without any attempt at camouflage.

It was the undertaker's wife.

She was surprised to see my mother standing there, looking so healthy.

"My daughter told me that you were sick," she said. "And I came over to ask if I could help out any."

"That's nice of you," my mother said. "But I'm not sick." I knew that my mother looked puzzled, though I could not see her face.

The undertaker's wife was looking directly at me, standing somewhere behind my mother, trying to be hidden. The expression on her face did not make me feel comfortable.

"My daughter told me that your son told her that you were sick, so I came right over. Obviously, you're not sick. I'm sorry to disturb you."

The undertaker's wife took a couple of steps backwards.

"I appreciate your coming over, but I'm not sick. Would you like some coffee?" my mother said.

"Oh, no," the undertaker's wife said. "I've got something on the stove."

Though suddenly I felt like a sinking ship, I still had enough curiosity to wonder what the undertaker's wife was cooking in the funeral parlor.

I had never really thought about them eating in there before, but of course they had to eat, and to eat you need to cook and she cooked breakfast, lunch and dinner in a place where dead people were briefly stored before something permanent was worked out for them.

I wondered how bacon and eggs tasted in a funeral parlor. I wondered how difficult it would be to eat ice cream in there. I didn't think there would be a big problem with it melting, even if it were a hot day.

"Well, I'm sorry that you came over for nothing," my mother said. "I'll have to get to the bottom of this."

She did.

I was already there waiting for her.

All she had to do was turn around.

The next morning for my funeral-viewing pleasure, they held the funeral for a dead child. I was up bright and early and standing on my chair.

The funeral unfolded like the petals of a flower whose ultimate blossom was a small coffin coming out the door of the funeral parlor and on its way to the hearse and that final place where the hearse would take it and come back empty and the child wouldn't need its toys any more.

I of course had no idea that it was the funeral for a child until they brought the little coffin out; except for that one occasion I never knew who was being buried. I had no way of knowing if it was a man or a woman or a young person or an old person or just a person inbetween who had gotten unlucky.

The coffins were always closed and I did not know the specific nature of their contents. All I knew was that somebody dead was inside.

So I was stunned when the little coffin came out. It only needed two pallbearers. They carried the coffin as if it were a feather of death. I suddenly felt very uncomfortable because the coffin was my size. I didn't know if there was a dead little girl or a dead little boy inside. I know that this may sound horrible, but I half-wished that there was a dead little girl inside because a dead little boy was too close to home for me.

When the full impact of the child's funeral had modified itself into an unwholesome curiosity and interest in detail, I looked around for child mourners that were my age and the size of the coffin. There were none. There was not a single child.

That seemed very strange to me. Didn't the kid have any friends? God, what a poor kid, I thought, not a single friend. I could imagine the kid with no one to play with. I shuddered twice: once because the kid was dead and a second time because the kid was friendless.

There were about thirty people out there watching the small flower-bedecked coffin on its brief journey to the hearse which took care of the child ever having the possibility of a friend.

I was suddenly very sad because the child had never gotten to play hide-and-go-seek or kick-the-can or statues. The child had only played games that you play by yourself like playing with its dolls or the little boxed games that have animal heads you hold in your hands with two empty holes where the eyes should be and you roll two little silver balls around and around until you think you're going to go crazy before you give the animal some eyes or perhaps the child went on solitary tricycle rides past other children playing together who would have nothing to do with this dead kid.

I didn't know what fate was back, then, but if I had known I would not have wanted that kid's fate, not for all the tea in China, which was something people said all the time in 1940, but you don't hear it very much in 1979.

If you were to say, "Not for all the tea in China," right now, it would attract a lifted eyebrow, but back then it meant something. You were communicating.

I was really disturbed by the total lack of child mourners. I made a vow that I would be nicer to people, especially kids. I would start off that very day dedicating my energy to the gathering of many new friends and the instant renewal and replenishing of old friendships.

Under no conditions did I want to end up like that poor hapless child with nobody but adults at its funeral. Today I would be as friendly as I could with the undertaker's daughter.

I would even . . . I would even touch her hands. The worst thing in the world would be if I were to die and she wouldn't come to my funeral. That would be the final blow. Too bad it wasn't winter, so I could wear mittens. No, I shouldn't think like that. I promised myself that I would somehow hold her hands, so that she would come to my funeral.

They put the little coffin in the back of the hearse and placed around it wreaths and bouquets of flowers that seemed to swallow it whole. If you were alive and playing hide-and-go-seek, the back of that hearse would be a good place to hide. No one could find you in all those flowers.

WHERE WAS THE UNDERTAKER'S DAUGHTER? suddenly hit my mind like the first whack of a spanking. She wasn't at the funeral, but then I thought she obviously hadn't been a friend of the dead kid or she would be out there in a tiny black dress, dabbing a moon-white handkerchief to her eyes.

After the hearse had driven off and all the mourners had followed in its shadow like the morbid tail of a black kite, I thought some more about the undertaker's daughter and the child just on its way now to the cemetery where it would stay after everybody else came back. I didn't know the full dimensions of forever, but I knew that it was longer than waiting for Christmas to come.

I knew that forever was longer than 39 shopping days until Christmas.

Yesterday when I was playing with the undertaker's daughter and eventually fled the touching of her hands, that dead child must have already been in the funeral parlor getting ready for today. While we were playing outside, they could have been taking the blood out of that child and replacing it with embalming fluid.

I wondered if the undertaker's daughter had seen the dead child when it came in, and if the dead child had been a girl, she'd thought: *Well, here's somebody I'll never play dolls with* or she already knew that the child had no friends and so she didn't think about playing with her at all.

That's an awful thought, isn't it? but that's what I thought about while still standing on my chair perch staring at the sudden emptiness that had once been the funeral of a child.

I wondered why the undertaker's daughter wasn't afraid of dead people and then I thought somebody who prefers *Grand Central Station* to *Inner Sanctum* was capable of anything.

When I heard somebody stirring in the house a little later on, I got off my chair and pulled the window shade down. I put the chair back where it belonged. I didn't want anybody today criticizing my interest in funerals.

I was going back to bed and think all over again what I had seen today, but when I thought about that dead child lying in a coffin hidden by flowers and on its way to the cemetery, going back to bed did not seem like a good idea at all. I decided to spend as much time as possible the rest of the day standing on my feet, just to keep in practice.

A few months later, we moved and I never saw the undertaker's daughter again. She probably grew up, went to college and got married, then kids, etc. Maybe her hands even got warm.

I should probably think about her more often than I do. Actually, this is one of the few times that I have thought about her in years, maybe even longer.

The whole time that I lived beside the funeral parlor and watched the funerals like garden parties where I was always the uninvited guest seems to me now like a dream.

The undertaker's daughter has become a character in that dream. Did I really stand on a chair in my pajamas and watch funerals for pleasure? Did we really live in an apartment that had once been an active part of a mortuary? Did I dream the undertaker's daughter and her hands which were like white daisies growing on top of Mount Everest? Did I really hide from them until one day I saw the funeral of a dead child who had no friends and, not wanting to end up that way, courted her hands as if they had the desirability of warm mittens on a freezing winter day?

Yes, and I remember:

Finished with the undertaker's daughter and still carrying my sack of beer bottles, I'm halfway to the pond now where the people will arrive soon and start taking their furniture off the truck and setting up their highly original house beside the pond.

Childhood thoughts of early death continue to unravel in my mind, perhaps unpeel is a better and more accurate way of looking at it, like peeling an onion into a smaller and smaller circle with tears growing in my eyes until the onion is no more, all peeled away and I stop crying.

About five years after I left the dream-like address of an apartment beside a funeral parlor, I was living someplace else. World War II wasn't quite over. It was hanging on by the skin of its teeth, but you could feel that the end was very near.

For all practical purposes the War was over except that people were still getting killed every day and they would continue to get killed every day until the War was actually over.

The days were running out for the Japanese Empire as the days of my childhood were running out, and every step I took was a step that brought me nearer to that February 17th, 1948, orchard where my childhood would fall apart just like some old Roman ruins of a childhood, so we just sat around: the Japanese Empire and my childhood listening to each other breathing away the end.

The new place where I was living was two addresses away from, and approaching, the pond. The next address would take me a hundred miles to live in a dingy yellow apartment where the most important and expensive tube in the radio burnt out and we were too poor to afford another one, so at night our little Welfare family just sat around and looked at one another until it was time to go to bed.

There are no words to describe how important a radio was in those days.

The next address after the radioless apartment would be the auto court and out the front door of the cabin on the way to my beloved pond and its fishing furniture.

Meanwhile: Let's go back the two addresses and I'll tell a story of dead toys and silence. The new someplace I was living looked like an old house that rented for twenty-five dollars a month. Thank you, Welfare! We lived there long enough for the seasons to come and go once.

There were walnut trees in the front yard. There were apple and cherry trees in the back yard, which also contained a large building that was part garage, storage place and woodshed.

We didn't need the garage because we were too poor to own a car, but we were rich enough to use the woodshed. My mother cooked on a wood stove and we used wood to heat the house.

I always hated to chop wood.

The place also had a lot of lawn that needed to be mowed and I always hated to do that, too. In the spring we put in a garden, which I worked at with great hesitation. I was inbetween stepfathers at the time, so my mother did most of the work in the garden.

Let's face it: I was a kid who didn't like to do his chores. I tried to keep as much space between me and work as I could. I don't think I was lazy because I did a lot of other things, but they were always the things that I wanted to do, and I tried not to compromise my values.

I always liked old people, so I spent as much time with them as I could. They fascinated me like spiders, which I had a great deal of affection toward also. I could spend an hour with a spider web and be quite contented, but show me some weeds that needed pulling from the garden and I would exit a long large sigh like a billboard of desperation.

Late in the spring of 1945, a new kid moved into the house next door to "ours." He was older than me and really a good kid. He was the kind of kid other kids looked up to and wanted to be friends with.

I think he was twelve and he was a boy scout and

shortly after moving in next door, he got a paper route because he had a bicycle and was ambitious. He was preparing himself for a positive life of accomplishment.

The bicycle looked brand-new even though it was prewar because he took such good care of it. I was not to have a bicycle until a couple of years later and my bicycle always looked shitty because I didn't care about its appearance. My bicycle started off by being blue but afterwhile it was so dirty that you couldn't tell what color it was and most people probably didn't care to begin with. The color of a kid's bicycle would not rank very high if you were to make a list of things people are interested in.

The boy next door always kept his clothes neat. With my clothes, half-the-time you didn't know if I was putting them on or taking them off. They were somewhere in the middle of coming and going simultaneously.

His parents really loved him.

I could tell by the way they talked to him.

My mother just barely tolerated my existence. She could take me or leave me. Once in a while she would go through short periods of intense affection toward me. It would always make me quite nervous and I was glad when she went back to just tolerating my existence.

You must pardon this cartoon-like Oedipus interlude because my relationship with my mother is not the point of this story.

The boy, being older than I, created the relationship between us. Older kids define the role younger kids act in their friendships.

He became a sort of abstract older brother to me. He was always kind and understanding to me, but he created the distance between us. I would like to have seen him a couple of times a day, but we saw each other three or four times a week. This was his choosing. He controlled the amount of time we shared.

I didn't feel bad about it except that sometimes I wished I were older. Maybe that would have made a difference, probably not. Our interests were not that similar. He was interested in hard work and the satisfaction and products gained from it.

I liked to look at spider webs and listen to old people talk about the days when Teddy Roosevelt was President and watching members of the Grand Army of the Republic marching down the street in ever decreasing numbers toward the Twentieth Century.

You don't get the same material success from listening to old people talk as you do from having a paper route. I was always a good listener.

The boy kept his bicycle on the front porch if there was any chance of it raining but if the weather was good, he parked it under the long, drooping branches of a Queen Anne cherry tree.

The day the boy was killed in an automobile accident, the bicycle was parked under the cherry tree. It rained that same night. If he'd still been alive, he would have taken the bicycle and put it on the front porch. His parents were in the accident but they had not even suffered a scratch.

They came home by themselves just about twilight.

They were driving the same car the boy had been killed in that afternoon. It had been hardly damaged at all in the accident. The chances of anyone being killed in that accident were easily 1 in a 1,000,000. It was the type of accident that it's even rare to get injured in.

The boy was dead.

His parents got out of the car.

The entire neighborhood was watching them. Everybody knew what had happened because it was on the radio.

Some people looked out furtively from behind curtains and others just walked out on the front porch and stood there gawking.

I was in the branches of an apple tree when they drove up. I was about twenty feet above the ground. I had climbed the tree because I didn't know what else to do. I was sitting up there thinking about the boy being dead. Earlier I had gone into the woodshed and cried for a long time. I sat on the chopping block and cried my eyes out.

I wasn't crying any more when they drove up and got out of their car. Accidentally concealed, I was very close to them and I knew that they couldn't see me. I was in a deep green section of the tree that was like a room and a window formed in the leaves and I looked through the window at them getting out of the car.

She got out first.

Then he got out.

She closed her door but he didn't close his.

He stood there beside the open door of the car, not moving.

They just stood on opposite sides of the car, staring at their house. They didn't say anything and then he slowly closed his car door and they went into the house.

They turned on one light in the front room. They left the rest of the house dark. One of our neighbors, a very kindly woman, left her house across the street and came over and knocked on their front door.

They were very slow to answer.

"Can I help?" the woman said.

"No," the boy's mother said.

"I don't know what to say," the woman said.

"I know," the boy's mother said.

"If you need any help, I'm right across the street," the woman said.

"Thank you," the boy's mother said. "I think we'll just get some sleep. We're tired."

Everybody in the neighborhood had been watching this. Nobody else came over that night. A few moments later the one light in the house went out.

I climbed very slowly down from the apple tree.

It rained that night.

The bicycle got wet.

The next morning the boy's father took the wet bicycle from underneath the long fruit-lush branches of the Queen Anne cherry tree and put it in the house.

They moved at the end of the month.

The neighbors watched silently. Nobody came over to say good-bye, not even the woman who had visited them the night their son had been killed. I looked over at her house but she wasn't watching. She was nowhere in sight.

When they moved, they didn't have the bicycle. It was not loaded on the moving van. I guess they must have gotten rid of it when I wasn't looking.

The house was dark and vacant for what seemed like an eternity, but it was only a week. The new tenants were very cheerful and friendly. They were too cheerful and friendly. They held weekend beer parties and the driveway and the parking in front of their house overflowed with cars like a waterfall of pre-World War II metal.

The cars had the uneasiness of a dirty joke that is not funny, but perhaps it was only my imagination. Why shouldn't people have a good time? The War was almost over. We were tired of it. Sometimes I would climb up in the apple tree and quietly weep:

So the Wind Won't Blow It All Away
Dust . . . American . . . Dust

The last stop on the way to the pond was that yellow dingy Welfare apartment where the most expensive tube in the radio burnt out, leaving us with silent nights far distant from Christmas carols.

The apartment also had a gas stove in the kitchen.

We were all terrified of gas, especially my mother. She had a mind like a gray library filled with gas-leak death stories.

It was a stove that you had to light with a match and we were scared to death of it. Every meal was a nightmare with my mother having to build up her courage to cook. We usually had dinner around six, but with that gas stove, dinner arrived on the table as late as midnight.

Every meal was an exhausting experience that left

us all completely drained right down to the bone where our marrow turned to dust caught in the vise of gas.

The worst it ever got was when my mother couldn't emotionally handle cooking any more and for one week, we had cornflakes for breakfast and the rest of the time we ate sandwiches.

We of course had no money and this was where Welfare had stashed us away. We lived there for three months and the radio was broken the entire time, so we just sat around in silence, waiting for the gas to get us.

My mother would wake up three or four times every night and check the stove for gas leaks. I was going to school at the time and I would ask the other kids what was happening on the radio.

They could hardly believe that I was not listening to the radio every night. It was inconceivable to them that somebody didn't have a radio.

Sometimes in the evening I would sit in front of our broken radio and pretend that I was listening to my favorite programs. My mother would pretend to read the *Reader's Digest,* but I knew that she really wasn't reading the magazine. She was just sitting there, listening for a gas leak.

The walls of the apartment were like dingy yellow roses and that's perhaps another reason why I disliked that apartment so much. It reminded me of all the funeral flowers that I had seen five years ago or was it twenty years ago? before I was even born.

The War seemed to have gone on forever, so that's why 1940 seemed such an incredible distance away, but when I stared at those walls long enough 1940 came closer and closer, and I could see the funerals moving in slow motion like old people waltzing in a movie.

I had very few friends because I was so exhausted all the time from the fear of dying by gas that it was very difficult for me to concentrate on anything or have the interest in trying to make friends.

So for that period of time, I just looked at other kids after I asked them what was on the radio. That was about the best I could do. Once I was awakened by the sound of my mother crying. I got out of bed. The apartment was dark except for a light shining under the bathroom door. She was in there crying. When she wasn't crying, she was just sitting in there repeating over and over again: "Gas, gas, gas, gas." Then she would start crying again.

I went back to bed and wondered if I should cry. I thought about it for a long time, and decided not to. My mother was crying enough for both of us.

While we were living in that apartment, a child died in the neighborhood. She was about eight years old and one of three sisters who lived half-a-block away in a large house that had a yard cluttered with an enormous amount of toys. There were enough toys in their yard for an armada of children.

I'll bet there were at least nine balls in that yard, along with a convoy of tricycles and scooters. There were about ten Christmas trees of broken toys or toys deeply in trouble and on their way to being broken. It was only a matter of time and time was running out for them.

I wondered how those girls avoided serious injury from falling over their toys and breaking their necks or cutting their heads off with broken toys.

But everything went along smoothly until one of the girls died. Strangely enough, she did not die from a toy-related injury. She died of pneumonia which was always an ominous and frightening disease to me. Whenever I heard the word pneumonia, my ears perked up. To me it sounded like an awful way to die. I didn't want my lungs to slowly fill up with water and then to die by myself, drowning by means of myself, not in a river or a lake but in me drowning. I always had a feeling that you died from pneumonia when somebody was out of the room. You'd cry for help, but they wouldn't be there and when they came back, you'd be gone: drowned!

Whenever I heard of someone dying of pneumonia, young or old, I was obviously agitated. If I ever got pneumonia, I wanted whoever was there to tie a very long string on my finger and fasten the other end of the string to their finger and when they left the room if I felt I was dying, I could pull on the string and they'd come back.

I wouldn't die alone if there was a long piece of string between us.

Anyway, she died of pneumonia and Thank God, it wasn't me. When I heard she had died of pneumonia, I *really* said my prayers that night. I promised to be so good that I would make a saint seem like a sack of coal.

The day after she was buried all the toys in the front yard of their house disappeared and were very slowly replaced with totally different toys, but for a while that front yard looked like a toyless desert. I wondered why this had happened and finally I heard the story.

Her living sisters were afraid of their own toys because they didn't know what toys had belonged to the dead girl and they didn't want to play with the toys of somebody who was dead. They had played so freely and intensely that they could not separate the toys of the living from the toys of the dead.

Nothing their parents said could change their minds, so it was decided to give all the toys away to the Salvation Army where they would be changed into Christmas presents for the unsuspecting.

All the sisters had blond hair that was yellow like the apartment we lived in. Whenever I see a blond woman, I almost always think of that long-ago apartment that always teetered on the edge of either poisoning or blowing us up.

I wonder why I don't talk about my own sisters.

I guess this story is not about them.

Once my mother had a date with a man who was an unemployed roofer. I stayed at home and waited out her date. I read the *Reader's Digest* that she pretended to read. It had nothing to do with my life. There wasn't a single thing in there that reminded me of my existence.

I guess some people lived like the *Reader's Digest*, but I hadn't met any and at that time it seemed doubtful that I ever would.

My mother's date turned out to be quite short.

She came home around ten, early.

I heard the unemployed roofer's truck pull up outside. Maybe it helped being a roofer if you were four feet eleven, but it hadn't helped him because he didn't have a job. I knew that something was wrong because my mother slammed the truck door.

"Aren't you asleep yet?" she said when she came angrily in.

I tried to get on her good side, so I told her that I had been reading the *Reader's Digest*. I don't know why I thought that would put me in her good graces.

I was a strange kid.

I guess you could safely add *very*.

My mother just looked at me when I told her I had
been reading the *Reader's Digest.* It had not worked. I
decided that it was time to go to bed and went very
quickly there.

A few moments later I could hear my mother in
the front room, repeating over and over again, in a
hissing whisper: *"Gas, gas, gas, gas."*

Looking back at it now, here in the forty-fourth
year of life, my mother was the only leak in that apartment.

The next morning I got out of bed and put my
clothes on very quietly, like a mouse putting on a Klee-
nex, and went over to the house where the little girl
used to live before she died of pneumonia.

There were no toys in the front yard.

This was a couple of days after all the toys had
been removed and given away at the vehement re-
quest of her very living sisters.

I stared at their absence.

I stared at their silence:

So the Wind Won't Blow It All Away
Dust . . . American . . . Dust

The sun had reversed its boredom and now had
grown interesting as it began its descent which would

soon open the beginning doors of night and the wind had died down making the pond as still and quiet as sleeping glass.

I had just reached my fishing dock and put down the gunnysack of beer bottles when I heard their truck coming down the road on the other side of the pond.

Ah, now my evening would really begin.

I got my fishing pole and carried it in one hand, the gunnysack of beer bottles slung over my shoulder with the other hand, and started on around the pond, which was about 3/4's of a mile in circumference.

I think the origin of the pond had been to get dirt to build the overpass, so that the trains could run under it. Once this pond had been just another field but now it was an overpass and a place for me to fish and an open living room for furniture.

I walked around the pond in the opposite direction from the route I had taken to the sawmill night watchman's gold mine of beer bottles.

There was a finger of water that branched off the pond that I had to walk around. The finger was forty yards long and about twenty yards wide. The water wasn't very deep in the finger and it was a great place for bluegills to spawn. The fishing was very good there, but you had to have some courage to fish that watery index off the pond because a strange old man had built a shack there.

All the kids I knew were afraid to fish there because they were afraid of the old man. He had long white hair like General Custer in an old folks home, denied the dignity and ceremony of meeting a few thousand Indians at the Little Big Horn.

He also had a long white beard that had a yellowish streak down the center caused by a constant overflow of chewing tobacco cascading out of his mouth.

He was the type of old man who looked as if he ate little children, but I had absolutely no fear of him. I met him the first time I was taken to the pond by a brand-new friend who asked me if I wanted to go fishing. I noticed a shack on the little finger-like bay off the pond.

I saw a man standing in front of it.

He was in the distance a ways, so I couldn't figure him out.

He had built a very sturdy little dock on the bay and he had a small boat tied up to it. He walked over from the shack to the dock and stood there looking at the water for a few moments. He didn't look up.

"Who's that?" I asked.

"A crazy old man," my new friend said. "Don't go over there. He hates kids. He hates everybody. He's got a big knife. It's as big as a sword. It looks like it's got rust on it, but it's really dried blood from kids.

"The fishing is really good, but no one goes over there. If that old man caught you, I don't know what would happen to you," he said.

"I'll be back in a minute," I said.

That little statement got me quite a reputation for being very brave and also crazy. I didn't mind the reputation from either end you looked at it. The distinction made me a sort of cockeyed hero, but that was all to end in the orchard that coming February.

The old man was very surprised when I walked up to him in a very friendly and relaxed style and said, "Hello." He was so surprised that he answered like the flipside of a well-mannered coin: "Hello."

"How's fishing?" I said.

"Good," he said. "But I don't fish."

I looked down into the water and it was filled with spawning bluegills. The bottom of the pond was a ballet choreographed by courting bluegills. There were hundreds of bluegills there. I had never seen so many fish before.

I was really excited.

"Do you live here?" I asked, knowing of course that he lived there, but also knowing that it was important for him to say so because it would make him feel more comfortable, at ease to establish his own territory thus to make me a young, non-threatening guest.

"Yes," he said. "I've been living here since the Depression."

When he said: Since the Depression, I knew everything was going to be OK.

The old man had built a shack out of packing

crates. It was maybe eight by six feet and had a stove-
pipe coming out the side. It was summer and the
screen door was closed to keep the mosquitoes out.
I couldn't see into the shack because the way the
screen door filtered, obscured the fading light of almost sundown.

He had a small table beside the shack with a bench
that was a part of it. The table was made out of packing-crate wood and scrap lumber.

Everything was very clean and neat around the
shack.

He had a small patch of corn, maybe forty stalks,
and he was growing some potatoes and some green
peas. There were also about a dozen tomato plants
that were covered with small delicious-looking tomatoes.

He had built a small washbasin that was just a
bucket stuck through a hole cut into a shelf that was
nailed to the shack. When he wanted to wash, he just
took the bucket from the hole in the shelf and got
some water from the pond.

The shack had a flat tarpaper roof.

I talked to the old man for a few moments.

I think he was impressed by the fact that I wasn't
afraid of him. Also, old people just tended to like me.
I had a quality that appealed to them. Maybe they liked
me because I was interested in them and listened to
what they had to say. It could have been that simple.

I asked the old man if I could come back and visit him sometime. He responded by walking over and picking a really beautiful tomato and giving it to me.

"Thank you," I said, starting to take a bite out of the tomato.

"Wait, before you do that," he said, walking over to the shack and opening the screen door. I got a brief glimpse at the interior of his dwelling. All of his furniture seemed to be variations on packing-crate themes.

He came back out of the shack with the largest pepper shaker I had ever seen. "Tomatoes taste best with pepper on them," he said, offering me the shaker.

"You're not afraid that it's poison, are you?" he said.

"No," I said, putting some pepper on my tomato.

"You can come back anytime you want," he replied.

I took a bite out of the tomato.

"What do you think of tomato with pepper on it?" he said.

I've been eating it that way ever since.

He went and got himself a tomato.

Pretty soon tomato juice was mixed in with tobacco juice in his beard, which began to look like a poorman's rainbow.

When I got back to where I had left my new friend, he was gone. He came over to the cabin at the auto court that evening to see if I was still alive. He was very surprised when I answered the door.

"Jesus Christ!" he said. "You're still alive."

Then he asked me if I had seen the sword covered with all the dried blood of thousands of pond-slaughtered kids whose bones were buried under his shack like millions of loose toothpicks.

"It's not a sword," I said. "It's a huge pepper shaker."

The kid didn't understand that, but he was very impressed anyway with what I had done.

I returned to visit the old man many times after that and to take apart and put back together his life like a huge puzzle in my mind, examining very carefully each piece and the totality of their effect.

The old man had been in World War I and was gassed by the Germans. Needless to say, when he mentioned the word gas, I was instantly fascinated and then he told me that it wasn't automobile gas or cooking gas, but poison gas and the Germans were sons-of-bitches for doing that to him because now he had only one lung and he couldn't do very much with his life except live here by the pond until one day the sheriff would come and tell him to move on and he'd have to find another pond somewhere.

The old man lived off a small pension that he got from The Government because he'd lost a lung in World War I. Other than this fact I didn't know anything else about him. He never talked about his family or ever being married or current and long-ago friends. I didn't know where he was born or anything about him. In his little packing-crate shack there were no personal items that gave a single clue to his past.

The old man had only things that he could use: clothing, cooking utensils, dishes and silverware, jars for storing food and some tools. He didn't have anything else.

He didn't have any old letters or a catfish postcard exploiting the possibilities of photography. He had made all his own furniture except for his stove out of packing crates and scraps of odd lumber.

The inside of his shack was so simple and honest that it was almost like a glorified kids playhouse. He was living the kind of hermit life kids dream about living. He was an ancient breathing statue of Huckleberry Finn.

The old man measured carefully every movement that he made. He didn't ever waste a single gesture. Maybe it was only having one lung that made him so premeditated. I don't think he even blinked without first thinking about whether or not it was necessary.

Sometimes for reasons that were completely unknown to me I wished that he had a calendar. I had a feeling that he didn't know what day, month or year it was. I thought that he should at least know what year it was.

What was wrong with that?

It wouldn't hurt him to know that it was 1947.

The two things that he took the most pleasure in and that were the only incongruity in the personal history that he acted out at the end of a tiny bay on a small obscure pond were his dock and his boat.

Perhaps once he had something to do with the sea.

But I would never find out because he never spoke of it.

The dock was a thing of beauty to behold. It was perfectly constructed like a harpsichord and polished like a silver plate. It was about nine feet long and a yard wide. The pilings were finely carved timbers. Each one of them looked as if it had taken a year to carve. There were six of them. That means he must have started work on them in 1941, or so it seemed to me when I looked at them.

The dock itself was three ten-inch planks that were about two inches thick. They were also hand-carved and then finely polished until a king could have eaten off them. It would have been interesting to watch a king eat directly off a dock.

I would imagine that each plank took perhaps two years' carving and polishing, so that's six more years and now the construction of the dock reaches back to 1935, when I was born.

Maybe he started it on the day I was born.

Once I asked him again how long he had lived beside the pond and he was very hard-pressed to give me an exact time. "I guess it's been a long time. Since the Depression," he said, finally and somehow confirming my idea that he had started the dock on the day I was born.

Then I asked him when he had started working on the dock.

After an equally long pause, he said, "About the same time."

Yup, that confirmed it!

Every time I saw the dock after that, I felt good and considered it an unknown birthday present from him to me, though I never mentioned this to him.

Now: I'll talk about the boat.

It was like a little brother to the dock. It was totally handmade from an elegant wood that was varnished to a beautiful sheen like finely diluted sunlight. It was a very small boat. Maybe 4 1/2 feet long and was, as I said earlier, a kid brother to the dock.

Sometimes I felt as if the old man was too big for such a small boat, but that was only a theoretical curiosity because I never once saw him in the boat.

It was always tied carefully, meticulously up to the dock. So what he had created was a holograph of boating which was not intended to actually move. It was just something to look at that pleased him very much and pleased me also because I thought it was another unknown birthday present from him to me.

In the background of the dock and the boat was a packing crate shack and a small patch of corn, green peas and tomatoes.

This was his life and time on earth.

The only vice the old man had was chewing a lot of tobacco. It stained his long white beard like a delicate garden constructed of a million tiny imperceptible daffodils.

Often when I looked at calendars back then, I thought about him lost in the geography of time, but finally not caring. Little did I know that I would end up the same way very soon:

So the Wind Won't Blow It All Away
Dust . . . American . . . Dust

The old man saw me coming a few months later with my fishing pole and my sack of beer bottles. He was sitting on his little packing-crate picnic-table bench, eating supper. His dock and boat were at total rest, total peace a few feet away from him. If he had been listening to some quiet dinner music, it could not have been any more peaceful than his dock and boat.

It looked as if he were eating some variation on the stew theme.

"Hello, there," he said, cheerfully. "Come to catch some of my bluegills?" He did have the best fishing in the pond right there.

"No," I said. "I'm on my way to the other side."

He looked across the metal dish he was eating from to the other side of the pond where the people were still coming down the road in their pickup filled with furniture. It would take them a while to get there because the road was very bad and they always drove extremely carefully because they didn't want to lose any of their furniture.

At one place in the road, there were some miniature Grand Canyon ruts and the people took about five minutes to get through them and every time their truck just barely made it, but they drove the ruts so carefully that not even a lamp fell off.

Those ruts would give me enough time to be at their fishing place when they arrived, so I could watch them take their furniture off the truck from the very beginning piece. The first thing they would take off would be the couch and I would be there watching them.

"They're coming," the old man said around a bite of stew in his mouth. He did a good job of balancing the stew in his mouth, so that I could understand what he was saying.

"Yeah," I said. "They're coming."

"They come every evening this year," he said. "They came only four times last year, and they never came before that. Last year was the first year."

I was very surprised when the old man said last year.

I wondered if he knew last year was 1946.

"When they came last year," he continued. "They didn't bring any furniture with them. Just themselves. That's not a good place for catfish where they set all that stuff up. I wonder why they do that?"

The old man looked away from their approach and took a spoonful of his stew, which starred a lot of potatoes, featured carrots and peas, and from where I was standing, it looked as if a hot dog sliced very thin had a minor role in his stew. Floating in the center of the stew was a big dollop of catsup.

He ate off the ledge of the catsup, working his way to the rim of the metal dish, so the catsup was slowly sinking into the stew like a strange red island in the middle of an equally strange sea.

After the bite, which dashed some stew down his beard like lava coming from a volcano, he returned to watching their approach.

He paused before he said the next thing.

"I've never seen people bring their furniture when they go fishing. I've seen people bring camp stools, but not all their furniture."

When he said this, it was not a form of criticism. It was just a simple observation that led to another bite from the movie on his plate called *The Old Man and the Stew.*

"Maybe they like to be comfortable when they fish," I said.

"I suppose so," he said. "Wouldn't make much sense to bring all that furniture with them fishing if they didn't enjoy it."

Then he stewed up again. This time he took an extraordinarily large bite. The runoff poured into his beard like Krakatoa.

"Well, I got to be on my way," I said, so that I could be waiting for them when they got there. I liked to watch them unload the furniture and set it up from the very beginning. To me it was like watching a fairy tale unfold in front of my very eyes.

You don't see stuff like that very often and I didn't want to miss any of it, not even a single lamp. They had three of them that they set up. They looked just like any other lamp you'd see in a real house except the people had converted them from electricity to kerosene. It must have been interesting watching them do that. I wonder where they got the idea in the first place.

That's something that you just don't think up out of the ordinary.

Most people, I should say all people except them,

just used the regular kerosene lamps you could buy in the store, but that type of thing obviously wasn't for them.

I wonder which one of them mentioned it to the other one first and what the expression on their face was and the next thing they said. I tried to imagine those words, but I couldn't because I wouldn't know what to say.

Would you?

But whatever was said in reply was the correct answer, the right thing and agreed upon and done.

The old man and his stew turned like a page in my life and then they were gone with his final words echoing in my mind as I headed toward the place where I would be there before they arrived and started setting up their furniture.

"If they want to catch catfish," the old man echoed. "They should set up their living room about fifty yards down the pond, right next to that dead tree. That's the best place for catfish in this pond."

"They do all right where they set up their furniture," I answered.

"Well, they'd do better for catfish if they put their living room in front of that dead tree."

What?

I can still hear those last words now a third of a century later, and they still sound just as strange now as they did back then.

"I'll tell them," I promised the old man, but of course I didn't tell them. They liked that place best for their furniture and they caught their share of cat-fish, so who was I to rock the boat?

I also don't think they would have listened to me anyway, and I certainly didn't want to make them angry at me because frankly they were the most inter-esting thing happening in my life.

They were better than any radio programs I heard or movies I saw that summer.

Sometimes I wished there was a set of them like toys that I could take home with me and play with: Carved wooden miniatures of the man and the woman and all their furniture and the truck (it was all right for that to be metal) and a green cloth that was shaped just like the pond with everything on it the way it actu-ally was.

I also wished that I had miniatures of the old man and his shack and his garden and of course the dock and his boat.

What an interesting game that would be.

Sometimes I tried to think of a name for it just before I fell asleep but I never could think of a good name for it and afterwhile it got lost in my dreams be-cause I couldn't keep up with it.

I arrived at the place where their living room would be set up at the pond's edge just about a minute or so before they got there.

While the minute passes before they get here with their furniture, there will be a huge INTERRUPTION like a black wet *Titanic* telegram or a telephone call that sounds like a man with a chain saw cutting up a cemetery at midnight or just the very rude distraction of death itself, the final end of all childhoods including mine which started to dramatically begin its descent when I passed the restaurant that February rainy afternoon in 1948 and should have gone inside and gotten a hamburger and a Coke. I was hungry, too. They would have been a welcome addition to my existence.

There was not a single reason in the world for me to walk past the restaurant and look in the window of the gun shop next door. But I did and the dice were getting ready to be thrown.

There was a beautiful-looking .22 caliber rifle in the window. I had a .22. Looking at that gun made me think about my gun, and when I thought about my gun, I thought about the fact that my gun didn't have any bullets. I had been planning on getting some for the last couple of weeks.

If I had some bullets, I could go out and shoot.

I could go to the junkyard and shoot bottles and cans and any abandoned old thing that looked attractive through my sights or there was an old apple orchard that had rotten apples still clinging to its leafless branches. It was fun to shoot rotten apples. They exploded when a bullet hit them. It was the kind of effect that kids love if they're slightly bloodthirsty for one reason or another and can dump their aggressions on passed-away objects like rotten apples.

I had a friend who liked to shoot apples, too, but he didn't like to go to the junkyard to practice the little decisions of destruction that a .22 rifle can provide a kid. But I couldn't shoot anything one way or another if I didn't have any bullets.

Some bullets . . . . or a burger, a burger . . . . or some bullets . . . . paddled back and forth in my brain like a Ping-Pong ball.

The door to the restaurant opened just then and a satisfied customer came out with a burger-pleased smile on his face. The open door also allowed a gust of burger perfume to escape right into my nose.

I took a step toward the restaurant but then I heard in my mind the sound of a .22 bullet turning a rotten apple into instant rotten apple sauce. It was a lot more dramatic than eating a hamburger. The door to the restaurant closed escorting the smell of cooking hamburgers back inside like an usher.

What was I to do?

I was twelve years old and the decision was as big as the Grand Canyon. I should have gone to neutral territory to think it over instead of just standing right there in the battleground of their beckoning.

I could have gone across the street to a magazine store and looked at comic books while I thought about how seriously I wanted a box of apple-splattering bullets or a delicious hamburger with lots of onions on it.

I could have thought about it while looking at comic books until the owner of the store started giving me the evil eye because obviously I was not a potential comic-book purchaser. I was just a kid hanging out with Superman and Batman while I made up my mind.

Too bad Superman couldn't have told me what to do.

SUPERMAN: Kid, go get a burger.

ME: Yes, sir!

SUPERMAN: And don't forget the onions.

ME: How did you know that I liked onions?

SUPERMAN: If you're faster than a speeding bullet and more powerful than a locomotive and able to leap tall buildings with a single bound, onions aren't that hard.

ME: Yes, sir!

SUPERMAN *(flying away)*: Be kind to your kitten! *(I would have to think that one over because I didn't have a kitten. Anyway, not one that I could remember. Maybe Superman knew something that I didn't know. Of course he did!)*

ME: I promise, Superman!

What did I have to lose?

Yeah, everything would have been different if Superman would have told me to get a hamburger. Instead I walked across the street to the gun shop and bought a box of .22 shells. The hamburger had lost. The sound of instant rotten apple sauce had won.

I have replayed that day over and over again in my mind like the editing of a movie where I am the producer, the director, the editor, scriptwriter, actors, music, and everything.

I have a gigantic motion picture studio in my mind where I have been working constantly on this movie since February 17th, 1948. I have been working on the same movie for 31 years. I believe that this is a record. I don't think I will ever finish it.

I have, more or less, about 3,983,421 hours of film.

But it's too late now.

Whereas I could never find a name for my pond game, I've always had a title for my movie starting with the day I bought the bullets instead of the hamburger. I call my picture *Hamburger Cemetery.*

After I bought the bullets, I didn't have any more money for a hamburger, so I started home. The box of bullets felt very good in my pocket. When I got home I would show them to my gun. I would load and unload my gun a couple of times. That would make the gun happy because guns like bullets. They are nothing without bullets. They need bullets like a camel needs the desert.

My gun had an interesting story about how it got into my life. I knew this boy whose parents didn't like him because he was always getting into trouble. He was fourteen, smoked, had a reputation as a well-known masturbator and had been picked up by the police half-a-dozen times though he had never been formally charged with anything. His parents always got him off.

His father had some thread-thin political influence that was left over from having had a bright future in local politics about ten years ago. He had lost his political future when he was arrested the second time for drunk driving and running over an old lady who broke like a box of toothpicks being stepped on by an elephant. She was in the hospital so long that when she got out, she thought it was the Twenty-First Century.

But he still had a few political debts owed him—before he ran over the old lady there was talk in high places about him being the next mayor—and he collected them whenever he went and got his son out of jail.

Anyway, the boy's parents didn't like him and after the last time he was arrested they decided not to let him sleep in the house any more. From now on after that, he was to sleep out in the garage. He could take his meals in the house and bathe and go to the toilet there, but those were the only times they wanted him in there.

To make sure that he got the point of their dislike, they did not provide him with a bed when they exiled him to the garage. That's where I come in and the gun comes in.

The boy had a .22 caliber pump rifle. I had for some unknown reason, I can't remember why, a mattress.

Just after his parents Siberia-ized him to the garage, he came over to visit me. I'll never totally know why because we were not that good of friends. In the first place, his reputation as a prodigious masturbator did not weigh well with me. I had jacked off a few times you know, but I was not interested in making it a career.

Also, he had eyes that were born to look at things that he could steal. I of course stole a few things, but I wasn't interested in stealing everything. And, finally, I didn't like his smoking all the time and trying to get me to smoke. I just wasn't interested in smoking but he kept insisting that I smoke with him.

Though he was fourteen and I was twelve and he was bigger than me, for some strange reason he was almost afraid of me. I encouraged his fear by telling him a few gory lies about my prowess in hand-to-hand combat with other twelve-year-old kids. I also told him that I had once beaten up a seventeen-year-old. That really registered with him.

"It doesn't matter how big they are. You hit them in the right place and they all fall. You just have to know that place," I said, finishing up my tale of Jack Dempsey-like heroics that convinced him into being a minor coward around me, which I enjoyed enormously but not enough to have him for a friend to bully.

As I said earlier, he just had too many things going that were not in his favor.

And then he arrived one day and told me his story of parental rejection and how he had to sleep in the garage and he didn't have anything to sleep on.

The cement floor was cold.

"I don't know what I'm going to do," he said.

I knew what he was going to do. The words had barely escaped his mouth when I had it all planned out. What was to form an eternal breach between him and his parents and eventually lead him to doing three years in the pen for stealing a car and then a marriage with a spiteful woman ten years older than him who had five children who all grew to hate him, causing him to gain his only and ultimate solace in this world by buying a telescope and becoming an extremely incompetent but diligent astronomer, was to work to my brief advantage.

"Mommy, where's Daddy?"

"Looking at the stars."

"Mommy, do you hate Daddy, too?"

"Yes, child. I hate him, too."

"Mommy, I love you. Do you know why?"

"Why?"

"Because you hate Daddy. It's fun to hate Daddy, isn't it?"

"Yes, child."

"Why does Daddy look at the stars all the time, Mommy?"

"Because he's an asshole."

"Do assholes always look at the stars, Mommy?"

"Your father does."

He had his telescope in the attic and he was always confusing his constellations. He could never get it quite straight between what was Orion and what was the Big Dipper. For some strange reason he couldn't accept that the Big Dipper looked like a big dipper, but at least he wasn't in jail for stealing cars.

He worked hard and gave his wife all his money and she went to bed with the postman every chance she got. It was barely a life but being always confused about the Big Dipper gave it a fingernail-clipping continuity and meaning. "How could it be the Big Dipper if it looks like a big dipper?" was the way he approached it.

But all that was years in the future and now he

was standing in front of me bedless and telling me all the details.

Changing the subject completely, I put my plan in effect by asking him if he still had that old .22 rifle of his.

"Yes," he said, looking slightly bewildered at the turn of mental events. "What does that have to do with anything? What am I going to do? I'll catch pneumonia out there in the garage."

I successfully concealed my instantaneous revulsion when he said the dreaded word pneumonia. I had more serious things on my mind than to be rattled by the idea of pneumonia.

"No, you won't," I said.

"How do you know?" he said.

"I've got a mattress," I said.

He looked at me.

"I've got a mattress, too," he said. "But my folks won't let me take it out of the house into the garage."

Good! I thought: My plan is a certain success.

"I've got an extra mattress," I said, emphasizing the word EXTRA. He was impressed, but he knew that there was a catch to it. He waited.

I made it simple and sweet using the English language like a brain surgeon ordering a sequence of nerve events with his scalpel.

"I'll trade you my mattress for your .22."

His face showed that he didn't like that idea. He

took out a twisted and hunchbacked cigarette butt. It looked as if he had found it in the Hugo novel.

Before he could light it, I said, "I just read someplace that it's going to be a . . . . . very . . . . . cold . . . . . winter." I dragged the key words out until they sounded as long as December.

"Ah, shit," he said.

That's how I got the gun that led me to making the fatal decision to get a box of bullets instead of a hamburger.

If his parents hadn't made him go live in the garage, I never would have traded my mattress for his gun. Even if they'd still made him go live in the garage, but had given him a mattress, I wouldn't have had that gun. I got the gun in October of 1947 when time-sequenced nature was beginning to close the pond down for winter.

When the first cold rainy winds of a big autumn storm blew across the pond, everything changed, but of course none of this has happened yet.

It is the future.

The present is watching their truckload of furniture drive/rattle down the road toward me, but somehow they never seem to get any closer.

They are like a mirage that refuses to have any responsibility toward reality. It just stands there satirizing actual things. I try to make it respond like reality but it refuses. It won't come any closer.

They and their truck are pasted like a child's drawing against the fourth dimension. I want them to come, but they won't come, so I am catapulted into the future where it is November 1948 and the February-17th apple orchard event is history. The court found me not guilty of criminal negligence in the shooting.

A lot of people wanted me sent to reform school, but I was found innocent. The subsequent scandal forced us to move and now I'm living in another town where nobody knows what happened in that orchard.

I am going to school.

I'm in the seventh grade and we are studying the American Revolution, but I have no interest in the American Revolution. I am only interested in everything that I can find out about hamburgers.

Somehow I believe that only a complete knowledge of hamburgers can save my soul. If I had gotten a hamburger that February day instead of bullets, everything would have been different, so I *must* find out all that I can about hamburgers.

I go to the public library and pour over books like intellectual catsup to gain information about the hamburger.

My desire for hamburger knowledge dramatically increases the level of my reading. One of my teachers gets alarmed. She calls in my mother trying to find out the origins of my gigantic intellectual leap.

My mother can only help by saying that I like to read a lot.

This does not satisfy the teacher.

One day the teacher asks me to stay after school. The teacher is becoming obsessed by my newly-found reading level.

"You're reading a lot," the teacher says. "Why?"

"I like to read," I say.

"That's not good enough," the teacher says, her eyes brightening. I'm beginning not to like this at all.

"I talked to your mother. That's what she also told me," the teacher says. "But you don't think I believe that, do you?"

I'd had teachers before who were strict disciplinarians and wouldn't think twice about whacking a kid, but this teacher was rapidly becoming dangerous right in front of my eyes.

"What have I done wrong?" I say. "I just like to read."

"That's what you think!" the teacher yells, loud enough to summon the principal who takes her away to his office, sobbing hysterically.

Following a period of recuperation, a month's sick leave, total rest, the teacher was transferred to another school. After a series of substitute teachers, we got a new permanent teacher who didn't give a damn about my reading, so I continued gaining the reading tools to aid in my exploration of the hamburger and possible redemption through a complete knowledge of its origins, quirks and basic functioning.

Looking back on it now, I guess I used the hamburger as a form of mental therapy to keep from going mad because what happened in that orchard was not the kind of thing that causes a child to have a positive outlook on life. It was the kind of thing that challenged your mettle and I used the hamburger as my first line of defense.

Because I looked older than I actually was—I was thirteen, then, but I was tall for my age, so that I could easily be mistaken for fifteen—I passed myself off as a high school student who was a reporter for the school paper and doing an article on hamburgers.

This gave me access to almost all the fry cooks in the new town where we had been forced to move. Ostensibly, I interviewed them about their experiences cooking, but always worked the interview around to their involvement with hamburgers. The interview would start out being about one thing and would always end up being about hamburgers.

A bright young high school reporter (me): When was the first time that you cooked a hamburger?

A Mexican fry cook approaching forty the hard way: Do you mean professionally?

Reporter: Yes, professionally or just as an amateur.

Mexican Fry Cook: Let me think. I was just a kid when I cooked my first hamburger.

Reporter: Where was that?

Mexican Fry Cook: Albuquerque.

Reporter: How old were you?

Mexican Fry Cook: Ten.

Reporter: Did you enjoy cooking it?

Mexican Fry Cook: What was that question again?

Reporter: Was it fun cooking your first hamburger?

Mexican Fry Cook: What kind of article did you say this was?

Reporter: It's about cooks here in town.

Mexican Fry Cook: You sure ask a lot of questions about hamburgers.

Reporter: You cook a lot of hamburgers, don't you?

Mexican Fry Cook: But I cook a lot of other things, too. Why don't you ask me about grilled cheese sandwiches?

Reporter: Let's finish up with hamburgers. Then we'll move onto other things: grilled cheese sandwiches, chili.

Mexican Fry Cook: I've never been interviewed before. I'd love to talk about chili.

Reporter: Don't worry. We'll talk about it. I'm very certain my readers want to hear everything you know about chili, but first let's finish up with hamburgers. That hamburger you cooked when you were ten years old was an amateur hamburger, wasn't it?

Mexican Fry Cook: I guess so. No one paid me to cook it.

Reporter: When did you cook your first professional burger?

Mexican Fry Cook: Do you mean when I got paid to cook my first hamburger?

Reporter: Yes.

Mexican Fry Cook: That would have been my first job. 1927 in Denver. I went to Denver to work in my uncle's garage but I didn't like working on cars, so my cousin had a little cafe near the bus depot and I went down there and started helping him out cooking and pretty soon I had a shift all my own.

I was seventeen.

I've been cooking ever since, but I cook a lot of other things than hamburgers. I cook—

Reporter: Let's finish with the burgers first and then we'll get onto other things. Did you ever have any remarkable experiences cooking a hamburger?

Mexican Fry Cook (now beginning to show a little concern): How can you have a remarkable experience cooking a hamburger? I mean, you just put the patty on the grill and cook it. You turn it over once and put it on a bun. That's a hamburger. That's all there is to it. Nothing else can happen.

Reporter: What's the most hamburgers that you ever cooked in a day?

Mexican Fry Cook: I've counted a lot of things in

my life but I've never counted hamburgers. People order them and I cook them. That's all I know about it. I mean, sometimes I'm busier than other times and sometimes when I'm busy people order a lot of hamburgers, but I've never counted them. I've never even thought about counting hamburgers. Why should I count hamburgers?

Reporter (undaunted): Who is the most famous person you ever cooked a hamburger for?

Mexican Fry Cook: What's the name of the paper you're writing for again?

Reporter: The Johnson Union High School Gazette. We have a large circulation. A lot of people out of high school read our paper instead of the *Johnson City Herald.*

Mexican Fry Cook: Do your readers want to know this much about hamburgers? I had some very interesting experiences in the War, cooking in the South Pacific. Once I was cooking breakfast on Kwajalein when a Japanese bomber—

Reporter (interrupting): That sounds very exciting but let's finish up with the hamburgers, so we can get onto other subjects. I know that talking about hamburgers may seem dull to you a professional, but my readers are fascinated by hamburgers. My editor told me to find out as much as I could about hamburgers. Our readers eat a lot of hamburgers. Some of them eat three or four hamburgers a day.

Mexican Fry Cook (impressed): That's a lot of hamburgers.

Reporter: In my article I'll mention the name of this restaurant and you'll be getting a lot more business. I wouldn't be surprised if this place became famous. Who knows. You might even become part owner because of this interview.

Mexican Fry Cook: Did you get the spelling of my name right?

Reporter: G-O-M-E-Z.

Mexican Fry Cook: That's right. What else do you want to know about hamburgers? What the hell! If people want to know about hamburgers, I sure as hell won't stand in the way.

Reporter: Have you ever felt sad cooking a hamburger?

Mexican Fry Cook: Only if I'd spent all my money on a girl or if a girl left me. Then I'd feel sad even if I was cooking pancakes. The most trouble I have in this world is with girls. I always get girlfriends who give me a lot of trouble. They take all my money and I feel bad afterwards, but some day I'll meet the right one, I hope. In the meantime, yeah, girls make me feel sad when I'm cooking and that includes hamburgers.

I'm dating a girl now who's a beauty operator. All she wants me to do is take her out to fancy restaurants and nightclubs. I have to work two shifts to keep her in restaurants and nightclubs, and you can bet your life that she won't eat here.

I once asked her if she wanted to eat dinner here. Of course I wasn't cooking. It wasn't my shift, but she said, "Are you kidding?" Three hours later she ate so many shrimp at this fancy seafood place that I had to hock my watch the next day. She wouldn't eat here if this was the last place on earth.

I stood there with my notebook imitating as if I were taking down notes about his love life that he was really getting into now, but they weren't notes. They were just nonsense symbols and useless abbreviations in my notebook. They could not be used for anything, but whenever he mentioned hamburgers my notes became as bright and clear as a searchlight.

Reporter (interrupting the boring tragedy of his life. He really wasn't a very good-looking man. The only reason women would go out with him was that he worked sixteen hours a day cooking hamburgers and he would spend all his money on them): Did you ever feel happy cooking a hamburger?

Mexican Fry Cook: If it was the last hamburger of the day, and I was going out on a date afterwards, I might feel happy because I was getting off work and was going to maybe have some fun with a girl.

I ingeniously ended the interview by keeping him away from cooking breakfast on Kwajalein during the War and a Japanese bomber— Also, his chili ended up being very much left out in the cold. As I was leaving the cafe, he began to have second thoughts about the interview. "When is this interview going to come out?" he said.

"Soon," I said.

"Do you really think people want to know so much about hamburgers?" he said.

"It's the latest rage," I said.

"I didn't know that," he said.

"Keep those burgers coming," I said. "And you'll be a very famous person."

"Famous for cooking hamburgers?"

"No one ever heard about Charles Lindbergh until he flew across the Atlantic, did they?"

"Yeah," he said. "But cooking hamburgers is a lot different."

"Not that different," I said. "Think about it."

"OK," he said. "I'll think about it, but I can't see what hamburgers have to do with Charles Lindbergh. I don't think they have anything in common."

"Let me put it another way," I said, rapidly approaching the door on my way out. "Lindbergh took some sandwiches with him to eat when he flew across the Atlantic. Right?"

"I guess so," he said. "I think I remember something like that."

"Well, none of them were hamburgers," I said. "They were all cheese sandwiches."

"All cheese?" he said.

"Not one hamburger," I said, nodding my head solemnly. "Everything would have been completely different if he had taken three hamburgers with him."

"How do you figure that?" the Mexican fry cook said. "If he took hamburgers with him, they'd just get cold and a hot burger tastes a lot better than a cold burger."

"If Charles Lindbergh had taken three cold hamburgers," I said. "With him when he crossed the Atlantic all by himself in *The Spirit of St. Louis,* he would have been famous for the cold hamburgers and not the actual flight itself, right?"

Before he could reply to that I had closed the door to the cafe from the outside. I had a feeling that whatever girl he saw that night, no matter how many orders of shrimp she ate, she would make him feel better.

I interviewed about two dozen fry cooks in my quest for burger Satori. I went to meat markets and interviewed butchers about the quality of hamburger meat, personal feelings and reminiscences and anything odd they might tell me about the making of hamburger.

I went to bakeries where the hamburger buns were baked and interviewed bakers to find out everything I could about the baking of hamburger buns and any stories related to their baking.

An old baker who had heart trouble told me that

he always prayed when he put the hamburger buns in the oven to bake. I asked him if he prayed when he took them out. He said no.

I wanted bizarre stories about hamburger buns!

I searched high and low for burger information.

I interviewed over fifty chosen-at-random victims to tell me their personal experiences eating burgers. I wanted unusual burger stories. I wanted happy burger yarns and amusing incidents concerning the burger.

I wanted tales of hamburger terror.

I collected a dozen file cards dealing with people who got sick eating hamburgers. A woman told me that she once got so sick eating a hamburger that she fell off the front porch.

There was no extreme that I wouldn't go to find out more about the hamburger.

I looked for hamburger references in the Bible. I was certain that there must be an overlooked reference to a burger in the Book of Revelations. Maybe the Four Horsemen of the Apocalypse liked hamburgers.

My days and nights were nothing but fields of burgers for months and months after we had to move away from the February-17th incident with the rifle in the apple orchard.

Well, the truck and its load of furniture are still pasted like some kind of greeting card to a mirage which is the past. I should let them advance and take their rightful places beside the pond.

They are only about a hundred yards away from the pond and all I have to do is let go of them and they will drive right up here where I am sitting.

But for some strange reason, I won't let the people drive up to the pond and take their furniture off the truck and go about their evening's fishing a third of a century ago.

I'm quite certain they are dead by now.

They were in their late thirties back then, and they were so huge and fat that they probably died of heart attacks maybe twenty years ago when they were in their early fifties.

They both had that early-fifties-heart-attack look to them.

First, one would die and then the other would die, and that would be the end of them, except for whatever I write down here, trying to tell a very difficult story that is probably getting more difficult because I am still searching for some meaning in it and perhaps even a partial answer to my own life, which as I grow closer and closer to death, the answer gets further and further away.

In my mind I can see two extra large graves in the middle of nowhere with not a single piece of fishing furniture in sight.

It's totally over for them now: no more truck, no

more each other, no more couch right beside the edge of the pond with them sitting there fishing into the dark, illuminated by three electric lamps converted to kerosene and a fire coming from a small wood stove with no pipe because you don't need a pipe when there's no roof or house or room, just the outdoors beside a pond in perfect harmony with their fantasy.

I'm going to leave them in the past, driving against reality for a little while longer. They don't know how slowly they are travelling to the pond because they've been dead for so many years now.

They will remain for a while longer two American eccentrics freeze-framed in grainy black and white thirty-two years ago at sunset:

So the Wind Won't Blow It All Away
Dust . . . American . . . Dust

Davivd didn't like to shoot at the junkyard. He said it was boring. He was two years older than I and my secret friend. I was a sort of social outcast in school because of my obvious poverty and ways that were sometimes hard for other classmates to understand. Basically, my only claim to fame was my lack of fear of the old man who lived at the pond.

That kind of fame has its limitations.

You're not going to be voted the most popular kid in your class because you're not afraid of an old man who has only one lung and lives in a packing-crate shack beside a pond that doesn't even have a name.

But I was smart and a year ahead in school and attending junior high.

David and I did a lot of things together but we always did them alone. I was not admitted into his social group. I wasn't invited to any parties that he gave or to drop by his house. We always met on the sly.

David was an enormously popular kid: the most outstanding athlete in school and class president. Whenever anything was voted on, he got it. His grades were straight A's.

He was tall and slender and had fine blond hair and all the girls were madly in love with him. His parents worshipped the ground he walked on. Whereas a lot of other kids got into some kind of trouble, he always got into achievement and glory. He had everything going for him. His future was unlimited.

I played a hidden role in his life.

He liked the odd paths of my imagination.

He could talk to me about things that he couldn't talk to other kids about. He told me that he wasn't as confident and self-assured as everybody else thought he was, and that sometimes he was afraid of something that he couldn't put his finger on.

"I'm scared of something, but I don't know what it is," he once said. "It bothers me all the time. Sometimes I get very close to knowing what it is, but then when I can almost see it, it fades away and I'm left alone, wondering what it is."

He was also the best dancer in school and sang "Blue Moon" at student body assemblies. His version of "Blue Moon" made the girls' hearts beat like the hearts of excited kittens.

David went out with a girl who was a cheerleader and president of the drama club and played the leading role in all their plays. By any standard, she was the prettiest girl in school.

I admired her from a distance, but I had a strong feeling that she had no idea we shared space on the same planet. Their going out together was the biggest single topic in school, but he never once mentioned her to me.

He and I would meet at odd times in a constant but almost accidental pattern. We saw each other two or three times a week but seldom were our meetings worked out in advance.

They just happened.

The day after I got the bullets when I should have gotten the hamburger, I bumped into him at the bicycle rack at school.

He was of course alone. He had been talking to

another kid as I walked up, but he finished his conversation with him and he left just as I arrived.

So there we were alone together again.

"Hi," he said. "Let's go for a ride."

His bicycle was in perfect condition. His spokes and chain shined like silverware. Mine were muddy and rusty. The paint on his bicycle looked brand-new. My paint just looked.

He led the way and somehow we were riding along a street where not many other kids lived or rode their bicycles. It was almost a kidless zone.

We didn't say anything as we rode along until he started talking. I always let him initiate the conversation. He was the king of our friendship and I was his vassal. I didn't mind. I had other things to think about. Though he seemed to be the crystallization of excellence and normality, I found him almost as odd as I was.

Finally, he spoke: "I had a dream about it last night," he said.

"Could you see it?" I said.

"No, just before I can see it, the damn thing disappears and I wake up feeling strange and unhappy. I've had dreams about it all week," he said. "I wish I could see it just once. That's all I ask."

"Maybe you'll see it someday," I said.

"I hope so," he said.

We bicycled by a cat.

The cat didn't pay any attention to us.

It was a huge gray cat with enormous green eyes. They were like very small ponds.

"I got some bullets for my gun," I said. "Do you want to go shooting tomorrow?"

"Not at the junkyard," he said.

"No, the orchard," I said. "We'll shoot rotten apples."

"That sounds like a good idea," he said. "I've been feeling so bad recently because of those dreams that I'd like to shoot some rotten apples."

Then he smiled. "Yeah, I'll shoot some rotten apples and then I'll feel better."

"It beats doing nothing," I said.

We pedalled another block and then we saw another cat. This one was smaller than the first one, but it was gray, too. Actually, it looked identical to the first cat except for its size and it also had enormous green pond-like eyes.

"Did you see that cat?" he said.

"Yeah," I said. Then I knew what he was going to say next but I let him say it first.

"It looks like that other cat, but it's smaller," he said.

Those were the exact words that I knew he was going to say.

"I wonder if they're related," I said.

"Yeah, maybe so," he said. "The big cat's the

mother and the small cat is the son or daughter."

"Makes sense to me," I said.

"For some strange reason those cats make me think about those people who brought their furniture to the pond last summer," he said. "Remember when you took me to see them?"

"Yeah," I said.

"They were really strange people. I wonder why those cats made me think about them," he said.

I wondered about that, too.

I put the two cats together in my mind and I couldn't figure out why they made him think about the pond people and their furniture. The cats' eyes reminded me of ponds but that was as far as I could travel with it.

"You got to know those people real well," he said. "Why did they bring their furniture with them?"

"I guess they just wanted to be comfortable while they fished," I said.

"They came there every night, didn't they?" he said. "What did they do with all the fish they caught? I mean, they were both huge people but nobody could eat that much fish. When I was there with you, they caught about thirty fish and they kept them all. Those people couldn't eat thirty fish night after night. That's fifteen fish apiece."

What David was talking about was something that had never really crossed my mind before. What did they do with all those fish? because they always kept every fish they caught. They even kept the smallest ones. They put all the fish on a big stringer in the water and fastened it to the shore with a railroad spike. They always brought a special very heavy hammer with them to pound the spike in with.

It was a part of their ritual.

That means that every week they must have eaten at least 105 fish apiece and some of the fish were big catfish and sometimes they caught bass that weighed up to five pounds.

They always cooked dinner at the pond on a wood-burning kitchen stove, but of course they didn't need a pipe because there wasn't any ceiling to their kitchen.

As we pedalled along, I was thinking about how they ate everything for dinner but fish. They cooked a lot of hamburgers and pork chops, and liver and onions, and they cooked potatoes in various ways and sometimes she baked cornbread and every once in a while a pie, but she did not cook a single fish.

Every caught fish always went on the stringer and back into the pond where it was anchored to the shore with a railroad spike.

What did they do with all those fish?

Did they eat them for breakfast?

That would be fifteen fish apiece every morning for breakfast or if they ate them at lunch it would be the same amount of fish, even if they divided the fish between breakfast and lunch that would still be seven or eight fish apiece for each meal. That's a hell-of-a-lot of fish and I don't think people can eat that much fish.

Maybe they gave the fish to their friends. I had to rule that out because these people didn't look as if they ever had any friends. Wait, that's not correct. I remember them once mentioning some friends they knew a long time ago, but you can't give fresh fish to people that you haven't seen in years.

If they gave the fish to their cat, it would have to be a lion. They didn't look like cat lovers either.

Out of the clear blue or I should say just-starting-to-rain February late twilight, David had opened a new mystery to me and a different viewpoint of the pond people.

What in the hell did they do with all those fish? It was too late now to find out because it was winter and bad weather had closed the pond down in October.

It was a mystery, then, and would always remain a mystery forever because I never saw them again.

Growing bored with too many fish for too few people, David changed the subject. "When did you say you wanted to go shooting rotten apples in that old orchard?"

Today was Friday.

Tomorrow would be Saturday: no school.

"How about tomorrow?" I said.

"Fine, maybe it will make me forget about that thing in my dreams," David said. "I sure wish I knew what it looked like. I can almost see it but not quite."

"Shooting some apples will make you forget about it," I said, trying to be understanding.

"Yeah," he said, but he didn't look as if he believed it too much. "Let's meet at the Crossroads Filling Station. Tomorrow at noon. How many bullets do you have?"

"A box," I said. "Hollow points."

"I'll bring a box," he said. "Hollow points. We'll shoot even-stephen."

The Crossroads Filling Station was often a meeting place for us. It was a small, tired filling station run by an old man who wasn't much interested in selling gas. He sold worms to passing fishermen and pop to thirsty kids during the summer.

As I said earlier, when David and I saw each other we were by ourselves, alone most of the time. We had a secret friendship:

So the Wind Won't Blow It All Away
Dust . . . American . . . Dust

I was there at the Crossroads Filling Station the next day with my gun and a box of bullets that could have been a hamburger if I had been lucky.

I arrived first and parked my bicycle and went and got a bottle of pop. I had my rifle under my arm. I was twelve years old and nobody paid any attention to a kid with a rifle standing in front of a filling station, drinking a root beer.

Needless to say, America has changed from those days of 1948. If you saw a twelve-year-old kid with a rifle standing in front of a filling station today, you'd call out the National Guard and probably with good provocation. The kid would be standing in the middle of a pile of bodies.

"Why did you shoot all these people?" would be one of the first questions asked after he had been disarmed.

"Because I don't like gym," would be the answer.

"You mean you shot all these people because you didn't like your gym class?"

"Not exactly."

"What do you mean, not exactly? What actually do you mean? There are twelve dead people here."

"McDonald's hasn't been putting enough of their special sauce on my Big Macs."

"You mean, you shot twelve people dead because you don't like gym? and you haven't been getting enough McDonald's special sauce on your hamburgers?"

The kid would look a little bewildered for the first

time after his interlude of carnage and then say, "You mean, those aren't enough good reasons? How would you like something like that to happen to you? Why don't you put yourself in my shoes?" the kid would say, getting into the back seat of the police car and most likely be on his way to parole eight years and seven months from now.

They'd let him out of prison when he was twenty-one, with a baby face and an asshole three inches wide.

"Going shooting?" the old man said, coming out of the filling station. He was rubbing his hands together because it was a cold, cloudy, damp day. It had rained all night and then stopped at mid-morning, around 9.

Everything smelled of rainy winter.

"Yeah," I said. "I'm going to try a little target practice."

"It's a good day for it," he said.

I didn't know exactly what he meant by that, but I said yes to humor him. Humored, he went back into the filling station to sit beside a pot-bellied stove and sell a few gallons of gas before dark.

He sold a lot of worms and a lot of pop there in the summer but because it was February, he would have to wait a few months for the fishing season to start and for it to get hot and pop-drinking weather.

I don't know why people didn't want to buy his

gasoline. He had a good location there at the Cross-roads. There are a lot of life's mysteries which will always remain unsolved.

He didn't seem to care much, so I guess it was all right with him. Maybe the filling station was just an excuse for him to sell worms. There was a big lake ten miles away and he sold a hell-of-a-lot of worms in the summer because the road to the lake went right past his filling station. They were big worms called night crawlers and he bought them from us kids for a penny apiece.

We'd go out at night and pick them up off lawns using a flashlight to see them. The lawns had to be wet to bring the night crawlers out. Rainy nights were of course the best and freshly watered lawns came in second.

I caught my share of night crawlers and sold them to the old man. I would bring in a bucket of worms and he'd count them out very carefully and then give me a penny for each one. He never paid for them with quarters or fifty-cent pieces or dimes. It was always pennies. He counted out the pennies as carefully as he counted out the night crawlers.

Every day during the spring and summer, there would be kids bringing in worms to be counted and leaving with pennies to be spent. It was very simple, earthy capitalism: What crawled out of the ground soon became an ice-cream cone. Also, the old man never turned away a worm, even when the fishing was slow out at the lake. He could always find room to count another worm and pay a penny for its counting, but most of the time he was very busy selling worms.

Gasoline was another story.

The old man's counting was constantly being interrupted by fishermen wanting to buy worms. He sold the worms in pint cartons with a bit of dirt and some wet moss in the cartons to keep the night crawlers fresh. Each carton contained a dozen worms.

When he was interrupted counting out either worms or pennies, he had a notebook that he wrote your first name down in, along with how many worms you brought in. He would count out all the worms and then count out all the pennies that he owed you.

If he was still counting out your worms when somebody drove up to buy a dozen, he would write down: Jack 18. That meant that he had counted out 18 worms and was still counting.

He would go out and sell some worms and then come back and start with 19. If he had counted out all your worms, say 175, he would write in his book: Jack Total 175, and then he would start counting out your pennies.

If he was interrupted when he was paying you, he would write this down in his notebook: Jack Total 175, 61 paid, and then he'd go out and sell some more worms and come back and start counting again at 62.

Our hands slowly filled up with pennies. They were always freshly minted. He went to the bank and got them. He wouldn't pay us with old pennies.

I don't know.

I think the only reason he had that filling station was that he liked to count worms and pennies. I can't think of another reason.

Can you?

He took care of his worm business in that part of the filling station that used to be the garage. Instead of putting cars up on the rack and finding out what was wrong with their brakes or transmissions or differentials or changing tires or doing anything that would help a car run better, he counted worms and pennies in the garage.

Where there should have been racks of tires, there were long wooden boxes filled with thousands of night crawlers and where there should have been cans of motor oil, there were stacks of pint boxes waiting to be filled with worms.

In his little office in the front, he kept a refrigerator to store the boxes of worms that were ready to sell. He had rigged the refrigerator so that the worms stayed cool in it but wouldn't freeze or suffocate. He called it his worm box. Because he spent so much time in the garage counting, he had a little bell outside the door of the office. There was a sign beside the bell that said: RING FOR WORMS.

Maybe that's why he didn't sell very much gasoline.

It was probably easier for somebody who wanted to buy gas to find a filling station that didn't have a sign out front that said: RING FOR WORMS.

I think a lot of people took advantage of that option because I doubt if he ever sold more than a few gallons a day and that would have been on a good day.

He had a huge cooler just outside of his office where he kept the pop. Every day in the summer he filled the cooler with big blocks of ice and the bottles of pop just floated there in the melting ice, making it the coldest and best-tasting pop in the world. That cooler of pop was a mecca for kids on a hot day. When you couldn't stand the heat any more, you knew that pop was waiting. The old man trusted kids. There was a tin can beside the cooler to put your nickels in or your pennies.

I wish that I could have a bottle of that pop right now.

David pedalled up to the filling station on his bicycle. He had his .22 across the handlebars. Again: it was not an unusual sight back in those days just after the War for kids to casually carry guns around with them.

"Want a pop?" the old man came out of his office and asked David.

"No, I'll wait for summer," David said.

"OK," the old man said. "Suit yourself."

He went back into the filling station to wait for summer.

We pedalled off toward the old abandoned apple orchard that was about three miles away. The day had grown darker and cloudier, but it wasn't very windy. The air was almost stationary with winter dampness. Everything had a slightly decayed, wet smell to it. This was in Western Oregon where the winters are usually just so much rain, days and days, weeks and weeks, months and months of just so much rain.

"How did you sleep last night?" I asked.

"I had that same dream," David said. "But it wasn't so bad. I wasn't afraid this time. I just had it and it went away. I couldn't see it, but I didn't really care."

"Well, I just dreamt about John Wayne," I said.

"What about him?" David said.

"Nothing," I said. "Just John Wayne doing all the things that he does."

"Were you in the dream?" David said.

"No."

"At least I was in my dream," David said.

"You're lucky," I said. "I was just watching it like a movie. I wanted to be in it, but I couldn't get out of my seat. I just had to sit there and watch it. I didn't even have a bag of popcorn."

There were very poor houses along the road to the orchard. People had built along there, I think, just after the First World War, but for some reason or another, it never really caught on as a place for people to live, so they just gradually moved away until now there were only people living in those houses who were very poor.

They had a lot of broken cars in their front yards that were never going anywhere again. The people just used the parts of those cars to try and put together cars that might work for a while. They were not gigantically successful at doing this.

All of their gardens had been crushed by winter storms and their corn patches were defeated and all akilter.

Sometimes dogs barked at us as we rode by, but the dogs were all so useless that they barely presented a threat. There were kids playing around the houses. The kids all looked defeated and out of kilter, too. Instead of being born, they just could have been ears of corn left over from last autumn's harvest.

Low, flat, gray smoke came from the chimneys of the houses. The smoke had a lot of trouble getting any distance into the air, so it just hung there like strange useless sheets that could have been hanging on an odd clothesline.

A kid about ten years old saw us coming and yelled at us when we pedalled by. "You sons-of-bitches all have bicycles!" he said. "I'll have a bicycle someday!"

Soon we had left his voice behind like a voice from a dream dreamt down the road, but I looked back into the dream and I could still see him yelling, but I couldn't hear a word. He was just another kid driven crazy by poverty and his drunken father beating him up all the time and telling him that he'd never amount to anything, that he would end up just like his father, which he would.

The old orchard was back in some hills about half a mile from the main road. We had to take a dirt road to get there. The road was narrow and very muddy and it was hard pedalling. There were no houses along the road. About the only thing there was were some abandoned farming equipment and broken-down fences that would never be repaired again.

The grass was a grayish yellow and had been beaten down by an endless series of hard winter storms that were our fate that autumn and winter.

The clouds were gradually lowering and it looked as if it might start raining any time, but we didn't care because we were Pacific Northwest kids and we were used to getting wet. It didn't bother us much at all. We were both wearing raincoats and rubber boots.

We continued pedalling up the road, slinging mud behind us off our rear wheels. It was very slow going. Sometimes we had to get off our bicycles and push them.

No one had used the road in front of us for a long time, not since hunting season. Then pheasant hunters went up there and banged away, but the season had been over for months now and the road had not been used since then.

At the end of the road was a burnt-down farmhouse and half a barn. One half was still standing and the other half had just collapsed because it was too old to hold hands any longer with the rest of the barn.

"I'm always in my dreams," David said.

Maybe our friendship was based on the fact that he always told me about his dreams because he was constantly talking about them. They were our chief subject of conversation and he always initiated it.

As we pedalled along, I thought about that. We had known each other since July and I had certainly heard a lot about his dreams, especially the nightmare that he couldn't see.

I guess he never told any of his teammates or his parents about the dreams. I was certain that I was the only person he ever talked to about his dreams. I don't think he even mentioned them to his beautiful girlfriend.

If I had a girlfriend like her, I'd tell her all about my dreams, but maybe the reason I didn't have a girlfriend like her was because my dreams were so boring.

But I'm certain he never told her any of his dreams. I guess their friendship was built on things other than dreams, though as I said earlier, he never mentioned her to me.

Once I asked him about her and he changed the subject to Joe DiMaggio's batting average. I didn't pursue it after that because I had absolutely no interest in Joe DiMaggio's batting average. I was a big fan of Ted Williams.

"You don't seem to be in your dreams," David said, as we neared the burnt-down old farmhouse.

"I try," I said.

"I don't even have to try," he said. "I'm just automatically there. I have no choice."

We got off our bicycles.

The first drops of heavy rain started falling, but there was quite a bit of distance between the drops. They were falling very slowly and you could almost walk around them if you were interested in doing that.

The trees in the old apple orchard were filled with rotten apples. We loaded our guns and started banging away. It was a tremendous lot of fun to watch the effect of a bullet hitting a rotten apple. They just simply exploded and the bullet continued on viciously scratching white grooves in the still-living branches of the apple trees.

We both had boxes of hollow points and they

could really show an apple who was boss. We shot up about twenty rounds apiece and then David decided to walk down to the other end of the orchard where there were some thick bushes because sometimes pheasants hung out down there. I think he liked shooting in the orchard rather than the garbage dump because he was interested in maybe shooting a pheasant, which he was never able to do.

So he went down to the other end of the orchard to see if he could find one to shoot. I sat down on a huge fallen apple branch and waited for him to come back. I sat there wondering why the people had let the orchard go back to nature.

Maybe when their house burnt down they just didn't care to live there any more because it was a sign of bad memories and the apple orchard was a character in their bad memories.

They weren't even interested in selling apples any more. A lot of bad things happen to people in this life that they just don't want to be reminded of, so they move away and try living someplace else where they can forget unpleasant things like their house burning down, and start all over again and build up some good memories.

The big drops of cold gray rain continued falling all around me and the sky was growing lower and lower. It seemed to want to touch the top of the apple trees like putting a gray tent over them.

I was getting a little wet but it didn't bother me.

I sat there continuing to think about David and our dream friendship.

I wondered how it had all gotten started in the first place. It's not an easy thing for a friendship to be founded on one person telling another person about his dreams, but they were the main ingredients of our friendship, and especially the one dream that baffled him so much, the thing that frightened him, the thing that he could almost see, but not quite.

There was something in his mind that kept it out of arm's reach. Though he tried and tried, he couldn't touch it, so he was constantly telling me all about what was not visible to him.

I was interested but not that interested, though I pretended to be because I wanted his friendship, even if it was based mostly on dreams.

Then I heard his .22 go off.

It snapped me alert and I heard the noise of a pheasant rooster coming my way. The bird sounded like a rusty airplane. The bird was coming right at me. I could see him skimming over the grass toward me.

Involuntarily, I snapped my gun up and got a shot off, quite obviously missing the bird that sailed right on past me, heading toward the burnt-down farmhouse and the collapsed barn.

There was a moment for the sound of the gun to disappear along with the pheasant. Then everything was very quiet, and I could hear the rain falling again, big February drops like small self-contained reservoirs.

The plopping of the rain would cause a beautiful green spring in a few months but I wouldn't be there to see it. I hadn't even stood up when I fired the gun. I just cracked off the shot and I had missed the bird by so much that I didn't even try for a second shot. I just turned my head and watched him disappear down around the collapsed barn.

Realizing that the bird and the accompanying shot had come from the direction David had gone in, I got up and yelled down the orchard, "You missed him!" I didn't think that he must already have known that because he heard me shoot.

Then I wondered where David was. He should have come back up this way by now. He always liked to get a second shot at a pheasant, so he would have wanted to track it down.

Where was David?

"David!" I yelled. "It came up this way! It's down by the barn!"

David did not answer.

Normally, he was very enthusiastic about stalking and shooting at pheasants with his .22, though I don't recall him ever having shot one, but he never stopped trying. They were like trying to see his dream.

"David!"

Silence

I started down there through the heavy wet grass. I knew that he couldn't be more than a hundred yards away.

"David!"

More silence

"David!"

Silence growing longer, heavier

"Can you hear me?"

I was almost there now—"David!"—and then I was there. David was sitting on the ground, holding the upper part of his right leg with both of his hands and there was blood spurting regularly between his fingers.

His face was very pale and his features had a dreamy expression to them, as if he had just awakened or maybe was falling asleep.

The blood was very red and it just kept coming. He seemed to have an endless supply of it.

"What happened?" I said, bending down to look at all the blood that was now covering the ground. I had never seen so much blood before in my entire life, and I had never seen blood that was so red. It looked like some kind of strange liquid flag on his leg.

"You shot me," David said.

His voice sounded very far away.

"It doesn't look good."

I tried to say something but my mouth was completely dry as if it had been suddenly sandblasted.

"I wish it would hurt," he said. "But it doesn't hurt. Oh, God, I wish it would hurt."

The bullet had severed the femoral artery in his right leg.

"If it doesn't start hurting soon, I'm going to die," David said. Then he kind of rolled very slowly over on his side as if he were falling out of the world's slowest chair. He kept holding his leg that was now just a sea of February orchard blood. He looked up at me with eyes that were disappearing right in front of me. They would be gone in a minute.

"Did I get the pheasant?" he asked.

"No," my voice blew out of the Sahara. It continued blowing. "I'm sorry. I didn't see you. I just saw the pheasant coming at me, and I fired. I didn't know where you were."

"I didn't get it, huh?"

"No."

"Just as well," David said. "You can't eat when you're dead. No good," he said. *No good.* He let go of his leg and rubbed his eyes with his bloody hands as if he were trying to see straight because everything had grown fuzzy. The blood on his face made him look like an Indian.

OH, GOD!

"I'll go and get some help. You'll be all right," I said. I'd just started to run when he stopped me by saying, "Do you know that thing in my dreams?"

"Yeah," I said.

"I'm never going to see it now," David said:

So the Wind Won't Blow It All Away
Dust . . . American . . . Dust

I was acquitted by the court of any negligence in the shooting. I told exactly what had happened and they believed me. I had no reason to shoot him. I was just supposed to listen to his dreams.

David was buried three days later on Tuesday and all the kids in school stopped talking to me.

He was a very popular boy and they retired his basketball jersey. There was a glass case full of trophies in the front hall of the gym and they put his basketball jersey in the case along with a photograph of him and a brass plaque that told his name and how much he was admired for his sportsmanship and academic qualities. The plaque also said that he was born March 12th, 1933, and died February 17th, 1948.

David would have been fifteen in a month.

We were off Welfare and my mother was working

now as a waitress. It was a small town and her tips stopped, so . . .

There wasn't much point in us hanging around there any more. I got in half-a-dozen fights at school. They weren't my fault. The only thing that was my fault was that I didn't buy that hamburger. If I had only wanted a hamburger that day, everything would have been completely different. There would be another person still living on the planet and talking about his dreams to me.

My mother kept telling me that it wasn't my fault.

"I should have bought a hamburger," I said.

She was very patient and didn't ask me what I was talking about.

We had this exchange a dozen or so times.

Finally, she said, "I don't know what you're talking about."

"It doesn't make any difference," I said.

Later on that year, after we had moved, and I had taken up my obsessive search for salvation by trying to find out everything there was to know about the hamburger, my mother said to me one day, right out of the blue, startling me because she hadn't made a single comment about my hamburger research, though she was quite aware that it was going on: "Maybe you should have bought the hamburger."

I had never told her about the hamburger decision I had made that led to the box of bullets, so I was surprised even more when she told me that I should have bought the hamburger.

"It's too late now," I said.

She went into the other room without saying anything.

The next day I brought a complete end to my hamburger research. I took all my notes and interviews and assorted documents down to the river that flowed by the new town we were exiled to and burned them in a picnic stove that was beside a very sad little Oregon zoo that barely had any animals and they were all wet because it was raining again as was the fate of that land.

An extremely wet and skinny-looking coyote stood on the other side of his Cyclone fence in a pathetic little compound and watched me burn too many pieces of paper dealing with the origin, refinement and other possibilities of the hamburger.

When all my papers were finally burned and the ashes stirred into oblivion the coyote walked away.

Leaving the zoo, I passed the cage of a black bear. He had a grizzled face. He was staring at the wet cement floor of his cage. He didn't look up as I walked by. I wonder why I still remember him after all these years. He's probably dead now. Bears don't live forever, but I remember him:

Well, there you have it and now I have released the two people from their paralyzed photograph of 32 years ago, and their truck filled with furniture is coming down the road toward the pond.

The truck rattled to a stop and they got out. They were not surprised to see me because I was their uninvited houseguest, almost every night.

"Hello," they both said in very slow unison that sounded as if it had originated quite close to Oklahoma. It was not a big friendly hello nor was it a little unfriendly hello. I just said a simple hello hello. I think they were still making up their minds about me.

I was sort of on probation, but I felt as if I were making some progress toward developing a minor pond comrades-in-catfish friendship with them. I had all summer to get to know them. I would outlast them.

Last week they asked me if I wanted to sit down on their couch with them, though that was very difficult because they both were so big that they practically took up the entire couch themselves. I barely made it on the couch with them like the last final squeeze of toothpaste from a tube.

They were both in their late thirties and over six

feet tall and weighed in excess of 250 pounds, and they both wore bib overalls and tennis shoes. I haven't the slightest idea what they did for a living because they never said a single word about what kind of job they did.

I had a feeling whatever they did for a living, they did together. They were the kind of people who looked as if they were never apart. I could see them coming to work together, working together, having lunch together and always wearing the same clothes. Whatever they did required that they wear bib overalls and tennis shoes.

I could see them filling out employment forms.

Under the line that asked about previous experience. They just put down "bib overalls and tennis shoes."

I also had a feeling that whatever they did, they came directly from work to the pond. I don't think they changed their clothes because different, but always matching pairs of bibs and tennis shoes were their entire wardrobe.

I could imagine them even having special overalls and tennis shoes for church with the rest of the congregation sitting apart from them.

Well, whatever they did for a living hadn't made them rich because the furniture on the back of their truck was well-worn and looked as if it had not been very expensive to begin with. It looked like ordinary used furniture or the stuff you'd find in any furnished apartment where the rent was cheap.

Their furniture was a replica of the furniture that I had lived with all my twelve years. New furniture has no character whereas old furniture always has a past. New furniture is always mute, but old furniture can almost talk. You can almost hear it talking about the good times and troubles it's seen. I think there is a Country and Western song about talking furniture, but I can't remember the name.

After their perfunctory hello to me, they took the couch off the truck. They were both so efficient and strong that the couch came off the back of the truck like a ripe banana out of its skin. They carried it over to the pond and put it down very close to the water's edge, so they could fish right off it, but still leaving enough space so as not to get their tennis shoes wet.

Then they went back to the truck and got a big stuffed easy chair. The chair did not match the couch which was an Egyptian-mummy-wrapping beige. The stuffed chair was a blood-fading red.

She took the chair off by herself while he stood there waiting to take something off himself. As soon as the stuffed chair was on its way to join the couch by the pond's edge, he got two end tables off the truck and put them on each side of the couch. By this time she had gone back and gotten a rocking chair and set it up.

Then they took a small wood cookstove off the truck and they began creating a little kitchen in the corner of their living room.

The sun was just setting and the pond was totally calm. I could see the old man standing on his boat dock across from us watching. He was motionless as they unloaded their furniture. Everything was shadowy on his part of the pond and he was just another shadow textured among thousands of other shadows.

They took a box of food and cooking things off the truck and a small table to use for preparing their evening meal. The man started a fire in the stove. They even brought their own wood. He was very good at starting fires because the stove was hot enough to cook on momentarily.

Redwing blackbirds were standing on the ends of the cattails and making their final night calls, saying things to other birds that would be continued the next morning at dawn.

I heard my first cricket chirp.

That cricket sounded so loud and so good that he could have been a star in a Walt Disney movie. Walt should have sent some scouts out and signed him up.

The man started cooking hamburgers.

They smelled good, but I did not pay the attention to them that I would the following February and the long months that I mulled over hamburgers after the shooting. To me now they were just the good smell of hamburgers cooking.

The woman got three once-electric floor lamps that had now been converted to kerosene use off the truck. The kerosene worked real nice, though of course the lamps were not as bright as they would have been if they used electricity.

There was another interesting thing about those lamps. The people had never bothered to remove the cords. They were still fastened to the lamps. The cords didn't look wrong, but they didn't look right either. I wonder why they didn't take them off.

The woman put a floor lamp next to each end table beside the couch and lit them. The light from the lamps shined down on the end tables.

Then the woman got a cardboard box off the truck and took two photographs out of the box. They were in large ornate frames. I believe one photograph was of her parents and the other photograph was of his parents. They were very old photographs and tinted in the style of long ago. She put them down on one of the tables.

On the other table she put an old clock that had a heavy somber ticking to it. The clock sounded as if eternity could pull no tricks on it. There was also a small brass figure of a dog beside the clock. The figure looked very old and was a companion and watchdog for the clock.

Did I mention that she put a lace doily on the surface of that table before she put the dog and clock there?

Well, I have now, and there was also a lace doily on the end table that held the photographs of their parents. I might add that their parents were not wearing bib overalls and tennis shoes. They were dressed formally in perhaps the style of the 1890s.

There was another kerosene lamp burning on the worktable beside the stove where the burgers were cooking, but it was a traditional lamp. I mean, it looked like a kerosene lamp.

The man was also boiling some water for Kraft dinner and there was a can of pears on the table.

That was going to be their dinner tonight: 32 years ago.

The smoke rising from the stove sought desperately for a pipe but not finding one just drifted slowly around like an absentminded cripple.

Their living room was now completely set up except that I have forgotten to mention the *National Geographic* magazines that were on both end tables. Sometimes when the fishing was slow they would just read the *National Geographic* while waiting for a bite.

They drank a lot of coffee from a huge metal coffeepot that he was now filling with water from the pond. They also drank the coffee out of metal cups. They put a lot of sugar in their coffee. Every night they used a pound box of sugar. You could almost walk on their coffee. An ant would have been in paradise if it drank coffee.

While they were setting up this living-room ritual of life beside the pond, I sat in some grass nearby, just watching them, saying nothing.

They hardly spoke either and this evening, their conversation was mostly about people who weren't there.

"Father, Bill would have liked this place," she said.

They always called each other Mother or Father when they called each other anything. They did not spend a lot of time talking to each other. They had spent so much time together that there probably wasn't much more to be said.

"Yes, Mother, he would have been happy here. This is a good pond."

"I don't know why people have to move all the time, Father."

"Neither do I, Mother."

He flipped over a hamburger in the frying pan on the stove.

"Betty Ann moved in 1930," he said.

"That means Bill must have moved in either 1929 or 1931 because they moved a year apart," she said.

"I don't know why either of them moved," he said.

"Well, don't forget: we moved, too," she said.

"But it was different with us. We had to move," he said. "They didn't have to move. They just could have stayed there. They could still be there if they wanted to be," he said.

She didn't say anything after he said that.

She just busied herself with the living room beside the pond, futzing like women do when they want to think something over and it needs time.

More crickets had joined in with the first cricket, but the new crickets were not star material. They were just ordinary crickets. No one from Hollywood would ever come to Oregon and sign them up.

I could barely see the old man across the pond on his dock staring at us, but he was fading very rapidly away. When night gets started, it just won't stop.

"How's the Kraft dinner?" she asked, sort of absentmindedly.

She had a feather duster in her hand and was dusting off their furniture that had gotten dusty because of the long gray destroyed road that had taken them to this pond in Oregon in late July 1947, the second year after the sky stopped making all that noise from endless flights of bombers and fighter planes passing overhead like the Hit Parade records of World War II, playing too loud on a jukebox that went all the way to the stars.

I was so glad the War was over.

I stared into the silence of the sky that used to be filled with warplanes.

"It's OK," he said. "I always thank the Kraft people for inventing Kraft dinner because you never have any trouble cooking it. A lot more things should be like Kraft dinner. Nice and Easy. Take it nice and easy is my motto."

"I guess it would be just as well if we don't think about Bill and Betty Ann any more," she replied to his observation about Kraft dinner. "We're never going to see them again, anyway. We got a postcard from them in 1935. I was happy they got married. We haven't heard a word since. Maybe they went to work in a plant during the War. They could be anywhere now, but I think they would have liked this place."

The man was dishing up the Kraft dinner and hamburgers. They would have their dinner and then do some fishing. They would eat their dinner off cheap plates on the couch. When they started eating, they never said another word to each other until they were finished.

"Maybe they don't even fish any more," he said, bringing two plates of food over to the couch where she had just sat down. "People change. They give up fishing. A lot of people are interested in miniature golf. Maybe Bill and Betty Ann don't feel like fishing any more."

"I suppose," she said. "But we're too big to play

miniature golf, not unless they wanted to use us for the course, Father."

They both laughed and fell silently to eating their hamburgers and Kraft dinner.

I had become so quiet and so small in the grass by the pond that I was barely noticeable, hardly there. I think they had forgotten all about me. I sat there watching their living room shining out of the dark beside the pond. It looked like a fairy tale functioning happily in the post-World War II gothic of America before television crippled the imagination of America and turned people indoors and away from living out their own fantasies with dignity.

In those days people made their own imagination, like homecooking. Now our dreams are just any street in America lined with franchise restaurants. I sometimes think that even our digestion is a soundtrack recorded in Hollywood by the television networks.

Anyway, I just kept getting smaller and smaller beside the pond, more and more unnoticed in the darkening summer grass until I disappeared into the 32 years that have passed since then, leaving me right here, right now.

Because they never spoke during dinner, I think after they finished eating they probably mentioned a little thing about my disappearance.

"Where did that kid go, Mother?"

"I don't know, Father."

Then they rigged up their fishing poles and got some coffee and just relaxed back on the couch, their fishing lines now quietly in the water and their living room illuminated by kerosene-burning electric floor lamps.

"I don't see him anywhere."

"I guess he's gone."

"Maybe he went home."

RICHARD BRAUTIGAN was born on January 30, 1935, in the Pacific Northwest. He was the author of ten novels, nine volumes of poetry, and a collection of short stories. He lived for many years in San Francisco, and toward the end of his life he divided his time between a ranch in Montana and Tokyo. Brautigan was a literary idol of the 1960s and early 1970s whose comic genius and iconoclastic vision of American life caught the imagination of young people everywhere. Brautigan came of age during the Haight-Ashbury period and has been called "the last of the Beats." His early books became required reading for the hip generation, and *Trout Fishing in America* sold two million copies throughout the world. Brautigan was a god of the counterculture, a phenomenon who saw his star rise to fame and fortune, only to plummet during the next decade. Driven to drink and despair, he committed suicide in Bolinas, California, at the age of forty-nine.